ADVANCE PRAISE FOR *THE WINTER PEARL*

"Molly Noble Bull has written a charming story with twists and turns for a character the reader will really root for."
—Lauraine Snelling, bestselling author of the
Red River of the North series, *Ruby* and
The Healing Quilt.

"*The Winter Pearl* is a jewel of a novel!
I literally couldn't put it down and found myself reaching for a tissue more than once. Molly has beautifully blended a heart-stopping adventure and a glorious romance filled to the brim with God's love and redemption—all set against the backdrop of the Old West.
I can't wait to see more from this talented author."
—Diane Noble, award-winning author of
The Last Storyteller

"I cared about Molly Noble Bull's heroine, Honor McCall, from page one of *The Winter Pearl* to the end of her satisfying and surprising journey where she discovered the precious pearl of grace set in a filigree of hope, redemption and forgiveness."
—Tamela Hancock Murray, award-winning inspirational author of *Love's Denial*

"A sweet pearl of a story that offers the redemptive message of Christ's love and forgiveness. Journey with Honor and Lucas as they ultimately find both."
—Pamela Griffin, author of novellas within *A Prairie Christmas* and *Christmas Homecoming*

THE
WINTER
PEARL

MOLLY NOBLE BULL

Steeple
Hill®

Published by Steeple Hill Books™

STEEPLE HILL BOOKS

Steeple Hill®

ISBN 0-373-78529-1

THE WINTER PEARL

www.SteepleHill.com

Printed in U.S.A.

To my husband, Charlie Bull.
To our family—Bret, Burt, Bren, Jana, Linda,
Bethanny, Dillard, Hailey and Bryson.
And to our pastor, Rev. Jerry Scott.

But to God give the glory.

Chapter One

❧

Falling Rock, Colorado
Late October 1888

"I'm not one to go without a woman for long, missy."

When Honor McCall had first heard her uncle say those words, she'd been sitting beside him in the wagon on the drive from the farm to the cemetery in nearby Falling Rock. She'd trembled then. Now, standing at Aunt Harriet's grave and digesting what Uncle Lucas must have meant, she realized she'd never stopped shaking.

She did *not* want to marry her late aunt's husband. If only the God that Aunt Harriet had told her about would provide her with a means of escape.

Although her aunt had been a Christian all her life, Lucas wasn't allowing a funeral service. There was no one to attend the burial because only the grave diggers knew about the death. It was surprising that Lucas had driven Honor to the cemetery to watch the men dig the hole. Knowing him, that was more than she'd expected.

As the diggers lowered the crude, wooden coffin into the ground, Honor saw a flash of gray behind a group of trees. In a moment, it became a young man in a gray suit, coming toward them, and she knew she'd never seen him before.

Her heart knotted. Lucas would not be pleased by this turn of events.

The stranger had thick brown hair and broad shoulders that reminded her of Lucas. Though her uncle was at least twenty years older, both men were tall and well built. But the young man's clothes looked spotless, and he held what appeared to be a black Bible in one hand and an umbrella in the other. While Lucas, also in a gray suit, had liquor stains down the front of his jacket, and he gripped a half-empty whiskey bottle as though it were glued to his right hand.

Dreading a confrontation, Honor wished the young man would just go away. At the same time, she hoped he would stay. There was something in his presence that made her feel safe.

She'd been so overwhelmed by the death of her aunt, she'd hardly noticed the weather. Now she felt the nip of a fresh norther that had just blown in. Dark clouds gathered, and an icy wind stirred the pines that surrounded them. Her shivers deepened.

When the younger man reached the graveside, Lucas glowered at him. "What do ya think you're doing here, mister?"

"My name is Jethro Peters, but my friends call me Jeth. I'm just visiting here in Falling Rock. I live over in Hearten. I'm the pastor there, and when the diggers told me someone died, I came to see if I could be of help."

Lucas studied the minister, his eyes wide and his mouth hanging slack, the way it always did when something un-usual happened to him. After a moment, his thick eyebrows drew together. His face turned red, and a crease appeared in the center of his forehead.

"Your kind ain't welcome here," he said, his voice rough and gravelly. "We don't need no preacher."

"Yes, Uncle, we do." Honor could hardly believe she'd found the courage to speak up. She knew she could be beaten for her words, but for her aunt's sake, she'd had to say what was in her mind.

Lucas scowled. "What did you say, girl?"

"I said that we need a preacher here today—at least, I do." Her voice was hardly more than a whisper. "Aunt Harriet was a Christian, and she would have wanted someone to say a prayer over her grave and read from the Good Book."

"I would be glad to do it," Jeth Peters said softly, "if you will allow it, sir."

Honor expected Lucas to curse the preacher and drive him away, but strangely, he kept silent for a few moments, staring at the younger man. Then he looked down at his dirty black boots. "All right," he mumbled. "Say what you have to and read from that there book you got. Then git. I ain't never had no use for do-gooders."

Jeth Peters nodded. In a clear voice, he read from the Bible. When he finished, he said a prayer.

The Bible reading sounded strange to Honor's ears, but the prayer made her feel warm all over. She longed to say "Amen" loud enough for her uncle to hear, but decided against it. One more word could set Lucas off, and that might embarrass the minister.

Rain started to fall before the diggers had finished cover-ing the grave.

The minister opened his black umbrella and offered it to Honor. "Here," he said. "We wouldn't want you to catch a cold."

Honor shook her head. "I couldn't take your umbrella, sir, but thank you for offering. And thank you for coming today. I'm sure it was just what my aunt would have wanted."

"My pleasure."

The preacher's wide smile lifted her spirits for an instant. Then thoughts of what Lucas might do to her at home washed away those good feelings.

"Will you take my umbrella if I stand under it with you?" the young man asked.

Stand under it with him? He obviously had no idea how dangerous such an act could be for her. The young minister couldn't know that Lucas would never allow her to stand close to any man, especially a man of the cloth. But defiance suddenly gripped her.

To her own surprise, she lifted her head and said firmly, "Yes. I would be happy to share your umbrella with you. It is kind of you to ask."

Lucas took a swallow of whiskey from the bottle without comment. She wondered if he was aware of what had been said. Or was he too drunk to have really taken in what was going on? No matter, sooner or later, he would insist that Honor pay for the things she'd said and done here today, of that she was certain. She shivered again.

Jeth stood under a spreading pine, watching as the young woman and her drunken companion climbed into the wagon. She'd called the man Uncle. Other than that, Jeth hadn't learned anything about them. Still, he wanted to know more, especially about her.

Her eyes were honey brown, fringed with long dark lashes, and her skin was as pale as alabaster—and flawless. So was her softly rounded figure, in his opinion. Her hair had been hidden under a cotton bonnet, but a few dark auburn curls had escaped—enough for him to know that her hair was long and probably very soft to the touch. And she'd smelled as sweet as rosewater. His experience as a pastor had taught him to notice things about people that other folks might miss—like the fact that the young woman's face, despite all its beauty, didn't contain any laugh lines.

It wasn't surprising that a deep sadness appeared to encase her; her aunt had died. But Jeth wondered if perhaps joy wasn't something she knew very little about—even in the best of times.

Was she married? Betrothed? He hadn't had such thoughts about a woman since before he met his late wife....

Jeth glanced away. A lump now dwelled in his throat as well as his heart. Pain, sudden and strong, blocked out everything. When he glanced back, the wagon had disappeared beyond a clump of pine trees.

In the four-room cabin Honor called home, the stale odor of alcohol surrounded her. Aunt Harriet had always kept the place clean and neat, but no matter how often she'd scrubbed the pine floors, Lucas had always found a reason to complain.

Honor glanced at the black iron skillet, hanging over the cookstove. The tears that she'd been holding in all day spilled down her cheeks. Quickly, she wiped them away. Memories of her aunt standing in front of the stove, cooking for her family with that very skillet saturated her mind.

Her gaze traveled to the door of the room Aunt Harriet had shared with Lucas. He was in there now—passed out on the bed, if she was lucky. Dabbing her eyes with a white handkerchief, Honor straightened her back. Lucas could come in here at any moment, but he wouldn't find her crying—not ever. It had been heartbreaking to say good-bye to Aunt Harriet, but now Honor's strongest emotion was a desperate fear—fear of being alone in the house with Lucas.

He had started to look at her in peculiar, leering ways shortly after her fifteenth birthday. She'd managed to stay out of his presence and avoid his attention most of the time. But what would happen now that her aunt wasn't here to protect her?

At that moment, Lucas tottered out of the bedroom on shaky legs, eyeing the table and the whiskey bottle in the center of it. Holding the back of a kitchen chair for support, he reached for the bottle, tipped it back as he drank. Then he wiped his wet mouth with the back of his hand.

He'd started drinking before breakfast that morning. Now, he reeked of whiskey—even his sweat seemed to give off fumes.

Standing in front of the stove, trying to appear calm, Honor thought about Lucas and his lustful glances through the years. She knew she would only encounter worse in the future. She was like a caged animal searching for a way out.

Lucas glared at Honor. "After what happened at the cemetery today, you owe me for not beating you the minute we came in the house."

She looked at his big hands. A shudder ran down her spine. His hands were strong and deeply tanned from the Colorado sun.

His face was bronzed, too, and with his high cheekbones and straight nose, some would still call him handsome, though his thick brown hair had thinned on top.

Some would call him successful also, since Lucas knew farming. Honor gave him his due in that regard. Yet when she looked at him, all she saw were a rough, unshaven face and bloodshot, blue eyes, with a twisted malevolence lurking behind them.

"Your aunt was sick for six months before she died, and I ain't had no woman since she took to her bed," Lucas began ominously. "But I aim to do the right thing by you. So we'll drive into town in the morning and get hitched. But not by no preacher. Don't even ask."

Lucas studied Honor's face—like a bobcat with a rabbit in its sights. "You're willing to marry me, ain't ya, girl?"

Never! Honor's mind screamed, but she swallowed. "Yes, Uncle," she said softly.

"And from now on, call me Lucas. It ain't fittin' for my future wife to call me Uncle."

"Very well, Lucas."

When he slammed the empty bottle on the kitchen table, it shattered. He laughed. "You've lived here for free long enough," he said. "It's time you paid for your keep. Now, pick up them broken pieces of glass."

She wanted to shout at him, to tell him she would never marry him. *Never!* She would yell and scream and fight to her last breath before she'd let him touch her. But she bit her lower lip. What good would yelling do? Lucas was big and powerful, and he had no mercy in him. Her only chance was to escape from him.

Honor took the broom from its place beside the woodstove. Sweeping up the tiny bits of glass, while he looked on, she made her decision. She would run away at the first moment of opportunity that she saw. In his drunken state, Lucas might not notice that she was gone for a while.

"Now," he demanded, "fix me my supper."

"I'm— I'm out of potatoes for the stew, Uncle," she said, feigning a light tone. "I'll need to go out back and get some."

"Then be quick about it. I'm hungry."

Honor still wore her best dress, the tan one she'd worn to the burial. When she wrapped her shoulders in her brown woolen shawl and pulled on her brown and yellow print bonnet, she snatched the vegetable basket from the shelf by the back door. Without another glance at Lucas, she went out.

The root cellar was to the right of the garden. If he was watching now, when his mind cleared Lucas would remember that she had turned in the opposite direction. Honor prayed he wouldn't notice. Walking, then running, toward the wooded area behind the house, she discarded the basket as she fled.

The cool October air smelled of nuts and pinecones. The wind murmured through the bare branches of the trees, tossing the soft curls around her face. Below her bonnet, her long auburn hair blew every which way.

Honor darted a fearful glance behind her. Nothing moved. She slowed her pace, tying the ends of her knit shawl in a knot. The soft garment did little to shield her from the slicing breeze, but it was better than no covering at all.

By the time Honor reached the turnoff that led into town, her breath was coming in deep gasps. She knew better than to stay on the road. If Uncle Lucas had a shred of wits about him, he would look for her there first. Besides, she couldn't take the chance of being spotted. Travelers moved along the road all the time. Her best bet, she decided, was to follow a line of trees.

Darkness had painted the sky a grayish-black by the time she arrived in Falling Rock. The bare trees looked like skeletons in the dim light of three street lamps. It was late enough that all proper folk were off the streets. The only men and women in public now would be those inside the Silver Nugget Saloon on the corner—or those standing outside that establishment. Honor skirted around and behind the saloon, making her way toward the church. Her aunt had told her that the building was kept open day and night. She would be safe there.

Honor hoped that by now Lucas would have passed out. Her best chance for escape hinged on his not coming after her until morning—and on her not being seen by anyone else. There were plenty of men around who thought like Lucas, and a young woman of barely nineteen years would be a quick target for them. Her aunt had cautioned her that such men were always out there.

As soon as she entered the church, Honor found a pew toward the middle of the chapel, and stretched out on it. Anyone who came in would not be likely to see her. She couldn't afford to fall asleep, but it was nice to rest her bones.

A sudden growl of hunger rumbled from her belly, loud enough to be heard if a stranger stood nearby. Yet her cravings went beyond her need for food. Peering at the dim outline of the pulpit at the front of the small church, she longed for a home, a place in the world. She also wished for someone who would love her unconditionally—the way her aunt had, before she died. Beyond that, Honor dreamed of never having to see Lucas again. If she'd known how to pray, she would have asked God to grant her requests.

Honor pressed her back against the hard wooden pew, wondering if the minister she had met that morning had a wife and children. She scarcely remembered her own parents. They had died of a fever before Honor reached the age of three. Her aunt Harriet, who lived in Colorado, had taken her in four years before she married Lucas. Were it not so, Honor might have spent her growing-up years in an orphanage. Although sometimes she wondered if that would not have been better than living in a house with the likes of Lucas Scythe.

Sitting up, Honor rubbed the palms of her hands across the oak pew and felt the strong yet rough texture of the wood. Her aunt had taken her to church every Sunday— until Lucas put a stop to it.

Harriet Scythe had been a churchgoing woman and a member of the choir, too. Lucas must have known how leaving the church would injure her, but then, hurting others appeared to give him a great deal of pleasure.

Her aunt had once told Honor that the folks at church had thought Lucas was a decent man before they married. Honor had wondered if he'd only pretended to be good and kind. Maybe he'd thought Aunt Harriet had money, since she'd inherited the cabin and the family farm. In any case, he'd managed to fritter away what little she once had, drinking and gambling at the saloon in town.

Aunt Harriet had never complained about anything. But her bruised arms and swollen, red eyes had told Honor all she needed to know.

As Honor sat in the church, remembering, her eyes grew heavy. She yawned, and stretched out again on the pew. Despite herself, a few minutes later, she was asleep.

A sound woke her just before daylight. She jerked, finding herself half on, half off the pew. Pulling herself back onto the wooden bench again, she stiffened and became still. She held her breath.

Had someone entered? Was it Lucas? Honor coiled into a tight ball. The church was silent once more. A few minutes later, she slept again.

Something brushed her face. Honor was instantly awake. She sat up, looking around. A soft *thump* sounded, and she turned in time to see a white cat disappearing behind a stairway leading to the choir loft. Honor sighed in relief. It wasn't Lucas.

Aunt Harriet would say she should pray if she hoped to survive this terrible ordeal. But if there really was a God, He seemed far away to Honor. She was on her own in getting out of this trouble. Since she would not go back to the cabin, *not ever,* and she couldn't remain in Falling Rock, Colorado, Honor had to get away. Yet where would she go? And who would take her in?

Tears gathered at the corners of her eyes, but before they could fall, Honor sniffed. There didn't appear to be a safe place in the world where she could rest her head, but she refused to cry. She had to think.

She needed a job, but employment choices for a young woman were few. She didn't have enough skills to become a schoolteacher, and she wouldn't become a saloon girl. So what did that leave? Nothing that she could think of.

A bookshelf, attached to the back of the pew in front of her, held two hymnals, one new and one old and worn. Honor took the new songbook in both her hands. The brown cover smelled fresh. She opened to the first page. In the pale light of early morning, she squinted at the dedication.

This hymnal is given to the Glory of God in memory of my dear wife, Selma, the love of my life.

Honor ran her fingers down the smooth, white page, studying the inscription. Were there really men in the world who could love a woman the way this nameless husband seemed to have loved his wife? Men were good at pretending. Lucas had taught her that. She put the hymnal back on the shelf and turned to gaze out the windows.

The morning sun still hid beyond the horizon, but the eastern sky was bright. A golden light edged the hills at the end of the street and it glinted on a collection plate in the center of a table directly under a window.

Would there be money in that plate?

Of course not. What pastor worth his salt would leave money in an unlocked church? That would be like opening the door to every outlaw for miles around. Still, what if money *was* left there? And what if she took some?

Honor hated to even consider the thought. Her aunt would have said that such musings were sinful. Yet Honor remembered her aunt also telling her that the collection money went to pay for the pastor's keep and to help the poor and needy. Well, who needed money more than Honor?

The right thing to do would be to wait until the preacher came in for the day and ask him for financial help. But if she waited, she could miss the early morning stage out of town.

Biting her lip, she deliberated. Thieves deserved to go to hell. Sinful thoughts came from the devil. Lucas never allowed Aunt Harriet to pray openly or study the Good Book, but she'd managed to teach Honor the Ten Commandments. And Honor knew stealing was a sin.

But what if she vowed to pay back all the money someday? Considering recent events, surely God would understand.

On the chance that money waited in that silver plate, Honor crept to the window. Even at a distance, she could see several coins and a number of bills. Her throat tightened. Her fingers shook as she reached her hands forward and scooped up all of the money they could hold. As she turned back to the wooden bench, she heard someone coming.

Trembling, she slipped into the nearest pew and stretched out to hide. The faint *tap, tap* of footsteps on the brick floor drifted up from the entry of the church. Honor dared not move.

Chapter Two

※

A man and woman whispered to each other as they moved down the aisle of the church. Honor held her breath. Now what? The squeak of old wood told her that they had selected a pew not far behind her. The scent of lilacs filled the air.

"Annie," Honor heard the man say. "I know your poor old bones are tired, because mine are, too. But, honey, do you really think it's all right for us to sit in here 'til the stage leaves? Why, we ain't even members of this church."

"A church is God's house, Simon, no matter where it is," the woman answered. "Besides, I reckon if you put something in the plate—under that there winder—it should take care of everything."

Honor froze. If the man named Simon came over to the window to put money in the plate, he might be able to see her crouched on the pew. Slowly, not making a sound, she inched along the pew, out of the light coming in from the window and into the shadows.

"Well, Simon. Are you gonna put something in or ain't you?"

Simon groaned. "Oh, all right. I'll put in a coin or two if that will satisfy you."

"Thank you, dear."

"So now I'm 'dear,' huh?"

Another squeak of the wooden bench indicated that the man had left the pew and was headed for the window. Honor shut her eyes. A minute later, the bench creaked again. She didn't feel safe, but at least she hadn't been discovered yet.

For the next hour, Honor learned more about Annie and Simon than she cared to know. Their conversation held no interest for her, but it assured her that they were harmless. The elderly couple planned to visit their daughter in Pine Falls. Honor wondered if she had enough money to travel that far. She still hadn't counted her loot.

Loot? Why, I'm nothing more than a common thief, she thought.

A lump lodged in her throat when she contemplated what she'd become. Not in her worst nightmare had she ever envisioned that she would stoop so low.

Simon's offering in the silver plate couldn't possibly add up to the amount of money Honor had taken. A feeling of shame swept over her. She wanted to tell God she was sorry for what she'd done, but she didn't know how. The only prayer that Honor knew was one Harriet had taught her before they stopped going to church, and years had passed since she'd recited that one.

But she remembered how it began. *Our Father, who art in Heaven.*

The sun had risen over the horizon now and was beaming through the east window. Inching back along the pew, closer to the light, Honor reached for a hymnal. When Lucas wasn't around, sometimes her aunt had enjoyed singing hymns as she did her daily chores. She said that church music gave her strength.

Strength. Honor could use some of that.

Flipping through the songbook, she didn't find any of the hymns her aunt had once sung, but she noticed some blank sheets of paper near the back of the book, titled "Note Pages."

She considered using one of the sheets to compose a note, a letter to members of the church. And what better place to write it than the back of a hymnal? She reached for the pencil that was in a slot on the bookshelf, and began to write.

Dear Church People,
I hated to steal the money from the collection plate, and I wrote in the hymnal, too. I know I did wrong, but I was once told that the collection money went to the minister and to the poor and needy. Well, I'm poor and might need money more than the preacher does.

You see, I have to leave town today. If I don't, my uncle will beat me and force me to marry him. He might even kill me.

Thank you for leaving the money in that plate so I could find it when I needed it the most. If I knew how to pray, I would tell God I am sorry for what I did. Since I don't, would you folks please pray for me?

As soon as I can find a job, I promise to pay back everything I took, a little at a time.
Yours truly,
H.

* * *

Honor placed the songbook back on the shelf. She was wondering if there was a way for her to count her money without making a sound, when the bell in the tower suddenly pealed six times. Honor flinched each time. Somebody had to be pulling the rope to ring that bell, but she hadn't heard a sound above her all night long. Yet, someone other than Annie and Simon was nearby. The minister? If he came down and saw her in the church or the churchyard, might he stop her from leaving?

The bench behind her squeaked, cutting off her racing thoughts. Honor didn't move a muscle.

"Wake up, Simon," Annie said. "It's time to go."

"What? Oh. Well, I wasn't asleep no-how."

"You were, too."

"No, I was just resting my eyes," Simon insisted.

"You can rest your eyes when we get on the stage." There was fond exasperation in the woman's voice. "Get up now, Simon. We have to get out of here. It's six o'clock. The stage leaves at six-thirty, and we still have to buy our tickets."

The bench creaked several times. Then Honor heard the *tap, tap* of their shoes as they moved back up the aisle. When the heavy front door of the church closed, Honor cautiously sat up and began to quietly count her money.

She had ten dollars and fifty-one cents, more than she had dreamed of finding. She could go to Pine Falls, for sure. That much money might take her all the way to Denver.

She'd almost reached the entry of the church when she saw the shape of a man in the shadows to the left of the door. Though she couldn't actually see him, she felt him—and there was something in the air between them, a kind of regret. Was it coming from him? Or was it her distress?

Guilt engulfed her. Did he know what she'd done? Would the man try to stop her to recover the money? She hesitated by the door, waiting to see what he might do. But he never said a word.

"I'm sorry," Honor whispered.

Without saying more, she raced out the door and down the path toward the livery stable where stagecoach tickets were sold. Once the stage pulled out, she would never have to see Lucas or Falling Rock, Colorado, again.

Honor waited in the carriage with Annie and Simon for the fourth passenger to arrive. The silver-haired couple looked older than she had expected, and she learned that their last name was Carr. Honor couldn't help liking them, but she wished they weren't so talkative.

The red velvet interior of the carriage looked new, and, although the back of the seat was wooden, the bench was padded.

Honor had heard that within a year, the railroad would be coming to Falling Rock. Tracks were being laid throughout the state, and stagecoaches could soon become outdated. A stagecoach had brought Honor to Colorado after her parents died, but she was too young to have a clear memory of that journey.

Now, fidgeting with the small velvet bow at the neck of her dress, she waited for the fourth passenger. She wished she had a hat with a net veil like Annie Carr's little black one. Honor also admired the string of pearls around the older woman's neck.

Aunt Harriet had had a pearl necklace that she'd inherited from Honor's grandmother, but one day it vanished. Lucas was behind the disappearance, of course.

Proper ladies wore pearls and store-bought hats, not homemade print bonnets like Honor's. But there wasn't much cause for Honor to worry about becoming a lady now.

The driver had explained that the fourth passenger would be delayed as a result of unforeseen circumstances. Honor hoped whoever it was would hurry and be done so they could leave. Lucas could come looking for her at any moment.

When she heard a *click* at the door, she looked up expectantly, and then recoiled. *Lucas!* Trembling, she pressed back and covered her mouth with her hand to keep from shrieking.

In the next moment, she saw that it was the minister who'd prayed at her aunt's grave, standing outside the carriage in his gray suit. He looked so much like a younger version of Lucas that for an instant, she'd thought he *was* her aunt's husband.

Standing in the street, with one hand on the door handle, the handsome young man smiled warmly at the passengers in the carriage. "Sorry to have kept you nice folks waiting. Jeth Peters," he said, leaning through the door, offering Simon Carr his hand, which the older gentleman took in a friendly shake. Jeth identified himself as the pastor of a church over in Hearten.

When Simon finished introducing his wife, Annie, Jeth turned his gaze on Honor for the first time. His smile fell away. "I want to express my sympathy once again for the loss of your aunt," he said.

Annie and Simon glanced at each other, then at Honor. She recognized the expression of sympathy in their eyes.

"Reckon we're sorry, too, miss," Simon said.

Honor's heart squeezed. "Thank you." She ducked her head, trying not to look at Jeth.

Was he the man from the church who'd hid in the darkness? Had her sin been discovered? Did he know what she'd done? When Honor glanced up, finally meeting his sky-blue eyes, the warmth in them suggested he wasn't concealing thoughts about her. But who could be sure?

Jeth climbed into the carriage and took a seat beside Honor. "I don't believe you told me your name at the burial yesterday. May I know it now?"

"My name is Honor. Honor Rose McCall."

"Honor." He smiled. "I like that."

Why had she told him her real name? She could have lied. Now it would be easier for Lucas to find her.

"Honor is a good character trait to have," he went on, "and one we should all live by. Are you on your way to Pine Falls?"

"Yes," Honor said a little too sharply, and pressed her lips together.

Jeth turned his gaze to the Carrs. "And where are you folks headed?"

"We're going to Pine Falls, too," Annie said, "and we'll be gone for quite a spell. We'll be home by Christmas, though." She turned to her husband. "Won't we, Simon?"

"We sure better."

Annie Carr looked back to Jeth. "Did I hear you say you were a preacher?"

A grin started in Jeth's blue eyes. "That's right."

Annie's wrinkled lips turned up at the edges in reply. "Reckon you could answer some questions about the Bible?"

"Watch out, Preacher," Simon put in. "My Annie is a longwinded woman when it comes to Scripture."

Jeth chuckled under his breath as Annie Carr began asking her questions. Honor glanced out the window on her side of the coach.

A quaint little log cabin with a peaked roof stood on a hill. It reminded Honor of the clock her grandmother had sent to Aunt Harriet for a wedding gift. Grandma McCall was dead now, but when she sent the present, she wrote that she'd bought it from an Amish wood-carver during a visit to Lancaster County, Pennsylvania.

Painted statues of a little man and woman inside the clock had captivated Honor as a child. She'd spent hours in front of the clock, sitting cross-legged on the floor, waiting for the toylike couple to come out of their little house to check the weather.

Sometimes, the statues stayed out on their front porch for a while. At other times, they went right back inside and shut the door.

Honor was like that, too.

She'd been a happy, winsome child who loved playing in the sunshine—until Lucas came into her life. After that, she went inside herself and only came out occasionally to see if things had changed. Nothing ever did.

An image of Honor and Lucas sharing a house together as man and wife flashed through her brain. Her heart constricted.

Lucas couldn't force her to marry him, but if he found her, he would whip her. Could she survive another of his beatings?

Aside from fearing him, she was disturbed and disgusted by the thought of seeing Lucas again. She knew she would always feel that way.

The stagecoach rocked, bumping Honor against the door. Holding herself stiffly on the bench, she gazed out the window again. They would be driving south from Falling Rock through what the ticket agent had called "rugged country." There was to be a stop in Hearten, then on to Pine Falls. Some of the trees were leafless. Others were alive with all the fall colors—red, orange, yellow, gold and shades of rusty brown.

The ticket agent had explained that traveling through the hills would not be easy. The roads were rocky and there were numerous low-water crossings. Nevertheless, Honor loved the beauty that surrounded her.

"God gave us a good world to live in, didn't He, Miss McCall?"

It was Jeth Peters who spoke, and Honor turned to face him, nodding a quick reply. She hadn't realized the minister was sitting there watching her. She wondered how long he'd been doing so.

"I noticed you looking out at the scenery," he continued, "and I figured you must enjoy the magnificence of nature as much as I do."

"Yes." Glancing away again, she squeezed her hands together tightly. She didn't care to talk. She hoped he'd take the hint.

"White-topped mountains are peaceful looking," he said. "Aren't they?"

She turned back again, nodded, and then looked away once more.

"It's real peaceful over in Hearten, too, where I live," he went on. "The stage will be stopping there before going on to Pine Falls. Hope you have time to look around before you have to get back on the stagecoach. Have you taken this route before, ma'am?"

"No, I haven't."

"Then let me prepare you."

When he leaned a bit closer, she flinched and pressed her shoulder against the side of the carriage. A hint of puzzlement crossed his face, but then his expression became sober.

"The first creek will be easy to cross," he explained. "But some of the rivers ahead are deeper. The currents will be swifter."

"Are you trying to scare me, Preacher?" she asked.

"Not at all." He chuckled, and a twinkle gleamed in his eyes. "Still, a person should know what to expect."

They crossed the first creek easily, just as Jeth had predicted. The banks held only a trickle of water. What he'd said about the rivers worried her, though, because she'd heard that a stagecoach could be swept away by the rapids in an instant.

Annie and Simon Carr had fallen asleep. Simon snored; the echo of it filled the carriage.

Jeth laughed softly, sharing his amusement with Honor. She smiled back, giving herself permission to relax. The stress she'd felt since Aunt Harriet died slowly began to melt.

The ride had been bumpy since they'd left town that morning, but now, all at once, it felt like the carriage hit something large and hard. The coach rocked and tilted to the left. Annie and Simon were jolted awake as they tumbled toward the door. With the stagecoach canted to on one side, Honor slid across the seat, landing in Jeth's arms.

"Oh, I'm sorry," she exclaimed.

He gazed down at her, and she felt the warmth of his smile.

If the man weren't a minister, Honor would say he enjoyed their brief encounter. Then the rig straightened, and she returned to her half of the padded bench.

Squeaking and jerking, the stagecoach continued down a road, which really wasn't much more than a set of deep ruts. Then the vehicle stopped. The driver got down from his perch and came to the window on Jeth's side of the carriage.

"We're gonna be going up a steep hill," the driver told him. "And the horses could sure use some help pushing the load if you two men are of a mind to lend a hand."

"Of course we'll help." Jeth glanced at Simon. "At least, I will."

"Reckon that makes two of us," Simon added.

"Now, you be careful, Simon," Annie warned. "You ain't as young as you used to be."

"Neither are you, my dear."

When the two men exited, the driver turned his gaze on the women. "Both you ladies better sit on Mrs. Carr's side of the coach. 'Cause you'll be thrown to her side anyway, once we start up that hill."

Honor considered offering to help push. She certainly felt fit enough. But Aunt Harriet would have said it wasn't ladylike to do such a thing, and Honor didn't want to draw more attention to herself or to be judged improper.

The stagecoach slowly moved upward at a steep angle. Honor fell against the back of the seat and held down the skirt of her dress to keep it from slipping up and showing her ankles. If she had thought the journey jolted her back and forth before, she needed a new word to describe the ride from that point on.

At the top of the hill, the carriage stopped again. Honor checked the condition of her clothing. The tan dress had been her aunt's wedding gown, and the wide lace collar looked soiled—no doubt the result of her dash into town through the woods and a night spent sleeping in it. The pearl buttons that went up to her chin appeared clean enough, but her sleeves were dirty.

After she'd bought her ticket, she'd placed her remaining paper money in the lace-edged cuff of her right sleeve.

After the rough ride to the top of the hill, she wondered if she still had the bills. Pressing her fingers against the cuff at her wrist, she felt the stiff wad and breathed easier.

Honor moved back to her original seat. She smoothed the wrinkles from her skirt, then stuck her head out the window to see what the world looked like from the top of the hill. She saw three riders coming up behind them at a fast gallop, and her pulse began to race. They wore masks. For a moment, she couldn't react.

Outlaws.

"Jump back inside!" she heard the driver shout to Jeth and Simon Carr. "I'm gonna try to outrun 'em."

Both doors flew open. The stagecoach lurched forward—starting off at a fast pace, while the two men crouched on the floor.

"Get down!" Jeth yelled to the women. "Both of you."

Honor jumped to the floor beside Jeth, Annie Carr right behind her. The men pulled pistols from their belts.

Honor hadn't expected Jeth to be armed—he was a preacher. However, she felt relieved, knowing he carried protection.

"Will we be able to outrun 'em?" Annie asked in a shaky voice.

"Yes, ma'am," Jeth replied. "I think so. At least, I hope so."

Every muscle in Honor's body tensed as the carriage rolled on down the hill. Clinging to the edge of the bench, she tried to imagine the driver and the man riding shotgun whipping the horses, urging them to run even faster. She could only hope the two men driving the stage could outrun their pursuers.

The carriage took a sharp curve, wobbling and swaying back and forth over the big rocks. Honor was tossed against Jeth again and again, and he jostled against her.

She felt a sudden jolt as the carriage lurched sharply. "What's happening?"

Jeth peered out a window. "We lost a wheel! I can see it rolling down the hill."

The carriage swerved to the right. The screeching cry of iron against rock rang out. All four passengers tumbled to the side of the stagecoach. Honor could scarcely breathe until Jeth pulled her out from under Annie. The crippled rig careened down the hill, half rolling, half dragging. They were coming close to the edge of a cliff. Annie screamed.

"Move out of my way, Miss McCall!" Jeth shoved Honor to one side and crawled to the door.

The stagecoach lost speed, then banged against the side of an embankment. They were all thrown to and fro. The rig slid a few more feet. Then stopped.

"Praise the Lord!" Jeth released a big breath of air and wiped his brow. "Someone must have cut those horses loose. Anybody hurt?" He glanced around and smiled. "Guess not. What a blessing."

"We're safe, then?" Honor asked, feeling a first rush of relief.

Jeth shook his head and cocked his pistol. "Now we'll have to deal with the outlaws."

Honor shrank to the floor as shots blasted from both directions. Jeth placed his hand on her back to keep her there. At the ring of a bullet hitting metal, Honor glanced out the window just as a rifle flew by.

"The stagecoach driver lost his weapon," Jeth announced.

Jeth and Simon aimed their pistols at the three riders who had caught up with them. Before the two men inside the carriage could discharge a single shot, the outlaws surrounded the crippled stagecoach.

"Everybody out with your hands up," a bandit with gray hair shouted down from his horse. "And be quick about it."

Jeth tucked his pistol in the waistband of his trousers. "Do whatever they tell you to do, Miss McCall," he whispered. "This is not the time to try anything risky."

Honor stepped down from the stage and stood between Jeth and Annie Carr. When she raised her hands above her head, she noticed that the edge of one bill protruded from the cuff of her dress.

Two of the robbers had dismounted. A young-looking man with a pimply face above a red bandanna held a basket that reminded Honor of the one she had discarded back in Falling Rock. Another outlaw stood beside him, aiming a gun at the hostages. The man with gray hair remained atop a big, reddish horse. He held a rifle on the group as well.

"Put all your money and valuables in the basket there," he ordered them. "And hurry up, or you'll be sorry."

When Honor thought nobody was watching, she attempted to push the money back in the cuff of her dress. The next moment, everything went black.

Chapter Three

✤

Lucas awoke with a jerk. Someone was pounding on his front door.

"All right, all right," he shouted. "Hold on to your horses. I'm comin'!"

He sat up. A massive headache made him wish he were still flat on his back. He pressed a hand over his forehead and looked around. He was shivering on the hard kitchen floor. Had he been there all night?

He stumbled to his feet. His legs felt like jam. Slowly, he made his way to the door and opened it. An icy wind swept inside. His shoulders shook from the cold.

The grave diggers he had hired stood on his porch. All three men wore dark clothing, gloves, and something furry-looking covered their ears.

"Mr. Scythe," the tallest one said. "Remember me? Hector Brown?" He motioned toward the other two. "And these are my brothers, Joey and Abner. We hate to bother you at a time like this, but you forgot to pay us for burying your wife yesterday." He handed Lucas a sheet of paper.

"A bill?"

Hector nodded.

"Oh, yes. The money." Lucas searched for something to say, to stall for time. "You'll have to excuse me. I ain't feelin' well today."

Hector nodded again. Joey and Abner just stood behind their brother, staring at Lucas.

Lucas shook his head. If it ain't one thing, it's somethin' worse, he thought. "Wait here, and I'll go see what I can do."

He started to close the door, to shut out the chill, but when he saw the hard look of warning in Hector's eyes, he left it open.

Lucas stormed into the kitchen and grabbed the cookie jar, one of the places Harriet liked to hide money. He removed the wooden lid of the clay pot and tossed it on the floor. Then he poured out the contents of the jar. Broken cookies, crumbs, and a sprinkling of sugar spilled onto the table. A few coins clinked together. They rolled around and stopped.

He scooped up the money and counted it. Thirty-six cents. He winced. The diggers expected more. Well, there was nothing he could do about that now.

Lucas pasted a smile on his face and walked back to the door. "Here's thirty-six cents. Sorry, I know it ain't enough. But it's all I've got until I sell them calves I've been feedin'. This'll have to hold you 'til then."

Hector Brown stepped forward, filling the doorway. "We expected to be paid in full. When will we get the rest?"

"As soon as I can find the time to drive my calves into town and sell 'em." Lucas grabbed the door and began to swing it shut as he spoke. "I'll keep in touch. And much obliged to ya."

"Wait, Mr. Scythe." With the toe of his black boot, Hector prevented the door from closing all the way. "We'll be back. You can be sure about that."

When Lucas finally closed the door, he leaned against it for a moment, listening to the three men depart. He felt hungry as well as cold. Thirsty, too. For something stronger than cow's milk or water.

Now, where was that Honor-girl? "Missy," he shouted. "Get in here!"

No answer.

"Don't play games with me. I ain't in the mood."

Lucas grimaced. That girl was never around when he needed her.

As he moved toward the kitchen, he glanced in a mirror on the parlor wall—then stopped and looked again. His eyes seemed more red than usual. His face had a drawn, pasty look.

He remembered why he was wearing his gray suit—to attend the burial of his wife—but he couldn't recall arriving at the graveside, much less leaving it. Come to think of it, he'd been having a lot of memory problems lately.

Lucas laid two small logs in the woodstove. When he had managed to start a fire, he pulled out a kitchen chair and sat down. Honor must be out in the garden, he decided. Reaching out, he held his hands in front of the fire, to warm them while he made his plans.

First, he'd get Honor to fix him something to eat. Then he would look for any other hidden money. Harriet had always hidden money from him, but she must have put it somewhere else this time.

Later, he would drive into town, buy a couple of bottles of whiskey, and maybe pay Miss Ruby a visit. His slow smile became a chuckle.

He vaguely remembered asking Honor to marry him, but he would worry about getting hitched some other time.

Lucas went out onto the back porch. "Missy! Come in here this minute!"

Calves bellowed. Chickens squawked from the henhouse. But not a sound from Honor. Lucas spent the next ten minutes searching the farm buildings, but he was unable to find her.

She could have hiked into town to buy supplies, he supposed. He'd noticed the flour sack was almost empty. Yeah, that must be what she done, he convinced himself.

Cursing his late wife for selecting a hiding place he couldn't discover, Lucas tore up the house and barn looking for money. Honor could clean up the mess when she got back from Falling Rock.

His breath became rapid from all the labor in his quest, and he felt a little shaky. He wanted alcohol—bad. He wouldn't hold out much longer without it.

Honor had been gone a long time. Too long. How much time did it take to go into town, buy a few things on credit at the general store, and walk back to the farm? Was that girl really shopping? Or had she left with the rest of his money?

The word *left* roared inside his head. Lucas stiffened, and he felt rage rising in his blood. "Why, that little—"

The truth hit him like a sock in the jaw. His late wife had hidden money, and Honor had taken it. The muscles around his mouth tightened. She'd robbed him. He still didn't want to believe it. Lucas balled his hands into fists. *Yes, that's what happened.* He would like to strangle her.

Hadn't Harriet always saved every penny she could get her hands on? And wouldn't she have told Honor where she kept it? His late wife had called Honor her cherished niece, her sweet little Rose of Sharon.

Lucas swore, kicking a kitchen chair. The chair banged the back wall, then fell on its side on the floor. Those two had *always* plotted against him. Whispering behind his back. Exchanging glances when they thought he wasn't looking.

"But no more!"

Lucas picked up the cookie jar and threw it across the room. The clay pot crashed against the iron stove, smashing into hundreds of tiny pieces.

Grabbing a loaf of bread from the bread box, he tore off a chunk and crammed it in his mouth. Then he reached for a slice of jerky and gobbled it down. Lucas looked at the clock on the wall. It was almost noon. Honor had a head start on him. If he expected to catch up with her and recover his money, he would need to ride out as soon as possible.

Jeth lifted Honor gently onto the back of the wagon. Then he climbed up, wrapped her in a warm blanket and sat down beside her.

The outlaws had disappeared as soon as they'd collected their spoils. The passengers and the crew were left behind with the crippled stage. Jeth had ridden one of the stage-coach horses into Hearten for help, returning with blankets, two wagons, a local doctor, and a few other folks from Jeth's church.

Jeth glanced at Dr. Harris, seated up front in the wagon and taking the reins. The doctor had examined Honor and bandaged her head as soon as he'd arrived. Now he was acting as their driver. Annie and Simon were in the other wagon.

Jeth cradled Honor's head in his lap as the doctor cracked his whip. The wagon rolled forward slowly.

A cold breeze whistled around them. When locks of Honor's long auburn hair blew across her eyes, Jeth pushed them back from her face.

Her thick mane looked shiny, and the strands felt soft in his hands. Jeth frowned. He shouldn't notice such things. He yanked his hands back as if her hair had scalded them.

When he looked down at her again, he felt a grip of fear. Honor looked pale. She hadn't moved at all, and now seemed gravely ill.

Lord, he prayed. *You know all about this young woman, and I'm sure You have a plan for her life. Heal her, Lord, I pray— spirit, soul and body—to Your honor and glory.*

Lucas carried his riding gear into the horse stall. His gray mare pulled back her ears, as she always did when she was about to be saddled.

"You turning on me, too, Lady?"

The horse blew out through her nose, making a gentle, snorting sound. Lucas put down his load and stroked the animal's head. Merely touching her velvety nose softened him a little.

"Easy, girl." He reached down and patted the mare's round belly. "You're getting big, ain't ya? I'll be riding ya nice and slow today. So don't fret none. Gotta take care of that colt inside ya, don't we."

The mare snorted again.

An image of Honor flashed before Lucas. His gentleness vanished. Wait 'til I get my hands on that girl. She'll be sorry for running out on me, he vowed.

Lucas arrived in town at three and went straight to the saloon. He hoped to buy a drink on credit.

Standing at the bar, he grinned at the bartender. "A shot of whiskey, Mitch. Just put it on my bill."

"Sorry, Lucas," Mitch said. "Your credit is all used up."

"I sure am dry. Couldn't you spare me one shot?"

"Not unless you're willing to wash dishes."

"I reckon I could." Lucas hid his hands in his pants pockets so Mitch wouldn't see how they shook. "But I have a couple of things I need to do here in town first."

"Then I suggest you go and do them. This here saloon will still be open when you get back."

Lucas had been counting on that drink to make it through the day. Knowing he wouldn't get a drop without working for it made him even thirstier. He licked his lips. He could almost taste whiskey in his mouth.

"Well, if you ain't gonna give me nothing to drink," Lucas said, "will you at least give me a little information?"

"Yes, I can do that." Mitch wiped a glass with a white cloth. Then he put it on the counter and cocked his head. "What kind of information?"

"That niece of mine has done run off with all my money. Would you have any idea where she might have went to?"

The bartender shrugged. "I wouldn't know. The sheriff might." Mitch glanced toward one of the tables. "He's sitting right over there."

Lucas had never liked Sheriff Manning. Years ago, the sheriff had made it clear he had no use for Lucas Scythe. Still, if the sheriff knew something, it wouldn't hurt to ask.

There were two local men at the round table in the corner with the lawman. Lucas ambled toward them.

Sheriff Manning was leaning back in his chair, drinking from a beer mug. His fat belly hung over his belt, and his blue shirt was stretched to the limit. Some of the buttons looked like they might pop off at any moment.

"Well, Scythe," the sheriff said, "what dragged you to town in the middle of the day? Whiskey?"

Lucas stiffened.

The other two men grinned.

Arms at his sides, Lucas clenched his fists. His jaw hardened. He should punch all three of them out for their taunting. They had it coming, even if he landed in jail. However, to get the information he needed, he had no choice but to rein in his anger.

"My niece, Honor, has done run off with my money, Sheriff. She's a low-down thief and that's the truth."

"Well, well. What a shame. Have you tried paying that girl for the work she does for ya, Scythe?"

"She gets room and board."

"Room and board." The sheriff exchanged a glance with the other men at his table. "Maybe she thought she deserved more. Ever think of that?"

The other men looked straight at Lucas, waiting for him to answer.

Lucas felt his face heat up, and fury burned like hot coals inside him. He cleared his throat, trying to keep calm. He'd learned the hard way that if he hoped to be looked on favorably by the sheriff and others in the community, he must pretend to agree with them, whatever the cost.

"Any idea how I could find her 'fore she spends all I got?"

"If your niece had money, she might have taken the stage to Pine Falls or on to Denver," the sheriff said. "Or she could have taken the stage to Cold Springs. Who knows?"

Slim Perkins sat across from the sheriff. He set his mug on the table. "Since Ben Kraken sells stagecoach tickets down at the livery, he might know."

Why hadn't Lucas thought of that? "Thank you kindly, Slim."

Lucas glanced toward the door. His absentmindedness appeared to be growing by the minute. He swallowed, wishing for a drink. "I best go on over there and see what Ben can tell me, then." He looked back. "And I'm much obliged to all of ya."

Nobody at the table made a comment. They merely watched him go like they all had a secret they weren't willing to share with him. Lucas turned, clenching his jaw. If he hoped to find Honor, he'd better just walk away.

Lucas brushed through the swinging doors, but he stopped before stepping off the covered porch in front of the saloon. Snowflakes were floating down, melting before they hit the ground. The chilly air and the refreshing sight of falling snow lifted his spirits. He straightened his shoulders and turned up his collar against the wintry breeze. If he expected Ben to provide him with answers, he would need to look composed.

Glancing up and down the street, he took in his town. Until now, he'd seldom seen the place in daylight.

Falling Rock reminded him of Cold Springs, the town he grew up in. He had never realized the similarity until now. Trees lined both sides of the street, and snow-tipped mountains towered in the distance. Neatly dressed people strolled in and out of the hotel and the general store.

Looking down at the gray suit he'd worn since Harriet's burial, Lucas wished he'd cleaned up a bit before leaving the cabin. A week ago, he wouldn't have cared. Now, he did. He should look respectable if he expected folks to give him the information he wanted.

Lucas started down the street and turned left at the corner. He'd almost forgotten he would have to pass by the church to reach the livery. He considered turning back, selecting a different route, then decided he just wouldn't look at the little church with its whitewashed walls and stone porch. Not this time. As a child, he'd had his fill of church and religion.

Yet when he reached the small structure, he found himself peering inside the open doorway. Harriet had once been a member of that church. He guessed she must have been considered a member until the day she died.

A middle-aged man in a dark suit came out and stood on the porch. The preacher? Lucas didn't want to find out. He stepped up his pace. Hurrying down the street, he didn't look back.

By the time Lucas reached the livery stable, his breath was coming in gasps. Then he coughed.

The room used for blacksmithing jobs smelled of smoke. Ben Kraken stood in front of a heavy anvil mounted on the stump of a big oak tree. He was hammering a piece of iron into a horseshoe.

"Good afternoon," Lucas said from the doorway.

Ben must have heard him, but he kept on working. His hammer hit the metal again. *Whop!* The metal glowed red-hot.

Even on such a cold day, the room was sweltering. Lucas unbuttoned the top button of his jacket and stepped inside. Ben raised the heavy hammer again. When it came down against the soft metal and the anvil, another loud metallic bang rang out.

Lucas stepped closer. "I said hello."

"I heard ya." Ben glanced at Lucas out of the corner of his eye. "Good afternoon. Or it will be—if you came in to pay what you owe me."

Lucas felt his temper rising, but he feigned a pleasant expression. "My niece run off with all my money, and I come lookin' for her. What else could I do?"

Ben Kraken lifted the hot iron with a pair of long-handled tongs and dropped it into a tub of water. The water sizzled. A puff of gray smoke spiraled upward.

Lucas took a step back from the tub. He had a deep need to punch Kraken in that big nose of his until it bled. Hearing Ben speak in mocking tones and with such a lack of respect was galling. Nevertheless, to get what he wanted out of the man, Lucas would hold back. For now. He could settle the score later.

"Do you know if Honor took the stage somewhere?" he asked in a calm voice.

"If I knew, I wouldn't tell you."

Lucas stepped forward again. His hands clenched into fists, and his wrath grew, but he held his tongue. Looking Kraken right in the face, he glared at him. "Why won't ya tell me, Ben?"

"Word gets around." Ben looked down at his work, ignoring the rage that Lucas could hear in his own voice. "The whole town knows how you treated your wife and that poor girl."

Ben pulled the horseshoe from the water with the tongs, then turned and thrust the metal into the forge. The blaze licked the iron, crackling and popping. Red and yellow sparks flew.

Lucas jammed his hands deeply into his pockets to prevent them from flying out as fists. "But if I don't get my money back," he pointed out, "how was you expecting me to pay ya?"

Ben dragged the iron from the fire. "Knowing you, I doubt I'll get paid anyway." The metal had turned a bright red. Heat radiated from it. Ben took the horseshoe back to the anvil and reached for the hammer. "Besides," he said, "if I can help that girl a little, I will."

Lucas gritted his teeth. Kraken was asking for it. He counted to ten, trying to calm down. Then twenty. At last he asked, "Did a stage leave for Pine Falls early yesterday morning?"

"As a matter of fact, one did. And somebody robbed it," Ben said. "I had to send out another coach to take the folks on to Pine Falls."

"Was anyone hurt?"

"If they were, I don't know about it," Ben said shortly.

"I guess I'll ride over to Pine Falls, then, and take a look around. See what I can find out. And thanks for your help."

"The best thing you can do for me, Scythe, is to get out of my livery stable. And don't come back without my money."

Lucas stood in the doorway, glowering at the back of Ben Kraken's head. He fought the desire once more to punch him and keep on hitting until Kraken cried for mercy.

Lucas turned and headed to the saloon. He *really* needed a drink now. If necessary, he wasn't too proud to wash dishes.

When he'd saved enough to buy a bottle of whiskey, he would ride on over to Pine Falls. The trip would take a day or two—maybe more. If he took it slow and easy, his mare should be able to make it all the way.

Maybe he would post a "Wanted" sign in the saloon. He thought for a moment. What should a sign like that say?

Pondering, he scratched his right ear. Twenty dollars. Thirty. That's it, thirty.

WANTED

Miss Honor McCall for stealing from Lucas Scythe.
Thirty-dollar reward for information on her
whereabouts.

Lucas spent the rest of the day and most of the night working at the saloon. When the bartender wasn't looking, he snatched a few drinks. During his supper break, he printed a sign on a piece of wood with some black paint he found in the storeroom.

He kept a close eye on Mitch. When Lucas saw the bartender escort a rowdy drunk outside, Lucas took a hammer, nails and the wooden sign, and sneaked to the pine wall at the front of the saloon where other signs were posted, looking for an available spot. A vacant square of discolored wall was right in front of the door.

Lucas nailed his sign to the wall with one whack of the hammer. Then he crept back to the kitchen and started washing dishes.

When the saloon closed for the night, Lucas stepped up to the bar to get his pay. Mitch handed him a few small coins.

"Is that all I get?" Lucas asked.

"Sorry, Scythe. I saw you steal drinks when you thought I wasn't lookin'."

"Have a heart, Mitch, and give me a whole bottle. I reckon I'll do anything to get it," Lucas wheedled. "Why, I'll promise to come in early tomorrow and work until closing time again if you'll give me a bottle of whiskey. Is that a deal?"

"You think you know how to get what you want, don't ya." Mitch shook his head like someone who didn't want to believe what he'd just seen and heard. "All right, I guess I could give you one bottle. But you better be here tomorrow. Early."

"You can count on me."

Lucas rode home, chugging down whiskey as he went. He finished the bottle before falling into bed. With nothing in his belly but liquor, he fell asleep immediately.

Honor opened her eyes and sat up. She was in a bed in a clean room, but had no idea how she'd gotten there. A sharp pain in her head and a wave of nausea caused her to consider lying back down, but she didn't want to give in to the discomfort.

Rose-print curtains framed the windows, and a cool breeze came into the small bedroom. A cast-iron stove stood in one corner, with a stack of wood nearby, but no warming fire blazed in it to take the chill from the air.

Glancing around, Honor noted a carved, wooden headboard, and a rose-cushioned chair with oak arms, placed beside the bed as if a guest was expected. A middle-aged woman of average build suddenly appeared in the doorway. She had salt-and-pepper hair and wore a white apron over a dark blue dress.

"Good morning," she said in a welcoming tone. "I'm Regina Peters, the reverend's mother."

Honor blinked. "Is it still morning?"

"It's morning, all right," came the cheerful reply, with a sunny smile. "But you arrived yesterday around noon."

"Yesterday?" Honor pressed a hand against her forehead and felt some sort of bandage. She wanted answers—explanations, though she barely felt able to ask questions.

"What happened to me?" She lay back against the soft pillow.

"You were on the stagecoach coming from Falling Rock when the stage was robbed," the woman said. "Afterward, they brought you to Hearten, to my boardinghouse to rest up, and I dressed you in one of my nightgowns."

Although she'd never seen Mrs. Peters before, there was something about her that reminded Honor of Aunt Harriet. Maybe it was the warmth in her gray eyes and the way the edges of her mouth lifted when she smiled. There was kindness in the woman's face—just as there had been in Aunt Harriet's—and Honor felt drawn to her.

At the thought of her late aunt, a wave of sadness swept over Honor. Her beloved only relative had died, and Honor had run away from...

Lucas. She sat up in bed again, her heart pounding.

Mrs. Peters came to the bedside and pressed her hand gently on Honor's shoulder. "What's wrong, honey?"

"Nothing," Honor answered quickly. "Has anyone been asking for me?"

"No. But if you're upset, I can't blame you. Bumps on the head are no fun. Being robbed isn't, either."

"Robbed?" Honor's hands began to shake. "Was I robbed?"

Mrs. Peters nodded.

Honor remembered getting out of the stagecoach, but nothing after that. She'd planned to mail whatever money she had left back to the church in Falling Rock, but now she had nothing and no way to begin to repay what she'd stolen.

"I know you must have a lot of questions," Mrs. Peters said softly. "And I'm sure my son will answer every one of them just as soon as he gets back to the house."

"Where is Reverend Peters?"

"He went over to our church to check on things. A preacher's work is never done. But he'll be back before you know it. The church is just down the road." Mrs. Peters patted Honor's shoulder again. "Why don't you lie down and try to rest until he gets here? Or would you like something to eat? I have warm chicken soup in the kitchen. Would you like some?"

Honor shook her head. "Maybe later. But thank you for asking."

"You know," Mrs. Peters said, "according to my son, you're a very nice person."

"Me?" Honor put her hand to her chest.

Mrs. Peters nodded. "My son is a pretty good judge of character, and I just know he's right about you."

What would Mrs. Peters say if she knew Honor had robbed the collection plate from a church? The preacher might *think* he was a good judge of people, but he wasn't. Nobody knew that better than Honor.

Chapter Four

✤

Honor woke the second time that day to the scent of roses. A white vase filled with flowers sat on a table at the end of her bed. She guessed that Mrs. Peters had brought in the arrangement while she slept. When she heard a noise in the hallway she turned her gaze to the doorway.

Jeth Peters entered the room. "So, how are you feeling?" he asked warmly.

"Fine." Honor tried to return his smile, but all she could think about was how stiff he looked. With his hands behind his back and his legs planted apart, he reminded her of a toy soldier—one of the tin men she played with as a child.

She liked the look of his dark curly hair and his blue eyes, but he seemed so self-conscious and uncomfortable in her presence. Could it be that all preachers turned into toy soldiers when alone in a room with a woman? Honor pulled the covers higher on her neck lest he become even more embarrassed.

"You took a big whack on the head," Jeth said. "We've been worried about you."

We? Who did he mean? Could Lucas have come here while she was sleeping? A chill ran down her back. "Who's 'we'?" she asked.

"Me, my mother, Mr. and Mrs. Carr, the stagecoach driver, and almost everybody else in Hearten." He moved to the table at the end of her bed and pulled a pink rose from the arrangement. "Mama sure likes flowers. In the spring and summer her garden is full of them." Jeth offered her the rose.

Honor waved a hand, refusing his gift. Lucas had given her aunt flowers whenever he'd wanted something in return. Honor had nothing to give.

As Jeth continued to hold out the pink flower, she saw that it was made of silk. So the scent she'd noted was rosewater. How had she not realized such an obvious fact immediately?

Honor looked back at Jeth. "Would you mind telling me exactly what happened? I still don't remember much."

Jeth returned the flower to the vase. Facing her, he again stuck his hands behind his back. "When you got off the stage, one of the outlaws caught you trying to hide your money and hit you over the head with the butt of his gun. Our entire congregation is praying for you."

"Was anyone else hurt?"

He shook his head, and she saw his shoulders relax a little. "The rest of us did exactly as the robbers said to do— especially after we saw what happened to you."

Jeth paused, as though he expected her to reply. When she didn't say anything, he stepped to the window near the foot of her bed and turned his back toward her.

Honor sat up. The pain in her head had faded slightly. "The elderly couple—Annie and Simon—" She swallowed. "Can you tell me...?"

He turned briefly, gazed at her, and then peered out the window again.

Honor wondered what he found so interesting out there. All she saw was brownish-green grass, trees, and a few clouds in a blue sky.

"What would you like me to tell you?" Jeth prompted.

She hesitated; she'd almost forgotten what she had planned to say. "Oh, about the Carrs. How are they?"

"They're fine. Except that, like you, they lost all their money."

When he turned back to face her, Honor flinched. It had happened again. For a moment, she had thought she was looking at her uncle instead of at Jeth. Why did she keep seeing a resemblance? The two men were nothing alike.

"The stage company honored the Carrs' tickets," Jeth continued, "and they caught another stage to Pine Falls." He took a step toward her. "They sure hated to leave before they found out how you were doing." A wrinkle appeared on his forehead. "How *are* you doing?"

"My head hurts. Other than that, I'm all right."

"Frankly, I'd be a little surprised if your head didn't hurt—after the smack you got."

A jumble of questions swirled in her head, but in her present state, she had trouble sorting them.

"You said the stage company honored the tickets of the other passengers?" she finally managed to ask. "Will they honor mine?"

"Of course." White teeth gleamed in his smile. A lock of thick brown hair fell across his forehead. "In fact," he added, "your ticket is waiting for you down at the stage office here in Hearten. As soon as you're able to travel again, you can pick it up."

"I'm ready now."

"No, Miss McCall, you're not." He shook his head firmly several times. "Dr. Harris wants you to stay in bed for the rest of the week." Jeth stepped to her bedside and touched her forehead. "Well, at least you don't have fever."

His palm felt rough on her skin. Weren't preachers supposed to have smooth hands? The only real work they had was to preach a sermon on Sunday and preside over a funeral or wedding every once in a while.

He stepped back from the bed and adopted his soldier stance again, hands behind his back. "When you're well enough, we'll see about getting your ticket."

"But I want—"

"No 'buts.' Doctor's orders. In the meantime, try to enjoy your stay here—and my mother's cooking."

"I have no money to pay—"

"We know, and it's all been taken care of."

"How?" Honor felt a twinge of alarm. "Who paid for my room and board?"

"The Lord did," he said.

That sounded too unlikely to be believed. "Would you please explain how God was able to do that?" she asked.

"The money came directly from the collection plate at our church," Jeth explained. "But it really came from the Lord."

"Why would God give me anything?" she asked.

"Because He loves you, that's why."

Honor shook her head doubtfully. The preacher must be just talking his line. God could never love someone like Honor McCall.

After Jeth left her room, Honor considered what he'd said, and she thought about the terrible irony of her situation. She was being supported by money from one church's collection plate, after stealing from the collection plate at another church.

She'd done a terrible thing. Yet God was rewarding her with goodness. It didn't make sense.

The sun shone high in the sky by the time Lucas woke up. When he climbed out of bed and crossed the room to draw the curtain, he saw two riders coming up the road.

Not those grave diggers again, he hoped.

As the riders grew closer, he realized they weren't the Brown brothers after all. One of them looked too small to be a grown man, and the other was heavy and stout, with carrot-colored hair and a red beard.

No matter who they were, Lucas wasn't in the mood for visitors. He closed the curtain and turned back to his bed. When a knock sounded at the door, he considered ignoring it, but curiosity captured him. He got up and headed through the kitchen to the small parlor.

Lucas opened the front door. Cold air blew inside. A thin layer of frost covered his front porch. And a man and a boy he'd never seen before stood there, staring into his face.

"Mr. Scythe," the man said, "I'm John Crammer." He glanced at the skinny, blond boy. "This here is my little brother, Bobby."

The brothers wore tattered dark coats and caps. Puffs of smoke seemed to come from their mouths, their breaths visible in the wintry air.

"Someone told us you put a sign up in the saloon," John Crammer said, "offering a reward for information on Miss Honor McCall. Is it true?"

"It shore is. Have you seen her?"

"Maybe." John took a step forward as if he expected to be invited inside. His black boots crunched on the icy porch. "I seen a young woman get on the stage yesterday headed for Pine Falls—the one what was robbed."

"Was she my niece?"

"I can't rightly say, sir, but I think so. I knew Honor when we went to school together in Falling Rock—but that was back before she dropped out."

Lucas held the door open only a crack, to keep out the cold wind. "My late wife taught Honor to read and write here at home. My Harriet was a former schoolteacher, you see, and a smart woman." Lucas had kept Honor close to home most of her life. Not many in town knew her. Apparently, John Crammer was an exception.

John shifted his weight from one leg to the other. "Mighty sorry to hear about your wife's death," he said.

Lucas nodded, studying the pair. The boy had a mass of curly blond hair beneath his black cap. Though Lucas's mind was still cloudy, he intended to remember John and Bobby Crammer.

"So, do I get my thirty dollars?" John asked. "I could shore use it, seeing as I'm about to get married."

"You'll get nothing from me until I know exactly where Honor is," Lucas replied firmly. "But if you're wantin' to make a little money, I might have a job for you."

"What could that be, sir?"

"I need to be gone for a few weeks, looking for my niece. If you and the boy would look after my place and my cattle for me until I get back, I'll give you one of my milk calves and call it even."

"I reckon that sounds like an honest trade," John said. "We accept. When are you leaving?"

"Today."

* * *

At noon, Mrs. Peters returned to Honor's bedroom. She placed a wooden tray on the bedside table, then removed a blue cloth that covered a white bowl. The aroma of chicken broth made Honor's mouth water.

"Hungry?" Mrs. Peters asked in a perky voice.

Honor glanced at the older woman's radiant smile and friendly expression and couldn't help smiling in return. "Yes, ma'am, I would like some. Thank you for asking."

Jeth's mother chattered away as Honor ate her soup, talking about herself and her son. Honor learned Mrs. Peters was a widow and owned the only boardinghouse in Hearten, Colorado. Honor also discovered that Jeth rented a room there. In addition to being a pastor, he farmed the six acres behind the rooming house and was the handyman for all house repairs.

Now Honor understood why his hands were rough.

"My son is a widower," Mrs. Peters said suddenly, simply.

Honor met her gaze. "I didn't know."

Honor hoped to hear more details, but instead of continuing to speak, Regina Peters gestured for Honor to lean forward. Then she reached for the pillow behind Honor's back.

"Jethro lost his wife in a terrible fire that burned down the parsonage," Mrs. Peters said as she fluffed the pillow. "My son hasn't fully recovered from the pain of it yet."

Honor looked into the older woman's eyes again. "How terrible."

"Yes, it was." Mrs. Peters placed the pillow behind Honor's head and put gentle pressure on her shoulder, encouraging her to relax. Then she pulled the covers up to Honor's neck, tucking her in as if she were a small child.

"Jethro was visiting his former in-laws, Reverend and Mrs. Andrew Fields, in Falling Rock, when the grave diggers told him about your aunt's death, Miss McCall. Ordinarily, Reverend Fields would have been the one to visit the gravesite, but he's been a little under the weather the last week or two. So Jethro went in his place."

"I don't know Reverend Fields, but I'm sorry he's sick," Honor said. "And I hope he's feeling better now?"

"Yes, let's pray so."

After Mrs. Peters left the room, Honor started thinking about Jeth again. Was he the man who had stood in the vestibule of the church on the morning she stole the money? Did Jeth know she was a thief? If so, why had he played innocent and acted nobly? There must be a reason.

She needed to leave Hearten as soon as possible. She couldn't go on being a burden to these good people much longer.

It was Honor's plan to move to Pine Falls. She had a lot of money to pay back. But first, she needed to find a job.

From the edge of the bed, she glanced out the open window. Jeth and his mother were in front of the boardinghouse, sitting in a wagon. A moment later, the team of brown horses started down the dirt driveway, Jeth at the reins.

A gust of wind rattled some papers on the table at the foot of the bed, sending them spinning. The vase of flowers stopped them from whirling to the floor. Honor crawled to the end of the bed, gathered the papers, stacked them, and placed a book on top, to keep them from scattering again. She was turning away when her eye fell on the title at the top of the first page: "Sermon for Sunday."

Had the sermon been left deliberately? Was Reverend Peters hoping to convert her? More likely, it was an oversight. Still, she wondered....

Honor glanced toward the bedroom door. If she was going to leave now, this might be her best opportunity to get away without being noticed.

Swinging her legs around, she rose out of bed. When her feet touched the soft rag rug, she felt as if the carpet had grown wings and was about to fly away. To keep from falling, she grabbed the bedpost and waited for the wave of dizziness to disappear.

Several moments later, the flying carpet became a rug again, and she reached for her tan dress. Pulling the garment from the hook on the wall, she saw that it had been cleaned, freshly ironed, and smelled faintly of rosewater. She buried her nose in the sweet scent, grateful for Mrs. Peters's kindness. Honor's shoes, bonnet and shawl were on a shelf by her dress—and those items, too, had all been cleaned.

Honor still felt slightly woozy. Jeth had said Dr. Harris wanted her to stay in bed for a week. For a moment she was tempted to follow medical advice and climb back under the covers. But no, if she planned to make her escape, she had to do it now.

Jeth and his mother were indeed generous to have done so much for her. Aunt Harriet had always valued giving thanks, and Honor couldn't leave town without writing a thank-you letter.

After quickly buttoning up her dress and gathering her bonnet and shawl, Honor went downstairs. In the entry hall, she noticed dark wood paneling. A small maple desk stood against one wall, and writing materials lay on the desktop. Honor sat down to write.

Dear Reverend and Mrs. Peters,
You have been more than kind to me, and I appreciate all you have done. But it is time for me to leave now. I

hope to have left on the noon stage by the time you
get back.
Yours truly,
Honor McCall

The minute she stepped out the door and onto the wide,
front porch, a rush of cold wind whipped around the corner of the big, old house and slapped her in the face. The air
smelled like rain. For a moment, she doubted her strength,
and her resolve weakened. Perhaps she should have stayed
in bed.

Another norther must have blown in while she was re-
cuperating in the bedroom upstairs, and she wasn't dressed
warmly enough. She longed for her old woolen cape, but
she'd left that back at the cabin with Lucas. Still, she was determined to leave now.

Honor stepped into the wind, head lowered. The ends of
her long hair flew below the print bonnet. Draping her shawl
over her bonnet and around her shoulders, she continued
up the road on shaky legs. Since she never reached her destination, Jeth had said that Honor's ticket was being held
until she could pick it up. All Honor knew was she'd never
been to Hearten before and had no idea where to find the
ticket office.

Wagon tracks went to the right. She turned to the left as
droplets of frozen rain hit her cheeks. Honor took a dozen
steps, then slipped and fell. Quivering from the dampness and
cold, she tried to rise and slipped again. Her head began to
spin. The next moment, a blanket of darkness shrouded her.

Lucas rode toward Pine Falls, in search of Honor. He'd
found a little food in the root cellar on the farm and had
wrapped it in a potato sack to bring along. He was taking a

route that avoided Falling Rock—too many debts waited for him there. His plan was to make a stop in Hearten, pick up a couple of bottles of whiskey, and move on.

There were no saloons in Hearten. The whole countryside was dry, though he'd heard of several ranchers who brewed spirits on the side. Maybe he could find one of them.

His mind seemed clearer now, and he'd been thinking about the minister from Hearten, who had been at the cemetery. The preacher had reminded him of somebody. Try as he might, Lucas couldn't think who.

When he was a child, his mother had read to him from the Good Book. Since the preacher carried a Bible, maybe that was what stirred his recollections. All he knew for certain was that seeing the reverend had caused him to recall events he would rather not remember.

His mare, Lady, moved into a soft trot. A frosty breeze whipped Lucas's ears. He pulled up the collar of his brown jacket. He had never thought he would miss Harriet. But he did. With a jolt, he realized he missed his mama and his childhood home, as well.

Lucas had ridden a horse named Old Smokey to school every day when he was a boy. He could almost see his mama standing at the kitchen door, waving goodbye to him and his big sisters as they sat astride the big gelding. Back then, Lucas was known as Lawrence Smith, but it had been years since anybody had called him by his real name.

His mama had wanted him to become a Christian and get a good education, but he'd fulfilled neither of those goals. Maybe he would have if he'd stayed at home instead of running away when he was barely fifteen.

Both his parents had been churchgoers, but his father was a hypocrite. Every time Pappy got drunk, he'd beat Lucas severely. Mama never said a word about the old man's drinking, but she scolded Lucas when she found him behind the barn one day, sipping spirits with his friends.

As soon as he was big enough, Lucas had joined a cattle drive. He'd admired the strength he'd seen in his first trail boss, Adam Scythe. He wanted to be just like him. Before signing with the outfit for the next drive, he'd changed his name to Lucas Scythe. Like Lucas's father, the trail boss had been a hard drinker, and Lucas had thought drinking would make him a man. In the end, he had become more of a drunk than Pappy.

Mama would have been disappointed if she'd known how her only son turned out. That was why Lucas never went back to Cold Springs for a visit. No point in making Mama feel worse by showing her what her son had become. Lucas swallowed an ache in his throat. Word had reached him that his parents died years ago, but he'd never checked out the rumor.

Patches of ground were visible under the melting snow. From a distance, the earth had a reddish color—like Honor's hair.

Missy. At the thought of her, Lucas's face hardened. When he found that girl, he'd teach her a lesson. She deserved a few knocks for taking his money and heading out of town. Then he would marry her. Why, she was young enough to have babies. He'd always wanted a family, but Harriet couldn't have children.

Lucas slowed Lady, then pulled her to a stop. He wanted to think. Miss Ruby Jones lived on the far side of Falling Rock. If he looped around, he could ride out to her farm without being seen. Maybe he would pay her a visit before riding on to Hearten.

He never saw Ruby much after Harriet got sick and not at all toward the end, but Lucas intended to visit her now.

Would she agree to see him? After all this time, she could have found someone new. He looked forward to being with her again, especially since Ruby always kept plenty of whiskey in the cabinet in her parlor, but if she turned him away, so be it.

When Honor opened her eyes, Jeth Peters was sitting in a chair near her bed, watching her.

"So, you're awake." He smiled.

Remembering her fall in the snow, she glanced under the covers and saw that Mrs. Peters must have removed her wet clothes and helped her into a flannel nightgown. Relieved and grateful, Honor pulled the quilt around her neck again.

"Now," Jeth said. "Would you mind telling me what you were doing walking around in a freezing rain without so much as a coat on?"

"First, sir, you tell me why you left one of your sermons in my room." She motioned toward the papers on the table. "Did you think I needed to be preached to or something?"

"I didn't know I left my sermon in here. I've been looking everywhere for it." He reached for the stack of papers. "I came in once to check on you earlier and I must have left my sermon notes then." His forehead creased. "And, Miss McCall, will you please stay put for a while? I'd like to rest up for a few days before I have to rescue you again."

Chapter Five

✛

Jeth sat in the chair beside Honor's bed, entertaining her with amusing stories about Timmy, a mischievous little boy in his congregation.

Honor was chuckling softly, when a tall gentleman with white hair and wearing spectacles suddenly appeared in the doorway. The little black bag he carried identified him as a doctor.

Jeth stood and crossed the room. "Dr. Harris. Thank you so much for stopping by, sir."

The men shook hands, then Jeth smiled and gestured toward Honor. "Miss Honor McCall, I would like to present Dr. Alvin Harris. He's the one who examined you after the robbery and bandaged your head."

Honor nodded. "I'm glad to meet you, Doctor. Thank you for all your help yesterday—or whenever the robbery took place."

"I'm glad to meet you, too, Miss McCall. And the stage robbery was yesterday. Though somehow it seems longer ago than that, doesn't it? How are you feeling?"

"Much better than when I first woke up, thank you."

"I hope you'll get better and better, young lady."

Jeth stood beside Dr. Harris. Honor thought he'd looked uncomfortable from the instant the doctor had come into the room. Nervous and slightly flustered, like a guilty child.

Jeth motioned toward the chair. "Please, Doctor, won't you sit down. I should go downstairs anyway and tell Mama you're here."

"I know he's here." Mrs. Peters stood in the doorway. "But do go down and wait for us in the parlor, Jethro. I know Dr. Harris will want to give you a report on Miss McCall's health as soon as he's had time to examine her."

"Yes." Jeth walked to the door. "That's just what I'll do."

The snow had vanished. Though a cool wind whistled down from the mountains, the day was clear and sunny. But even if it had been cold and icy, the valley would have reminded Lucas of springtime as he rode into the pasture in front of Ruby Jones's farmhouse. Everything about her had that effect on him.

How many times had Ruby insisted there was something almost magical about her farm? Especially her house, with its white shutters and all the fancy gingerbread trim around the eaves. In the next breath, she would talk about how unhappy she was. How tired of being "the other woman" in Lucas's life. Her moods moved back and forth faster than a lady's fan on a hot summer night.

He had stopped seeing Ruby after it became clear that Harriet was dying, and she'd said she understood. But did she still care? Or had she found someone new? With Ruby, it was hard to tell what she was thinking, and they hadn't been together in almost two months.

He never knew whether Ruby was going to kiss him or hit him over the head with a frying pan. Raising his collar against the chill, Lucas wondered what she would be like this time.

"Reckon I'll find out soon enough," he thought.

A white picket fence circled what Lucas called her dollhouse. Since he was here the last time, she'd painted her home butter yellow. A man would go insane in an overdecorated house like hers. Lucas unsaddled Lady, tied her to a tall pine out front, and gave her some water from the nearby well.

As he started up the stepping stones leading to Ruby's front porch, the door flew open. Ruby burst out onto the porch, arms outstretched, and waited for him. Her laughter, like music, floated toward him. Ruby had never lost her sense of grace or her ability to pull in the sun with one of her smiles.

"Oh, Lucas. I'm *so* glad you stopped by. I haven't seen you in ages and ages."

Since he didn't see a frying pan in her hand, he moved forward.

Ruby had been a dance-hall girl until she'd inherited the farm from a great-aunt. Though almost forty, she looked younger. Dressed younger, too. Ruby was one of those women who refused to grow old—always trying to turn fall into early springtime. She almost got away with it.

She probably expected Lucas to marry her now that Harriet was gone. They'd been keeping company for almost ten years. But marriage to Ruby wasn't in his plans.

Yet already, the sweet scent of her floral perfume drew him closer and closer. Around her, he always felt like a hooked trout on a short line.

Ruby's smile evaporated, and she sent him a sorrowful look. "I regretted hearing about Harriet's death. You have my deepest sympathy, Lucas."

"Thank you."

Just as suddenly, her grin reappeared. "But, as they say, life must go on." She grabbed his hand. Pulling him forward, she opened the door. "Hurry now. We have a lot to talk about."

"I need a drink first."

"Later."

Lucas stopped as soon as he walked into the house, and then he coughed. An overpowering odor of perfume choked him. The air reeked. His eyes watered. He wished for a handkerchief.

The parlor had been rearranged since the last time he had seen it. New yellow chintz curtains hung on all the windows. Orange and yellow paper flowers in white vases were everywhere. He took a moment to absorb it all.

"Like it?" she asked.

"Maybe. Now, about that drink—"

"Please, Lucas." She squeezed his hand. "Tell me what you really think. It's important."

Breaking free of her grasp, he surveyed the rest of the room. "Where's that there chair I always sit in?"

"Over there." She pointed to an overstuffed chair near the fireplace.

"It used to be blue."

"Now it's yellow."

"I can see that." He looked around again. "Where's the cabinet that you keep the liquor in?"

"I've rearranged a little. I'll explain more in a minute. We should discuss a few things first."

Here it comes, he thought.

"Would you like to sit down?" she asked.

He looked down at his dusty clothes, then at the yellow chair. "I ain't sitting in no chair like that. I might get it all dirty."

"Maybe you'd be more comfortable if you washed up before supper. The kettle has enough hot water left to warm the tub, and the clothes you left last time you were here are clean and ready for you to put on."

"I reckon I'd be more comfortable if you gave me a drink." He looked around again. "Now, where did you say that cabinet was? I don't mind helping myself, if you'll point the way."

"I said I'd explain later. I'm going to get the kettle. There's already a big bucket of cold water upstairs. Make yourself at home. I'll be right back."

She floated from the room on the balls of slender feet like the dancer she'd always been.

Lucas moved across the room to the china closet and opened it. He saw only white dishes.

"Looking for something?" Ruby's voice came from behind him.

He whirled back around. "The whiskey. I was looking for the whiskey."

"I—I don't happen to have any down here right now."

"Don't have none? Why not?"

"I told you. I'll explain after a while."

"Well, you're sure taking your sweet time about it, ain't ya?"

Ruby wore a white apron edged with ruffles over her green dress. A dark green ribbon tied back her long brown hair. At hardly more than a hundred pounds, she looked like a doll herself. Except for a few wrinkles around her chocolate-colored eyes, she appeared almost as young as Honor. Regardless, she was a long way from nineteen. Lucas intended to keep that in mind when selecting a mother for his future child.

"So if you would like to go upstairs now and take a bath," Ruby said, "you'll find cloths for washing and drying next to the washtub." She handed him the kettle. "I'll have supper ready by the time you finish, and then we can talk."

Ruby was up to something. He'd seen that look before. Still, a hot bath appealed to him. And who knows? Maybe I'll find me some whiskey up there, he speculated.

Lucas took the stairs to the guest bedroom. Like the downstairs rooms, everything had been changed since his last visit. Sheer, yellow curtains replaced the blues ones he'd seen on the windows before, and a lacy, white bedspread covered the double bed. A tub for bathing stood in the middle of a circular rag rug. The bucket of cold water waited near the rug. Lucas put the kettle next to it.

His feet hurt from walking his horse a mile or so back, and he wanted to sit down and take off his boots. The only chair looked as fancy as the bedspread. Seated on the edge of the bed, he pulled off his boots, and Harriet's warning filled his mind.

Don't empty your boots on the floor, she'd always said.

Old, naggin' women are all alike, he told himself. That's why I'm gettin' me a young one—like Honor.

Lucas poured dirt from his boots onto the floor until nothing more came out. Then he let them drop. *Thump. Thump.*

Now where would Ruby have put the whiskey? She must have a bottle or two hidden somewhere.

A chest of drawers stood against the north wall. He pulled out the top drawer and threw out what was inside, tossing everything on the floor.

When he didn't find any bottles, Lucas jerked out the second drawer and repeated the process. Then the third drawer and, finally, the fourth.

Heat warmed his face. His muscles tensed and anger welled inside him. Now he *really* needed a drink.

Crouching down, Lucas looked under the bed. Nothing. His jaw tightened as he got to his feet again. He snatched the covers and threw them on the floor.

"Where's that whiskey?" Lucas bumped his toe on the iron bedpost. "Ouch!"

Hopping on one leg, he reached down, grabbed his toe and held it. He'd thought his feet hurt before, but nothing compared to what he felt now.

A yellow trunk, decorated with painted flowers and vines, stood at the foot of the bed. He threw back the lid and removed dresses, petticoats and delicate undergarments. Near the bottom, his hand touched a hard object under a frilly, pink nightgown. He pushed the gown to one side. A dark-colored flask, flat on both sides, caught his attention.

He grabbed it and unscrewed the top. The smell of whiskey filled the room. Lucas lifted the flask to his lips and swallowed. The golden liquid burned its way into his stomach. He sighed deeply and took another gulp.

"Lunch is almost ready," Ruby called from downstairs.

"Be there in a minute," he shouted back.

Lucas dropped his dirty clothes on the rag rug. First, he poured cold, then hot water into the wooden tub. At last, he climbed into the warm water, carrying the flask with him.

Ten minutes later, Lucas, in tan trousers and a fresh blue shirt, came downstairs. He felt better after bathing and putting on clean clothes. Just not as good as he would feel after he had a few more drinks.

The dinner table was covered with a blue linen cloth. Ruby set out her best white china. Lucas sat down and reached for the platter of fried chicken.

"Not yet, Lucas."

"Why not?"

"We haven't said the blessing."

"Blessing? When did you start that?"

"A few weeks ago. I go to church every Sunday. You should, too. I was baptized."

"Baptized? You?"

She nodded. "I'm a saved Christian now."

He wondered if she still drank, but didn't ask.

Ruby folded her hands like she was about to pray. When Lucas didn't fold his, she sent him a scolding glance—like his mother used to do when he was a child.

Lucas groaned and folded his hands.

"Thank you, Lucas," she said.

After Ruby said grace, she handed him the chicken.

"What am I getting to drink?" he asked.

"Did I forget to give you your tea?" Casually, she pointed to the steaming cup by his plate. "Oh, there it is." Her smile held a hint of amusement. "Drink up while it's hot."

"Tea ain't what I want, and you know it."

"Sorry. It's all I have on hand. Now, will you please pass the mashed potatoes?"

After lunch, they moved into the kitchen for apple pie and coffee. Lucas enjoyed her desserts, but he would like some alcohol better.

Did Ruby intend to pour him a shot of whiskey or not?

"Have you finished your pie yet?" she asked.

He took the last bite and swallowed. "I have now." He wiped his mouth with a blue-and-white checkered napkin.

Ruby got up and stood by her chair. "I would like to go out and see your mare before we have our talk." She pulled a carrot from a bowl on the kitchen table and held it up for him to see. "This is for Lady. I remember how she likes carrots."

She gathered several other things and placed them in a wicker basket. None was a bottle with liquid in it. So he didn't pay much attention.

"Shall we go?" she asked.

"I reckon. The sooner we go, the sooner we'll get back and I can have that drink."

They went out into the sunshine, and Ruby rushed over to his mare. The basket swayed back and forth on her arm as she fed Lady the carrot.

"Hello, girl," Ruby said. "How are you doing?" She turned and smiled up at Lucas. "Horses have such soft noses, don't they?"

"I ain't never thought much about it."

It was a lie. He *had* thought about it. But he'd always considered it unmanly to let anyone know how he felt.

His saddle, blanket and other equipment had been dropped together under a pine tree. Ruby picked up one of his saddlebags. Then she pulled a small book from her basket and slipped it in the bag.

"Hey! What do you think you're doing?"

"I got this Bible from the preacher at my church in town. The inscription inside said it belonged to Harriet. She must have left it at the church. I thought Honor might like to have it now." She stuffed a small wooden box in with the Bible.

Lucas reached for the bag, taking it out of her hand. "What else are you puttin' in there?" He peered inside.

"That string of pearls you gave me last Christmas. I know you stole it from Harriet, and I think the pearls should go to Honor now."

For all Lucas cared, she could take the book and necklace and throw them in the creek. Then he had a second thought. Were the items worth something? Could he sell them? Lucas always needed money.

Ruby moved over to his gray mare again and patted the animal's swollen belly. "Don't you just love babies?"

"I like colts. They make me money."

"Always money." She turned and smiled at him again. "What about human babies? Wouldn't you like to have one?"

"I never gave it much thought," he said, knowing it was another lie. "Harriet couldn't have no children."

"I can. At least, I hope I can."

Lucas tensed. "Are you—are you in the family way, Ruby?"

"Not yet. But I'd like to be." She moved toward him and put her arms around his neck. "Will you marry me, Lucas?" She beamed up at him. "You always said you would. Someday. And someday is here. Please, Lucas, say yes."

"You know better than to pen me in, Ruby. I've been penned up for too long as it is." He took hold of her arms and removed them from around his neck. "I don't want to get married."

To you, he thought.

"Don't say that!" Ruby covered her mouth with the palms of her hands. "Not now!"

Lucas tensed. "The only thing I want is a good shot of whiskey."

"But you promised..."

"I don't want you, Ruby. You can't have no babies. If you could, you would have had a couple by now."

Her eyes widened. "How can you say such a cruel thing?"

"'Cause it's true."

Her mouth turned down at the edges. The softness he'd seen in her face a few minutes earlier vanished. Slowly, her jaw tightened. She looked hard, yet strong...and beautiful.

Anger boiled inside him, threatening to bubble up. His face and neck heated quicker than a kettle on a hot stove. Didn't Ruby know enough to back away while she had the chance?

"What makes you so sure I'm the one who can't have children?" she taunted. "Did you ever wonder if maybe it's you, Lucas? Maybe if Harriet and I had been with a *real* man, we could have had all the babies we wanted."

He stiffened. His hands became fists.

Ruby screamed. "Don't!" She got down on her knees. "Please, Lucas! Don't hit me."

He wanted to. Oh, how he wanted to. After what she had said, she deserved it. And yet...

His chest heaving with suppressed rage, Lucas turned toward his mare. The muscles in his face were as stiff as iron. Slowly, he saddled his horse.

When he'd mounted, he looked down. Ruby rocked back and forth on the ground, crying.

"Goodbye, Ruby. And thank you kindly for a mighty fine meal." He pulled out the flask and held it up for her to see. "Thanks for the whiskey, too."

Lucas took a swig from the flask. Then he turned his mare toward Hearten and rode away.

He would sell the items that had belonged to Harriet. Honor didn't deserve them after what she did. Besides, he needed money. Otherwise, he might need to find a temporary job before going all the way to Pine Falls.

Jeth didn't feel like sitting in the parlor on one of his mother's ornate, store-bought chairs while he waited to hear what Dr. Harris had to say about Honor. Pacing back and forth in the entry hall in front of the double doors, he paused only long enough to check his pocket watch.

He thought of Honor's letter—the one he had discovered on the desk near the door. What if he hadn't noticed it in time? She could have died—frozen to death in the icy rain.

Miss McCall could still be seriously hurt and might need weeks to recuperate. Yet she'd written him a thank-you letter before wandering off in the cold. She must be one of those modern girls he'd been reading about in the newspaper.

The reporter had written, "These young ladies will feel more comfortable in the twentieth century when it finally arrives than they ever felt in the nineteenth."

Jeth headed for the kitchen. He respected Honor's independent spirit, but to his way of thinking, her judgment was misguided.

He poured himself a cup of coffee, sat down at the table and looked around. Where was the doctor? Jeth drummed the fingers of one hand on the table. The man should have finished examining Honor long ago.

At the sound of creaking from the stairway, Jeth glanced toward the door, put down his cup and started to rise from his chair.

"No, don't get up," his mother said from the doorway. "We can entertain the doctor in here as well as the parlor."

Dr. Harris stood behind his mother, his hands on her shoulders. Jeth liked the picture they made. At over six feet, the doctor barely fit under the lintel of the door and he looked even taller next to his mama.

Jeth had always thought the doctor was sweet on his widowed mother. But so far, Dr. Harris hadn't declared himself.

Mrs. Peters gestured toward the chair across from Jeth's. "Sit down, Alvin, and I'll get the coffee."

Dr. Harris settled into the chair and leaned back, folding his hands over his chest. Jeth wondered what the doctor must have thought when he found him alone in a room with a young, unmarried woman. He should have been standing in the doorway instead of seated in a chair by her bed. Now he wanted a report on Honor's health, but the doctor looked tired.

"Alvin was up all night with Mr. Sloan's mother," Mrs. Peters explained. "The dear woman isn't doing too well. So we need to keep praying, Jethro, and have patience. Wait on the Lord."

Jeth nodded, drumming his fingers again. "Yes, we certainly do."

The doctor's eyes were closed and he was snoring softly. It was amazing that he could fall asleep so quickly, and it would be a shame to wake him, but Jeth needed to hear how Honor was doing and didn't know how much longer he could sit and wait.

Jeth cleared his throat.

The doctor jerked forward. His eyes popped open.

Mrs. Peters placed a steaming cup of coffee before the doctor. "Here ya go, Alvin." She poured fresh coffee into Jeth's cup and returned to the stove.

Steam from both cups curled up and disappeared into the air. The doctor reached for his cup and took a swallow of the hot liquid. He made a sighing noise of contentment.

"Well, Doctor," Jeth prompted, "what can you tell us about Miss McCall? Is she going to be all right?"

"She's still dizzy and sick to her stomach. The pain in her head bothers her, too." The doctor took another mouthful of coffee and swallowed. "Though she's improving nicely,

I've told her to stay in bed for at least a week. She didn't like hearing that, and I can't blame her. It's no fun, staying in all the time with nothing much to do but look out the window. I'm counting on you and your mother to keep her from being bored. Can you find the time to do that, son?"

Jeth had a few more humorous anecdotes involving Timmy and the other children from his congregation that he could relate. He hoped they would amuse Honor.

"Yes, sir," Jeth said. "I think I can."

"I know you can," Dr. Harris replied approvingly. "A young man like you can do anything he sets his mind to do." The doctor looked over at Jeth's mother and smiled. "Isn't that right, Regina?"

"I believe so," she said.

Dr. Harris turned back to Jeth. "Your mama and I might have some news to tell you." He winked, then nodded toward Regina Peters. "Come on over here, woman, and let's get this job over with."

Jeth saw his mother's cheeks turn a rosy pink as she came to the doctor's side. Dr. Harris pulled a chair next to his own and draped his arm across the back. "Sit right here, Regina, where I can keep you close."

She ducked her head shyly, then sat down and blushed some more.

Jeth's grin grew and he felt excitement at what he thought would be good news. "Are you two getting married?"

"You betcha," the doctor said.

"When?"

"Right after the first of the year."

Jeth rose from his chair. "Congratulations." He went around the table and hugged them both. "I couldn't be happier." He gave his mother an extra squeeze. "But why wait?"

The doctor grinned at Regina. "Your mama said she has some things she has to do first. Promises to keep." Dr. Harris turned his smile on Jeth. "And we want you to perform the ceremony. Will you, son?"

Jeth nodded. "I would be honored. Welcome to the family, Doctor."

"Welcome to my family, son." The doctor patted Jeth on the back. "I guess you'll really be my son soon, won't you."

"Yes, sir. I guess I will."

Jeth was glad his mother had found love again after all these years, and he'd always liked Dr. Harris. But he couldn't help wondering what would become of the boardinghouse after his mother married.

Should he start looking for a new place to live?

Chapter Six

❦

Late-afternoon shadows darkened the cream-colored walls of Honor's bedroom. She barely noticed. Turning on her side to examine Jeth's face, she struggled to keep the heavy, brown and rose-colored patchwork quilt over her shoulders. The wood-burning stove wasn't lit, but she felt warm and safe under the covers.

Again, Jeth sat in the chair by her bed. His dark, curly hair looked thick and shiny. Lights flickered in his blue eyes.

Honor owed Jeth and his mother a huge debt of gratitude for finding her on the road when they did. However, she still hoped to leave as soon as possible. Next time she wouldn't write a letter revealing her plans. Nor did she intend to give any information about her past.

Jeth leaned forward as if he had something important to say. "Are you all right, Miss McCall?"

He placed his hand on her forehead as he'd done before, and she felt his rough fingers.

"You don't have a fever, ma'am. I sure am glad."

She thought he looked a little flustered as he removed his hand. Had touching her face embarrassed him?

"Mama said you haven't been sleeping well—that before you really came to yourself, you tossed and turned a lot. Once she heard you scream like you'd just had a bad dream. As a pastor, I would like to help, if I can. Is something bothering you?"

"Nothing's bothering me," she lied. "But what happened on the stagecoach was frightening. The dreams are probably the result of that, don't you think?"

"That's possible, of course."

He cocked his head, and she wondered if he truly believed her explanations. Or did he know her for the thief and liar she actually was?

"Would you like me to send a message to your uncle so he'll know what happened to you?" he asked. "I think it might help."

"My uncle?" Honor stiffened. "No! Don't write him!"

She thought his steady gaze had a skeptical edge to it, and she immediately regretted her response. It had been too emotional, too strong. She should have spoken more calmly, given logical answers. Forcing a smile, Honor tried to swallow the lump in her throat.

"I would rather you not tell my uncle about the stage robbery or where I am," she said softly, at last.

"Why not?"

She quickly searched her mind for an answer, a lie. "We quarreled and shouldn't see each other for a while."

"Very well." Jeth frowned. "But you should know that I disagree with you. I think you should contact your uncle as soon as possible." A skeptical expression remained on his face. "Nevertheless, I will honor your wishes."

Her problems with her uncle went far beyond a mere quarrel. Still, it would be too embarrassing if churchgoing people like Jeth and his mother knew the real reasons she never wanted to see Lucas again. Not only would it hurt to admit that Lucas was an evil man, but also Honor didn't want the Peters to know about her sins.

"Do you have any other relatives who I might contact?" Jeth placed his elbow on the arm of his chair and propped his chin in his hand. "Like a mother and a father?"

"My parents were missionaries living in Mexico when they died of a fever. I was too young to remember them. My two older brothers died when my parents did. My aunt and grandmother were the only relatives I had."

He grew silent, but an expression that Honor identified as concern seemed to soften his eyes. Had her words affected him, perhaps more deeply than she could comprehend?

"It couldn't have been easy growing up without parents."

"No," she said, "it wasn't."

His face looked tight and pinched, and he folded his hands loosely between his knees. "I never knew my father. He died soon after I was born. But at least I have a mother."

"I had an aunt." She looked away from Jeth. "Until now."

In spite of a harsh life at the hands of her uncle, memories of her aunt's humor and warmth filled her mind. She never knew how Aunt Harriet managed to rise above all her troubles, but she always did.

As more happy memories rose, Honor looked up at Jeth and smiled. "She told me things about my parents I'll treasure forever."

All at once, Honor had the desire to share some of those treasures with Jeth. "My aunt said my father called me his little Rose of Sharon, and sometimes Aunt Harriet did, too."

Jeth had been gazing down at his black boots, but at her words he looked up into Honor's eyes and smiled. "Rose of Sharon," he repeated. "Why would they call you that?"

"My mother's name was Sharon, and my middle name is Rose. For them, it might have seemed right to call me by that name." She smiled. "The Rose of Sharon part could also have come about because one set of my grandparents was from Scotland. Rose sounds Celtic, don't you think?"

"I wouldn't know, but you certainly have a Scottish look about you."

Honor blinked. "Do I?"

He grinned. "With all that long auburn hair and those honey-brown eyes, I would say so. Rose of Sharon is the name of a flower that grows in Mama's garden. But did you know the Rose of Sharon is also mentioned in the Bible?"

"No, I didn't."

"The term is found in the first verse of the second chapter of Song of Solomon."

"I don't know much about the Bible."

He glanced down at his boots again. "I see."

"But if it's there, I guess that explains where the name came from." She wondered if he was surprised to learn that she wasn't a Bible scholar? Could it be that he was disturbed to realize she wasn't a churchgoer, either? He should have guessed how things were at her home by what Lucas had said and done at the cemetery.

"As I said, my parents were missionaries," she continued. "Aunt Harriet said the Good Book was very important to them."

The young pastor seemed to have disappeared into another void of silence. Had she revealed more than she should?

At last, Jeth looked up again. He smiled, but to Honor his expression seemed counterfeit.

"Mama and I have been talking," he said. "We would like to offer you employment."

Employment? Honor was shocked. Who would want to hire her to do anything? She started to sit up, then remembered the importance of modesty and slipped under the covers once more. "Why me?" she asked.

"Mama needs someone to help around the rooming house here. And I need a helper to do odd jobs at the church."

She lifted her head off the pillow, staring at him. "Just how odd are these jobs?"

He laughed. Leaning back in his chair, he appeared to relax—like he was enjoying himself. Then the humor slowly faded. A serious expression replaced the smile on his face. "Your duties at the church would mostly involve delivering food and messages."

"And to whom would I be expected to deliver these things?"

"Members of our church." Another brief smile surfaced. "The job could include cooking. You can cook, can't you?"

"My, yes. I've done a lot of that."

Jeth nodded. He slapped the wooden arm of his chair lightly, then he rose and went to the door. Honor thought he planned to leave, but he turned back and stood, as usual, with his hands behind his back and his legs spread.

"I know you can read and write," he said. "You wrote us that note. But can you read well enough to teach someone else?"

"Of course."

His face relaxed.

Feeling a blush rising, Honor focused on a brown square of the cotton quilt. "I might not be perfect, but I can read."

"Sorry," Jeth said. "I never intended to hurt your feelings or embarrass you. However, these days, some folks can't read. I'd like you to help the adults in our congregation who want to learn, so they can read the Bible."

"My late aunt was a schoolteacher before she married, and she made sure I learned to read and write. I also do figuring and numbers."

His head cocked. "So, will you accept the job?"

"I'm not sure. I'll need time to think about it."

"Take all the time you want." He pulled out his pocket watch and checked it. A small smile turned up the edges of his mouth, and a twinkle appeared in his eyes. "As long as I have your answer today, that is. Shall we say in one hour?"

Honor hesitated, considering his proposal. One hour? Was the man serious or teasing her? With Jeth, she never knew.

Before he left her room, Jeth told her more about the jobs. Honor gave him her decision. She would accept both positions...temporarily.

What other options did she have? Moreover, Jeth and his mother needed her, and they had been helpful and kind. She had to pay them back in some way.

Honor also set a task for herself: she would pay back the money she owed by Christmas. She wouldn't make much, but with her room and board furnished, she should be able to save a little. She didn't know if it would be enough to pay back her entire debt to the church by her deadline, as she so hoped, but she certainly planned to try.

* * *

The next afternoon, at a lake near Hearten, Lucas stopped to water his mare. He was thirsty himself, and his backside ached from the long hours of riding. Shifting in the saddle provided only some relief. Before dismounting, he leaned forward and pressed his hands on the saddle horn, taking most of his weight in his legs.

Cold and damp, Lucas got down from his horse. A wave of guilt swept over him, along with a thin sprinkle of frosty rain. Thinking about Harriet and all that had happened, his mind and heart were troubled, but he pushed away the memories. They demanded too much of him. Lucas didn't need to change. He was fine the way he was.

Yet, he wished he'd never hit Honor and Harriet—or any woman, for that matter. Lucas always regretted his sins when he was sober, which was a good reason to have another drink. He pulled the flask from the inside pocket of his jacket.

He planned to pay a visit to the Sharp Ranch, hoping to find work. He chortled at the thought. If they needed someone to help them brew the alcohol they were so famous for, he was the man. Now, there was a job that he would like.

When he looked up again, he saw a skinny cowboy riding toward him on a swaybacked, bay gelding.

Lucas thought of the Bible and the necklace in his saddlebag. Maybe the cowboy would be willing to buy them. Lucas could probably get more money if he sold the pearls in Pine Falls, but if the cowboy bought the Bible, he'd have cash right away.

Every day, Dr. Harris paid a visit to Honor. A week after the stage robbery, he announced that she was well enough to do light housekeeping and to work at the church for a few hours a week.

Just getting out of bed was a chore for her. She couldn't imagine what an entire day of work might be like.

Mrs. Peters had given Honor several dresses, and they all fit perfectly. Honor wouldn't have to wear her late aunt's tan wedding dress again until Sunday, when the family attended church. She put on a green, wool dress with a white cotton collar.

Honor had doubted that she was the right person for her new job since the day she accepted it. She worried still more as she combed her long hair and twisted it into a tight bun at the nape of her neck. Gazing at her reflection in the oval mirror with the maple frame, she concluded that she looked presentable.

After helping with breakfast in the big kitchen and dusting the upstairs bedrooms, Honor's back hurt. Tendrils of her long red hair had pulled free of her bun and were falling in her eyes. Pushing them away with the back of her hand, she sighed deeply. If only a chair had been tied to her back so she could sit down and rest whenever she wanted.

Later, when Honor served the noon meal, Jeth didn't join the other boarders in the big dining room. She wondered if perhaps he ate at the hotel in town. She hadn't seen him at breakfast, either. Then she glanced out a window and saw him talking to his mother on the lawn outside.

In the kitchen after the middle-of-the-day dinner, Honor and Mrs. Peters, wearing long white aprons, stood in front of a tub of soapy water. While Jeth's mother washed the pots, pans, plates, cups and silverware, Honor rinsed the items in a bucket of fresh water and dried them with a white cloth.

Mrs. Peters looked up from her dish-washing and glanced out a window. "Have you noticed how cold it's getting outside? Look at the wind, blowing the branches of the trees.

It could be snowing by nightfall." She dried her hands on her apron. "Miss McCall, I've been meaning to tell you a little about the folks who live here. Now seems as good a time as any."

"All right, ma'am."

"Of course you already know my son, the minister. And since you dusted upstairs this morning, maybe you met Mrs. Clark and Mrs. Davis?"

"No, ma'am, I didn't."

"They probably went out for their morning stroll. They are sisters, you see, and very sweet. I know you'll like them. Both are widows. And as I said, they live upstairs. I live upstairs, too. And besides your room, there are also two vacant rooms above the stairs and one available room downstairs. As you know, Jethro and Elmer live down here on the first floor. You probably haven't met Elmer yet, but you will.

"Dr. Harris lives in town but eats most of his meals here," Mrs. Peters explained. "Sometimes we have as few as four or five at mealtime. Counting you and I, that would make six or seven. Or we could have a dozen or more at every meal. You just never know. But there's always plenty to do."

Honor nodded. "I can see that."

"Oh, and that reminds me. I need flour and a few other things from the store. Baker's Grocery and Mercantile is just down the road. Jethro promised to drive into town to get what I need. And, Miss McCall, I want you to accompany Jethro today when he drives into town."

Why did Mrs. Peters call her son Jethro when he preferred Jeth? And why did she think Honor needed an outing? Yes, she was tired, but regardless of her current physical condition, Honor was capable of finishing a day's work without a long break.

"Besides, honey," Mrs. Peters continued, "you look worn out."

"I'm all right, ma'am, really I am."

"Nonsense. You've worked hard today and deserve rest from your labors. Now, run along. Jethro will be leaving in a few minutes, and I expect you to go with him. You can wait for him in the parlor."

Honor returned to her room to wash her face and comb her hair. Then she went downstairs and entered the parlor to wait for Jeth. It was the first time she'd visited that part of the boardinghouse, and she stood in the doorway for a moment to take in the large, well-decorated room.

The parlor windows were edged with heavy, green drapes. Three overstuffed, gold chairs separated the sitting area from a pump organ. A bookcase lined the north wall, and a sturdy-looking desk with a lamp stood in one corner.

The *snap* and *crackle* of a fire burned in the fireplace, and there was a scent of smoke and pinecones in the air. Honor felt a sense of peace just looking at the red and yellow flames.

She settled onto the hunter-green settee and gazed at the organ. She wondered who played it. When she heard footfalls, she turned toward the sound. Jeth stood in the doorway. Honor smiled. He didn't smile back.

"What's wrong?" Honor stood. "Did I forget to pin back my hair or something?"

"It's not your hair." His jaw firmed, and his gaze shifted to the ceiling. When Jeth glanced back at Honor, a hint of anger gleamed in his eyes.

"What is it, then?" she asked.

"It's your dress."

"My dress?" Honor glanced down at the gathered skirt of her green outfit. "What's wrong with it?"

"It's—" He glanced away again. "It was Selma's, my late wife. She wore it on the day I asked her to marry me. She'd left some of her clothes here at the boardinghouse to be mended. That's why some of her dresses weren't burned in the fire."

Honor stared at him. "Why wasn't I told?" She continued to peer at him, waiting for him to say more, anything.

He stood before her and remained silent.

"I'm so sorry," Honor said finally. "I—I didn't know." She spun around, heading toward the stairs. Before she could reach the first step, Jeth grabbed her arm.

"Whoa! Where are you going?"

"To my room—to change into something else."

"No reason for that." His grin looked forced, but at least he was smiling. "I told Mama to give Selma's clothes to a person who needed them. It surprised me, that's all, seeing you in the green dress. But I'll get used to it."

"You won't have to get used to it because I'm returning all the dresses. And again, you can't know how sorry I am about this." Jerking free of his hand, she continued toward the stairs.

"No, wait! Please."

Honor glanced back.

"Selma would have wanted you to have her things." His face looked kind and tender. "Really. That's the sort of person she was."

"I'm sure your late wife was a nice person, but I won't wear her clothes. I just can't. I guess that's the sort of person I am." Honor raced up the first three steps, then paused. "Don't wait for me, Preacher. I won't be driving into town with you after all."

Honor hurried up the stairs and into her room. Why had Jeth's mother given her the clothes in the first place? She should have known how Jeth would react when he saw Honor wearing them.

She hadn't owned a new dress in ages and had especially liked the green one. Now she wanted to throw the garment on the bedroom floor and stomp on it.

But fine clothes were much too precious to treat carelessly—even dresses that had once belonged to someone else's late wife. Still, Honor found it difficult to understand how this situation could have happened. She folded the green dress, put it on the shelf next to her bed with the rest of Selma's clothes, and changed into her one and only—the tan dress that had once belonged to Aunt Harriet.

Selma. Wasn't that the name mentioned in the dedication—the one written in the new hymnal back in Falling Rock? After contemplating the possibility, Honor became convinced it was. Suddenly, a new question shut out all others.

Was she jealous of this woman, this Selma Peters? Jeth Peters meant nothing to her. Furthermore, Honor would be moving on soon. She would probably never see him again. And yet...

Jeth's mother flew into Honor's bedroom with a bundle of clothes in her arms. Honor turned, focusing her attention on the trees outside her window—anything to keep from looking at Mrs. Peters.

"I know now, Miss McCall, that I should never have given my late daughter-in-law's dresses to a lady who lives around here. But you were the first person I've found who was thin enough to wear them." The woman paused before speaking again. "Can you ever forgive me?"

Honor swallowed, then slowly turned. "Yes, ma'am, I can forgive you. But please don't expect me to wear that woman's clothes."

"Of course not." Mrs. Peters held out the stack of garments. "Here are some of my dresses. They're old and too small for me now, and they will be much too big for you. So make all the alterations you need to. I'll never wear them again."

Honor cleared her throat, reflecting on what she should do. She lacked clothes. Mrs. Peters was offering her several outfits that looked warm. Perhaps this wasn't the time to allow pride to control her thinking.

"Thank you, ma'am." Honor faked a smile, taking the clothes from her. "I'll gather up your son's late wife's things and return them to you later today."

"There's no hurry," Mrs. Peters said softly.

"Yes, ma'am, I'm afraid there is."

The woman nodded, then grew silent. "There are needles and spools of thread downstairs if you need them. And I'll be happy to help you with all the alterations."

Honor produced a weak smile. "You're very kind."

As soon as Mrs. Peters left, Honor changed into one of the dresses—a threadbare blue wool with a wide collar. The garment was too big in the waist for Honor, but it had a matching sash. Honor pulled the sash tight and tied it in a bow in front.

I guess this dress is good enough for a thief like me, she thought. Then she hurried downstairs.

When Jeth climbed onto the wooden seat of the wagon, a cold wind whipped around him. Reaching for the reins, he thought of his earlier conversation with Honor McCall.

He shouldn't have mentioned the green dress. A thoughtful minister would have known she would be upset. Jeth should apologize.

Was he becoming fond of this young woman, Miss Honor McCall? He shook his head, replying to his own question. He merely felt sorry for Honor because of what the robbers did—because they hit her in the head with the butt of a gun.

Yes, Honor needed a man in her life, but it had only been two years since...

Selma. He still hated to admit his wife was dead. Besides, it was much too soon for Jeth to consider...

Was he considering?

This young woman needed prayer, not Jeth Peters. He'd been praying for her and intended to continue.

"Heavenly Father, You are the Lord my God, and You answer the prayers of those who turn to You. Please help me to help Miss McCall find You, Lord, and deliver her out of this trouble she is in. In the name of Jesus, Amen and amen."

Jeth pulled down his hat. He snapped the reins. The team of brown horses moved forward at a brisk pace. He would visit the sick in his congregation and finish all the chores his mother had asked him to do. He wouldn't think about Honor's soft, pink lips or her long, auburn hair.

But he knew it would be hard to keep that promise.

An hour later, Honor stood at the kitchen window, looking out as she stirred cake batter with a wooden spoon. The temperature had dropped since morning. An icy wind scattered dry leaves on the back porch. Shivering, Honor felt the cold seep in through the crack under the door.

A dapple-gray horse appeared at the top of the hill. Honor froze for a moment, then, dropping the spoon into the batter, she moved to the window. The approaching rider wasn't close enough to identify, but the gray mare had a round belly. And Lucas had a horse exactly like the one coming over the rise.

Chapter Seven

❧

Lucas!

Honor crouched in the pantry closet, afraid to move. Had Lucas come to the boardinghouse to drag her away? Or to beat her as he'd abused her aunt?

She'd left the chocolate cake batter behind and raced to the mess room where food supplies and medicines were kept. Mrs. Peters had said the walls in the rooming house were thin. Even with the door shut, Honor would probably be able to hear most of what took place in the kitchen. If she wasn't careful, others might also hear her. She didn't intend to move.

Honor heard a knock at the back door.

She tensed.

More rapping sounds followed.

"Just a minute," Mrs. Peters shouted.

When Jeth's mother passed in front of the storage room where Honor was hidden, the older woman's rapid footsteps tapped the pine floor. The *squeak* of a door indicated she'd opened it.

A blast of cold air seeped under the mess room door. Shaking from the cold as well as fear, Honor waited to hear the caller's name.

"Well, Elmer," Mrs. Peters said. "Come in and warm yourself. It's getting cold out there, isn't it."

"Yes, ma'am, it sure is."

Honor freed the breath she'd been holding. Lucas wasn't the person at the door after all. She could come out—pretend she hadn't heard the man knocking. However, she hadn't calmed down enough yet. Her heart still pounded inside her chest.

"And Elmer," Mrs. Peters said, "you don't have to knock at the door when you want to come in. You live here now. All you have to do is just walk right in."

"Sorry, ma'am. I forgot."

There was a short pause before anyone spoke again.

"It could snow tonight," Mrs. Peters said.

"Yes, I reckon it could."

Honor heard another *squeak* and a muffled *bang.* She relaxed a bit and stopped shaking. Someone finally closed the kitchen door.

"Have a seat at the table there, Elmer. Would you like a cup of coffee?"

"Yes, I would."

"Well, make yourself at home," Mrs. Peters said. "How's the mare you bought working out?"

"Mighty fine."

"That's good. Now, sit there and rest while I warm up the pot." Mrs. Peters paused before speaking again. "I don't know what happened to the girl who was working in here. She's new, you see. In fact, this is her first day on the job.

Her name's McCall. Miss Honor McCall. Sweet little thing. I don't guess you've met her yet, have you?"

"No, ma'am, I reckon not."

"You will. With you living here at the boardinghouse, I'm sure you'll run into her, sooner or later."

Honor heard the scrape of a chair, followed by footsteps, and assumed someone had left the kitchen. She opened the door a crack. The cake batter would probably go flat if she didn't finish mixing it soon. If Elmer was still there, she supposed she should introduce herself.

A man was sitting at the kitchen table, near the archway that led to the hall. By hiding behind a high cupboard, Honor was able to study him without being seen. He was tall and skinny with protruding front teeth and red-brown hair. When he lifted his cup, she noticed his dirty, freckled hands. She wrinkled her nose. He needed a bath. Even from across the room, she could smell him. He wore tan trousers and a filthy tan jacket, and Honor judged him to be middle-aged.

"Hello, there." Faking a smile, she stepped from behind the cupboard. "I'm Miss McCall."

The man turned and stared. "Hello." He took a sip of coffee.

"I work here."

Elmer set down his cup without smiling. He wasn't much of a talker, which suited Honor just fine. She finished mixing the cake, popped the pan into the oven and washed and dried the dishes. Then she glanced at the safe box with its perforated, tin doors. This was the only cupboard in the kitchen where the cake would be protected from mice. When the cake was done, she placed it in the safe box, wiped her hands on her white apron, and eyed Elmer to see if he needed anything.

"Ma'am." Elmer pulled an envelope from the pocket of his dirty jacket. "I almost forgot I had this." He cleared his throat. "Mrs. Peters says your last name's McCall. Is that right?"

"Yes."

"Then I guess this here letter is for you."

"Letter?" Honor gasped, and a shiver trailed down her back. Did Lucas know where she was?

"Thank—Thank you, sir."

Honor took the letter without looking at it. The mere thought that it might be from Lucas tied her stomach in knots. A wave of the jitters followed.

"Ain't ya gonna open it?"

Honor blinked several times before focusing on Elmer. "What did you say?"

"That there letter you got. Why don't you go on and open it?"

She'd almost forgotten Elmer was still watching her, and with his mouth gaping open, too. She shook her head and dropped the letter into the pocket of her apron, without looking at the return address. She glanced at Elmer. "I thought Reverend Peters always brought in the mail."

"Whenever I can, I pick it up of a morning. I work on a ranch a ways on t'other side of town. Sometimes I stop at the post office. I reckon the preacher come to town after I done rode out."

"Yes. I see."

Honor nervously wiped her hands on her apron. A moment later, she realized that she was pacing in front of the stove. "I guess I'll—I guess I'll go up to my room now so I can read my letter."

On her way up the stairs, Honor pulled the envelope out of her pocket. The printing was large and she smiled in relief. It wasn't from Lucas. Honor would know his small, scratchy handwriting anywhere.

As she climbed the stairs, she saw that the letter came from Simon and Annie Carr, the couple she had met on the stagecoach. Honor opened the envelope and stopped to read it in the hallway outside her room.

Dear Miss McCall,
We are still visiting our daughter in Pine Falls and are not going back home until Christmas. Please thank Reverend Peters for writing a letter and telling us you are feeling better. Hope you still are.

Our friends here in Pine Falls told us about a man what was asking about you, ma'am. We never seen him, and we do not know his name. But he shore is trying to find you. If we ever do see him, miss, should we tell him where you are staying now and all?

"No!" Honor trembled from head to toe, thinking, don't you dare tell him a thing!

An hour later, Honor was swishing the broom back and forth across the wood floor in the entry hall. She'd already written a letter to Mr. and Mrs. Carr and told them not to reveal her location to anyone.

When she heard the sound of footfalls on the steps outside, she went to one of the windows that framed the front door and looked out. Jeth.

For a moment, she wondered if she should tell him about the letter she'd gotten from the Carrs. Then she decided not to, since he would probably want to read her letter, and then expect her to tell him about Lucas. She was still exasperated with Jeth over the incident with Selma's dress. She didn't want to explain anything to him.

Jeth opened the door. An icy wind whooshed inside. Standing before her, his breath looked like a puff of whitish smoke. She'd thought he was alone, but then she saw a small boy with big, green eyes beside him, wearing one of the warmest smiles she'd ever seen on a child. His dark coat looked two sizes too big for him. Black, curly hair edged his brown wool cap.

"Miss Honor McCall, meet Timmy Rivers," Jeth said. "His parents are members of our church. He's the little boy I've been wanting you to meet."

A smile formed on her lips. Timmy was the little boy that Jeth had told stories about when she'd first woken from unconsciousness and came to herself.

"Hello, Timmy," she said.

"Hello, Miss McCall. I'm very glad to meet you." He offered her his tiny hand.

Honor smiled. "I'm glad to meet you, too."

His hand felt icy when she shook it. Timmy should be wearing mittens on a cold day like this.

Bending down to the child's level, her smile lingered. "What brings you out here today?"

"My mama has the sneezes."

"The sneezes? I'm sorry to hear that."

"She'll be all right, though. Dr. Harris said so when he came to our house a while ago. Reverend Peters is taking care of me so Mama can rest."

"That's probably a good idea." She brushed snow from the shoulders of his jacket with her fingertips. "Let's go into the kitchen now, Timmy, and see if we can find something good to eat and drink, shall we? It's warmer in there."

As she ushered the child down the hall, she sent Jeth a hard glance. She wanted him to know that, despite the boy, she hadn't forgotten the tension between them.

Jeth must have known she would warm to a child no matter how she felt about him. Could he have invited Timmy over deliberately to provide a buffer?

No, she thought not. Timmy had said his mother was sick. Still, Honor wasn't ready for a truce.

Jeth followed them into the kitchen. "How about heating up the coffee?" he asked.

The muscles around her mouth tightened. "Very well." But her expression softened when she gazed back at Timmy. "And what would you like, young man? We have cookies and milk. Would you like some?"

"Yes, ma'am, I sure would."

Jeth removed his heavy, woolen jacket and draped it over the back of his chair. Then he sat down at the table.

"You're still upset with me," he said, "aren't you."

Ignoring his question, Honor turned to Timmy. "Just put your coat and cap on the back of a chair like the reverend did."

"Yes, ma'am."

Honor went over to the sideboard and started putting cookies on a white plate. Timmy hung up his coat and trailed right behind her.

"Timmy," she said, "I hear you have a birthday coming up. Is that right?"

"Yes, ma'am, it is."

"And how old will you be?"

"Six."

"Six years old? Why, that's big, isn't it? What do you want for your birthday?"

"A new kite. I busted my old one."

"That's what Reverend Peters was telling me." Leaning over, she offered him the platter of cookies. "How did it happen?"

"Playin'." He grabbed three cookies from the platter. "I was just running down the road one day trying to get my kite to fly...and it happened."

Timmy put one of the cookies in the pocket of his wool breeches and held the other two, one in each hand. Honor tried not to smile. When she glanced at Jeth, he appeared to be holding back a grin as well.

"So what exactly happened?" she asked.

"Well, I just kept on running. I didn't see the old speckled hen and her baby chicks when they ran across in front of me. Guess I wasn't lookin'."

"You didn't step on one of the babies, did you?" Jeth asked.

"No, but I almost did. Anyway, the old hen fluffed out her feathers and started chasing me. She was real mad. I ran so hard my kite hit the trunk of a tree."

"You weren't hurt, were you?" Honor asked.

"No, but my kite sure was." His expression matched the sound of his crestfallen voice. "And it was the best one I ever had, too."

"How many kites have you owned, Timmy?" Jeth asked.

He shrugged, a cookie lodged in his jaw. "Just that one." The words came out muffled through his mouthful.

Honor and Jeth both laughed, but she recovered quickly.

"So why don't you sit down now, Timmy, and I'll pour you that glass of milk?"

The child nodded. "All right. And can I have some extra cookies to take home—for later."

"Take all you want. But you have to agree to ask your mama before you eat them. Promise?"

Timmy grinned. "Yes, ma'am, I promise."

Later, Timmy went outside to check on Mama Cat and her litter of baby kittens living in the barn. Honor and Jeth continued to sit at the table a while longer, drinking their coffee.

"So far, it's been a warm winter." He glanced out a kitchen window. "Just a trickle of cold rain and snow now and then. But it sure looks like snow's coming. Maybe tonight."

"That's what your mother said." Honor moved to the stove and stoked the flames to warm the coffee. When she heard his chair move, she looked back at Jeth. "Is it too hot in here for you?" she asked.

"Not at all. I like it warm and cozy like this."

He fingered his empty cup. She wondered if something was bothering him—like the fact that he'd scolded her when he'd seen her wearing his wife's dress.

"I really am sorry, ma'am, for mentioning the green dress the way I did. As a Christian, I should have known better. But when I saw you wearing Selma's clothes, I kind of flew over the chicken coop—so to speak."

She knew she should accept his apology. Someday, she probably would. Now, all she felt was embarrassment.

A few minutes later, steam sizzled from the pot, and the smell of coffee filled the room. Hurrying to the woodstove, Honor poured hot coffee into their tin cups and handed one to Jeth. Taking hers in both hands, she settled into the chair across from him. A smile wasn't in her.

Honor reached for the sugar bowl. "So what happened in town today?"

"I visited Miss Lucy Jordan."

She dropped two lumps into her cup and stirred without looking at him. "Who's she?"

"A member of our church."

"How nice for a single man like you." A fresh blush warmed her cheeks when she realized what she'd said.

He grinned. Had she amused him?

"Miss Jordan lives with her mother."

A *ping* startled her. Glancing down, Honor realized she had bumped the metal spoon against her tin cup. She set her spoon on her crumpled napkin and rose from her chair, hands flat on the table.

"I baked a chocolate cake. Would you like a slice?"

"No." He covered her hand with his. "I want you to sit back down. There's something else I need to say."

"Oh," she said, inching her hand free.

"I told you there are folks in our church who have been wanting to learn how to read. Well, Lucy Jordan is one of them. She knows your name now, Miss McCall, and that you'll be her teacher. And she's very excited. When can you start?"

"When would you like me to?"

"As soon as we can arrange it."

Jeth took a sip of coffee, then wiped his mouth with the back of his hand. Honor stilled a shudder. How many times had she seen Lucas wipe his mouth in just that way?

"I want you to drive into town with me in the morning so you can meet your new student. And don't worry about your duties here at the boardinghouse. I'll tell Mama that you're meeting Miss Jordan tomorrow and will be teaching her once a week."

"What time do you plan to leave?" she asked.

"Is right after breakfast too soon?"

"After breakfast will be fine."

When Jeth left to drive Timmy home, Honor cleared the table and washed the dishes, but her thoughts focused on her future tutoring student. Honor tried to imagine what Miss Lucy Jordan might be like, and all sorts of pictures played in her mind.

Jeth had explained the importance of a first meeting. Honor wanted to look her best and would stay up late and alter another of his mother's dresses.

In the big dining room that evening, the long table was filled with people. The supper guests included Mrs. Clark and her sister, Mrs. Davis, Elmer, a Mr. Lott, Dr. Harris, and, of course, Jeth. The scent of a beef roast and spicy baked potatoes wafted around them.

Honor planned not to look at Jeth. She would simply do her job and go back to the kitchen, she told herself.

The table was covered with bowls and platters of food, but there was space for one more something directly in front of Jeth's plate. Holding a heavy bowl of green beans in both hands, she intended to place it on the table and walk away. But standing behind Jeth, she realized there wasn't enough room between him and Dr. Harris to squeeze a bowl through. Somebody needed to move out of her way.

Gathering her courage, she cleared her throat. "Would one of you gentlemen please move so I can put this bowl on the table?"

Both men turned and smiled.

Jeth moved way over—as if he expected her to put a washtub on the table. "Is this far enough?"

Everybody looked at Honor and laughed.

Her cheeks burned. "Yes, that should do it."

Jeth rose from his chair. "That looks heavy. Let me help you."

Honor shook her head, glowering at him. "No, thank you, Preacher. I can do this all by myself."

She stepped forward on shaky legs. The bowl tipped slightly. Beans spilled to the very edge. Jeth reached out and steadied the bowl.

"Thank you," she said stiffly.

"You're welcome."

Knowing that all eyes were on her, Honor was flooded with embarrassment. She set the bowl near Jeth's plate and stepped back.

"Please, everyone," she said. "I'm sorry for causing a stir and interrupting your supper. Now, if you will excuse me, I need to get back to the kitchen."

Honor hurried to the door before she caused another disaster. She'd almost reached it when she heard a chair move, then footsteps. Jeth was right behind her.

She raced into the kitchen. Out of the corner of her eye, she saw Mrs. Peters standing at the stove, stirring a pot of something. Honor headed for the mess room, thinking nobody would bother her there.

"Miss McCall," Jeth said from behind her. "I'm so sorry. I've hurt you again. I was joking. We all joke with one another here at the boardinghouse. But you're new and didn't know. Can you ever forgive me?"

Honor turned and glared at him, with tears in her eyes. "It doesn't matter. Forget about it. I'm just a maid here anyway."

"Children!" Mrs. Peters clapped her hands. "What are you two fussing about?"

"I'm sorry, ma'am," Honor said. "This is all my fault. I'm making a mess of everything." She glanced toward the hall leading to the stairway. "If you will both excuse me, I need to go to my room now. I'll be back as soon as I can."

Jeth followed her to the stairway. Before she reached the first step, he took her arm gently and held it.

"Go on up if you like, Miss McCall. You deserve a recess. And I think you're doing a fine job here at the boardinghouse. I know you'll do well as my assistant over at the church, too."

Honor forced a quick smile. "Thank you, Reverend." Then she dashed up the stairs, and didn't look back.

The next morning, Honor sat beside Jeth in the wagon. The last thing she wanted was to ride into town with him, but she was obligated to fulfill her agreement to tutor members of his church. And how else would she get to town on such a chilly day?

The brown plaid dress that she'd altered hugged her slender form, and she wondered if Jeth noticed that she'd taken special care with her hair and clothes to appear neat and well-groomed. Now, if only she could stop shivering.

Snow fell softly around them and the thin material of Honor's dress did little to protect her from the cold.

Jeth pulled a woolen blanket from a box under the bench of the wagon. "Here. Wrap this around you. And if this isn't enough, I have another blanket or two I can give you."

"One will be fine. Thank you very much."

"I'm buying you a winter coat as soon as we get to town."

"You will not!" Honor grimaced. "I won't hear of it. When I can afford a coat, I'll buy one—and not until then."

"I think the Lord wants you to have a coat today, Miss McCall, and so do I."

"We'll see about that."

"Yes, we certainly will."

By the time they reached the general store, the snow had stopped. The roofs of the houses were dusted with a layer of white. Icicles hung like silver ornaments from the eaves of the houses and the other buildings along the main street.

The town was bigger than Falling Rock, and there was a quality of warmth and friendliness shining in the faces of everyone who Honor saw. Could part of the reason be that she hadn't seen a single saloon?

Lucas had once complained that Hearten was bone-dry. At the time, Honor hadn't known what that meant. Then Aunt Harriet explained that alcohol wasn't sold in Hearten. That fact gave Honor a sense of security and reassurance.

She'd considered staying in the wagon while Jeth went into Baker's Grocery and Mercantile. But thoughts of a warm building and a roof over her head prompted her to follow him inside.

The store was divided into sections by display tables covered with a variety of items. Glass canisters filled with licorice and hard, brightly colored candies were placed beside boxes of bullets and hunting rifles. Shoes and ladies' hats were near a grocery counter, and shelves of food lined the back wall. A stairway led to the second floor, where Jeth had said the store-owner and his family lived.

Another counter stood in one corner of the big room. A sign above it read United States Post Office in big black letters.

Jeth ambled to a part of the store where coats and capes of various colors and sizes hung on wooden wall-pegs. He picked up a brown coat with a dark brown fur collar. "This looks about your size, Miss McCall. Why don't you try it on?"

A thrill shot through her. The coat was lovely.

Pressing her lips together, she shook her head. "I told you. I'm not buying a coat until—"

"Let me pay for it. You can reimburse me out of your salary. Employees do things like that around here all the time."

She opened her mouth to refuse, then closed it. The coldest winter months were ahead.

"Try it on," he urged.

She studied him for a moment. "All right."

Honor slipped her arms into the coat, buttoned it, and felt truly warm for the first time since she'd left the rooming house.

"Thank you, Reverend." His thoughtfulness overwhelmed her. "I've never owned a coat I liked better than this one. But remember, I will pay you back."

"Of course."

Honor wasn't accustomed to receiving gifts and kindnesses from anyone except her aunt, and she wanted to escape before she started to weep. Turning, she headed for the entry door.

The street in front of the general store was wet and filled with slush. She stood on the wide front porch until Jeth came out. Then she helped him load the items he'd bought into the back of the wagon, and together, they covered everything with a piece of canvas.

"I'll need to wait for the mail," he said. "Mr. Baker is sorting it now. As soon as it's ready, we can go."

"All right."

Jeth stepped back onto the porch, but Honor lingered by the wagon for a closer look at the town of Hearten. She glanced down the main street. A rider appeared in the distance.

A drop of freezing water, coming from the roof, dampened the top of Honor's head. Gazing up, she saw that the icicles were melting, and stepped under the covered walkway. Jeth still waited there—in his usual stance, hands behind his back and legs apart.

"Thank you again for the coat, Reverend."

"You are most welcome."

Honor turned back toward the road. A sandy-haired boy in a gray jacket rode up on a big, red horse. He looked to be about nine or ten years old.

The boy stuck out his chin, as if he had important things to do. Evidently, the child didn't see Honor and Jeth standing in front of the store, because he never glanced in their direction.

Honor noticed Jeth studying the boy and especially the animal. When the child went inside, Jeth turned to her. "Ever seen that sorrel horse before?"

"No, I can't say that I have."

"Are you sure?"

"Yes. Why?"

He shrugged. "Just wondered."

Jeth stepped from the porch and walked over to the hitching post where the red horse was tied. He squinted at the animal's markings and rubbed his hand across the brand, which read Lazy S. Honor wondered what he found so interesting.

She walked to the edge of the porch to view the horse from a different angle. The red gelding did look familiar. Had she seen the horse after all? If so, she couldn't remember where.

The store-owner came out with a handful of letters and nodded to Honor. "Ma'am." He gazed out toward Jeth. "Here's your mail, Reverend."

"Thank you, Mr. Baker," Jeth called back. "Would you please just give it to Miss McCall there? She works for my mother at the boardinghouse now."

"Of course." He handed the stack of letters to Honor. "Here you go, miss. And good day to ya."

"Good day to you, too, sir," Honor said.

Jeth continued to inspect the red horse, while Honor descended the wooden steps and climbed into the wagon. Surreptitiously, she inspected the mail, hoping she wouldn't find a letter from Lucas. When she didn't, she let out a deep sigh. He hadn't found her, not yet.

Honor glanced down at her new coat, brushing away a speck of moisture from the front of it. Thanks to Jeth, she felt warm now. That was something to be glad about.

Jeth still stood beside the red horse.

"Well, are you coming or not?" she asked.

"I have something else to do before we leave," he said without looking at her. "I hope you don't mind waiting a few minutes longer. If you get too cold, go back inside the store. I'll look for you there."

"No, I don't mind waiting. I'm warm enough right here."

"Thanks." Jeth turned sharply, walked across the muddy street and entered Sheriff Green's office.

What business did Jeth have with the sheriff? Honor felt her forehead wrinkle. Was he about to turn her in for stealing from the church in Falling Rock? Honor bit her lower lip, holding onto the hope that his business with the sheriff had nothing to do with her.

Chapter Eight

✤

Honor had hoped Jeth would tell her about his business with the sheriff, but when he returned, he simply climbed in the wagon and clicked the reins.

She lifted her chin. "Reverend Peters." Determination filled her. "I can't help but wonder why you went over to Sheriff Green's office. Did it have anything to do with me, or the boy on the red horse?"

"Sorry, Miss McCall, I'm not at liberty to discuss this with anyone right now. But it has nothing to do with you."

Honor nodded. "I see."

But she didn't. What was Jeth hiding?

Without another word, Jeth trotted the horses down a different road than the one that led to the boardinghouse.

"Are we going to Miss Jordan's now?" she asked.

"Yes. As I mentioned, I want the two of you to become acquainted before you start teaching her how to read."

Honor paused before speaking. "What is she like?"

Briefly, Jeth looked away from the reins and over at Honor. Then he peered down the road again.

"To some," he said, "it might seem strange that a well-bred lady like Miss Lucy Jordan never learned to read. But after her well-to-do father died, Miss Lucy spent most of her growing-up years on a remote farm with her invalid mother. By the time she was three, her mother was totally blind. A maid cooked their meals and cared for them. The maid, Maria, didn't know how to read or write, but she taught Miss Jordan to sew and do other handiwork.

"Miss Lucy was barely eighteen when her late father's money ran out, and Maria died the same year. She's been her mother's only cook and caretaker ever since then, and makes her living as a seamstress."

She noticed Jeth studying her again. Did he expect her to make a comment? Yes, she had thoughts regarding Miss Lucy Jordan, but she felt she should keep them to herself.

Honor knew about problems in life and appreciated all Jeth had to say about Lucy. She regretted that the woman had difficulties, but an unflattering image of Miss Jordan formed in Honor's mind long before the wagon stopped in front of a quaint, little house with dormer windows and green shutters.

She pictured Miss Lucy as an old maid of thirty or more with wrinkles and straight, greasy hair. As she and Jeth came up the walk, a young woman stepped out onto the porch of the cottage. Honor's image of her prospective pupil disintegrated.

Miss Jordan had short, golden curls and violet-blue eyes. A perky smile lit her pixielike face. Honor started to like her at once—until she noticed the look in Jeth's eyes when he gazed at Lucy. Plainly, he was fond of the young woman.

Lucy Jordan was petite, slim and ladylike in her pale blue, wool dress and matching slippers. Compared to her, Honor felt like an awkward giant.

Taking a step forward, Honor suddenly felt her feet slide out from under her on the icy front porch. She reached out to save herself, but there was nothing solid to grip for support. Two strong arms grabbed Honor from behind and held her.

"Easy there, Miss McCall," Jeth said. "It's slippery out here."

"I guess I found that out, didn't I." Honor glanced back at Jeth. While her face flamed, she forced a smile. "And thank you. So much."

"Please," Lucy said. "Come in out of the cold. Both of you. It's safer inside."

Lucy led the way into a cozy parlor decorated in white and shades of blue. "I have hot tea and cookies."

"Nothing for me," Honor said, "but thank you for offering."

Lucy smiled at Jeth over her shoulder. "And you, Reverend? Would you care for something?"

"Frankly, I'd love tea and cookies."

Miss Jordan and Jeth shared the blue velvet settee, and they were soon deep in conversation. Honor sat in an overstuffed, blue and white striped chair, surveying the formal dining room beyond an arched doorway, trying to avoid witnessing the tender and admiring expression in Jeth's blue eyes when he looked at the engaging Miss Jordan.

The long rectangular dining table and heavy oak chairs looked tasteful and expensive. White lace curtains added charm. Honor barely heard what was said in the parlor.

"Is this agreeable with you, Miss McCall?" Jeth asked.

Honor's cheeks heated again because she hadn't been paying attention. "Agreeable? With what?"

"We were discussing when you would start the lessons."

"Oh, well. Whatever you both decide is fine with me."

"Thank you, Miss McCall," Jeth continued, "for being so cooperative."

Would Jeth be driving Miss Jordan to the boardinghouse for the lessons? The trip would give him plenty of chances to spend time with the young seamstress—if he wanted to, of course.

"Miss Jordan can't leave her mother alone for long," Jeth explained. "So I'll drive you here to the cottage on Monday, Miss McCall. If the weather is bad, I'll also pick you up afterward. Miss Jordan has been kind enough to allow us to have all our future lessons here on Mondays, as well. It's quiet at the cottage and more private than it would be at the rooming house. If later you have other students, they will like it here, too, I'm sure. Is this arrangement all right with you?"

"Of course." Honor nodded. "It wouldn't be right to leave Miss Jordan's poor mother alone."

In the wagon on the drive back to the boardinghouse, Honor caught Jeth looking at her before he turned off the main road.

"I would gladly pay a penny for your thoughts," he said.

"You would be wasting your money." Honor tried to smile. "I have no thoughts. My mind is a blank."

What a lie. She'd been thinking about Jeth and Miss Lucy since she'd left the Jordan home, recalling how cozy they had looked together in the parlor.

"Maybe I was thinking about the boardinghouse," she said. "It looks very impressive even at this distance."

"Yes, it does."

The big, white, two-story house with its red-tile roof and reddish-brown shutters was imposing and picturesque, surrounded by trees, on gently rolling grounds covered by a thin layer of snow. Snow-capped mountains rose behind the house, and hills framed the structure on both sides. Beyond the barn, Honor saw cow pens, outbuildings and fields. A glassy lake directly across the road from the main entrance reminded her of a reflecting pool. A wooden gate guarded the private road that led to a circular drive in front of the house.

Jeth got out to open the gate. Honor waited, shivering in the wagon. After he'd driven through and closed the gate, they wheeled slowly down the driveway.

When they stopped in front of the house, Jeth helped her from the wagon.

"The house is awe-inspiring," she said, noting the heavy brass knockers on the double doors made of oak. "Was it always a boardinghouse?"

"No, it wasn't. The house was built for a British lord and his family, but they didn't live in it long. When the family moved back to England, my grandfather bought the house and the land around it for a reasonable price."

"What an interesting heritage."

"Yes." He smiled. "We think so, too."

In the foyer, Jeth pulled a gift-wrapped package from under the maple desk and handed it to Honor. "Here, this is for you."

"But why?" Honor gazed at the pink bow on top. "It's not my birthday, and Christmas is over a month away."

"This is something you need." He smiled. "Please, go ahead and open it."

Honor took the package and tore back the paper. After the coat, she couldn't imagine why Jeth was giving her another gift. She unfolded the white tissue paper in the box and saw a black Bible with a gold cross on the front.

"Oh, it's lovely."

Honor had wanted a Bible to use for the reading lessons and she had hoped to borrow one. But she had never expected one of her own.

"I want to thank you for giving me this beautiful Bible, Reverend, but I can't accept it—unless I can reimburse you for the cost."

"I agreed to let you pay me back for the coat because you insisted. But the Bible is an extra copy I've had for a long time. I promised the man who gave it to me that I would give it to a person who needed it. That's you, Miss McCall."

She searched for a reasonable protest but couldn't think of one. Honor glanced toward the pine stairway. This would be an excellent time to exit the room before the tears of joy came.

That night, Honor took her Bible and sat in the chair by her bed. Pulling the oil lamp closer, she flipped to the first page. An inscription jumped out at her. Honor's forehead wrinkled. Had Jeth written this?

Honor gazed down at the page and noticed the same wide, free-flowing script she had found in the songbook back in Falling Rock—the one that held the dedication to somebody's late wife. Carefully, Honor read what was handwritten in the Bible. *To Miss Honor Rose McCall. Seek and you will find.*

Jeth! Clearly, he had written both inscriptions. Did he also know what she had done at the church in Falling Rock?

On Monday morning, a damp and cold wind lashed the trees in front of the boardinghouse. Seated in the wagon, Honor pulled up her coat collar. Today, she would tutor Miss Lucy Jordan in reading for the first time. She was eager to get the chore behind her.

Jeth took longer than usual hitching the leather harness to the team of brown horses. She wished he would hurry. At last, he climbed into the seat beside her.

"Warm enough?" He snapped the reins.

"I'm just fine."

"I should have gotten out the arched bracing and strung the canvas over the wagon long before now. I'll need to do that before I drive you into town again. Covered wagons are warmer and would protect you from rain and snow."

Honor tried to smile. Would Jeth ever stop worrying about her?

"You suggested that I begin my Bible reading with the Gospel of John," she said. "I thought you'd want to know I plan to do that. But I've also been reading in the Old Testament, and I have a couple of questions...." Her words trailed off when she realized that Jeth didn't appear to be listening.

"I'll be taking the long way this time." Jeth looked down the road ahead. "I want to drive by a ranch I know before delivering you to Miss Lucy's."

A slicing wind had pulled several soft curls from Honor's tight bun. The locks tickled her skin, whipping about her face and around the edges of her print bonnet. She pushed back her hair, considering the questions flooding her mind.

To Honor, the God of the Old Testament seemed harsh and nothing like Jesus. Yet at church on Sunday, Jeth had explained that the Bible was one book from Genesis to Revelation.

"The Lord is the same yesterday, today and forever," Jeth had said. "We cannot expect to completely understand God until we get to heaven and see Him face-to-face. We must accept on faith that everything in the Bible is good, right and completely true, and that the God of the Old Testament is also the God of the New Testament."

Honor was about to try again to ask her first question, when she remembered the letter from Simon and Annie. She should tell Jeth about it before discussing anything else. Still shivering, she pulled the envelope from the pocket of her new coat and leaned forward in the wooden seat.

"Sure you're warm enough?" Jeth asked.

Honor nodded, hugging her shoulders.

"Then why are you shaking?"

She shrugged. "Habit, I guess."

He lifted his head, and laughter boomed from deep within his chest. "If you change your mind, the blankets are still under the seat." He glanced at Honor, lifting one eyebrow in question. "What's that paper you've got there?"

"This?" Honor held out the envelope so he could see it. "It's—It's a letter from the elderly couple who we met on the stagecoach."

"The Carrs?"

"Yes. They said to thank you for writing them, and they wanted to know how I'm feeling."

"Well, aren't you going to read it to me?"

Read it to him? Honor cleared her throat. She'd hoped to avoid this, but couldn't see a way out now.

When she had finished reading, she waited—holding the letter tightly against her heart. Jeth would probably have questions she wasn't prepared to answer, though she doubted he would attempt to snatch the letter from her. At last she rested her hands on her lap, trying to relax.

"Who do you think is looking for you?" Jeth asked. "Your uncle?"

"There's a good chance it's him, all right."

"And what did you say his name was?"

"Lucas Scythe."

"So, what are you planning to do?"

Before she could answer, he looked off toward a red farm-house. Honor followed his gaze. A big, two-story house stood on a rise, set back from the road. New rooms appeared to be under construction. Smaller buildings circled the compound, and fresh lumber revealed that the cattle pens and lines of wood fences were also new. Honor glanced at the sign above the main gate: Sharp Ranch.

Jeth pulled the team to a stop in front of the sign.

"Why are we stopping here?" Honor asked.

"I hadn't been by this way in a while, and wanted to have another look around." He gazed at a plowed field across the road from the farmhouse. "That was the Sharp boy we saw in town the other day—the one on the sorrel horse."

"And you went across the street and talked to Sheriff Green. But you didn't tell me why."

"I still can't discuss it. But I hope I can tell you all about it very soon."

Honor resisted the urge to press the issue now.

"I hate to repeat rumors," he added, "but the Sharps are said to make liquor in a barn on their property." Jeth swung his whip above the horses and made clucking sounds. "Apparently, they are selling it to folks, making them drunk with the mixtures."

He clucked again, and the animals jerked forward. The horses trotted down a road that was little more than a pair of bumpy ruts.

Honor tried to push away her confused thoughts. Instead, she focused on the beauty of the hills and the snowy mountains in the distance.

The road took a sharp turn to the left. A tree loomed close to the muddy road. Its sweeping branches arched above their heads. Suddenly, she noticed that one of the lower branches was obstructing her view.

"Duck!" Jeth shouted, jerking back on the reins.

Honor ducked. The branch barely grazed the top of her head. Jeth stopped the horses.

"Are you hurt?"

She heard genuine concern in his tone. "No, Reverend, I'm fine," she assured him.

Honor watched as Jeth tied up the reins.

"I'm so sorry about the branch," he said. "If you hadn't ducked, you could have been seriously injured." Jeth shook his head. "Frankly, I didn't even see the thing until it was almost too late." Leaning over, he brushed a few dried leaves from her hair and bonnet. "As I think I told you, I don't take this road very often." He appeared to be studying her lips. "Are you really all right?"

"Yes." She tried to smile. "Yes, I am."

He moved closer. Her eyes widened and her breath caught. Honor touched the bow tied under her chin, and felt her cheeks flaming. She was sure he planned to kiss her, and she'd never been kissed by a man before.

His lips were inches away. "Are you saved, Miss McCall?" he asked.

Her eyes had been half closed, but they snapped open at his question. "Am I what?"

"Born again?"

"I don't think so. Should I be?"

"Yes." He backed away from her and settled into the seat on his side of the wagon.

She studied him for a moment before speaking again. "Did I give the wrong answer?"

"You told the truth, and that's always good."

Nodding, Honor fumbled for the blanket under her seat, needing the distraction. At the same time, she tried to digest exactly what he'd said and what it meant. Unfolding the plaid, wool lap-covering, she spread it across her knees.

She had wanted him to kiss her, and still did. Would it ever happen? In the meantime, she planned to learn what it meant to be saved and born again. Apparently these terms were important to Jeth. She also hoped for answers to her Bible questions and a solution to the mystery of the boy and the red horse.

Jeth cleared his throat. "I think it's time you contacted your uncle, Miss McCall. This Lucas Scythe. Let him know you're all right. I'm sure Simon and Annie Carr would be glad to tell him for you."

"They probably would. But I've already written and asked them not to."

"Not to?" He stared at her, shaking his head. "Why would you do that?"

"I told you. My uncle and I quarreled."

"Quarrels can and should be resolved. It's called forgiveness."

Forgiveness? She should have known Jeth would preach to her sooner or later. Wasn't that what ministers did?

"I'm not ready to see my uncle right now. And you promised not to tell him where I am." Honor studied Jeth searchingly. "You're still willing to keep that promise, aren't you?"

"Of course."

Jeth clucked the horses to attention, and the animals moved slowly down the road.

Honor would need to tell Jeth the truth about her uncle eventually—or part of it, at least. But her past was still too painful to think about much less discuss.

Lucas left his rented room over the grocery store and descended the stairway outside the building. He hesitated on the street and looked around. He'd been living in Pine Falls for three weeks, and this was his first day off since he had accepted work at Skip's Saloon. Today, he planned to make some progress in finding his runaway niece. If he also had a little fun along the way, all the better.

He pulled a handwritten map from the pocket of his jacket and studied it.

"Turn to the right when you're standing in front of that place where you live and facing the street," the man at the depot had written. "Then go one block and turn right again."

Lucas put the map back in his pocket and started walking.

Ed Carter, the depot manager, was a big man, several inches taller than Lucas. Carter had complained every time Lucas had walked in the door of the depot and he'd become especially disgruntled when Lucas had asked questions. Once Carter finally opened his mouth, his answers came out as more of a begrudging growl than words Lucas could understand.

Just looking at the man, Lucas knew Carter hated him. For Lucas, the feeling was mutual. But he'd decided to keep those kinds of thoughts and feelings to himself until he'd gotten the information he wanted.

Yesterday, Carter had leaned forward and reached across the counter. Lucas had thought the man intended to grab him by the collar and drag him over to his side to punch him. Lucas had fisted both hands, just in case. Then Carter had pulled back and slowly relaxed.

"Day after day, you come in here, mister," Carter had said, "asking me questions about that stagecoach robbery, wanting to know the names of those who were on that stage. Why?" Carter demanded. "Why is this so important to you?"

"I done told ya. My niece, Honor McCall, is missing. My wife is worried about her and sent me to fetch Honor home. Bring her back with me if I can. As I said, we think she was on that stage what was robbed. That's why I'm asking questions."

"And I've told you many times that I don't know who was on that stage. But Gregory Kline might know someone who can answer your questions. I gave him your name, and he said he was willing to talk to you." Carter handed Lucas the map. "Now, go talk to Kline in the morning at nine and don't come back here. Ever! You're bad for my business."

As Lucas left the depot, he'd felt a sense of satisfaction over the encounter with Ed Carter. At the same time, he was slightly surprised that he'd managed to hold in his anger.

Lucas stepped up his pace. He was finally on his way to meet Mr. Gregory Kline to find out what he knew. Lucas hoped to learn what had happened to Honor. And he especially wanted to know what had become of his money.

He hadn't sold the Bible or the pearls yet, but he had sold Lady to the man on the swaybacked horse back in Hearten. He hated to lose his mare, but in her condition, Lady was having a hard time carrying Lucas and his load. As a result of the sale, Lucas had enough to take the stagecoach to Pine Falls—with money left over.

He turned right at the corner and went down a side street. Ed Carter said that Kline lived in the middle of the block in a little white house with black shutters.

Gazing ahead, he saw a small cottage fitting the description. A white picket fence surrounded the house, and a man stood at the front gate. Lucas assumed he was Gregory Kline.

The man smiled when Lucas grew closer. "Are you Lucas Scythe?" he asked.

"I reckon I am."

"I'm Gregory Kline." He opened the yard gate. "Please, come in. My wife and I were expecting you."

Lucas licked his lips. He needed a drink. Was Mr. Kline a drinking man? Lucas sure hoped so. However, he decided to wait a while before asking, get to know Mr. Kline first.

The small living room was neat and clean, and a fire popped and snapped in the hearth.

"Sit there by the fire and warm yourself." Mr. Kline motioned toward an overstuffed brown chair with a wooden footstool in front of it. "Put your feet up if you've a mind to. We wouldn't care at all. My wife will be in with a pot of hot coffee in a minute."

Lucas sat down and looked around the room. He hoped to see a whiskey bottle or something that would indicate he would soon be drinking alcohol. His eyes focused on a large Bible—open on a table near his chair.

"I see you noticed our family Bible."

Lucas swallowed before trying to reply. "Yes, yes I did."

"If you haven't found a church home yet, we would sure like to have you come and pay ours a visit."

"Church home?"

On hearing the word *church,* Lucas felt his face and neck warm, and he stopped looking for whiskey. He wasn't likely to find any here.

"Do folks live right there in your church?" Lucas asked.

Mr. Kline grinned. "My, no. What I meant to say was, would you do us the honor of visiting our church on Sunday morning?" Still smiling, he hesitated. "What do you say? It's just down the street here, and I'm the pastor."

"You mean you're a preacher?"

"God willing, I am."

"Well, I don't know about church. You see, I'll probably have to work this Sunday."

"Then please come the first chance you get. We have services on Wednesday nights, too. But you're welcome at First Bible Church. Anytime."

"Thank you kindly, sir." Lucas swallowed again, wondering what to say next. Then he cleared his throat.

A rounded little woman with yellow hair, bright blue eyes, and a wide smile came into the parlor. She carried a silver serving tray.

"Here's my wife now." The minister got up from his chair and helped the woman set the heavy tray onto a small table near the center of the room. "Mrs. Kline, I would like to present our guest, Lucas Scythe."

"I'm glad to make your acquaintance, Mr. Scythe," she said.

Lucas nodded, glancing back at the coffeepot and tray on the round table. "Likewise, I'm sure."

He couldn't keep his eyes off the pot and the shiny metal tray. *Wonder how much the silver in it is worth?* he thought.

Mrs. Kline poured coffee into two white cups, acting the perfect hostess. The silver coffeepot and tray glittered in a beam of sunlight coming from a window behind her.

"Mr. Scythe is the one Ed Carter at the depot was telling us about," Reverend Kline said to his wife. "He wants to talk to folks who were on that stage that was robbed."

"Yes, I remember." Mrs. Kline walked across the room and handed Lucas a cup of steaming coffee.

Lucas took the warm cup from her. "Thank you, ma'am."

"Sugar and cream, sir?"

"No. I drink my coffee black." He motioned toward the table where she had left the silver pot and matching tray.

"That's a mighty fine coffeepot and tray you've got there, ma'am, and it looks expensive. Is it made of genuine silver?"

"Yes, it is. In fact, the inside of the pot is made of gold." Her smile deepened. "It was a wedding gift and came all the way from London, England."

"That's a gift you can be proud of," Lucas said, "ain't it." He glanced back at the preacher. "I hear you know somebody what was on that stage from Falling Rock. The one that got robbed. Is that right?"

The preacher nodded as his wife handed him a cup of coffee. "Two people on that stage have been attending our church, but I don't know them very well yet. What would you like to know?"

"I'm looking for my niece, Honor McCall."

"So I've heard," Reverend Kline said.

Lucas lifted the cup to his lips and took a sip. The hot liquid warmed his mouth.

"Honor is like a daughter to my wife and me. With Christmas coming and all, we've been hoping I can find her and bring her home before the holidays. I thought maybe if I talked to the ones who were on that stage, I might learn something that would help me find Honor."

"As I said, I don't know the couple who were on that stage very well."

Couple. Lucas hadn't known they were man and wife.

"They haven't been coming to our church long," the preacher went on. "But I'll be glad to talk to them and see if I can set up a meeting with you."

"If you wouldn't mind giving me their address, I could stop by and talk to them myself. Save you the trouble."

The preacher shook his head. "Well, I don't know about that, sir." He cleared his throat. "That's not normally the way things are done at our church."

The minister covered his initial reaction with a quick smile. Still, the flicker of distrust left its mark on Lucas, and he feared there might never be a meeting now.

There was nothing Lucas hated more than church and preachers. However, his only hope of meeting the couple who had been on the stage might be to attend church services on Sunday. Since he wasn't scheduled to go to work until five on Sunday afternoon, he really had no excuse.

"Maybe I could attend morning services at your church on Sunday after all. Now, when did you say I should be there?"

"Half past nine."

Jeth stopped the wagon in front of Lucy's cottage. Honor thought he appeared to be in deep thought. Was he thinking about Lucy? Uncle Lucas? Or the kiss they had almost shared?

The kiss.

A whisper of softness rippled through her as Honor recalled that Jeth had leaned toward her, dissolving the space between them. His blue gaze had gentled, and his mouth had moved closer and closer. She couldn't stop wondering what it might have been like if he'd taken her in his arms and held her. She blinked, holding back a sigh, as thoughts of actually kissing him touched every part of her.

Was it wrong to have such thoughts? Dreams? Now that Aunt Harriet was gone, there was nobody for Honor to ask.

What did it matter? With Lucas actively searching for her, she should probably leave Hearten by the end of the week.

Chapter Nine

❧

While Honor taught her reading lesson, Jeth drove his team of horses to a spot across the street from the sheriff's office. As he started to climb down from the wagon, he noticed a purse that Honor must have left on the wooden seat. Jeth decided to put it under the bench and out of sight.

He reached for the purse, and suddenly noticed the scent of lilacs coming from the brown material. Tender visions of Honor McCall filled his mind.

Her long auburn hair had been coiled into a bun at the nape of her slender neck that morning, and those big brown eyes of hers had never looked brighter or more appealing. And her pink lips...

Jeth drew in his breath. It wasn't proper to think about Honor's mouth. Yet he'd been doing it for days and most nights.

Jeth wanted to kiss her—to make her his wife. However, knowing what he knew about her spiritual walk, marriage was out of the question. Perhaps it would always be so. Yet he couldn't stop worrying about her and hoping that one day soon, things would be different.

He crossed the wet street to the sheriff's office and opened the door. Sheriff Green was leaning back in his chair and appeared to be sleeping. The sheriff had once told Jeth that his grandfather was a Cheyenne chief. Certainly his dark, rugged complexion and blue-black hair confirmed it.

As Jeth moved farther into the office, he bumped into a chair, knocking it against the wall. The chair hit the floor with a *bang*. The sheriff jumped and jerked his head around.

"Well, Reverend. Good to see you in here again." Sheriff Green glanced at the overturned chair. "Sit down if you can find a place, and stay awhile."

Jeth chuckled and hung his hat on the wall. Then, righting the chair, he settled onto it.

The sheriff gestured toward a coffeepot, hanging from a hook over an open fireplace. "I've got coffee if you want some."

"Smells good, but I better not. I drink too much coffee."

The sheriff gave a short laugh. "Are you saying you're a drinking man, Preacher?"

"Maybe." Jeth laughed. "But only if it's the right kind of drinking." He relaxed against the back of his chair. "So how's your robbery investigation going?"

"Oh, yes, the stage robbery." The sheriff looked down at a sheet of paper on his desk. "Let me see. It says that the last time you were here, we talked about the robbery. And you said you thought the red horse that the Sharp kid rides around town is the same animal you saw during the robbery. Is that right?"

"Exactly right."

The sheriff leaned back in his chair, rubbing his black mustache. "So what new information have you brought me this time?"

"I rode by the Sharp place before coming here and saw something that might interest you."

"Let's hear it."

"The Sharps have fixed up their place since I last saw it. The house has a new roof. A couple of rooms are being added to the original structure, and the fences are new, too. The Sharps look more prosperous than I remember. Do you know if the family inherited money lately?"

"Not that I know of, but I'll sure check. Still, I can't make an arrest merely because they're finally keeping their place from running down. Any rancher with brains in his head repairs his property."

Jeth frowned. "That's true. But I still think they're the outlaws. I know what I saw."

"I think they might be the robbers, too, Reverend. But you said the outlaws were wearing masks the day of the robbery, didn't you?"

"Yes, I did."

"I need proof of a crime before I can make an arrest. That's the law."

"It's against the law to rob stages and hit young women over the head with the butt of a gun. But that didn't stop the robbers, did it."

"It's *my* job to solve this case, and I will." The sheriff glared at Jeth. Then, his face relaxed. "Not that you'd do something like this—being a preacher and all, but we can't have our citizens going around taking the law into their own hands."

Jeth pulled out his silver pocket watch and checked the time. He didn't want to overstay his welcome. After a moment, he glanced back at the sheriff. Jeth respected Sheriff Green, but he knew—and the sheriff knew—the Sharps were guilty. Why didn't the lawman go ahead and put them in jail before they robbed another stage? Or did something worse?

Clenching his teeth, Jeth rose from his chair. The more he thought about the short arm of the law, the angrier he got. Someone needed to put a stop to these crimes, and apparently, nobody planned to do so.

He snatched his hat from the hook on the wall and headed for the door. "I'll see if I can find the proof you need, Sheriff. Somebody has to."

Jeth glanced back. The sheriff grinned and got up from his chair.

"Thanks for stopping by." Stretching long, skinny legs, Sheriff Green folded big hands around his wide leather belt and jerked up his trousers as though he expected them to slip down around his narrow hips. "Come back anytime." He placed a hand at Jeth's back and walked him to the door. "But remember, I need proof of a crime before I can make an arrest."

Yes, Jeth thought, holding in another burst of irritation. *I believe you mentioned that.*

"And another thing," the sheriff added. "I might be calling on you soon to serve as a special deputy."

"Special deputy?" Surprised by his comment, Jeth stopped and faced him. "You must be joking."

"I've never been more serious."

"Have you forgotten I'm the pastor of a church?"

"No, I didn't forget. But it's hard to find honorable men to serve as deputies these days. And you're about the most honorable around."

Special deputy? Jeth chuckled under his breath and turned toward the door. He could only imagine what his parishioners would say if he became a lawman—even for a short time. But if the sheriff wanted proof, Jeth would see he got it.

As Jeth stepped down from the wooden walkway, the soles of his boots dug into the thick mud mixed with ice. He ambled across the street, again noticing the red horse tied in front of the general store.

He wondered if the boy was riding the animal. It was possible that one of his older brothers came into town. Maybe Jeth would go over to the store and see what he could find out.

As soon as he stepped inside, Jeth saw the boy looking dreamily at jars of candy. Jeth sidled up to him.

The child looked up at him. He appeared to be clean enough in spite of the patches on his ragged clothes, and his black eyes snapped with a hint of intelligence. But the thick, sandy-colored hair that fell across his forehead needed cutting. Was the child's mother too busy to use the soup bowl and trim the boy's hair?

"Like candy, boy?" Jeth asked.

"Do I?" The child turned to Jeth and grinned up at him again. "Yes, sir, I sure do."

"I like candy, too, especially the red kind."

Jeth opened one of the canisters, and the scent of peppermint filled the air. He closed the glass jar and studied the boy.

The child still watched him. "You're that preacher, ain't you?"

"Yes, I'm Reverend Peters. Who are you?"

"Willie Sharp."

Willie offered Jeth his hand. Jeth shook it and smiled. Without knowing anything about the child other than his firm handshake, Jeth liked him immediately.

"Glad to know you, Willie."

"Same to you." Willie hesitated. "I knew you was the preacher 'cause I seen you there."

"You visited our church?"

"I did once. Mama came, too. But—But we don't go to church no more."

"I'm sorry to hear that. I would love to visit with you if you ever decide to come back. God would also be happy to see you there."

"You sound like you know God—personal like."

"I do, son. I really do. The Lord's my best friend."

"You're joking, ain't you?"

"No, God *is* my friend. And He would like to be your friend, too."

"Me?" The boy looked at Jeth long and hard, shaking his head. "Naw, He wouldn't want me." Willie turned to go.

"Yes, He would," Jeth called after him. "And before you leave the store, I want to buy you some of that candy."

"Candy?" The boy whirled around and grinned. "Do you mean that? Really?"

"Really. But remember, the candy's not from me. It's from God."

After the boy had mounted his horse and trotted out of town, Jeth thought about what the child had said. Maybe he would visit the Sharp Ranch soon and invite the folks to church. Not only would he be doing God's work, he might stumble onto proof the sheriff needed.

At four o'clock, Jeth and Honor started back to the boardinghouse. In the wagon, Honor's anxiety grew as she reflected on what the outcome might be if Annie and Simon told Lucas where she was staying. Yes, she'd asked them not to tell anyone where she lived. But how could she be sure they would do as she requested?

Annie and Simon could have already told Lucas what they knew before getting Honor's letter. Uncle Lucas might be on his way to Hearten now.

Though Honor hadn't told anyone about Lucas, she'd been having bad dreams, and they all featured him. She shook her head, as if that simple act would erase the disturbing thoughts and nightmares from her mind, but it didn't work. All her dreams were similar, and she couldn't stop thinking about them, like the one she'd had on the previous night, in which Lucas had chased her again. In the dreams, he was always chasing her. She'd run and run, hoping to get away. Then she would turn, and there he'd be, about to grab her. She would wake then, often in a bed soaked with perspiration. Sometimes, she'd wake up screaming. When that happened, Mrs. Peters always came to her bedside and comforted her.

Now Honor trembled. She shouldn't stay in Hearten any longer; even a few more days could be dangerous. Perhaps if she moved somewhere else, her fears and bad dreams would stay behind and she would never be bothered by them again.

She would tell Jeth and his mother she was leaving as soon as they got back to the boardinghouse.

Jeth reached below the seat for a blanket and handed it to Honor. "You're shaking. Wrap this around you."

"Thank you, Reverend."

A few minutes later, Honor stepped down from the wagon and stood on the back porch of the white, two-story house. Jeth opened the kitchen door.

"You're not shaking as much now," he said. "Hope it means you're warming up."

"Yes, it does." She went inside. "And I have something important I need to say to you and your mother." Glancing back, she added, "Can we sit in the kitchen and talk for a minute?"

"Talk? Of course." He gestured toward the table. "Why don't you sit here while I look for my mother?" Jeth disappeared through the connecting door that led to the big dining room. "Mama!"

"Yes?"

"We need you in the kitchen."

Honor sat down. A moment later, Jeth and his mother settled into chairs around the kitchen table.

"Well," Jeth said to Honor. "What was it you wanted to say?"

She'd planned to tell them she was quitting. Now the time had arrived, and she couldn't utter a sound.

"While you're thinking—" Mrs. Peters smiled "—I have some news of my own."

"Oh?" Honor's gaze shifted from Jeth to his mother.

"Dr. Harris and I are getting married after the first of the year."

"How nice." Honor forced a pleasant expression. "I mean, congratulations, ma'am."

"Thank you, Miss McCall."

"But she's not giving up the boardinghouse after the wedding," Jeth put in. "So at least we'll have a roof over our heads a while longer."

Mrs. Peter glanced at her son and feigned a scolding look. "You'll have a roof as long as you want one, Jethro. And you know it." She turned to Honor. "I plan to keep running the boarding as long as I'm able to do it, and you'll have a job here forever—if you want it."

"You're very kind, ma'am, but—"

"There's something else." Mrs. Peters pulled an envelope from the pocket of her white apron and laid it on the table. "Elmer brought the mail in earlier, and I got a letter from my niece, Margaret Starling. Margaret lives in Pine Falls and is my late sister's only child. We're very close. Why, I'm like her second mother now. She's in the family way and expecting to deliver soon. The doctor said this could be a difficult birth, and she asked me to come to Pine Falls and stay with her until after the baby is born to cook for her husband and help take care of her other children. I've decided to go."

"I'm glad, Mama. You should go," Jeth said.

"Thank you, Jethro." Mrs. Peters smiled at Honor. "I'm putting you in charge of everything here, Miss McCall."

"Me?" Honor shook her head. "Oh, no, Mrs. Peters. I'm not qualified. Besides—"

"Don't be so modest. You'll do a wonderful job of keeping everything going here. Still—" Mrs. Peters tilted her head to one side. "We'll need to find an older woman from our church to come here and stay while I'm away. It wouldn't do for you to live here without a chaperone. Remember, Jethro and Elmer are both single men. And as soon as I find a suitable chaperone, I'll be leaving on the next stage." Mrs. Peters sent another little smile toward Honor. "Now, what was it you wanted to talk about, Miss McCall?"

If Honor had felt speechless before, now she was doubly so. She swallowed and cleared her throat. How could she tell them she was leaving town after this revelation? Jeth and his mother had never needed her more.

Her gaze traveled to the mess room door. The last time Honor had been in the pantry, she had noticed that their supply of beans and rice were low. She'd intended to remind Mrs. Peters to put those items on her grocery list. However, barrels of beans and rice weren't important enough for a full-blown meeting with her employers. She would need to come up with something else. Then she remembered her Bible questions.

"I—I've been reading the Bible and have questions I would like to ask. Since both of you know a lot more about Scripture verses than I do, I thought you might be kind enough to help me."

"Of course we'll help you," Jeth said. "But from the expression on your face when we sat down, I assumed you wanted to discuss something more pressing." He eyed her carefully. "Honor, is something bothering you?"

Honor. He'd called her by her first name. She wanted to bask in the moment, but she felt their eyes on her. It was time to ask her questions. Unfortunately, she couldn't think of a single one.

Lucas arrived late for work at the saloon that evening, for the second time that week. He went directly to the kitchen and started washing dishes. Maybe Mr. Skipworth wouldn't notice the time Lucas came in. But if he did—

Lucas looked down at the torn blue shirt he was wearing and the brown trousers covered with patches. They were the oldest, shabbiest clothes he owned. Now all he needed to do was carry out his plan and lie a little.

Lucas picked up a beer mug and dropped it in the soapy water. Footsteps thumped the floor nearby. Lucas assumed a calm expression.

"Scythe!" Mr. Skipworth shouted from behind him.

Lucas looked around, keeping his hands in the water, pretending nonchalance. "Yes, boss."

"Why were you late again?"

"My sister got sick and died last night. The funeral's Saturday afternoon."

The tall, muscled saloon owner's cold gray eyes narrowed. "I'm sorry to hear that." He hesitated, and his eyes softened a little. "I—I guess you'll be wantin' off, then, won't you."

"No, sir." He dropped a soapy glass into a bucket of clean water. "I won't need to be off. I ain't going to the funeral."

"Why not?"

"I ain't got no fancy suit and tie. All I got is ordinary clothes—like the ones I got on."

"Would you go if you *did* have the right kind of clothes?" Mr. Skipworth asked.

"I reckon I would. I'd sure like to go. My family expects it, I guess."

Mr. Skipworth went over and looked out the only window in the kitchen. He wouldn't see much in the alley out back except trash heaped up and food left to rot. Mr. Skipworth opened the window, but when the stench rushed in, he quickly shut it.

"My own sister died a while back," he said. "I'm glad I went to the funeral. It meant a lot to my family to have me there." He turned from the window and stared at Lucas, lifting one dark, bushy eyebrow. "I'm gonna do you a kindness, Scythe. I hope you appreciate it."

Lucas pulled a glass from the bucket. As he dried it with a clean cloth, he looked at his employer. "And what's that, boss?"

"You don't have to come to work the day of the funeral."

Lucas shook his head. "You don't need to let me off. As I said, I ain't goin'."

"You're about my size, and I want to lend you my Sunday-go-to-meetin' clothes to wear on Saturday. You can bring them back when you come to work on Sunday evening."

"Why, thank you, sir. That's mighty nice of ya."

"You'll need proper clothes to wear to a funeral." He pointed a finger at Lucas. "And you better take care of 'em."

After a hearty breakfast at the boardinghouse the next morning, Jeth rode his brown gelding toward the Sharp Ranch to see Willie and his parents. He planned to make pastoral visits to several families. The Sharps were at the top of the list.

The country air was crisp and there wasn't a cloud in the sky. Trotting his horse, Jeth enjoyed the cool breeze on his face. He'd never minded the cold, but he was tired of snow and sloshy roads. Jeth was grateful that the day was clear and dry and that all the snow and ice had melted.

At the fork in the road, he guided his horse to the right. As he started down a road lined with pines and other evergreens, he thought about what had happened at the boardinghouse on the previous night.

At nine o'clock, he'd drifted into the kitchen for a glass of milk before retiring for the evening, and he'd caught Dr. Harris kissing his mother good-night in the entry hall.

Quickly, he had stepped back into the kitchen, waiting there until he saw the lamp hanging from the doctor's buggy shining in the lane outside.

He knew his mother and the doctor were engaged and planning to marry, but seeing his own mother lost in a romantic embrace had taken him by surprise.

In those quiet moments of waiting, Jeth had imagined what it might be like to hold Honor in his arms in the way the doctor had held his mother. Could he be jealous because they had love and he didn't?

The *tap* and *bang* of hammers and the raspy back-and-forth scrape of saws brought Jeth's attention back to the present. Lifting his head, he glanced at his surroundings. The compound where the Sharp family lived was fenced on all sides. The yard gate in front of the house was just ahead.

Jeth gazed at the carpenters up on the roof, and wondered how poor ranchers like the Sharps were paying for all this remodeling.

Jeth felt sorry for Willie and his mother and wanted to help them. They would be hurt if the older Sharp boys were put in prison. Still, righteousness and justice were important, too.

How could a mere human know what was right in all cases? Without the Lord, he knew such understanding would be impossible. Jeth closed his eyes briefly and prayed for wisdom.

He tied his bay horse to the fence in front of the rambling house and started up the rock steppingstones. Jeth gazed up at the men who were putting a roof on one of the new rooms. Most ranchers did their own carpentry work. Was he seeing the Sharp Gang without their masks for the first time?

"How's the work going?" Jeth called out.

"All right, so far," one of the carpenters shouted back.

Jeth nodded. He climbed three steps to the front door and knocked. A tired-looking, middle-aged woman opened the door, leaned on a broom and stared at him. Unpleasant odors came from inside the house, filling his nostrils. Spoiled food. Dirty laundry. Garbage. He tried to smile.

"Well," she said, one hand on her hip. "What can I do for you?"

"I'm Reverend Peters and my ministry is here in Hearten. I understand you visited our church, and I would like to invite you to come again."

"Not much chance of that."

He'd hoped she would offer him her hand in friendship. She didn't.

The green dress she wore needed ironing, and her stringy brown hair could use a good washing. His mother would probably say her unkempt appearance indicated she'd given up on ever finding happiness.

"Has Willie left for school yet? I met him at the general store yesterday, and I'd like to talk to him—if it's all right."

"Willie ain't here. Walked on over to the school. But come on in."

Jeth stepped across the threshold and looked around. Clothes had been draped on the backs of chairs and were spread all over the dining room table. The scent of spoiled milk and rotting vegetables wafted from the kitchen.

Mrs. Sharp hadn't invited him to sit down. This would be a short visit. Jeth moved to the fireplace for a better look at a line of photographs on the mantel. None of the faces in the pictures looked like the carpenters working on the roof.

"Is this your family?" he asked.

"What's left of it."

Jeth thought of Selma's death and empathy filled his heart. "Did you lose a loved one recently, ma'am?"

"My ma passed on when I was ten, and my pa died four months ago. Shot in the back at a saloon over in Pine Valley."

"I'm so sorry." He waited before going on. "Are these your sons?"

"All but the oldest. He's my husband."

Jeth glanced at the woman again. She looked too old to be Mr. Sharp's wife. She must have had a hard life.

"There's Willie." Jeth pointed to a photo of the child. "Nice boy. What are the names of the others in the pictures?"

She pointed to the man with streaks of gray at the edges of his hairline. "That's Frank, my husband." Her finger moved to the photograph to the right of her husband's picture. "This is my son, George. The next one is Harry, and you know Willie."

"Yes, I do. Nice family. Where are they now?"

"I've learned not to ask." She shrugged. "As I said, Willie's at school. Other than that, who knows?" She glanced down at a clump of mud in front of the divan and started sweeping. "Just look at this place. Livin' with a houseful of men ain't easy, I can tell you that. They ain't never around when there's chores to be done."

Jeth wondered if she was talking about having to hire men to work on the roof—not to mention the other repairs being done to the place.

"We would consider it an honor if you and your family visited our church." Jeth tried again. "Can we count on seeing you on Sunday morning?"

"I doubt it. I never know what's going to happen next around here."

Jeth put his hand on her shoulder and looked deep into her eyes. "Will you try to come?"

She hesitated. "All right. I'll try. But don't be surprised if we don't make it."

Chapter Ten

❧

On Sunday morning before the regular service, Honor chose to sit in the back row of the church. She'd come to this Scripture session to learn more about the Bible, not to be seen. She hoped that nobody would take notice of her, but when she sat down, the wooden pew squeaked.

A gray-haired lady directly in front of her, wearing a dark brown hat with a veil, turned and stared. Honor looked away, pretending she didn't see the woman.

She'd visited Jeth's church on the previous Sunday morning and listened to his sermon, but she hadn't been in a Bible study like this one in years, not since her aunt had taken her to church, before Lucas had come into their lives. Honor felt awkward and out of place.

Now Miss Lucy Jordan floated into the chapel and started down the middle aisle like a queen. The scent of her lilac perfume trailed behind her. Lucy wore a light blue, winter coat with a hood edged in white fur, and she carried a fur hand-warmer.

Honor had never seen an outfit as fine as Lucy's. Lucy drifted all the way to the front and took a seat in the first row. Then a small, middle-aged woman in a dark cape and walking with a cane made her way to the front and sat down beside Lucy. Honor assumed the woman was Lucy's mother because she'd heard that Lucy's mother was blind.

Honor glanced down at her clothes. She wore her tan dress underneath her brown coat. Again.

Twisting her white lace handkerchief around her finger, she longed for Aunt Harriet, or someone like her, someone who cared about her, to be with her.

Honor always felt uneasy when she was in a strange place. If only Jeth's mother were sitting next to her on the bench. But Regina Peters was in the other room, playing the organ while the children sang.

Honor had admired the organ in the parlor at the boardinghouse the instant she first saw it, and had wondered who played it. Now she knew. Mrs. Peters had volunteered to teach Honor to play the organ, but Honor didn't plan to stay around long enough for lessons. And Mrs. Peters would be leaving for Pine Falls soon, in any case.

Jeth taught this class. As the teacher, would he ask Honor direct questions? If he did, would she be able to answer them? She was reading her Bible daily, but she had a lot to learn.

The church organist opened with a tune Honor remembered from childhood, and everyone stood. A songbook lay beside her on the pew. Honor grabbed it and got to her feet. But how would she find the right page number in the hymnal when she didn't know the name of the hymn?

She flipped to a page near the middle. She doubted it was the right one. Nevertheless, she held the hymnal with both hands and gazed down at it.

She shouldn't have come.

When the music stopped, everyone sat down. Jeth strolled to the podium. Honor watched him as she put the hymnal on the bench beside her. Standing behind the darkly stained oak lectern, Jeth looked dashing in his navy suit and pale blue tie.

Honor felt Jeth's gaze upon her from across the room, as though he could see into her heart. Her cheeks warmed and she glanced at the Bible on her lap. When she looked again, Jeth appeared to be watching someone in the first row. Was it Miss Lucy Jordan?

"Today," Jeth began, opening his Bible, "we are going to study the meaning of true repentance."

Honor leaned forward. The topic sounded interesting.

"Turn with me in your Bibles to the Book of Matthew, chapter six and verses fourteen and fifteen."

Honor turned to the table of contents. *Matthew. Where is it?* She ran her forefinger down the page. Oh, there it was. Matthew. Now, what was the chapter and verse? Shaking her head, she closed her Bible.

"'For if ye forgive men their trespasses,'" Jeth read, "'your heavenly Father will also forgive you: But if ye forgive not men their trespasses, neither will your Father forgive your trespasses.'"

Jeth looked up from his reading. "We are told in the Scriptures to repent of our sins and forgive others for their sins against us. But do you understand the meaning of true repentance?" Jeth hesitated, looking out at the congregation as if he anticipated an answer to his question. "You see—" he took his Bible and gently tapped it "—it's possible to repeat the words 'I'm sorry' until the cows come home to be milked, without meaning them. Some appear to regret sinning because they got caught. Then they go right out and sin again and again.

"But Jesus said to the woman caught in adultery, 'Go, and sin no more.' True repentance means a change in behavior—being sorry enough not to make the same mistake."

Jeth paused again. "Like repentance, forgiveness is mandatory, if we want the Lord to forgive our sins. Is there a person in your life who has hurt you deeply?"

Yes, and his name is Lucas, Honor thought.

"And do you realize," Jeth went on, "that the Lord expects you to forgive that person—no matter what he or she has done?"

No matter what rolled around inside Honor's brain. Then *forgiveness is mandatory* took over. She grimaced. If Jeth expected her to forgive Lucas, he would have a long wait.

On Sunday morning, Lucas dragged himself to Reverend Kline's church, wearing Mr. Skipworth's heavy brown wool suit and tan plaid tie. Seated in the back row, as near to the door as he could get, he tried to relax. No, he wasn't attending a funeral, but he was in church. He hadn't lied about that.

He felt hot and uncomfortable in the borrowed suit. Perspiration trickled from his hairline. Lucas pulled a handkerchief from his vest pocket and dabbed moisture from his forehead.

He'd brought Harriet's Bible, hoping to sell it. What did Christians find so interesting about such an old book? He reached for the Bible and opened it, and a sudden urge to read what was written there surprised him.

Lucas glanced down. The top of the page said, Gospel of John, chapter three. But when he started reading, his heart pounded. He could hardly breathe.

He considered getting up and leaving, but he felt suddenly weak. He sensed that if he got to his feet, he would become dizzy and fall. He started to tremble. He'd never needed a drink more. Lucas closed the Bible and set it on the pew beside him.

Consumed with the desire for alcohol, Lucas paid scant attention to what was said during the service. Oh, he stood when the congregation stood, sat when they sat. But his mind drifted. Lucas could hardly wait for the service to end.

After the last hymn, Lucas was one of the first to reach the door. He'd lost interest in finding a buyer for Harriet's Bible, or even in talking to the couple who knew Honor, and he hurried outside. He'd only walked a short distance when he heard footsteps behind him.

"Wait," a woman called out.

Lucas stopped and turned. Mrs. Kline stood on a stepping-stone a few feet from him. She wore a dark green dress, and her golden hair fluttered about her face in the winter breeze. Hugging her arms as if she was cold, she came no closer, nor did she turn around and go back. What did the woman want?

She smiled. "You said you wanted to meet someone who was on that stagecoach, didn't you?"

"Yes."

"Then please follow me. They are waiting for you."

Lucas wanted to know the names of the people he would be meeting, but Mrs. Kline was already walking back toward the church.

In a room across the hall from the minister's office, an elderly couple sat in straight-backed chairs at a long table. During a brief introduction, Lucas learned they were Mr. and Mrs. Simon Carr. He took a chair across from them.

Mrs. Kline selected a chair next to Lucas, but after she sat there for a moment, she got up and reached for her purse.

"I'm going to leave you folks now so you can get acquainted." Smiling, Mrs. Kline left the room, closing the door behind her.

"Why were you trying so hard to find us?" Mr. Carr asked.

"My niece is missing," Lucas replied. "That's why. My wife and I think she might have took the stage to Pine Falls. The same one you folks rode on the day it was robbed. You *were* on that stage, weren't ya?"

"What business is it of yours?" Simon Carr asked. "We don't even know you."

"I reckon it's my business 'cause I need to find my niece. Honor has reddish hair and brown eyes, and she's nineteen years old. Did you see her?"

"Maybe. Maybe not. We ain't saying."

"If it's money you want," Lucas began, "I don't have much." He pulled his money clip from the pocket of his trousers and offered it to Simon Carr. "But I'm willing to give you what little I got."

Simon shook his head, looking irritated. "Put your money away. We don't want it. And we ain't got nothing to tell you about nobody."

"At least tell me if'n or not she was on the stage. I reckon you owe me that much."

"We don't owe you nothing, mister. And stop trying to find out where we live." Simon Carr stood and motioned for his wife to do the same. "If you keep on as you have been, we'll call the sheriff and have you arrested."

Lucas rose from his chair as well. The Carrs started walking toward the door.

"Wait!" Lucas said.

Mr. and Mrs. Carr stopped and looked back at him.

Lucas pulled out his Bible and held it out to them. "I have this here Bible. It's a real nice one, too. Genuine leather cover and all. I need to sell it. Would you good folks like to buy it? I'll sure make you a good price."

Annie Carr glowered at him. "What you need to do, sir, is read that Bible from cover to cover. Not sell it." Then she turned sharply and walked out the door with her husband.

After church, Jeth shook hands with Mr. and Mrs. Joe Miller, giving Violet Miller an extra pat on the shoulder. She was expecting a baby soon, and from the looks of the woman, the infant could arrive at any time.

Mr. and Mrs. Rivers stood directly behind them. But where was their son Timmy? Jeth could guess that the boy was playing with the other children and probably getting into mischief.

Jeth had noticed Willie Sharp and his mother when they came into the chapel. They'd arrived after the service had begun and left before it ended, but at least they'd made an appearance. Still, he wished he could have talked to them.

Glancing at the line of parishioners waiting to shake his hand, Jeth saw Lucy Jordan and her mother near the end. He wanted to get this handshaking business over with quickly so that he could leave with Honor and his mother. Although he liked Lucy, she wasn't easily discouraged, and would no doubt try to detain him.

"Please excuse me, Mrs. Jordan, Miss Jordan," Jeth said after he shook their hands at the door of the church. "I have things I need to do before I leave today."

"Of course."

It wasn't a lie. All Jeth's notes were kept in his desk, and he always had projects that needed to be completed before the evening service. Turning, he walked down a short hall. Three little boys stood in front of the door next to his office. Timmy Rivers, the smallest of the three children, pushed a strand of dark hair from his eyes and grinned at Jeth sheepishly.

In the instant before he'd seen Jeth, Timmy's hand had been reaching out, as if he'd been about to open the door to the bell closet.

"Timmy!" Jeth scolded. "What do you think you're doing?"

Timmy gazed up at Jeth with a look of remorse. Whether or not it was genuine, Jeth might never know.

"We wanted to see the rope that rings the church bell," Timmy said. "That's all."

"Were you planning to pull it?"

Timmy glanced down. "Yes, sir." He rubbed the toe of one shoe across the floor in front of him. "We're sorry."

Jeth smiled. "I appreciate your honesty. But I can't let you boys ring that bell. Do you know why?"

"No, sir."

"The church bell is only to be rung at certain times and only with my permission. Here at our church we ring it to call people to worship. We also ring the bell on special occasions—like anniversary parties and weddings. So I can't let you ring the bell now. It's not the time for it. But I will let you see the rope. Would you boys like to see it?"

"Yes, sir!" the boys said together.

Jeth opened the door to the windowless, little room where the rope was kept. The pale rope, hanging through a hole in the ceiling, looked almost white in the darkened bell closet.

"It takes a lot of strength to pull the rope enough to ring the bell," Jeth explained. "I usually have a grown man do it."

"What if two of us boys pulled together?" Timmy suggested. "Or three? Would three be enough to ring the bell?"

"It might." Jeth grinned again, amused at Timmy's determination and creative mind. "Two or three boys about your sizes just might be able to do it. Nevertheless, it's just not the right time."

Jeth closed the door and locked it with a key from his key ring. "Now run along, boys. Your parents are probably looking for you."

When the boys disappeared around the corner and into the sanctuary, Jeth walked next door to his office. A pile of papers lay on his desk. He pulled out his Sunday night sermon, but he didn't read it. Instead, he reached for his personal calendar and looked back over the week.

His visit to the Sharp Ranch had brought Willie and his mother to church that morning. Perhaps he would visit them again.

His glance fell on what was written on his calendar for the day he visited the sheriff's office. *Buy supplies. Buy Honor a coat.* Memories of Honor and his visit with Sheriff Green returned to his mind.

The sheriff wanted him to serve as a special deputy once all the clues to the stage robbery were in. At first, he'd disregarded the entire idea, but lately, he wondered. Should he consider doing it? Somebody had to help the sheriff out.

And if Honor was in danger—

He worried about her more than he should. Despite what happened at Falling Rock, she was so sweet and innocent, he couldn't stop thinking about her. On the other hand, maybe he should wash all thoughts of her from his mind— concentrate on a more appropriate young woman, like Lucy Jordan. At least he knew Lucy was a Christian.

Jeth liked Lucy Jordan, but he wasn't attracted to her as a man to a woman. Unfortunately, his interest in Honor went beyond friendship into uncharted waters he wasn't willing to name yet.

Honor probably wasn't a true Christian, and she might never be. He put the calendar back on his desk and hurried out the door. Surely by now, Lucy would have gone home.

Mrs. Jordan sat in the buggy out front. But Lucy and two other young, single women stood at the door—waiting for Jeth.

"Did you finish whatever it was you had to do?" Lucy asked.

"Yes. Yes, I did." Jeth shifted from one leg to the other, wondering how to leave her company without being rude. "So, how are your reading lessons working out?"

"Miss McCall and I are just getting started—but we're doing fine. And I've already learned a lot."

"Good." He paused, searching for something else to say. "And how is your sewing coming along? I've heard glowing reports about the dresses you make."

"Really? Well, thank you very much. But lately, I've been getting behind. What I really need is a good seamstress to help me catch up with my sewing. But they are hard to find in a place like Hearten."

On impulse, Jeth suggested Honor for the job. Then wished he hadn't. He needed to talk to Honor as soon as possible.

Lucas had considered dropping the Bible in the nearest trash can, but thought again. Someone in Pine Falls was sure to buy it. He stuck the Bible in the inside pocket of the borrowed suit and hurried down the street toward his rented room above the store.

Ten minutes later, he tossed the suit and tie onto his bed with the rest of his belongings and changed into the clothes he'd worn when he left Ruby's farm. They were dusty and wrinkled. The entire room reeked of spoiled food and dirty laundry. Lucas didn't care.

Guilt flooded him every time he stopped to think about Ruby. The same thing happened when he thought of Harriet and Honor. Whiskey erased those unhappy memories.

Lucas got down on his hands and knees, peering under his bed. A cockroach crawled near his hand, but he took little notice. He pulled out two bottles of whiskey and put one beside the only chair in the room. Then he opened the other bottle and started drinking.

He gulped down half the bottle in one swallow. Then he wiped his wet mouth with the back of his hand. Maybe he should sit down before drinking the rest.

Soiled clothes were draped all over the chair. Lucas threw them on the floor and sat down. As he lifted the bottle to his mouth again, he realized he felt dizzy. He was also sick to his stomach.

Honor slipped out the back door of the church to avoid seeing Jeth and Lucy together. Then she walked around the building to join Jeth's mother in the buggy, which was parked in front.

Jeth usually drove the wagon into town, but they'd come to church in the black buggy. Apparently, the buggy was used on Sundays and special occasions.

Jeth's mother sat in the front seat, talking to Dr. Harris, who stood beside the buggy. However, the doctor turned and headed for his covered wagon before Honor reached them. Honor took the wooden bench behind Jeth's mother and settled herself to wait.

She gazed at the little white church with its painted wood siding, stained-glass windows and bell tower. Jeth stood just below the front steps, talking to Lucy Jordan and two other young women.

Honor refused to watch them. Strong emotions she couldn't name churned inside her, heating her cheeks.

"Jethro so loves to fellowship with the members of his congregation," Mrs. Peters said. "But he should be along shortly."

You mean he enjoys visiting with Lucy, Honor thought.

She'd hoped to get answers to her Bible questions. Now all she could think about was Lucy Jordan and her blue coat.

Why should Honor care if Jeth talked to Lucy or anybody else, for that matter? He had a perfect right to have a conversation with anyone he liked. After his mother returned from Pine Falls, Honor would be leaving Hearten. Still, seeing Jeth surrounded by young women upset her.

At the crunch of Jeth's boots on the gravel path, Honor looked up. He nodded to Honor, then climbed into the buggy beside his mother.

Honor nodded back halfheartedly.

"I saw Willie Sharp and his mother in church this morning," Mrs. Peters said to her son. "Did you?"

"Yes." Jeth untied the reins. "But I didn't get to talk to them."

"Don't be discouraged, son. There's always next Sunday."

"I know." Turning around in his seat, Jeth smiled at Honor. "Mama and I have been meaning to pay you the wages you've earned so far, Miss McCall. And now seems like a good time."

"Pay me?"

"Yes." Pulling bills and a few coins from his pocket, he handed them to Honor. "You've been doing a good job, too."

"Thank you." Honor was about to put the bills in the new drawstring purse she'd made, when she remembered the coat Jeth had purchased for her. "And here's a dollar back to pay on the coat. I'll have more to give you later."

"I like the way you do business."

The warmth in his blue eyes excited her.

"But one whole dollar is a lot to pay," he added. "You only made three. I'm willing to take less."

"That's very kind of you. But I want to pay one dollar toward my debt today."

"All right." He paused for a moment, then said, "Miss Jordan was impressed with the way you altered Mama's clothes, Miss McCall, and she wants to offer you a job, if you're interested."

"What kind of job?"

"She not only sews clothes for people, she alters them, and she's gotten behind. Miss Jordan said that if you would work for her at night doing alterations at the boardinghouse, she would pay you half the money she gets for each job."

Half? If Honor was going to be doing the alterations, why wouldn't she get all the money? Still, she supposed half was better than nothing, and she needed to increase her income if she hoped to save enough to pay her debt by Christmas.

"All right. Tell Miss Jordan I'll be happy to accept."

That night, Honor sat beside Jeth's mother in the back row for the evening service. They huddled as close to the woodstove as they could get. Still, Honor felt cold and uncomfortable. Little wonder. It had started snowing soon after the morning service, and still the soft white flakes drifted down.

Honor prayed daily now. She also knew one of the hymns they sang in church by heart, and most of her questions about the Bible were being answered from reading the Scripture. Yet the true meaning of what Jeth called "salvation" escaped her. A common thief could never be worthy of eternal life, she was sure, no matter what Jeth said to the contrary.

Honor glanced at Jeth, standing behind the podium, and realized she hadn't been paying attention. She sat up straighter. For the rest of the service, she planned to listen to every word Jeth spoke.

"A long time ago," he said, "Christians greeted each other in a special way." He smiled. "One would say, 'Jesus is Lord.' And the other would say, 'He is Lord, indeed.'

"Many, if not most people know who Jesus is," Jeth went on. "But you can know Jesus personally, and when you do, you will call Him Lord. Then, you won't have to wonder if you're saved. You'll know—for sure."

Of course, Jesus is the Lord. Everybody knows that, Honor thought, shaking her head. She assumed what Jeth had said was important, but had no idea what his sermon meant.

Honor tapped her fingers on her knees. Soon, the service would end, but not before Jeth gave an altar call. She'd told Jeth's mother she would step forward and join the church that night. Now, she regretted her promise.

She worshiped God and loved Him, and she was learning about Jesus from reading the Bible. But she couldn't forgive Lucas or feel worthy enough to become a born-again believer. And she still felt guilty for stealing money from the church in Falling Rock. None of that was likely to change.

All at once, Timmy walked toward her from a bench near the front of the church. Beaming, the little boy stood in the aisle beside Honor's pew. He looked adorable in his blue sailor suit, and his infectious grin melted her heart. She supposed he wanted her to make room for him. Honor inched over and Timmy sat down.

"I'm coming back to the boardinghouse, Miss McCall, so I can visit you again. Mama said I could."

Honor pressed her forefinger to her lips in a shushing gesture. The fact that Timmy wanted to sit beside her in church touched her deeply, but she wouldn't allow him to misbehave.

"Don't talk during the service, Timmy," Honor whispered. "We can talk later."

The child nodded and looked down at his hands folded in his lap.

Mrs. Peters leaned toward her. "Are you going to join the church tonight?" she whispered. "You'll feel better if you do."

Honor leaned closer to Jeth's mother and whispered in the older woman's ear, "Mrs. Peters, now what did you say I was supposed to do?"

"Walk to the front of the church at the proper time and tell Jethro you want to join this church."

"Just go forward?"

"Yes. You'll do it tonight, won't you?"

"Of course." A lump in her throat made swallowing difficult. "I said I would and I will."

Honor hated the thought of walking to the front of the church. Everyone would be watching her. What if she stumbled and fell? Or made some other mistake?

Why had she said she would do this? She glanced toward the entry door, wishing she could walk outside and wait in the buggy.

Jeth stood behind the podium, looking as handsome as ever. He'd said a lot of things about salvation and being born again. Now he was talking about joining the church. Apparently, salvation and joining the church were different, but Honor didn't understand what that difference might be. Jeth continued talking, but Honor couldn't focus on anything he was saying.

Mrs. Peters elbowed Honor in the ribs. "It's time to go forward."

Frowning doubtfully, Honor glanced at Jeth's mother.

"Go on," Regina Peters whispered. "It's time."

Honor rose from the pew. Stepping in front of Timmy, she stood in the aisle, hesitating a moment. As her aunt would have said, she needed time to gather her wits about her.

She felt everyone watching as she trudged toward the podium. Out of the corner of her eye, she noticed Lucy Jordan and her mother sitting near the front of the chapel. Now was not the time to fall on her face.

Chapter Eleven

❧

Honor crept down the center aisle of the church while the organist played "Onward Christian Soldiers." Jeth waited behind the podium. He grinned as she moved toward him, but she felt too unsure and shaky to smile back.

She'd never liked being the center of attention. Stepping forward to join the church made her feel more like an actress on a very big stage than a maid working at a boardinghouse.

Jeth was framed on both sides by large, bronzed vases filled with evergreen branches and pinecones. Woodsy aromas floating out from the arrangements did little to calm her nerves.

Jeth's commanding presence behind the podium made Honor think of a general about to send his troops to war. But she wasn't a Christian soldier. Nor was she prepared for battle.

Still smiling, Jeth stepped down from the platform. "What is your desire tonight, Miss McCall?" He took her trembling hands in his and held them. "Salvation?"

Honor swallowed. "I just want to join this church."

"I see." He released her hands, looking slightly disappointed. "Well, why do you want to join?"

"Because I want to learn more about God."

"Very well." Jeth nodded. "I'll introduce you to the congregation, then."

Honor was never able to remember anything else that was said inside the church that evening. It all vanished in a swirl of embarrassment and a sense of failure. She hadn't said what Jeth had wanted to hear.

Though she still didn't fully understand what the word *salvation* meant, she should have requested it, then joined the church. That was the pattern in this congregation, and it was what Jeth wanted. It was probably what she wanted. But it was too late.

Walking to the buggy after the service, she was still in a daze. She remained distracted when Mrs. Peters stopped to introduce her to a stocky, middle-aged woman.

"This is Mrs. Belinda Grant," Jeth's mother said.

Honor saw dark salt-and-pepper hair, but she noticed little else, until she heard Mrs. Grant's giggle. It caught Honor's attention and made her almost want to giggle back.

Mrs. Peters gestured toward the jolly woman. "Mrs. Grant is a widow, who will be moving into the boardinghouse tomorrow, Miss McCall, to serve as your chaperone."

Honor glanced at Regina Peters in surprise. "My what?"

"Your chaperone. Remember, I told you we needed one. It wouldn't do for a single woman to live at the boardinghouse unchaperoned. I'll be leaving for Pine Falls now."

* * *

Slowly, Lucas opened his eyes and glanced around. He'd done it again—passed out on the floor.

The odors in the room of rotting fruit and dirty clothes, gagged him. He coughed, then held his nose to block the smells. Lucas staggered to his feet, then braced himself against the wall. He opened the window and poked out his head.

An icy breeze diminished slightly the nasty odors coming from in the room and chilled Lucas to his bones. Shivering, he breathed deeply in and out. The fresh air revived him a little.

When he felt strong enough, he gathered the spoiled food and other garbage and threw the entire mess out the window. He would need to wash his dirty clothes if he expected the room to become livable.

Gazing out the window again, he tried to ignore the smelly rubbish and trash on the street below. But he couldn't overlook the hunger calling from his belly. He was unable to remember the last time he had had a real meal and he supposed that he should eat before reporting for work at the saloon.

The sky had turned to gold, and the sun sparkled above the mountains, indicating early morning. But hadn't he arrived from church around noon?

Lucas shook his head. He must have slept all day and all night, missing work—again. Mr. Skipworth would not be pleased. In fact, unless Lucas came up with a good excuse for not showing his face at the saloon, he would be fired.

Lucas dressed and prepared for work. On his way out, he grabbed the borrowed suit and tie. As he tossed them over his arm, the Bible fell to the floor. He kicked it out of the way and raced outside. Downstairs, on the street in front of the store, he turned and went into a little shop for food. He bought a small loaf of bread and two sausages. Then he hurried down the street. As he moved along, he ate his meal and planned the lies he was going to tell his boss.

The saloon wasn't open in the morning, but sometimes Mr. Skipworth left the door unlocked. If it was open now, Lucas could sneak in and do a few chores before his boss arrived. The effort might be enough to enable him to keep his job.

His brain seemed hazy and off course. Still, he should come up with another plan in case this one didn't work.

Lucas could say he had to bury his other sister, Clara. Or perhaps a brother or an uncle might work better this time. For all Mr. Skipworth knew, he could have several brothers and uncles, five sisters or more.

His "my sister just died" excuse had worked once. Why not again?

Lucas went down the narrow alley behind the saloon. Cans and boxes heaped with garbage lined both sides. The sickening odor was strong.

He reached for the doorknob and jiggled it a little before giving it a turn. The door opened and he went right in.

The dishes must have been washed and put away before closing time the previous night, meaning he couldn't do his job now. Still, clean glasses had to be put on the bar out front before the saloon opened for business. He would do that.

Lucas tossed the borrowed suit and tie on a barrel, got a big wooden tray from the cupboard near the hand pump and began putting glasses on it. The tray could easily hold twelve glasses, but Shorty, another man who worked at the saloon, had said to never put more than ten on at one time. Well, Shorty wasn't here. Lucas placed two more on the tray. This would save him an extra trip to the front.

He lifted the tray. It seemed heavier than he had expected. How could two extra glasses make such a difference? He set the tray on a table by the stove.

Lucas removed one of the glasses, poured a shot of whiskey into it and gulped it down. The drink did him so much good that he decided to have another, and another. At last he sat down on the cold floor, leaned against the cupboard and drank directly from the bottle.

Some time later, the sound of people talking alerted him that he wasn't alone. He straightened up and looked around. Little sunlight entered the darkened room's one window, but anyone who came in would see him sitting there.

"I'll get the oil for the lamps," he heard Shorty say.

Footsteps sounded on the wooden floor, and they were getting louder. Lucas got to his feet and kicked the partly filled bottle under the cupboard. Gold liquid spilled out and sloshed on the floor. The odor of whiskey would be impossible to miss.

Shorty came into the room.

"What are you doing here?" he whispered.

"I'd asked ya the same question," Lucas said. "You never come in this early."

"I'm helping the boss with a few things. And keep your voice down, will ya? He might hear." Shorty sent Lucas a look of disgust. "You smell like whiskey. Why are you here?"

"I—I came in early to help out."

"Came in early? You've got a lot of gall showing your face here at all, Scythe, after not coming in for work."

"My, my sister died and—" Lucas struggled to form his lie.

"Your sister died the last time," Shorty scoffed. "You better dream up a better story."

"It was my other sister. And what's so terrible about missing one night of work?"

"One night? Are you crazy? Today's Tuesday. You haven't showed up here since Friday."

"It was my other sister what died. The funeral was yesterday."

"If you know what's good for you, you'll get out the back door and never come back. I don't think you'll want to know what the boss might do if he finds you here."

"But he owes me money," Lucas whined.

"Unless you're wearing padded trousers, I would leave before he kicks you out," Shorty advised.

"Shorty!" Mr. Skipworth called from the bar area of the saloon. "Hurry up with the oil and get in here. I need help."

"I'll be right there, boss!" Shorty glared at Lucas. "This is your last chance, Scythe. If I don't go out right now, he'll be back here to find out why. And I won't be responsible for what might happen next."

"But what about the money and—?" Lucas pointed to the wrinkled suit and tie, draped over the beer barrel. "And I need to return his clothes."

"Leave 'em and go." Shorty moved to the door. Opening it, he held the door wide for Lucas. "Don't even think about the money. From the looks of that suit, you owe him some."

Lucas staggered to the door and went out. When he turned around, Shorty slammed the door shut.

Lucas squinted at the morning sun. Only a few clouds overhead broke up a blue sky. He walked back down the alley, trying to formulate a plan as he went. If he sold the pearls, he might have enough to live on for a while, but sooner or later, he would have to find another job if he expected to continue living in Pine Falls and searching for Honor.

He turned right and went on. At the corner of the street, tables and chairs had been placed outside, in front of a small café. People in coats and hats sat drinking coffee and talking. Lucas thought it was much too cold to be at an outdoor restaurant, but apparently, the folks sitting there didn't agree.

His gaze fell on a pretty young woman with dark hair seated alone at a table. She reminded him of his sister, Clara, but of course it couldn't be her. Strange, he'd just been talking about Clara. The table next to hers was vacant. He took it. Lucas could use a cup of coffee.

The young woman turned and eyed him carefully. He knew he'd been peering at her and decided to apologize.

"Forgive me for staring, ma'am," he began, "but you remind me of my sister. I ain't seen her in a long time, and she'd be a lot older than you are by now."

She nodded and looked down at her coffee.

"You wouldn't happen to know anybody who might be interested in buying a pearl necklace, would ya?"

She glanced his way again. "I might. Have you got one to sell?"

"I sure do. And the pearls are real, too. Genuine. I also have a nice Bible for sale. Would you like to see it?"

"Yes." She leaned toward him as if she expected him to hand the items to her.

"Well, I ain't got them with me right now," Lucas said. "But if you'll tell me where you live, I'll come by later and show you what I got."

She shook her head. "That's impossible. But if you would like to bring them here to our café, I work every afternoon between two and five."

Lucas glanced at the red door of the restaurant. "You mean you own this café?"

"My husband and I do." She rose from her chair. "If you will excuse me, I must go inside now and see how things are going. I would like to see the pearls and the Bible, though, if you decide to bring them by."

"I'll try to be here this afternoon."

As she walked inside, he realized she was expecting a baby.

Lucas didn't wait for coffee, but hurried back to his room to get the pearls. They were in a wooden box, tucked under a shirt in the chest of drawers.

He raced inside and pulled out the drawer. He'd forgotten that since he'd last opened it, he'd removed his last clean shirt. The box was there, but it was open—and the pearls were gone!

On Wednesday after an early lunch, Honor helped Jeth harness his horses to the buggy and load his mother's bags in the back. Mrs. Peters would be catching the noon stage for Pine Falls.

Jeth's mother settled into the seat up front with her son. She wore a new, navy wool traveling-dress, one that Miss Lucy Jordan had made, and a store-bought blue hat with a veil. Honor thought the woman looked lovely and smelled as sweet as roses.

"You look so nice in your new dress, ma'am," Honor said, "so stylish, too."

Jeth's mother cocked her head. "Do you really think so?"

"Oh, yes, I do."

Mrs. Peters smiled her thanks, then turned to her son. "We should go now, Jethro. I wouldn't want to arrive too late and miss the stagecoach."

Honor glanced at Jeth. He wore a new suit, dark brown with a matching vest. He'd said he needed a new suit to preach in, but Honor hadn't known he'd already bought one.

Mrs. Belinda Grant sat with Honor in the back seat of the carriage. They had removed their white aprons for the trip to the depot, but they still wore their ordinary work clothes under their coats.

Dr. Harris was waiting for them at the depot—all slicked up in what also looked like new clothes. He wore a brown suit, tan boots and a tan hat. Looking more like a cowboy than a doctor, he was checking his pocket watch when the buggy stopped.

Jeth was tying the reins when the doctor rushed up and lifted Regina Peters from the buggy. He let her down slowly, looking into her eyes the entire time. Then the doctor kissed her on the forehead before setting her on her feet.

"You're gonna write me, aren't you, sweetheart?" Honor heard him ask.

"Every day, my love," Mrs. Peters said.

"I'm going to miss you," the doctor said.

"I'll miss you, too."

Hand in hand, they walked to the stagecoach.

Honor glanced at Jeth. He didn't appear to be as touched by their sweet goodbye as she'd been. Maybe he wasn't affected at all. Then she noticed his tight jawline, and thought he looked downright aggravated. Did romantic overtures make him uncomfortable? Honor watched him hustle around to the back of the wagon, where he got his mother's carpetbags and carried them toward the stagecoach.

Dr. Harris turned and met him halfway. "Let me help you with those."

"That's all right, Doctor. I've got 'em," Jeth said curtly.

When his mother was loaded on the stagecoach and the carriage was on its way toward Pine Falls, Jeth shook the doctor's hand. "Glad you came," he said.

"I wouldn't have missed it for anything."

Honor knew Jeth liked and respected Dr. Harris. She couldn't understand why he suddenly seemed so resentful toward the man his mother loved and planned to marry.

Jeth had told her that he'd never known his father. Was that the reason he was acting so coolly now? Could it be that he felt left out? Lonesome? Betrayed? His mother had someone now, but he no longer had anyone.

After almost a week of warm, sunny days, cold weather returned to Hearten. Honor stood in front of the kitchen window, washing the lunch dishes in a metal tub, wondering if it was going to snow again.

The warm, soapy water made her skin itch. Mrs. Belinda Grant thought Honor suffered from too much lye soap and had suggested that she stop washing dishes. But with all she had to do, that was impossible. Mrs. Peters had been gone for days and wasn't expected back until shortly before Christmas.

Honor worried that Lucas could arrive at the boarding-house at any time and without warning. Hearten was only half a day's ride from Falling Rock. Lucas would look for her here if she didn't move on soon, but she'd pledged to stay until Mrs. Peters returned. She intended to keep her promise. As she rinsed a plate in a bucket of clear water, it floated slowly to the bottom, just as her hopes of leaving town before Lucas found her seemed to sink.

Since Mrs. Belinda Grant had moved into the boarding-house to serve as Honor's chaperone and helper, Honor had found that she liked the widow very much. Still, she wished the woman wasn't such a matchmaker and chatterbox.

Mrs. Grant was constantly saying things such as, "The reverend has sure taken a shine to you, hasn't he, Miss McCall?"

Honor disregarded the woman's words. She was fond of Jeth, all right. If things were different, maybe he was a man she could love. But anyone with eyes could see that Jeth was interested in Lucy Jordan. Understanding this gave Honor an even greater reason for wanting to leave.

Honor finished the dishes, put them away and wiped her hands on her white apron. Jeth was repairing a board fence out back and hadn't come inside for his noon meal. She'd prepared a lunch for him and now she would have to take it out to him. It seemed odd, eating outdoors in the cold when he had a warm kitchen available to him, but she pulled on her coat and the brown, wool bonnet she'd made. Folding up a red-and-white checkered tablecloth, she covered Jeth's tray of food with it, and walked out the back door.

A gray horse was penned near the red barn. Elmer's mare. Normally, Elmer rode out on his mount right after breakfast and didn't return to the boardinghouse until after dark. But Elmer hadn't gone to work today. He had a fever and a cough, and Mrs. Belinda Grant was caring for him.

Seeing the animal up close for the first time, she set the tray on a wooden barrel in a clean corner of the fenced area and walked over for a better look. The mare turned away when Honor started toward her. The animal's belly was round and full. Honor predicted the mare would soon have a colt.

Kicking up her hind legs, the horse trotted to the far side of the pen. Honor stepped around for a better view of the animal and read the mare's brand.

L. S. Lucas Scythe? It *was* her uncle's brand. Her throat tightened. Elmer's horse had once belonged to Lucas, just as she'd thought.

A taste of fear rose in her throat as she kept looking at the mare that Lucas had called Lady. She took a deep breath. How had Elmer gotten the mare? Gaping at the horse, memories of Lucas riding the animal filled her mind, and all her old terrors returned like a flood. Honor gazed back at the boardinghouse. She'd tried to put Lucas out of her mind, but no matter what she did or how brave she pretended to be, her uncle was always just a thought or a bad dream away.

Honor wanted to go to Elmer's room without delay, to find out how and where he'd gotten the mare, to see if he could tell her something about Lucas.

She glanced at the tray on the barrel. First, she would need to take Jeth's lunch to him. Then she would go to Elmer's room and find out what he knew.

Beyond the wooden gate, Jeth was repairing fences in the pasture. The ground looked hard and unyielding, still half frozen from the recent snow, as Honor unfastened the hook and opened the gate. Jeth, working in the far corner of the property, turned, waved and started toward her. Honor waved in return and carried the lunch tray to a level spot under a big oak tree. She spread out the checkered cloth on the cold ground and began unpacking the food.

"Well, hello," Jeth panted, towering over her, his face shining with perspiration. "Is that fried chicken I smell?"

She nodded. "Your mother told me you like it. But I can't understand why you like picnics on a cold day like this."

Jeth grinned. "Cold air makes me feel like working. If I went inside to eat, I might get lazy and decide not to come back out. I could convince myself to take the rest of the day off." He gestured toward one corner of the tablecloth. "Won't you join me? Looks like there'll be plenty."

She shook her head. "I really should get back."

"Nonsense. We'll call this an employer-employee business conference, and we really do have things to discuss."

"I guess I could for a minute." Honor sat down on the cloth.

Jeth took a place across from her. "Are you all right, Miss McCall? You look a little upset."

Honor forced a smile, trying to push away all thoughts of Lucas and the brand on Elmer's mare. "I'm just tired, I guess. Nothing to worry about."

"Good." He gave a pained expression mixed with amusement and moved to a different corner of the cloth. "This ground is colder and harder than I expected."

"You're right." Honor giggled. "It is."

She reached for the tin and opened the lid. The aroma of fried chicken rose in the air. She placed a plate in front of Jeth and handed him the chicken.

"I hate making decisions," she said offhandedly. "You choose. White meat or dark?"

"Dark." Jeth grabbed a drumstick. "This looks good." He took a bite and swallowed. "Tastes good, too. So you hate making decisions, huh?"

Honor blushed. "Maybe *hate* isn't the right word."

"My late wife, Selma, disliked making decisions, too."

Honor leaned forward. Jeth had never really talked about his wife.

"I thought Selma was never going to give me an answer after I asked her to be my wife. She wouldn't say 'yes' but she wouldn't say 'no,' either."

"What caused her to finally agree to marry you?"

"I challenged her." He grinned. "I said, give me an answer now, or forget I ever asked."

"And then?"

"She said yes."

Honor smiled. "And then the two of you got married and lived happily ever...." Honor gazed down at the tin of chicken. If only she could retract her words. "I'm sorry. I should never have said that. Please forgive me."

"Of course I forgive you. Don't think of it again. And we did live happily until...until the day she died."

His blue eyes looked sad. She wished the subject of his late wife hadn't come up. Maybe it would be best if she went back to the house before she said something worse.

She got to her feet, brushing a wet clump of dirt from the skirt of her blue wool dress. "I have to go. I have things to do, and I better get started." Then she realized that Jeth hadn't mentioned what he wanted to discuss. "We haven't had our business discussion yet, have we."

"I would love to have you stay," he said, "but it's cold out here. If you need to go on, I'll understand. We can discuss business later. And don't worry about the cloth and the food tray. I'll bring them up to the house when I finish for the day."

As Honor walked back to the house, she thought about Jeth and his late wife. He must have loved Selma very much, and she must have been devoted to him. And why not? Jeth was a man any woman would be proud to call her husband.

Honor swept through the kitchen and down the hall to Elmer's door. She knocked, and when nobody answered, she peeked inside.

Elmer Coffee lay in an oversize bed, snoring. A black bucket filled with hot coals had been placed nearby. Water boiled from a pot on top of the coals, and a thin layer of steam filled the room.

Honor backed out and closed the door. She would talk to Elmer when he was awake and feeling better.

She went into Mrs. Peters's room at the head of the stairs to clean. While sweeping, Honor got down on her hands and knees and reached for whatever dust might be under the bed. She hit something hard. Dragging the object, she discovered a six-shooter and a box of bullets.

She wondered why Jeth's mother felt the need to keep a firearm under her bed. Were those in the boardinghouse in danger of some kind? Or was this simply a good place to keep a gun?

The pistol in her hands felt heavy. That didn't surprise Honor. She'd been around guns since she was a little girl and knew how to use them. After cleaning under the bed, she slid the six-shooter and the box of bullets back where she had found them.

As she mopped the hall outside Elmer's door, waiting for him to wake up, she still wondered about the pistol. Should she mentioned the gun to Jeth? Question him about it? She shook her head. No, she would say nothing.

She was thinking about Jeth's sky-blue eyes—flecked with a deeper blue she'd noticed—and how they crinkled at the edges when he smiled, and suddenly, an image of Lucas's blue eyes came to her. Honor flinched. Stepping back, she tripped over the mop bucket, stumbled and almost fell. The metal pail banged the pine floor, the sound reverberating around her. Water spilled, spreading across the hall.

"Mrs. Grant," Elmer called from his bedroom. "Is that you out there?"

"No, sir, it's me, Honor McCall. I'll be right in, as soon as I clean up this mess."

Chapter Twelve

❧

Honor put the mop in the bucket and pushed it beside the paneled wall near Elmer Coffee's room. Was Coffee really his name? Or had he acquired the name because he enjoyed drinking that particular beverage?

She'd thought a lot about what she would say to Elmer and still hadn't come up with a plan. She hoped an idea would pop into her mind once she saw him face-to-face.

Honor turned the white porcelain knob. The door squeaked. Elmer lay on the bed, looking up at the ceiling. What was it about this man? Being near him always made her wish she was in another place.

She opened the door wide, the way a proper young woman should. "Sir," she whispered. "Are you awake?"

Elmer flinched. In the dim light coming from the window near his bed, he jerked around, glaring at her. "You ain't Mrs. Grant. I thought she was my nurse."

"She is. But Mrs. Grant went into town to buy groceries. I thought I would look in on you to see if you wanted anything."

"I need Mrs. Grant." He coughed. "Tell her—" He coughed again. "Tell her to come in here as soon as she gets back."

Honor nodded. Then she just stood there, wondering how to say what she needed to say. "I—I saw your horse a while ago."

"She ain't hurt or nothing, is she?"

"Your mare's fine. And there's plenty of hay and grain in the pen with her."

He lifted one eyebrow. "What about water?"

"The water trough's full to the top."

His face relaxed. "That's good."

Honor cleared her throat. "The brand on that gray mare of yours looks different from any I've seen around here. Did she come from somewhere else?"

"I bought her from a man what was on the road from Falling Rock." His voice sounded gravelly, and he coughed several more times into his hand. "Said he was going to Pine Falls."

"Pine Falls? That's a long ride from Falling Rock. Why do you think he was going there?"

"He said he come a-lookin' for somebody. His niece."

Honor stiffened. *Lucas.* She tried to swallow but couldn't.

"Why was he looking for his niece?" Honor managed to ask at last. "Was she lost?"

Elmer shook his head. "Runned away. That's what Mr. Scythe done said. He was hoping to bring her back home."

"So how did you end up with his gray mare?"

He glared at her. "What business is it of yours, missy?"

Missy. Lucas had called her by that name. She forced herself to swallow, then lifted her head. "I just wondered," she said calmly. "That's all."

"Well, since you're itchin' to know, he said his mare was tired and couldn't make it all the way to Pine Falls in her condition. So he sold his mare to me and went right to the depot in Hearten and bought a ticket on the stage. Why, he was done gone in less than an hour."

"You didn't tell him where you live, did you?"

His eyes were full of suspicion. "Matter of fact, I did," he said. "What's it to ya?"

Honor clenched her hands into fists to hold in her anger. "Well." Her breath caught; she could hardly say more. "It's like I said. I was curious, that's all."

"Curious, huh? Well, it ain't any of your concern, but the mare was done bred when I bought her. Mr. Scythe wants to see the colt after the mare foals. Maybe buy it."

"You—You mean he'll be coming here?" Honor felt the blood drain from her face. "To—to the boardinghouse?"

"Reckon so."

A wave of terror swept over her. Her fingernails bit into the palms of her hands. She needed to control her emotions—at least enough so that Elmer wouldn't notice.

"The mare should foal by Christmas," Elmer explained. "And Mr. Scythe said he'll be back this way to see the colt after the first of the year."

Honor swallowed, hoping to dissolve the bitter taste in her mouth. Lucas was coming back to Hearten around New Year's Day. She *must* be gone before then.

Jeth had gathered the tablecloth and all the picnic gear and carried it inside before going back to work. In the kitchen, he'd looked for Honor. Then he heard her talking to Elmer and assumed she must be busy.

Walking back toward the field behind the boardinghouse, he glanced at Elmer's gray mare. Honor had looked toward the horse pens several times while they were talking earlier. He wondered what she had found so fascinating and why she had seemed nervous. He'd wanted to pull her into his arms and hold her—kiss her—until all her fears disappeared.

Was he beginning to care more for Honor than he should? He knew she wasn't the kind of woman the Bible said he should be looking for as a future wife. And yet...

Most merciful Father, he prayed. *I know You want me to help this young woman, but You also know that she pleases me greatly. I would like to make her my wife, Lord. If there is any way that my desire for her can result in Christian marriage, let it be, I pray. In any case, not my will but Thy will be done.*

Lucas had inspected the chest of drawers in his room a dozen times, searching for the pearls. On Wednesday afternoon, he tried again. This time, he threw the four drawers upside down on the floor. But when he looked under them, the pearls were still not there. He pushed one of the oak drawers out of the way with the toe of his boot. It landed in a nest of dirty clothes.

Lucas had been unable to find the pearls, and he hadn't found a job to replace the one he had lost. More and more now he thought about the Kline's silver coffeepot and tray—the one they had gotten as a wedding gift. How much might those items be worth?

Lucas had expenses. Besides robbing people, what else could he do to get the money he needed? How could he survive without at least a pint of whiskey every day?

He reached under his bed for a bottle and his hand touched something soft. More dirty clothes. He cursed when he realized his last bottle was gone. At least he had what was left in his flask.

The mere thought of liquor made him thirsty. His hands were shaking again as he reached for the flask on the table by the bed and drank.

One swallow was all he could have now. Gotta make it last, he thought. He put the flask back on the table.

Stealing from the pastor and his wife no longer seemed like a dim possibility. It appeared to be his only alternative.

Through a man Lucas had met at the saloon, he'd lined up a buyer, a Mr. Scott. All that remained was to go in and take the silver objects without getting caught. The Klines would be attending church tonight, Lucas knew. There'd never be a more perfect time.

That evening, Lucas stood behind a tree outside the Klines' home, waiting until they left for the Wednesday evening service. At last, the couple walked out their front door, looking like shadows in the semidarkness.

"Did you remember to lock the door?" Lucas heard Mrs. Kline ask.

"Sorry, dear. I guess I forgot again." Reverend Kline turned back toward the door. "We don't have much time. The service starts in thirty minutes, and I still need to look over my sermon. Do you really think locking up is necessary?"

"Yes, I do. The sheriff said locking doors prevents crimes. We certainly wouldn't want to make it easier for a sinner to sin, would we?"

"No, of course not." He started up the steps to the front porch, then glanced back. "I won't be long, and then we can be on our way."

With shaky fingers, Lucas pulled the flask from the inside pocket of his jacket and took a swallow. He wanted more, but he restrained himself. When he put the container back in his pocket, his hand touched the cork from one of his bottles of whiskey. Lucas always kept a cork or two in his pocket for luck—a habit he'd learned from his pappy. He felt safe knowing the corks were there.

The minister locked the door and turned toward his wife. The couple moved through the yard gate and down the street toward the church on the corner.

As soon as they were out of sight, Lucas went around to the back of the house, opened a window and crawled inside.

The house was dark. He dared not light a lamp. Lucas took one step and his foot hit a solid object. He tripped and fell forward, landing on the hard floor. He wasn't hurt, but he'd made a loud *bang*. The neighbors might have heard something.

Maybe he would light a lamp after all. The soft glow shouldn't invite much attention. It was better than stumbling around in the dark.

All at once, a Scripture verse from his childhood came into his mind. Something about letting your light so shine before men that they may see your good works. He chuckled. *Good works.* He pulled a match from his pocket. Yes, stealing was wrong, but for him it was necessary.

He felt around for the table where he remembered seeing an oil lamp. After more fumbling, he found it. He lit the lamp and grabbed its base and then moved from room to room with the light, looking for the silver objects.

Thirty minutes later, he had found what he had come for, plus a few other expensive-looking items. He wrapped them all in a bed sheet, carried the load through the window and placed the bundle beside the outer wall of the house. Then he went back inside to put out the lamp.

Outside again, he lifted the sack of stolen goods over his shoulder and hurried back to his room.

* * *

Around midnight, a loud rap sounded at Lucas's door. Mr. Scott had arrived, as expected.

Holding a lamp in one hand, Lucas opened the door, and the man stepped inside. Mr. Scott was tall and fearsome looking, with a bald head and a missing front tooth.

"S-sit there," Lucas stammered, indicating the only chair.

"I'd rather stand. What have you got for me?"

"Silver and a little gold." Lucas opened the sheet and spread out the items on the bed. He picked up the coffee-pot and shone the lamp so Scott could see the gold inside. "This is genuine silver and the pot is lined with gold. The spoons, forks and knives are silver, too. How much will you give me for the pot and the tray?"

"Throw in the silverware, and I'll give you ten dollars."

"I expected more."

"That's my final offer. Take it or leave it."

"I...I guess I'll take it."

"That's a smart answer." Mr. Scott pulled out a money clip and started counting out the bills. He put ten dollars in Lucas's hand, then wrapped the sheet around the items again and cinched the bundle into a makeshift sack. "Let me know when you have more to sell."

"I will."

Mr. Scott threw the sack over his shoulder and started to walk off.

"One more thing—" Lucas said.

"Yes." The man half turned, displaying his broad chest at an angle.

Lucas felt intimidated, but he refused to stop now.

"I'm here in Pine Falls looking for my niece, Miss Honor McCall, and ain't been able to find her." Lucas cleared his throat. "I think she took the stage some weeks back—the one what was robbed between here and Falling Rock. I need to find the driver of that stage and the man who rode shotgun. Mr. Carter down at the depot won't tell me nothing. Can you get me the names of everyone on that stage and where they live? I need to know in the worst way."

"I can find out, all right, but it'll cost ya. Are you willing to pay?"

"I'm willin', but ain't able right now. I'm still lookin' for a job, you see."

"As soon as you find one or steal more things to sell, let me know. I'll have information for you by then. And I sure enjoyed doing business with you."

After Mr. Scott went out the door, Lucas moved toward the table where he'd left his flask. His boot hit something, and he shone his light on the floor. Harriet's Bible lay where he'd dropped it.

He never intended to visit another church and doubted he would be able to sell the Bible anywhere else. For sure, not to Mr. Scott. Still, he'd keep trying. He put the Bible on the table next to his flask, then opened the flask and drank. He'd earned the right to finish what was left. After all, he now had the money to buy more.

Ten dollars. As he thought about it, he realized his success as a robber was not as sweet as he had believed it would be. He wondered what the Bible meant by letting folks see your good works. The only works Lucas showed were bad ones.

Honor crossed the cold, windy field leading from the boardinghouse to the church. Her brown snow boots crunched on the icy ground, and she pulled her coat tightly around her.

Jeth had delivered her bundles and boxes to the church for the country fair soon after daylight, when he drove there in the wagon. All she had to carry was her purse and a flour sack containing a few other items she would need.

"The church sponsors a country fair to raise money for the orphanage every year," Belinda Grant had explained a week ago, after breakfast one morning. "Everybody in Hearten is invited. This year's theme is Winter Wonders."

The event was held in several rooms in the church, and Honor had volunteered to head the project to get the barn and church rooms ready because she thought it would please Jeth. At the time, she hadn't realized just how much work that would mean. Now she knew.

In addition to her other duties, Honor had to cook special food, organize games for the children, make toys and Christmas ornaments, and work on a dozen other projects in preparation for the fair. Sleep was no longer a part of her schedule.

Honor looked up at a darkened sky. If there was such a thing as chocolate buttermilk, it must look exactly like those clouds. A frosty raindrop landed on her upturned nose, and Honor bolted. From the look of the sky, what had started as a light sprinkle could become a downpour. Were those snow-clouds she saw overhead instead of rainy ones? Maybe. She raced on.

She was huffing and puffing by the time she reached the church. Exhausted, but excited and ready for work, she went directly to the storeroom. A big box filled with materials for making decorations waited on the bottom shelf. Honor dragged the heavy box out of the storage area and into the room where the children sang songs and learned about the Lord.

As she opened the wooden box, her stomach growled, reminding her she'd skipped breakfast. If she hoped to finish on schedule, there wasn't time for a noon meal, either. And she'd forgotten to bring a lunch.

The morning skipped by quickly. As soon as she finished one project, she started on another.

For one of her decorations, Honor pulled out a big ball of cotton and placed it on the table beside her. Next, she reached into her bundle and got out a glass jar containing paste she'd made by mixing flour and water. She planned to transform the cotton into tiny snowflakes.

Dabbing a snowflake with a bit of paste, she pressed the delicate fluff onto the wall around the doorway. When she'd attached a few more, she stood back to view her work. Yes, the room was going to look very different and beautiful. The children would love it. She would worry about how she was going to remove the cotton balls at a later date.

At the tap of boots on the pine floor, she glanced up. Jeth appeared in the doorway. Honor's mouth gaped open. As an afterthought, she covered her lips with her hand and faked a coughing spell.

"You better take something for that cough, Miss McCall. Frankly, I think you look tired. You have dark circles under your eyes. Have you been getting enough rest?"

"You look very nice, too, Reverend."

He laughed. "I wasn't trying to insult you. Can we start all over? Maybe I should go out and come in a second time. You see, I came here to invite you to have lunch with me in my office."

She shook her head. "Too busy."

Crossing his arms over his chest, he stood watching her. "As your boss, Miss McCall, I have a job I want you to do."

"All righty." With a perky flair, Honor pulled a black slate and a piece of chalk from the box. Holding the chalk between her thumb and forefinger, she hesitated. "Well, what is it? I plan to write down whatever you say."

"I already told you. You're having lunch with me."

"That's the job you have for me?"

He nodded. "It'll soon be noon." He checked his pocket watch. "I'll expect you in my office in five minutes."

Honor took the ball of cotton and tossed it into the box. "There. Now, I'm ready to go." She wiped her hands on a white cloth.

She thought about the box filled with supplies. The blue socks she'd been knitting for Jeth were inside. She'd intended to take them back to the boardinghouse to work on them there, but she'd forgotten. It wouldn't do for him to see his present before Christmas. Honor leaned over and slammed down the lid.

"What have you got in there?" he asked teasingly. "Explosives?"

She sent him an innocent stare.

"Come on," he insisted. "Admit it. You're hiding something. Confess. It's good for the soul."

She blinked, fluttering her eyelashes for maximum affect. "I can't imagine what you're talking about."

Merriment shone in his expressive blue eyes. Perhaps he was enjoying himself. She hoped that was true.

"I always thought you had a sense of humor under that serious exterior of yours," he said. "Now I know for sure."

Honor smiled but didn't say anything.

He liked her. She was sure of it. Honor knew she liked him. Dare she allow herself to think the word *love?*

She shook her head, rejecting that possibility. She would never be good enough for a man like Jeth Peters. It was time to face reality.

Chapter Thirteen

✤

"Is there anything I can do to help so you can leave sooner, Miss McCall?" Jeth asked. "I don't know about you, but I'm getting hungry."

"Thank you, but everything's been done."

"I'm looking forward to having lunch with you."

Honor smiled. "I know I'll enjoy it very much."

A heavy rain pelted against the windows. Honor went over to see they were shut firmly enough.

When she'd turned back around, she pointed to the tiny balls of cotton that she'd pasted to the blue wall. "Thought you'd like to see what I'm working on."

Jeth focused on the wall. Frowning, he peered at the bits of white fluff. "What is it?"

"The first of many snowflakes." She motioned with her head toward the dots. "What do you think?"

"I think I want to be far away from here when you try to remove the cotton from that wall."

She laughed. "It shouldn't be *too* hard." She shrugged as though she had a plan, which she didn't. "Were you joking? Or did you really fix lunch?"

"I did part of the work. I spread out the tablecloth and helped Mrs. Grant set the table. Then I drove her back to the boardinghouse."

Honor clucked her tongue. "You must be exhausted."

"I am."

He laughed, and she joined in.

Jeth offered her his arm. "Shall we go?"

Honor hooked her arm through his and gazed up at him. "Let's."

Honor smelled the scent of fried chicken as soon as she stepped into Jeth's office. A greater thrill was the company of a charming man like Jeth.

Evergreen branches and fall leaves had been placed in a white, china vase in the middle of a desk that doubled as a dining table. Straight-backed chairs were at each end of the desk, and the top of a low bookcase had been converted into a buffet table. Appetizing aromas wafted from steaming bowls of food. Red candles, white dishes, crystal glasses, and a red-and-white checkered tablecloth gave the entire room a welcoming air. If Honor didn't know better, she'd find the setting…romantic.

"So what do you think?" Jeth asked.

"I think everything looks lovely."

He gestured toward the serving area. "Would you like to eat now?"

"Of course. Why else would I be here?"

He handed her a white plate. "Do you always make a joke out of everything? You've been doing it a lot lately."

Gripping the plate in both hands, Honor thought of all the times she'd responded to one of Lucas's unseemly suggestions with a witty reply, hoping to deter him. Her sense of timing and humor had saved her sanity when she was a young teenager, but she couldn't tell Jeth that.

When they had filled their plates, Jeth followed her to the table. He put down his plate, helped Honor into her chair, and then lit the candles before sitting down to eat.

Everything seemed perfect. Yet the memories from her past had put her nerves on edge.

"What's wrong?" Jeth asked. "When you look like that, I can tell something's bothering you."

"Nothing's bothering me. As you said, I guess I'm a little tired."

On the following Saturday morning, when the worship service ended, Honor rose from her usual seat in the back row. Winter Wonder Day had finally arrived, and she'd made a mental list of all she had to do. With all the last-minute cooking and other preparations, she had intended to skip the fair's opening ceremonies, but Jeth had wanted her to attend.

As Honor made her way to the children's music and Bible study room, someone tapped her on the shoulder. Turning, Honor was startled to be staring into the eyes of John Crammer, a boy she had known from Falling Rock. Only, he wasn't a freckle-faced boy anymore. He was an overweight young man with carrot-colored hair, squinty brown eyes and a red beard.

Was John still the bully he used to be? Memories of taunting words and pigtails dipped in inkwells filled her mind.

"I knew I seen you in church this morning," John said. "What brings you to Hearten?"

"What brings *you* here, John?"

"The fair, of course. I come every year. But I ain't never seen you here before."

A pale young woman with blond hair and blue eyes stood slightly behind him. Though Honor couldn't remember her name, she recalled that the young woman was also from Falling Rock, and not much of a talker.

Ignoring John, Honor forced a smile and aimed it at the young woman. "Forgive me. I think I know you, but I can't remember your name."

"This here is Willa," John said proudly, gazing down at the young woman. "She's my wife."

Willa blushed, looking down at her shoes.

"We're here on our—" he grinned sheepishly "—our honeymoon and staying at the hotel."

"Congratulations." Honor started to back away. "But if you'll excuse me, I have work to do."

"Now, hold on a minute," John insisted. "I have some questions to ask you."

"What questions?"

"Where have you been all this time? My younger brother and I work for Mr. Scythe now. And he's been looking everywhere for you. Asking questions. Wanting to know who seen you last."

Honor tensed.

"Why, I reckon your uncle's traveled pretty near all over the state of Colorado looking for you by now. Even set a reward for the one who finds ya. Thirty dollars."

Honor was shocked. Where would Lucas get thirty dollars?

"As far as I know," he added, "he's still looking for ya—"

"I have to go."

Heart pounding, Honor raced down the short hallway to the door to the children's music room.

Would John tell Lucas what he knew in order to collect the reward? Knowing John, the answer was yes.

She'd promised Jeth and the Lord she wouldn't leave Hearten until Mrs. Peters returned. Once more, she prayed that she could keep her vow and still have time to escape.

"What's the matter?" Jeth demanded. "Is something wrong?" He stood looking at her from the doorway of his office.

Until that moment, she hadn't known he was there.

"I know something's the matter," he said. "You're shaking like a leaf."

"I—I'm not feeling too well this morning. I think maybe I'm getting sick."

"I'm not surprised with all the work you've been doing. Why don't you go back to the boardinghouse and rest? I'll get somebody to take over for you."

"Nobody else knows what must be done."

"Belinda Grant knows."

"Yes, but she's back at the boardinghouse, seeing to things there."

"When I drive you home, I'll ask her what your duties are. She's been as worried about you as I have. Better yet, you can tell me on the way."

"All right, I'll tell you. Can't fight you and Mrs. Grant both. But who will you get to take my place?"

His expression faltered, then he smiled. "Miss Lucy Jordan. She just volunteered to help out. I'll get her to do your jobs."

Lucy again. Honor should have known.

She didn't want anyone else to finish the tasks she'd worked on for so long—especially Lucy—and she wasn't really sick. She would feel guilty if she left. At the same time, she couldn't face more of John's questions. He seemed too eager for the reward to let her out of his sight. She would have no choice but to return to the boardinghouse and stay in bed for the rest of the day.

"Get your things," Jeth insisted. "I'm driving you back right now. And I'll be looking in on you later to see how you're doing."

A coughing spell erupted and Lucas drank a big swallow of whiskey directly from the bottle. Then he put the letters he'd written into the inside pocket of his jacket.

But would he remember to mail them? With his failing memory, he never knew.

He'd started drinking as soon as he got up on Saturday morning. As well as his coughing spells, he had a fever and felt slightly nervous over a job interview at another saloon. Liquor calmed his nerves, but walking also helped. He filled his flask with whiskey from the bottle and put it in the pocket with the letters. His hand still in his vest pocket, his fingers touched a bottle cork.

At least one lucky charm is still there, he thought as he left the room. I don't know what happened to the other one.

A thin layer of ice covered the stairway outside. He slipped, but caught hold of the icy railing in time to keep from falling. How he managed to descend those slippery steps without falling again and breaking his neck was a mystery to him. His late mother would have said God was with him. He had doubts about that.

Snow and ice covered the street and every rooftop. When he started walking, ice crunched under the soles of his brown boots.

Lucas strolled by the depot, coughing as he went. He hoped to catch one of the stagecoach drivers standing around. Maybe one of them remembered Honor. Two wooden signs hung on the entry door. He stepped closer to read them.

New Schedule
Departures: 6:00 a.m., noon
Arrivals: 1:00 p.m., 5:00 p.m.
Warning!
Be on the lookout for a band of outlaws who robbed
this stage line. Any information would be appreciated.

Apparently, they still hadn't found the robbers. Had any-one at the stage office ever heard of Honor? He doubted Mr. Carter would tell him, even if he knew.

Lucas pulled out his flask, took a gulp of whiskey and set out again. He had plenty of time before the job interview and he figured that he might as well enjoy himself until then.

Houses lined both sides of the street and laughing children raced about in a few of the front yards playing tag. Thanks-giving would be arriving soon, then Christmas. Lucas won-dered who Ruby planned to spend Thanksgiving with. Certainly not with him.

He'd almost forgotten about the holidays and now he wanted to keep it that way.

The main street was crowded and the brightly colored displays in store windows depressed him. Lucas hadn't been interested in spending time or money on gifts since he was a child in Cold Springs.

He stopped in front of a large store in the middle of the block. People holding wrapped packages milled around, talking, laughing, engaging in their daily chores. Who knew? Maybe one of them might be Honor. Lucas was determined to find her. She was the only thing he thought about now—other than whiskey. He would even forgive her for taking whatever money had been hidden as long as she gave back anything that was left.

Walking on, he soon found himself in front of the café he had visited before. Two carpenters were building a roof to cover the area in front of the main entrance. Lucas assumed the roof was designed to protect those seated at the tables from the rain and snow. Still, the weather was too cold for outdoor dining. Shivering, he sat down at one of the tables. Perhaps he would see the young woman—the one who had reminded him of his sister, Clara. At that moment he spotted the woman, strolling down the street with another woman, both wearing dark capes with hoods. The two women crossed the covered area where the tables were located and went into the café. Lucas noted that the young woman looked even heavier with child than the last time he'd seen her. Although he was unable to see the other woman's face, the way she moved reminded him of someone.

Lucas followed the women into the café. They were seated at a table at the other end of the room. A need to talk to them, to hear what they were saying, suddenly overwhelmed him. He put his flask in his pocket and looked for a table near theirs.

He coughed, and a wave of dizziness engulfed him. Lucas felt weak and shaky. On unstable legs, he made his way across the redbrick floor. A vacant table waited, right next to theirs, but before he could sit down, the world began to spin. His body swayed back and forth. He reached for the back of a chair to steady himself. The chair's legs scraped across the floor. He started coughing again, and both women turned to face him.

His mouth fell open. Lucas couldn't believe his eyes. The other woman was one of his elder sisters. He hadn't seen her in over twenty-five years. "Regina?"

"Lawrence, is that really you?"

He couldn't speak. He couldn't breathe. All the air in his lungs had been sucked out. Seeing Regina again after all this time brought him face-to-face with memories he had no wish to remember. He backed away from the table. Then he turned and ran out of the café.

Honor left the church grounds with Jeth. She didn't think John saw her, but how could she be sure?

Belinda Grant met them at the kitchen door of the rooming house. "What brings you two back here so soon?"

"Miss McCall is ill. She needs rest," Jeth said. "And Mrs. Grant, ma'am, will you see to it that she gets something to eat? Even if it's nothing more than soup?"

Honor hated it when people discussed her as if she wasn't there, and she didn't wait to hear more. Climbing the stairs to her room, she wondered what to do with herself. She preferred to keep busy; spending a day in bed when she felt perfectly healthy would not be easy.

She could read her Bible, but she knew with a sinking feeling, that nothing would stick. Her mind was too muddled. She kept thinking about John and the reward that he hoped to get if he told Lucas where to find her. He could be asking questions about her even now. If John learned where she was staying, Lucas would soon know, too.

What if John followed her to the boardinghouse? Would Belinda Grant answer his questions? Honor had never told the widow not to say anything about her because she'd never revealed that she was trying to hide.

Honor's eyes drooped—she couldn't keep them open. Perhaps she would climb in bed after all. She really did feel tired. Honor got into bed, clothes and all, and soon fell asleep.

Lucas tottered aimlessly up one street and down the next, drinking big swallows of whiskey—coughing, falling, getting back up. *Regina*. He fell down again.

Sitting in the snow, he lifted his flask and gave a toast. "Here's to ya, sis." He put the flask to his lips and drank. "You're one of the only ones who ever loved me." He got to his feet, then he stood, swaying.

What was Regina doing in the café with the young woman? What was she doing in Pine Falls? He'd heard she and her husband owned a boardinghouse. Didn't know where. Lucas also thought he remembered hearing that her husband died, but he wasn't sure.

Regina had aged since he last saw her, but she was still beautiful. He'd always thought she was the prettiest of his two sisters. As a child, she was his favorite. Now, he had nothing to say to her.

"What do ya think of your baby brother now?" He lifted his flask again. "Lawrence Smith."

Lawrence had been their father's name. Lucas suited him better. He raised the flask again. "This one's to Honor." He took another big swig of whiskey. "And you, too, Ruby."

Regina was a churchgoer. Had the sight of him, a drunk, disgusted and embarrassed her?

He started down the street again, but another coughing spell erupted. On wobbly feet, Lucas reached down, snatched two handfuls of melting snow and formed a sloshy ball. He drew back his arm and threw the snowball at a white picket fence. It hit the gate, splattering and running down.

Lucas was drunk, but he suddenly realized that the gate looked familiar. Looking around, he recognized the street in front of Reverend Kline's house. He should leave at once, before Mr. or Mrs. Kline came out and found him.

He turned and fell down in the snow, then tried to get up and slipped, crumpling again. Lucas coughed. He couldn't stop coughing. The whole world looked fuzzy. He felt fuzzy. Everything was spinning, whirling, circling. He blinked, trying to make the world stand still, but he couldn't. Then everything when black.

At four o'clock, Jeth returned to the boardinghouse, thinking about a conversation he'd had with John Crammer and the mystery of Honor's past. He went into the kitchen to speak to Belinda Grant, who was blending biscuit dough. He wanted a report on Honor's health. While they were talking, there was a knock at the door.

"Just keep on with what you're doing, Mrs. Grant," Jeth insisted. "I'll answer the door."

He strode through the dining room and into the entry hall. Through the etched glass in the double doors, he could see the sheriff, wearing a cowboy hat and a brown, fur-lined jacket, standing on the front porch.

Jeth forced a smile and opened the door. "Sheriff Green, come in."

The sheriff nodded. "Thank you, Reverend."

Sheriff Green wiped his wet boots and came inside. Jeth took his hat and coat and hung them on the hall tree.

"Why don't we go in and talk?" Jeth motioned toward the parlor.

The sheriff entered the room and sat on the settee.

Jeth took the chair across from him. "What brings you here today?" he asked. "Any news on the stage robbery?"

"As a matter of fact, there is." The sheriff pulled a sheet of paper from the inside pocket of his vest and unfolded it. "I got this letter from the sheriff over in Pine Falls, mailed a week ago." He cleared his throat. "Yesterday, there was a stage robbery a few miles out of Pine Falls. Two of the passengers were injured."

Jeth leaned forward. His mother could have been on that stage. "Was...was one of the injured a middle-aged woman?"

"No, it was two men."

"Praise the Lord." Jeth tried to breath normally again. "I don't want to imply I'm not sorry about what happened to the men, because I am. I intend to pray they will recover. However, I was concerned about my mother. Mama's in Pine Falls, visiting my cousin, Margaret Starling. She could have been on the stage."

The sheriff nodded. "I understand."

"What else can you tell me about what happened with the stagecoach?"

"A witness said one of the outlaws rode a big, red horse. That sure matches up with what you've already told me, doesn't it?"

Jeth nodded. "What about the brand?"

"Nobody got close enough to see one. But I've sent a man to keep an eye on the doings out at the Sharp Ranch. If I learn anything new, Reverend, I'll let you know. Oh, and another thing. Have you given any thought to becoming a special deputy?"

"I hadn't," Jeth said. "But now, I think maybe I might."

Honor woke and glanced around the room. Jeth sat in the chair by her bed, just as he'd done on the day that she'd arrived at the boardinghouse. When he saw that she was awake, he got up, went to the door and took his customary stance—hands behind his back.

Even when he stood at attention like a tin soldier, he reminded her of Lucas. Fortunately, the resemblance didn't bother her too much anymore.

Honor curled a strand of her long hair around her forefinger. "How long have I been sleeping?"

"All day, according to Mrs. Grant. She said she came in several times to check on you, but you slept right through it. How are you feeling?"

"Sleepy. I'm not really awake yet."

"Mrs. Grant has food warming in the oven for you," he said. "Would you like for me to go down and get it?"

"No." She started to rise. "I'll go down." She hesitated, choosing her words carefully. "I'm feeling more like myself now."

"You do look better. No more dark circles under your eyes."

In the kitchen, Honor ate her meal while Jeth drank a cup of coffee. After she finished eating, he got a look in his eyes that told her he was about to ask her more questions.

"There was another stagecoach robbery." Jeth shook his head. "The sheriff stopped by and told me. Two men were injured."

"People aren't safe anywhere these days, are they?"

"Apparently not. Do you remember the day we saw the young boy in town on the sorrel horse?" he asked.

"How could I forget? You never did tell me why you found the boy so interesting, or why you talked to the sheriff."

"I didn't have enough information then. Remember when I asked you about a red horse? Well, I saw an outlaw riding one the day of the first stage robbery. And the sheriff said a red horse was also seen at the site of the second robbery."

"Now that you mention it, I do remember seeing a red horse," she said, "just before I was knocked out."

He nodded. "I was hoping you'd finally remember."

Holding a cup of coffee in one hand, Jeth moved to the cookstove. Then he turned back to Honor at the table. "I met someone today at the fair. A man from Falling Rock. He told me that he works for your uncle. He's watching his place while Mr. Scythe is out looking for you."

Here it comes, she thought.

Jeth sat down in his chair again, watching her closely. "His name's Mr. John Crammer. Know him? 'Cause he sure knows you."

"I knew John as a child." She worked to keep her voice calm. "But not well."

"Mr. Crammer said your uncle has been looking for you. Said he even offered a reward for information as to your whereabouts."

"You— You didn't tell him anything, did you?"

He shook his head. "I didn't tell him a thing. But I wanted to."

"Wanted to?"

"I think your uncle has a right to know where you are, Miss McCall, no matter how many times you quarreled."

"I'm sorry, but I don't feel the way you do about this. And remember, you promised not to tell where I am."

"I'll never tell where you are unless you want me to, ma'am. But that doesn't mean I think it's right."

Chapter Fourteen

❧

Honor quaked in her bed. The room was cold, but that wasn't the only reason she was trembling. She'd had another horrible dream and she could still see it in her mind—see her uncle chasing her. Honor had thought the nightmares would end in time, but they hadn't. Now she wondered if they ever would.

She regretted missing church that Sunday morning and not hearing Jeth's sermon. She hated saying she was still ill when she wasn't. Her feeble excuse hadn't sounded believable, even to her. Could it be that her bad dreams would go away when she stopped telling lies?

She hadn't wanted to take the chance that she might run into John Crammer again at church. He'd seemed too eager to collect the reward Lucas was offering.

Still, her lies bothered her. Keeping God's commandments was becoming important to her, and she didn't like breaking them.

Honor threw back the covers, jumped out of bed and quickly went to the wood-box. Empty. Shaking her head, she dressed quickly. It would be warm downstairs by the kitchen stove.

Before leaving her room, she looked out the window near her bed. She saw Jeth's buggy slowly moving away, toward the wooded area beyond the house, and she hurried down to the kitchen.

After warming herself in front of the stove and eating a light breakfast, she put on her coat and her head-covering. Then she went out to gather wood. She was pulling a short log from the pile when the black buggy returned and stopped in front of the kitchen door. Honor groaned. Jeth must have forgotten something. Now she would have to try to explain why she wasn't upstairs resting.

But a man in a dark coat and hat jumped down from the buggy. At first she could see only the back of his head. Then he turned, and a red beard caught the morning sun. She recognized John Crammer. He was with his new wife.

What was he doing here? She had thought John would either be back in Falling Rock by now or attending church in Hearten. His visit to the boardinghouse could only mean trouble.

John Crammer lifted his wife down and placed her on the frozen ground by the steps. As they started toward Honor, she waved and tried to smile. She had no choice but to go forward and meet them.

"Is the pastor home?" John asked.

"No, he already left for the church. I'm surprised to see you here, John. To be honest, I thought you would have gone back to Falling Rock by now."

"We aim to go to church first." John held his wife's hand protectively. "In fact, we was on our way there now. But I have a question for the preacher, and thought I might catch him before he left for church."

Was his question about Honor? Did John think Jeth would tell him things about her that would help him collect the reward?

"But when I seen you standing by the woodshed, Miss McCall, I thought we best stop and say hello even if the pastor's done gone. So, why ain't you in church this morning?"

"I've been feeling poorly." Honor glanced down at the pine log in her arms. "And I needed wood for the stove in my room. It's cold in there." She waited, hoping John would say what else was on his mind and go away.

At last, she said, "I know you're in a hurry to get to the Sunday service. So I won't keep you any longer. But it was nice to see you again." She started to walk off.

"Wait a minute."

Honor stopped and looked up at him.

He pulled out his pocket watch and glanced at it. "We have time. Would you mind if we went inside and visited a while? I reckon we have some catching up to do, and I could use a cup of coffee."

The word *no* shouted through her brain. He'd probably want to know when she planned to leave Hearten and where she might go when she did. Honor hoped to end this conversation. John had tricked her when she was a child and he might try to do it again. She could end up saying more than she planned to.

She faked a coughing spell, hoping he would take the hint and keep the visit very short. "Do come in, then." She coughed again to underscore her point.

"Thank you. We'll go in, then. Won't we, hon?"

Willa blushed, looking embarrassed. "Whatever you say, dear."

Honor led John and his wife into the kitchen, settling them into chairs around the table. Then she put the pot on the stove to warm. Keeping busy meant more time to collect her thoughts before she had to face John Crammer.

"Coffee with cream and sugar?" she asked.

"Willa takes hers that way. I drink my coffee black."

Did John always speak for his wife? Honor wondered. Didn't she have a voice of her own?

When the coffee was hot and on the table, Honor took a chair next to Willa.

"So you ran away from home, huh?" John said.

"Not really." Honor's temper flared, but she tried not to let it show. "I'm old enough to leave home now. Why, Willa's about my age and she's already married."

"She's my wife."

Poor Willa, Honor thought.

"So if you ever leave Hearten," John said, "where would you go?"

"I have no plans to go anywhere. Why would you think otherwise, John?"

"Just making conversation."

He took a sip of coffee. "As I mentioned, my little brother and I are taking care of your uncle's farm for him 'til he gets back, and he's been gone a long while now, looking for you." He looked at his pocket watch again. "I guess we best go. It's getting late. Church starts soon." He rose from his chair. "Come on, hon." He stared back at Honor. "I reckon I'll ask the reverend them questions after church. But if not, I 'spect we'll try to stop by again before we leave town."

Honor forced a smile. "I'm sure Reverend Peters would enjoy visiting with you, but he's really been busy lately. It's hard to catch him."

"We'll take our chances, won't we, Willa?"

"Yes, John."

"As I said," he went on, "'spect we'll be back if we can spare the time."

Then they left. Honor didn't take a full breath of air until John's buggy had rounded the hill at the end of the lane.

As she was clearing the table, she noticed that he'd barely touched his coffee. Willa's cup was almost full, as well.

So, Honor thought, it was just as I thought. John wasn't interested in coffee.

She tossed her head and poured the black liquid into a bucket she would empty later. Her encounter with the man had been exhausting. Now she *really* felt tired. Perhaps she would go up to her room and read for a while, maybe take a nap.

She reached for the pine log. Besides, Jeth wanted her to rest, didn't he?

Lucas opened his eyes, coughing, and he found himself in a new world, but he had no idea where he was. A metal teakettle sat on a table at the foot of his bed, steam pouring from it.

He lay in a tidy bed, and the blue nightshirt he wore smelled clean and fresh. His hair and body had been washed. Yet all he wanted was a drink. He threw back the covers and started to get up.

"Not so fast, sir." The man's voice came from a corner of the room.

Lucas turned. "Reverend?"

The minister nodded. "You're not ready to be out and about yet, Mr. Scythe. You have a fever and a bad cough." Reverend Kline rose from his chair to stand near the bed. "But I'm glad you're awake. We've been worried about you."

"How long have I been here?"

"Two days."

"Two days? Why, I done missed my job interview. What day is it, anyway?"

"Monday."

Lucas swung his bare feet to the floor. "I gotta get out of here." A wave of dizziness overcame him, and he started coughing again. He pressed the palm of his hand to his forehead, suddenly aware of a pounding headache. "I gotta get out of here," he repeated.

The Reverend shook his head. "The doctor will want to see you first."

"What doctor?"

"Dr. Brown, the one who's been treating you. So please, lie back down. He should be here in a little while. Until then, just rest."

Lucas remained on the edge of the bed. His shoulders shook, and he was having a hard time breathing. The minister was bound to notice. Though he had no desire to get back under the covers, he wasn't sure he would be able to stand.

"How are you feeling?" Reverend Kline moved closer to look down at Lucas. "You had us all concerned."

"I'm all right. But I'd feel a lot better if I had me a shot of whiskey." He shrugged. "Sorry, Preacher. You being a man of the cloth and all, you probably ain't got none. That's why I gotta get out of here."

"Whiskey isn't what you need right now."

"But it would sure help my cough some. It always does."

"A doctor's what you need. The doctor who lives here in Pine Falls. And the one up there." The pastor pointed toward the ceiling. "You're in God's hands. So please, lie back down and let my wife and me take care of you. You would be doing us a great favor if you would let us help you."

"Why would helping me do you any good?"

"That's a long story. Remind me to tell it to you." He hesitated, looking at Lucas. "If nature calls you, I'll be glad to hand you a pot. Would you like it now?"

"As a matter of fact, I would."

Later, the minister reached for a small metal bell on the table by Lucas's bed. It gave out a soft tinkling sound when he shook it.

"Why did you ring that there bell?" Lucas laughed. "Is it time to go to school?"

The pastor chuckled. "I told my wife to bring you a tray of food when she heard the bell. You must be starved. Do you feel like eating?"

"I reckon I could tolerate a cup of coffee if you could see your way clear to put a little something extra in it." Lucas grinned sheepishly. "I shore am shaky, Preacher, and whiskey is powerful medicine."

"As you thought, we don't keep *that* kind of medicine in the house. But the doctor will give you plenty of good medicine when he gets here."

The minister turned toward the doorway as Mrs. Kline swept into the room, carrying a wooden tray. Lucas had never seen a smile as bright and warm as hers. For an instant, he almost forgot about how much he needed alcohol.

"Good afternoon, Mr. Scythe," Mrs. Kline said. "I'm so glad to see you're awake. We've been praying for you."

"Praying for me?"

"Of course. And I've brought your supper and a big glass of water."

Lucas's mouth felt dry, but not for water. Why didn't these people understand that?

"The doctor said he wants you to drink a lot of water."

She put the tray on the table by his bed and handed him the glass. "Here. It's good for what ails ya."

He *was* thirsty. Lucas reached out and took the glass from her. Lifting it to his lips, he drank.

"Don't drink too much at one time," Mrs. Kline warned. "The doctor said to drink a little, put down the glass, wait a minute or two, and drink again. He wants you to empty the entire glass. And if it stays down, you can have your supper."

Lucas wanted more of the water, but he put down the glass as she had requested. He couldn't figure out why they were treating him with such kindness. Didn't they know he was the thief who had stolen the silver coffeepot and tray?

On Tuesday morning, Jeth arrived at Baker's Grocery and Mercantile soon after it opened for business. When he walked inside, a tinkle sounded directly above his head. Looking up, he saw a bell nailed above the door, just like those used in big-city stores back East.

Well, what do you know? Mr. Baker is going modern, he thought.

Smelling the brine from the pickle barrel mixed with the fresh scent of baked goods, Jeth tossed his hat on a hook near the front door. Drifting toward the back of the store, he gazed at the items on display.

Mrs. Withers, in a dark gray hat, stood in front of the counter while Mr. Baker tallied her bill. Out of the corner of his eye, Jeth saw Mrs. Baker talking to Miss Sally Bennett. According to Belinda Grant, the forty-year-old Miss Bennett was the biggest gossip in Hearten.

Jeth turned his back on the women and looked at the sign above the storekeeper's head: Ring Sale—All This Month.

Rings. Just this morning Jeth had pulled open the top drawer of his dresser and found the small, purple-velvet box that he'd forgotten was there. It had been pushed to the back of the drawer, under a neatly folded stack of long underwear. When he'd opened it again, after all these months, a wave of grief had overwhelmed him. It was the first time he'd looked at Selma's engagement ring since she died.

The diamond had also belonged to his mother. But would it be right for Honor? Knowing it had once been Selma's, Honor could refuse to wear it. Jeth had put the box back in the drawer, but now he couldn't stop thinking about it.

Mr. Baker put Mrs. Withers's purchases in a burlap sack. "All right, ma'am, that will be fifty-nine cents."

The stout widow wore dark, plain-looking clothes, but Jeth had always admired the liveliness in her pale, gray eyes, as well as her dedication to the Lord.

"Can you put this on my bill, Mr. Baker?" she asked. "Money will be hard to come by until I sell the calves I've been raising."

"Of course. I'll be glad to."

"Thank you. You're very kind." Mrs Withers reached for the burlap sack.

"Would you like me to carry your sack out to the wagon for you?" the storekeeper asked.

"No, I can manage on my own. It's not heavy." She shook her head. "But thank you for asking. And I hope you and the missus have a nice day." She turned to Jeth and smiled. "And you, too, Reverend."

"Same to you, Mrs. Withers, and I hope to see you in church on Sunday."

"Don't worry. I'll be there."

When Mrs. Withers left the store, Mr. Baker turned to Jeth. "So what can I do for you today, Pastor?"

"I would like to look at those rings you have on sale," Jeth whispered.

"Rings?" Mr. Baker said aloud. "What kind of rings are you looking for?"

Jeth put his forefinger to his mouth. "Engagement rings. But please don't say anything about it. I haven't even asked the young lady yet."

"My lips are sealed."

The storekeeper pulled a box from under the counter and placed it on top. Jeth heard muted giggles coming from behind him. He expected Mrs. Baker and her friend to sidle up beside him and start asking questions, but they kept their distance.

A pearl ring caught Jeth's interest immediately. Honor had told him that her aunt had owned a pearl necklace that had once belonged to Honor's grandmother. Her aunt Harriet had promised Honor she would have it one day, but the necklace had disappeared long before her aunt died.

Jeth tried not to look at the pearl ring. His mother had taught him long ago that a wise shopper didn't show an interest in the item he intended to buy. Jeth picked up a diamond ring. Looking at it briefly, he dropped it back in the slot.

He lifted the ruby ring and examined it. "How much is this one?"

"Seventy-five cents. It's a genuine imitation ruby."

"Is the pearl imitation, too?"

"Yes, but of the finest quality."

"Do you have any real pearl rings?"

"Oh, well..." Mr. Baker hesitated. "No. But I can order you one. I have a catalog here somewhere. Excuse me a minute." The storekeeper went to the back of his shop and out of sight.

Jeth glanced over his shoulder. The two women had moved much closer to the counter and were whispering back and forth. When they saw him watching them, Sally

Bennett elbowed Mrs. Baker, and they ended their conversation. Then they grinned at Jeth.

Forcing a smile, Jeth drummed his fingers on the countertop. In his opinion, the women were up to no good.

A few minutes later, Mr. Baker returned, holding a thick book in both hands. He put it on the counter, then opened it to a marked page.

"Here it is." Turning the catalog around, Mr. Baker pointed to a drawing of a pearl ring. "Would you like me to order it for you?"

Jeth squinted at the page and read the information. The price was more than he wanted to pay. But the ring was exactly what he'd been hoping for. Honor would love it. "Yes, I would like you to order this one for me," he said. "Will it be here by Christmas?"

The storekeeper frowned. "Let me think. It's still mid-November." Mr. Baker turned and gazed at a calendar on the wall behind him. When he swung back around, he smiled. "Yes, sir. I'm sure it will be. Maybe sooner. I know a jeweler in Denver, and he handles rings like the one you want."

"Good." Jeth closed the catalog, sliding it back to Mr. Baker. "As I said, I hope you'll keep this purchase between the two of us."

"Oh, yes, Pastor. Nobody else will know."

As Jeth started for the door, he saw Mrs. Baker and Sally Bennett whispering and looking animated and excited. He hoped they had been discussing matters other than his purchase, but he doubted it.

Maybe Mr. Baker would take hold of the reins and demand they keep Jeth's secret. But knowing the storekeeper and his wife, Jeth found that possibility unlikely. If the tongue-wagging started, he would have to find a way to stop the story before it spread.

* * *

A rat the size of a big dog ran halfway across Lucas's bed and stopped. Lucas screamed. He could smell its vile breath. The rodent turned and snarled at him, showing long white teeth. Lucas shrieked again.

Reverend and Mrs. Kline raced into his room.

"What's wrong?" the minister exclaimed.

Lucas pointed a shaky finger toward the foot of his bed. He'd always hated rats. At the moment, he was too frightened to speak.

The minister put a hand on Lucas's shoulder. "What's the matter, Mr. Scythe? What do you see?"

"That...that big rat. It's daylight outside. Can't you see it?"

The reverend shook his head. "Nothing's there, believe me. You've had another bad dream, probably brought on by your fever."

"I...I ain't dreaming. My eyes are wide open."

"I know it's hard to believe, but there is no rat. Nothing's there. Your mind is playing tricks on you because of all your drinking. Remember, the doctor said you were to expect this." Reverend Kline put his hand on Lucas's forehead. "Your fever's high again, too."

"No matter what you say, this ain't all in my head, and it shore ain't because of no fever. It's real. I know what I seen." Lucas screamed again.

"What happened?" the reverend asked.

"It bit me! On the foot!"

Lucas began to weep, shaking all over. He couldn't seem to stop. Reverend Kline took him in his arms, as if he were a baby, and held him tight.

"Bless your heart," Mrs. Kline said, leaning forward and patting Lucas on the shoulder. She handed him a white handkerchief. "Here, sir, use this."

Through his tears, he saw compassion on her face.

"And remember," she added, "you're not alone. We're here, Mr. Scythe. And we're praying for ya."

"Yes, we are," the reverend put in, "and the Lord's here, too, watching over all of us."

Lucas sniffed and wiped his nose on the handkerchief. "Why would God waste his time on somebody like me? I ain't worth it."

"Oh, you're worth it, all right," Reverend Kline insisted. "And God loves you, Mr. Scythe. He truly does."

"How do you know?"

"The Bible says so, that's why. And it is impossible for God to lie."

Lucas cast a quick glance toward the foot of the bed.

"Is the rat still there?" the minister asked.

"Yes, but his mouth is shut. And he ain't as big now."

Reverend Kline folded his hands. "I'll bet if we pray together, he'll get even smaller. Maybe he'll go away completely. Will you pray with my wife and me, Mr. Scythe?"

"I ain't no praying man, Preacher. Never have been."

"You don't have to say or do anything if you don't want to. You don't even have to say 'amen.' But the wife and me—well, we're going to pray. And we'd love for you to join us."

Lucas didn't hear much of the preacher's prayer. But all at once, the rat started growing smaller and smaller. Trembling, he watched until the varmint disappeared.

Lucas must have gone to sleep. When he awoke again, it was dark outside. An oil lamp burned on the table by his bed, and the reverend slept in a chair nearby. The covers on his bed looked wrinkled, and his feet felt icy. Lucas hesitated to glance toward the foot of the bed to see why. The rat could have returned. When he finally looked, however, he discovered the blanket had pulled out from the edge of the mattress and his feet were uncovered.

Despite his fear of rats, Lucas sat up to fix his covers. When he did, the bed squeaked, and the minister stirred in his chair.

"Are you all right, Mr. Scythe?"

"I'm fine now, Preacher. Why don't you go to bed? I figure that there chair is mighty uncomfortable to sleep in."

"What about the rat?"

"I reckon he went back where he came from."

Reverend Kline chuckled softly. "How are you feeling?"

"As I said, I'm doing plenty fine. So why don't you go? Get some sleep?"

"You've had a bad night. Bad dreams. Tossing and turning. I think I'll stick around a little longer. Would you like something to drink—besides you-know-what?"

"I'm pretty dry at that. I reckon water might be powerful nice after all."

The minister poured water from a china pitcher into the empty glass. "I found a key in your pocket. Would it be the one to the place where you live?"

"I reckon. I have a room over Wilson's Grocery Store in the center of town."

Reverend Kline handed Lucas the water and watched while he drank. "I'll be going over to that rented room of yours this morning to get your things and haul them over here. Is there anything special you would like for me to bring you?"

"You don't need to bother, Preacher. About all I've got over there is dirty clothes."

"My wife is good at washing and ironing. And you'll be doing me a favor by letting me get your things."

"How?"

"It'll give me an excuse to go downtown and look around. Maybe do a little shopping," he whispered. "I need to buy an anniversary gift for the wife, but don't tell her I said so."

Lucas laughed with real amusement for the first time since he had arrived at the Klines' home. "Don't worry, Preacher. I won't tell her nothing."

"Did I mention that I mailed those letters you had when you came here?" the minister asked.

"What letters?"

"The ones I found in your pocket. There was a letter addressed to Mr. John Crammer and the other was to Miss Ruby Jones."

Lucas had forgotten he'd written any letters.

"While I'm in town," the minister went on, "would you like for me to check with the man who owns the grocery store downstairs? See if you have any mail?"

"Suit yourself. But I doubt I'll have any. I ain't never got many letters. Unless folks have something to fuss about, that is. Or want me to pay 'em some money." Lucas chuckled. "Now them are good reasons to write me, ain't they?"

Then he added, "But if'n I ever do get any mail, I reckon my landlord would bring it up to me. Slip it under the door or tote it on inside. I 'spect he's got a key, since he owns the place."

Chapter Fifteen

⚜

At three o'clock on the next afternoon, Reverend Kline came into Lucas's room carrying a book. A closer look revealed Harriet's Bible.

"I've brought your Bible."

"Why did you bring it in here?" Lucas demanded. "I've been meaning to sell it, but I ain't been able to find no buyer yet."

"My wife is washing all your clothes right now," the minister said, ignoring Lucas's comment. "Mrs. Kline should have them ready by nightfall." The minister set the Bible on the table by the bed.

"Get that book away from me," Lucas shouted. "I done told ya. I don't have no hankering for the Good Book."

Lucas grabbed the Bible and threw it as hard as his weakened condition would allow, barely missing the minister's shoulder. The Bible hit the chest of drawers and landed on the floor.

He expected the minister to be angry. His outbursts usually caused fear or anger in others. Without saying a word, Reverend Kline picked up the Bible and placed it right back on the table.

Lucas shouted out a curse, but the minister appeared not to notice. Reverend Kline had nerves as hard as an anvil. Lucas had to respect a man like that—even if he was a preacher.

On Monday morning, Honor went to Lucy Jordan's home to teach her weekly lesson. In Miss Jordan's living room, Honor finally met Lucy's blind, widowed mother, Mrs. Annette Jordan.

Wearing a violet dress, Mrs. Jordan looked a lot like Lucy, but her smile was sweeter. She was also small and dainty and had a fair complexion like her daughter, but in Honor's mind, the similarity ended there. The older woman's long dark hair was streaked with gray and piled on top of her head in a tight knot. Pearl earrings dangled from her ears.

Honor had loved pearls ever since she'd first dreamed of inheriting the string that had belonged to Aunt Harriet. After the necklace had disappeared, Honor had tried to put the pearl necklace out of her mind. But now, Mrs. Jordan's earrings brought all Honor's losses to the surface of her mind again.

Once, in a sermon, Jeth had told the story of the pearl of great price mentioned in the Bible. He'd said he thought the pearl was a symbol of Jesus and salvation by grace. Although Honor attended church services regularly now, terms Jeth used still baffled her. Some of Jeth's warnings frightened her, as well, so much so that she wanted to crawl under a pew and hide, especially when he stressed the importance of being saved from the fires of hell.

She didn't want to believe there was a hell. If there was such a place, Honor was probably doomed.

"May I touch your face?" Lucy's mother asked in a gentle voice, interrupting Honor's thoughts. "I know it's a strange request. But I can see people better when I do."

The question gave Honor an uneasy feeling, but when Mrs. Jordan gestured for Honor to come closer, she did. Kneeling before the older woman, she removed her bonnet.

Mrs. Jordan placed wrinkled hands on Honor's face, moving them as an artist might as she molded a piece of clay. "Oh, Miss McCall, you have high cheekbones, a wide mouth and soft skin. You are very beautiful."

"Oh, no, ma'am. I'm just average looking."

"Nonsense, you're lovely. My fingers never lie."

Honor couldn't help but smile. She hadn't received many compliments in her lifetime, and cherished each one.

Mrs. Jordan ran her fingers through the curls that had escaped Honor's bun.

"Shouldn't we start my reading lesson now?" Lucy asked from across the room.

"In good time, daughter. I want to finish looking at this pretty young lady first," Mrs. Jordan said. "Your hair is soft and thick, my dear." She brushed the tips of her fingers lightly over Honor's eyelids. "You have long lashes. What color are your eyes and hair?"

"I have brown eyes and dark, reddish-brown hair, ma'am."

"Ah, yes, auburn hair and brown eyes. A nice combination. Do you enjoy reading, Miss McCall?"

"Yes. Yes, I do."

"So did I, once. But now—" She licked her crinkled lips. "I miss reading the Bible. But thanks to you, young lady—" She folded her hands, put them in her lap and sent a smile in Honor's direction. "Thanks to you, my Lucy is learning to read. Soon she'll be able to read the Bible to me. What a joy that day will be."

While Mrs. Jordan talked, a current of warmth started in Honor's heart and spread throughout her body. Until now, instructing Lucy in reading had merely been a job. But Mrs. Jordan made teaching seem like a calling—a Christian ministry, as Jeth would say.

Honor wanted to continue talking to this dear lady, but she knew that she should start the lesson. Nevertheless, she would be eternally grateful to Lucy's mother. She'd helped Honor see herself in a fresh way.

After Mrs. Jordan had left the room, Honor sat down by Lucy on the couch and pulled a slate and a piece of chalk from her carpetbag. "I guess we can start now."

"Why don't we pray first?" Lucy suggested, and then immediately bowed her head. *"Lord,"* she prayed. *"Teach us what You would have us learn during today's lesson."*

When the prayer ended, Honor drew the letter *A* on the slate and gave the chalk to Lucy. "What are the long and short sounds of this letter?"

Lucy took the chalk between her thumb and forefinger. "Let me see." She tilted her head. "*A* gives its short sound in words like *apple*." Lucy put a small chalk mark over the *a*. "And it gives its long sound in words like *table*."

Honor smiled. "Very good."

Lucy produced the sounds of all the letters in the alphabet and read several verses from the Bible aloud. She wasn't the best reader Honor had ever heard, but she was showing a lot of improvement.

"You're reading well, Lucy. I'm proud of you."

"Thank you for saying that."

"It's the truth. I wouldn't have said it if it wasn't."

Honor put the slate and chalk back in her bag.

"You're in love with Pastor Peters, aren't you, Miss McCall."

Shocked by Lucy's question, Honor stared at her. Then she fumbled with the leather handle of her bag, wondering how to reply.

"I'm sorry," Lucy said. "I had no right to ask that question."

"Don't worry yourself about it." Honor rose. "But I really must go. I have shopping to do before I return to the boardinghouse, and I'd better get started."

"I'll walk you to the door."

Honor forced a smile. Forgiveness didn't come easy to her. But she planned to be extra nice to Lucy the next time they met.

After the lesson, Honor was picked up in the wagon by Jeth. "Would you mind stopping by the general store before you drive me back to the boardinghouse?" she asked when she'd taken her seat beside him. "I need to buy thread and a few other things."

"I wouldn't mind at all."

As soon as Honor stepped inside the store, a bell rang above her head. Several women were huddled around Mrs. Baker, talking, their backs to the door. When they heard the bell, they turned and looked at Honor, watching her for several moments.

Honor hated attention and knew she must be blushing. At last, they turned around and continued their conversation.

Honor dismissed the incident and went directly to the display of threads on a small table near the jars of candy. She selected spools of white and pale blue and dropped them in her carpetbag, intending to pay for them later.

Now, what else do I need? She puzzled, trying to remember. I should have made a list. Oh, yes, white material for a new blouse. She gazed at the piece goods area, close to where the ladies stood.

Taking her time, Honor surveyed every table as she meandered through the store. She needed shoes, and she picked up a pair of brown high-buttoned ones that she immediately saw were much too big. She put them back and moved on down the aisle.

From the rear of the store, she slowly made her way back to the table where cloth was displayed, hoping none of the women would notice her.

Honor ran the palms of her hands over rolls of white material, trying to decide which one felt the softest.

"Are you saying Pastor Peters ordered an engagement ring?" one of the women asked.

Honor paused to listen.

"Yes, that's exactly what I'm saying," Mrs. Baker answered.

Honor jerked her hands from the fabric as if it were hot. Did this mean Jeth was engaged? Or about to be? And who was the lucky bride? Lucy Jordan?

"Does anyone know who the pastor's lady-love is?" another woman asked.

"I can't say for sure, mind you," Mrs. Baker went on. "But I was told on good authority that…" Her words faded into a whisper.

Honor strained to hear more but couldn't.

The bell over the door chimed.

A gray-haired man whom Honor had seen at church came into the store. Honor didn't want to be caught eavesdropping. Grabbing her carpetbag, she quickly walked away from the group of women. She was about to open the door when she remembered that she hadn't paid for the thread.

Whirling, she snatched the spools from her bag, tossed them on the nearest table and dashed outside. She'd almost reached the wagon when a new thought hit her. Could *she* be the future Mrs. Jethro Peters?

Impossible.

She didn't smile when she climbed onto the seat beside Jeth, but she didn't frown, either. She simply sat there like a wooden statue, contemplating.

Three days later, Lucas lay in bed awaiting his breakfast. He licked his lips. Mrs. Kline was a good cook and he smelled bacon frying. Lucas was feeling better and had begun to get out of bed for a few hours each day. Now he reached for the pitcher on the table by his bed, and as he poured water into the glass, he thought about what he used to drink in the morning. It wasn't water.

Casually, he glanced out the window beside his bed. A woman in a dark cape was trudging through the snow outside. Lucas looked again. Could it be his sister? Opening the window wide, he leaned closer to it. A draft of frosty air made him shiver. Lucas hugged his arms close to his body and watched. He couldn't see the woman's face, but her purposeful gait reminded him of Regina.

The woman turned. She *was* Regina. Where was she going? Was she looking for him? Lucas doubted it.

Then Regina moved out of his line of vision. Lucas hoped she would turn around and walk by his window again, although he wasn't ready to talk to her face-to-face. He might never be.

Lucas partially closed the window, settled back in the bed, and pulled the covers around his shoulders. Reverend Kline had told him that if he hoped to recover from the fever, he should stay warm.

Reverend Kline also had left Harriet's Bible on the table. Lucas recalled that Regina had studied the Bible every day after she'd learned to read, and so had his eldest sister, Clara. Lucas was the black sheep of the family—just like Pappy. With those memories came the thought that a shot of whiskey sure would taste good right now.

Lucas gazed at the Bible again and saw a gold ribbon dangling from it. He'd been carrying that Bible around since the day Ruby had given it to him. Why hadn't he noticed the ribbon before?

Sipping his water, he wondered what the ribbon meant. Why was it there? He had no intention of reading the Good Book. However, the ribbon intrigued him.

He put down the glass, reached for the Bible and opened it. Holding the Bible with his left hand, he ran his fingers down the marked page. The silk ribbon felt soft to the touch.

Lucas looked closely. Some of the words had been underlined. He shook his head. Who had the audacity to write in a Bible? He'd always been taught that such behavior was shameful. His schoolteachers would have switched him if he'd underlined words in a school book. Still, he was curious to know what was written on that page.

His eyesight wasn't as good as it had once been. Squinting, he stretched his arms out almost as far as they would go and read.

For God so loved the world, that He gave his only begotten Son, that whosoever believeth in Him should not perish, but have everlasting life.

"I noticed you squinting," Reverend Kline said. "Are you having a hard time reading?"

Startled, Lucas glanced toward the doorway and closed the Bible. He hadn't known the reverend was watching.

"I ain't been reading. Just looking over this here book some, that's all." Lucas tossed the Bible back on the table by his bed.

Reverend Kline came closer, and pulling a pair of spectacles from the pocket of his shirt, he placed them over the Bible like a paperweight and glanced toward the window. "The house is a little drafty. We best close the window there by your bed, Mr. Scythe. It's getting cold in here."

Since Lucas made no attempt to do as he suggested, the minister leaned over the bed and closed the window all the way. "That's an extra pair of spectacles I've had for a long time," the minister added. "I thought you might like to have them. They'll make it a lot easier for you to read."

"I don't need nothing like that. 'Cause I ain't planning to do no more reading—at least not the Good Book. But if you have any of them 'shoot 'em up' stories, I'd be obliged if you would bring one of them in here so I could read it. I like to read about outlaws and cowboys and Indians." Lucas coughed. "When am I getting out of this here bed?"

"The doctor said you could be up and around as soon as your fever goes down."

Lucas glanced at the Bible again. "I noticed somebody's been marking in the Good Book," he said. "Guess it must have been my wife. This here book belonged to her 'fore she—" After telling everybody in Pine Falls that his wife was still alive, he almost let it slip that Harriet had died. "As I told ya, we raised her niece as our own. That's why I came here to Pine Falls, to find the girl. But nobody's done seen her. Least, I ain't found anybody what has."

"God knows where your niece is."

"How do you know that?"

The minister glanced at the Bible. "It's all right there—in God's Word."

Lucas thought of the underlined words again. "My pa would have taken me to the woodshed if I'd marked up an expensive book like Harriet done."

"I would never take someone to the woodshed for underlining verses in the Bible," Reverend Kline said. "In fact, I encourage those in my congregation to draw lines under Scripture verses they want to remember and read again."

"Still, it's a shame to mark up a nice book like that, ain't it? Books cost money. Mama always kept the family Bible out where folks could see it when they come for a visit. And when we were little, us kids weren't allowed to touch it."

"That's a shame. Children should be able to pick up the Bible and read it whenever they want to."

"I played in the dirt a lot when I was a kid, Preacher, and my hands was always needin' washing. What if I'd gotten dirt or mud all over Mama's book? What do you say to that?"

"I would have said, 'Lucas, the Bible is God's Holy Word. Read it as often as you can. The Bible teaches us how to live the abundant life. How to be happy no matter what troubles come our way.' But I would also have told you to wash your face and hands first."

"You sound like my mama." Lucas chuckled softly. "She was always trying to get me to wash myself. Used to take hold of my ear and half drag me to the bowl and pitcher."

The minister laughed. "My mother did the same thing to me when I was a boy, but she never pulled hard. Did your mother hurt your ear when she dragged you?"

"Naw. I just pretended it hurt so Mama would stop. Back then, I shore did hate soap and water. And I loved to get a rise out of Mama."

The preacher smiled. "I guess all young boys are pretty much alike. I never did like bathing until the Lord washed me clean once and for all."

"God gave you a bath? Why, I never heard of such a thing. What do you mean by that, Preacher?"

"Remind me to tell you about it sometime when you're feeling better. It's quite a story. That makes two stories I owe you."

Lucas smiled, wishing the preacher would tell the stories now.

He liked the Klines. They had been kind to him, and he thought they liked him, too. Why else would they bring a near stranger into their home and care for him? But they would hate him if they knew Lucas was the one who broke into their house and stole the silver tray and coffeepot.

After Reverend Kline left the room, Lucas put on the spectacles. They did make things less fuzzy around the edges. With a quick look to make sure Reverend Kline wasn't watching, he picked up the Bible and began reading. He told himself it was something he could do to pass the time...until he could leave this place for good.

Saturday was baking day. Honor and Belinda Grant were busy baking cakes, pies and cookies. Snow had fallen on the previous night. Honor had promised Jeth and Belinda that she'd help build a snowman as soon as the noon meal was over and the dishes were washed and put away.

Honor pressed down on the cookie cutter. Dough in the shape of an evergreen tree appeared on the flour-covered table where she worked. She was about place the bit of dough on the greased pan when she heard a knock at the front door.

"Just a minute!" Honor wiped her hands on her apron and started for the entry hall. "I'll get the door, Mrs. Grant."

"Thank you, Miss McCall," Belinda called back from the mess room.

Honor noticed that flour was dusted on the front of her apron, and some of it had turned the long sleeves of her dress a whitish-blue. She rubbed her itchy nose with her forefinger, then wished she hadn't. She probably had a white nose now and maybe a ghostlike face, as well.

Jeth had already opened the door by the time Honor got there. Miss Sally Bennett stood beside him in the entry, holding a tray.

"I baked a cake for you, Reverend," she said to Jeth.

"How thoughtful. Thank you, Miss Bennett." Jeth glanced at Honor. "Take the tray, will you, Miss McCall?"

"I'll be glad to."

"I want to help our guest with her cape."

Honor took the tray in both hands. Miss Bennett had just carried it in from the cold, yet the metal platter felt warm to the touch and seemed heavier than she had expected.

Snowflakes drifted to the pine floor when Jeth helped the middle-aged woman off with her furry, black cape. Honor fought a frown.

I just mopped and waxed that floor, she thought.

Jeth looked back at Honor. She forced a smile.

"That tray looks heavy." He took it from her. "Would you mind taking Miss Bennett into the parlor while I put the cake in the kitchen?"

"Of course. And please excuse the way I look, Miss Bennett. We're baking today."

"No apologies are necessary. I baked this morning myself." Miss Bennett pulled a lacy handkerchief from her purse. Reaching over, she wiped something from Honor's nose. "There, that should do it."

Honor felt her face heat.

The older woman dropped the handkerchief back into her purse. "Was it flour?" she asked.

"Yes, ma'am, it probably was," Honor responded. She gestured toward the parlor. "Please sit down. The settee is very comfortable, but anywhere you would like to sit would be fine."

"Thank you, but I've been here many times and know my way around." She glanced toward the most comfortable-looking chair in the room. "Mrs. Peters is a good friend of mine." She started to sit down, then stopped and glanced at Honor. "But of course, you wouldn't know because you're new in town, aren't you."

The sarcasm in her tone hurt. But it wouldn't be Christian to hit back. "Would you like something to eat or drink, ma'am? We have fresh cookies, and I could warm up the coffeepot."

"No, I wouldn't care for a thing."

The older woman's gaze found Honor's again. From the look on her face, perhaps Miss Bennett hoped to climb inside Honor's brain. The spinster finally sat down.

A photograph of Jeth's parents on their wedding day sat on the small table beside Miss Bennett's chair. She reached for the frame. After studying the picture for a moment, she offered it to Honor.

"Regina was so young when she married the pastor's father," Miss Bennett said. "I didn't know her then. But as you can see, she made a very beautiful bride."

"Yes." Honor nodded. "She certainly did." Honor crossed the room, photograph in both hands and returned it to its proper place on the table.

"Speaking of brides, have you heard the news, Miss McCall?"

"What news?" Honor found a chair and settled onto it.

"Pastor Peters has ordered an engagement ring for a young lady. And I heard Miss Lucy Jordan will be getting a very nice Christmas gift this year—if you know what I mean."

So, it's Lucy after all. Honor bit her lower lip. I knew it. She squirmed in her chair, trying not to look at Jeth's guest. Honor needed to leave the room before she did or said something she would regret.

Miss Bennett tapped her long fingernails on the table at her side. Then Jeth returned from the kitchen, all smiles. Honor rose, straightening the skirt of her dress.

"How have you ladies been getting along?"

"Just fine," Miss Bennett said, "haven't we, Miss McCall?"

"Yes, ma'am." Honor stepped to the door, looking down at the toes of her black shoes. "But if you will both excuse me, I have things to do in the kitchen."

"Don't forget," Jeth reminded her. "You promised to help me and Mrs. Grant build that snowman later."

Honor stopped and looked back at him. "Sorry. I won't have time to build a snowman. I have too much to do." Then she headed for the kitchen—determined not to cry.

Chapter Sixteen

❧

Later that same day, Elmer brought in a stack of letters and laid them on the kitchen table. "Give them letters to the pastor for me, will ya, miss?"

Honor nodded. "Of course." She reached for Jeth's mail. "I'll just put them on the pastor's desk."

"Did I hear someone say letters?" Mrs. Clark said from the dining room.

"Yes, ma'am," Honor called back to the boarder.

Mrs. Clark burst through the connecting door leading into the kitchen, followed by her sister, Mrs. Davis.

Elmer shook his head at them. "Sorry, ladies. All the mail that came in today was for the preacher." He turned and started down the hall toward his room.

Honor hoped the two women hadn't noticed her red eyes. She'd tried not to cry, but hearing that Jeth was engaged, or soon would be, to Lucy Jordan had affected her.

Mrs. Clark sat down at the table. Mrs. Davis did the same. Honor could see that both women were disappointed not to receive any mail. Although they had lived at the boardinghouse since Honor had arrived, she hardly knew anything about the two sisters and had been too busy to inquire.

"Can I fix you ladies something?" she asked now. "Coffee, cake, cookies?"

"Nothing for me, thank you," Mrs. Clark said.

"Me, neither," Mrs. Davis added.

The two widows were former schoolteachers and Honor had often wondered if they were twins. Their squinty eyes were different shades of brown, but they looked alike, although Mrs. Clark had more wrinkles and frown lines. The spectacles perched on their pointed noses were the same, and their dark wool dresses could have come from the same out-of-date fashion pattern. They both wore their hair in tight buns, and the texture and color was identical—salt-and-pepper, mostly salt.

Honor gazed at the younger, Mrs. Davis. "So how was your daily walk?"

Mrs. Davis glanced at Mrs. Clark as if she expected her older sister to answer for both of them. Honor couldn't know for sure, but she had a feeling that the younger woman had been doing that for most of her life.

"We enjoyed our stroll very much," Mrs. Clark put in. "We always do. And we saw so many trees that would make wonderful Christmas trees, too. Are you planning to put up a Christmas tree this year—here at the boardinghouse?"

Honor stopped, wondering how to reply. "I really can't say. As you know, I'm new here. I suppose I'll have to check with Reverend Peters to see what his mother did in the past. Besides, it's too soon to worry about a Christmas tree. It's not even Thanksgiving yet."

"No, but it will be in just a few days."

Honor nodded. "I know."

After the sisters left the room, Honor started toward Jeth's office to deliver his mail. Glancing down, she saw a letter from his mother on the top of the stack. As she placed the pile of mail on the table next to his lamp, one of the letters fell to the floor. Honor bent to pick it up, and glanced at the return address.

John Crammer. She looked again, hoping her eyes had deceived her, but the letter was from John all right. Honor had an overwhelming urge to open the letter and read what was written there. But she couldn't. She was a Christian now.

Honor went back to the kitchen, wondering what the letter might say. Had John told Lucas where she was living? The mere thought gave her a new case of the jitters. If he hadn't told yet, he would. John wanted that reward; he'd said as much when he visited the boardinghouse.

Her imagination had taken her prisoner again. The idea that Lucas might actually find her practically brought on a case of the vapors.

He could come here when she least expected it. Perhaps at night. And he could...

Just last night, she'd had another horrible dream. If she didn't stop dwelling on all this, she would go mad. Yet disturbing thoughts and dreams rose in her mind, again and again.

In the dream last night, she was gathering wood, as she had on the day that John Crammer and his wife came to the boardinghouse. Honor held two small logs. As she reached for the third, Lucas appeared. Fear engulfed her. Her heart pumped. Honor dropped the logs that she held. Evil gleamed in her uncle's blue eyes, and he held a log as if it were a club.

She turned to flee, but he grabbed her. She screamed. And then she'd wakened, trembling and perspiring.

If only she could put the frightening dreams and disturbing thoughts out of her mind.

In the kitchen now, Honor picked up a knife and moved to the slicing board. She tried not to think about her dream or her secret desire to marry Jeth Peters, and attempted to concentrate on slicing bread. But she had no idea how to stop the anger and discouragement she felt.

Belinda Grant rushed into the kitchen from the backyard, bringing a blast of cold wind inside with her, until she shut the door.

"It's freezing out there." Wiping her wet shoes on a mat by the door, she shook snowflakes from her hair and from her dark blue overcoat. "I wouldn't be surprised if we got a lot more snow before it's over tonight."

Belinda stomped her feet. Snowflakes drifted onto the pine floor. She unbuttoned her shoes, one black button at a time, and put them beside the door. Then her gaze fastened on Honor. "You're awfully quiet this afternoon."

Honor shrugged. "I've been busy. How's the snowman?"

"Perfect, just perfect. And he's so handsome."

"Handsome? How can a man made of snow be handsome?"

"Well, he is." Belinda's grin showed her excitement. "Just go out back and look." She pointed toward the back door. "I don't mind saying that I've never seen a better looking snowman." She paused and examined Honor slowly. "I wish you'd been there to help us when we made him."

Honor looked away. "I'm sure you and the reverend did a fine job without me."

"Have you been crying?" Belinda asked.

"Onions. I chopped onions a while ago."

"Yes. But have you been crying?"

Yes, she thought, tears looming close to the surface again. For years, Honor had tried to hold in her emotions no matter what happened, and she'd been successful. But she couldn't manage any longer. She needed someone to hold her, someone to tell her things would get better.

Honor felt the warmth of Belinda's kindness and wanted to tell her everything. Her true feelings for Jeth were too obvious to hide anymore, but she could never let anyone know about Lucas or what he might do if he found her. Her private monsters were between Honor and—

Who? God?

"What's the matter?" Belinda asked. "Is it the pastor?"

"He's going to—" Honor sniffed. "He's going to marry Lucy Jordan."

"How do you know that?"

"Miss Bennett told me."

Belinda patted Honor gently on her back. "What does *she* know? I think the pastor's in love with you."

"What makes you think so?"

"I have eyes in my head, and ears, too. It's obvious to me that Reverend Peters is *not* interested in Miss Jordan. If he was, he'd be courting her. He's known her for years."

"Then who is he courting? Certainly not me."

"But he *is* courting you. Can't you see that? Why do you think he drives you into town every time you need to go?"

"His mother tells him to. Or rather, she told him to before she left. And Miss Jordan lives in town. Maybe he goes there to see her all the time. We just don't know anything about it."

"He never drives Miss Jordan anywhere." Belinda took Honor's hand and led her to the table. "Sit down and let me fix you a cup of coffee. I think you need it."

Honor sat, trying not to cry again. A few minutes later, Belinda handed her a cup of coffee. Honor lifted the cup to her lips but had a hard time swallowing the warm liquid. Holding the cup in both hands, she studied her saucer, then took another sip.

She wanted to believe Belinda was right—that Jeth loved her...and would rescue her from her uncle. But if Lucy wasn't his intended, who was? Could Jeth be in love with another young woman, someone nobody knew about?

Belinda leaned toward Honor. "You're in love with Reverend Peters, aren't you."

Yes, I am. Slowly, she nodded.

Belinda smiled, displaying straight, white teeth. "I knew it all along."

If only Honor could tell Belinda—or somebody—all the things that troubled her. A thought came to her: Tell the Lord.

But surely He already knew.

That evening after supper, Honor looked at Jeth through the open doorway of his office. In the dim light coming from his oil lamp, he sat behind his desk reading one of the letters, with a serious look on his face.

Was he reading the letter from John Crammer or the one from his mother? She wanted to go in and find out, but knew she shouldn't. Instead, she lifted her chin and straightened her back, preparing to move on.

"Miss McCall, will you come in here for a minute, please?" Jeth motioned toward the empty chair in front of his desk.

Here it comes, she thought. She stepped into his office stiffly and sat down.

"I just got a letter from my mother and I thought you might enjoy hearing what she had to say. She has news that's very exciting."

Relieved, Honor leaned forward in her chair. "Has the baby been born?" she asked.

"No, but it should happen any day now." He picked up his unopened letter from John Crammer and fingered it.

A disquieting feeling shot through her. She hoped it didn't show. Jeth had never looked more like Lucas than at that instant. She was glad the resemblance no longer troubled her, but what he might say about John's letter did.

"I wanted to tell you about something amazing that happened to Mama in Pine Falls." He smiled. "I have an uncle I've never met by the name of Lawrence Smith. Uncle Lawrence ran away from home before my parents married and never came back—even for visits. Nobody knew what happened to him or if he was still alive. Then he just appeared briefly at the Starling Café one day. He ran away before Mama could talk to him."

"Has your mother talked to him since then?" Honor asked.

"Not yet. But she's looking for him. If he's still in town, she'll find him sooner or later. My mama doesn't give up easily."

No, she doesn't, Honor thought, and neither do you.

Jeth still held the letter from John Crammer. He studied the envelope. Honor wanted to leave before he opened it. She didn't care to hear what John had to say about Lucas or her.

"Thank you for telling me about your uncle. It's wonderful news. I hope your mother finds her brother again very soon." She stood. "But I guess I'll leave you now so you can finish reading the rest of your mail."

Lucas smelled dinner cooking. Pot roast and potatoes, he hoped. He felt better now that his fever had left him and he'd begun eating his meals at the table with Reverend and Mrs.

Kline. Over the last few days, his strength was rapidly returning. He still thirsted for whiskey, but the craving had weakened.

Lucas continued to read the Bible. Though he didn't understand much of it, he studied it—mostly to please the minister. He had to do something to pay for his keep.

"Dinner's ready," the minister's wife called.

When Lucas entered the kitchen, Mrs. Kline was standing in front of the woodstove, stirring a pot. White steam twirled up from it. The minister, at the head of the table, motioned for Lucas to sit down.

"How's the Bible reading going, Mr. Scythe?" he asked. "Are you understanding it better now?"

"I understand it when you explain it."

"Then maybe we should have a short Bible study after we finish eating."

"I think I best go looking for a job after we finish eating, sir," Lucas said. "I'm not gonna live off you folks forever. It ain't fittin'."

"You can move back to that room of yours over the store anytime you want to," the minister said. "We've paid for your rent three months in advance."

"Paid for my room?" Lucas stared at the preacher. "Why would you do that?"

"As I told you, Christians treat others as they would like to be treated. It's called the Golden Rule."

Lucas shook his head. "Don't make no sense to me."

"It will sooner or later. Just keep reading your Bible. Understanding will come."

Mrs. Kline placed the platter of roast beef in front of the minister and a bowl of roasted potatoes in the middle of the table. Then she sat down.

The pastor nodded to Lucas. "Let us give thanks."

The Klines folded their hands and bowed their heads. After a moment, Lucas did, too. He was staying in their home and should do as they did. Common courtesy taught him that much.

"Heavenly Father," the minister prayed. *"Thank You for all our blessings and for this food. Use this meal to the nourishment of our bodies as You use the Bible to nourish our souls. In the name of Jesus, Amen."*

A stack of white plates, a large fork and a sharp knife had been placed in front of the minister. Reverend Kline picked up the knife and sliced enough for three servings, then put a portion of meat on each plate. He handed a plate to Lucas. "Please pass this on down to my wife."

When all three had a plate in front of them, Mrs. Kline passed around bowls of potatoes, gravy and beans. Lucas hadn't seen such a feast since before Harriet took to her bed. At last, they started eating.

"You need a job, Mr. Scythe," the minister said. "Isn't that what you said?"

"Yes, sir."

"Well, it's my pleasure to be able to offer you one."

"You want to hire *me?* What kind of job?"

"We have an opening at our church. We're looking for a caretaker. Someone to clean the church, make minor repairs, and pull the weeds in the flower beds. Are you interested?"

Lucas smiled. "Yes, I shore am."

"When can you start?"

"Today, if you need me."

"Saturday will be soon enough. That's when we clean the church for the Sunday services. Can you be there by eight on Saturday morning?"

"You can count on me."

You can count on me. How many times had Lucas spoken those words without really meaning them? But things were different now. He wanted to do a good job for the minister. And he needed employment.

He thought about what he'd done to Mr. and Mrs. Kline, stealing from them, then accepting their hospitality. Until that instant, he'd never considered asking for forgiveness. Yet he found himself wanting to tell them what he'd done, even if it meant he would never see them again.

Lucas put down his knife and fork. "I have something to tell you good folks."

Reverend Kline's brows lifted. "And what might that be, Mr. Scythe?"

"I...I was the one what stole your silver tray and coffeepot. Then I went and sold them for money. I truly am sorry, though. Now, I reckon I best leave." Lucas put down his napkin and started to rise.

"Don't go!" The minister smiled. "Sit back down and finish your meal. Please."

Lucas stopped, standing by his chair. "Didn't you hear what I said, Preacher? I was the one who—"

"We know all that, Mr. Scythe."

Lucas stared at the minister. He couldn't believe his ears. "You knew?"

"We've known all along. The top from one of your whiskey bottles must have fallen out of your pocket the night you broke into our house. We discovered a cork exactly like that one in your pocket the day we found you unconscious in the snow."

My good luck charm, he thought.

Had the charm finally started working? Or had his good fortune come from somewhere else?

"Then, if you knew all this about me, why did you take me in, nurse me back to health, and do all those other things to help me? It don't make no sense."

"No, it doesn't, unless you know and love our God," the reverend said. "I was once just like you, Mr. Scythe. I was a poor boy, and my papa beat me almost every day. So I ran away and stole something from a man. When he caught me, I thought he would beat me and have me put in prison, but he didn't. I found out he was a godly man. He took me in and raised me as his own son. Even sent me to college, where I became a minister.

"The man said he was able to forgive me and love me because God first forgave him and loved him. So now I'm passing that on to you." The minister sent Lucas a soulful glance. "Has anyone ever hurt you, Mr. Scythe? Or have you ever hurt anybody?"

Too many to name, Lucas admitted to himself.

"If you've hurt others, you'll have some repenting to do," the reverend went on. "When you tell the Lord you're sorry and really mean it, He will forgive you and wash away all your sins."

"Is that the heavenly bath you were talkin' about?"

The minister laughed. "It sure is." Then his face turned sober. "Would you like to have what my wife and I have, Mr. Scythe?"

"Would I have to give up drinking?"

"That's not the way it works. You just have to repent and ask the Lord to come and live in your heart. Let God worry about your drinking and everything else. Would you like to do that—right now?"

Lucas shook his head. "I don't know yet. I'll let you know when I do."

"Don't worry about telling me. Tell Him."

"You mean God?"

The minister nodded. "He's the Creator of the universe, you know. And He loves you very much, Lucas Scythe." He paused again and smiled. "And don't forget. We're expecting you for Thanksgiving dinner."

The following afternoon, Honor sat at the kitchen table, writing her grocery list. The roast baking in the oven smelled delicious, and the biscuits were ready to pop in when the roast came out. She'd never thought she could run a boardinghouse, but she was doing it.

The supper crowd would be small that evening. Jeth, Elmer, Mrs. Clark, Mrs. Davis and Dr. Harris. Belinda and Honor would eat what was left over.

Jeth would have read John Crammer's letter by now. Honor wondered if he intended to mention it.

"Hey, there," Jeth said. "What are you doing all hunched over? Don't you know positions like that are bad for your back?"

Honor straightened. Surprised to see Jeth standing beside her, she manufactured a quick smile. Well, at least he hadn't sounded angry.

Jeth sat down at the table. "Supper sure smells good."

"It'll be ready by seven. Elmer should be here by then."

She wanted him to tell her about John's letter, to get it over with. Waiting to hear what Jeth might say and when he might say it worried her more than an honest discussion.

"I noticed you got a letter from John Crammer." She swallowed before going on. "What did he have to say?"

His smile disappeared. "That's what I came in here to talk to you about."

Honor stiffened. "Go ahead, then. Talk."

"Mr. Crammer said your uncle left Falling Rock, looking for you, a day or two after the stage robbery. Until recently, he didn't know where your uncle was. But a letter from Mr. Scythe arrived a few days ago, mailed in Pine Falls. Mr. Crammer wrote your uncle and told him where you were staying. Then he wrote me to let us know what he'd done. I think it's time that you wrote to your uncle, Miss McCall. You've waited long enough."

She rose from her chair. The very idea! She'd expected Jeth to tell her about his letter from John, but he had no right to come in here and tell her what to do. Who made him an expert on everything? He'd promised never to reveal her location to anyone. Was he breaking his promise now?

"Did John Crammer also tell you that he expects my uncle to give him a reward for finding me?"

"No, he never mentioned anything like that. And that reminds me, I've got your uncle's mailing address, if you want it." He hesitated. "So, what will you do?"

"I plan to finish cooking supper. Then I'll serve it. That's my job. What do you plan to do, *Preacher?*"

"I still think you're making a mistake not writing to your uncle. I really do."

"Why don't you write my uncle yourself since you think it's so important? I'm sure you would do a better job than I ever could."

Honor went to the stove, got the old quilt rags she used as pot holders, and opened the door of the oven. Her anger felt hotter than the heat coming from the cookstove.

"The roast should be cooked by now," she said, more to herself than to Jeth. "It's time to put in the biscuits."

As she carried the heavy roasting pan to the cabinet by the hand pump, she realized she wasn't as frightened at the thought of seeing Lucas as she had thought she would be. Had raw fury eclipsed her fears? Or did God have something to do with it?

Chapter Seventeen

❧

By nightfall, Honor's disagreement with Jeth had become a distant memory. Fear replaced her anger. Visions of Lucas with a club in his hand haunted her. The fact that the house creaked and the wind whistled through the shutters didn't help.

In the middle of the night, Honor went down to the kitchen for a glass of water. The boardinghouse was dark except for the lamp she held. She paused at the foot of the stairs, listening to the old house settle after each burst of the howling wind. Once, she'd worried that her uncle might find out where she lived and come after her. Now she knew for *sure* that he knew her location. So what must she do? Run away? Find a new place to hide?

A stagecoach ticket waited for her at the depot in Hearten, and she'd saved enough to live on for a while, until she found another job. But she felt that the money she'd put aside was the Lord's. It should only be used to pay back what she took from the church in Falling Rock. She couldn't, *wouldn't* steal from God again.

Still, she needed to feel safe. There might never be a better time to tell Jeth everything.

She shook her head. No, not now, she thought. I'll discuss all this with Jeth some other time.

She remembered the six-shooter and the bullets under Mrs. Peters's bed. Honor inspected the weapon every time she cleaned the bedroom, touching the cold metal, fingering the bullets.

She was a fair shot. Aunt Harriet had made sure that Honor had learned the correct use of firearms, though their target practice sessions had always been held in secret. How many times had Honor and her aunt sneaked out to the woods to practice shooting when her uncle was far from home?

Would it be wrong to borrow Jeth's mother's gun until the woman returned? And if necessary, use it?

Honor crept up the stairs. Then, after looking both ways, she darted into Mrs. Peters's bedroom at the head of the stairs.

As soon as she returned to her own room, Honor loaded the pistol and placed it under her bed along with the rest of the bullets. Still, she couldn't sleep that night. Tossing and turning, her thoughts returned again and again to Lucas and what he might do to her. Would he ravish her? Beat her? Or simply drag her back to Falling Rock and make her his slave?

Suddenly, she heard footsteps in the hall outside her door, and a chill snaked down her spine. Soundlessly, she lowered herself to the floor and reached under the bed for the six-shooter. Rolling on her side, she held her finger on the trigger. Heart pounding, she pointed the weapon toward the door. A *click* seemed to echo loudly when she cocked the gun.

"Who's there?" she demanded.

"It's just me," Belinda said softly. "Sorry I woke you."

Honor relaxed. "What are you doing up at this time of the night?"

Belinda giggled. "If you must know, I'm on my way to the privy."

"Oh. Well, be careful. It's cold and dark out there."

"Don't worry," Belinda called back. "I'm always careful. Go back to sleep."

How was Honor expected to go back to sleep when she hadn't been asleep in the first place? She removed her finger from the trigger and guided the hammer back in place. When she'd pushed the six-shooter under the bed, she got into bed. Yet memories of Lucas still haunted her. She didn't fall asleep until shortly before dawn.

There were so many people expecting a Thanksgiving meal at the boardinghouse that Jeth decided they should have the dinner at the church, in the adult Bible study room. On Thanksgiving morning, it took Honor and Belinda over a half hour to carry platters and white china bowls of food to the covered wagon and load them in the back.

The frozen ground was slick under their feet and dangerously rocky and uneven. Honor slid a few inches and staggered while she was transporting the mashed potatoes. A small amount spilled over the side of the bowl and fell on the icy ground.

"Now look what I've done!"

"Don't fret, dear," Belinda said. "It's not like you dropped the whole thing and broke the bowl. Besides, I heard some news that should perk you up considerably."

"What news?"

Belinda had reached the wagon, carrying a bowl of corn-bread dressing. "Well, yesterday at the store, I talked to one of the ladies who knows all the gossip going around about the ring the reverend ordered at Baker's."

"And?"

Belinda placed up her heavy white bowl in the wagon and reached back to take the potatoes from Honor. "Nobody but the pastor knows for sure who the engagement ring is for. And he's not telling. It could be anyone. Even you, Miss McCall."

"Well, it's not me." Honor reached over to cover the bowls with a linen cloth. "Besides, I'm planning to move away from here."

"Move away? When?"

"As soon as Mrs. Peters returns from Pine Falls. And I'm sure Reverend Peters must have guessed that by now."

"Have you told him?"

"Not in words, no."

"Then how would he know?" Belinda asked.

Honor shrugged.

Belinda put her hand on Honor's shoulder as they walked back to the boardinghouse. "Miss Honor, why don't you keep that bit of news about you leaving between the two of us for now? Give the reverend the chance to reveal who his future wife will be before you hand him your resignation. What do you think?"

"I have no plans to tell him anything until his mother comes back. But then, I'll be moving far away. And you're the only one who knows about it."

The Thanksgiving meal at the church appeared to be a huge success. Everybody raved about the food. Unfortunately, Honor and Belinda never found time to taste any of it.

When the last dish was washed, carried back to the rooming house and put away, Jeth insisted that Honor and Belinda sit at the kitchen table and rest.

"I'm warming up the leftovers and serving you ladies a midafternoon feast fit for a queen—or rather two queens." Jeth put a white washcloth over his left arm, clicked his heels together and bowed at the waist. "Chef Peters, at your service, ladies."

Belinda laughed, clapping her hands, and Honor joined in. Belinda started to get up out of her chair. "Are you sure you know how to do this, Reverend?"

"Absolutely. Keep your seats. I helped Mama boil water once and remember just how to do it."

Female laughter filled the room.

Jeth opened the door to the cupboard beside the stove and peered inside. "Where are the pots and pans? All I see in here are stacks of white dishes."

"The pots and pans are in the cupboard next to it," Honor informed him.

Jeth took three dishes from the stack and put them on the table. Then he pulled out more pots and pans than three people could ever use and lit the oven.

Honor gazed at Belinda. They burst out laughing again and didn't stop until they started eating. When they finished their meal, Honor offered to wash the dishes, but Jeth insisted on doing them.

At last, he sat down at the kitchen table, panting as if he'd run a mile. "And I still have to dry all those dishes and put them away," he said.

"I'll finish up," Belinda volunteered. "It's the least I can do."

"Thank you," he said. "That was hard work."

"You're not telling us anything we didn't already know," Belinda said. "How would you like to fix breakfast in the morning for fifteen people? Mrs. Clark, upstairs, likes her eggs hard on the outside and soft in the middle."

Jeth groaned. "No, thank you."

He laid his head down on the table, closed his eyes and feigned an attack of snoring.

"What would your future wife say if she knew you snored, Reverend?" Belinda asked. "If you ever marry again, that is."

Belinda had a mischievous gleam in her eyes. Honor knew that look. Belinda's next question to Jeth would probably include the word *ring*. She didn't want to be around to hear it.

Honor rose from her chair. Neither Belinda or Jeth appeared to notice.

"How's Miss Jordan?" Belinda asked Jeth pointedly. "I didn't see her at the Thanksgiving doings today."

"I have no idea how she is," Jeth said. "But I would imagine that she and her mother went to Denver to visit her aunt. They have been spending Thanksgiving there for years."

You would know, Honor thought and then cleared her throat. "Thank you for the meal, Reverend. It was very good. But I should go upstairs now. I still have sewing for Miss Jordan to do."

She didn't wait to hear any response. Honor hoped to be in her room and engaged in handiwork before Belinda and Jeth discussed the ring.

Lucas had Thanksgiving dinner with the Klines, and the next day he moved back to his room over the grocery store. How he'd changed since he left. His desire for alcohol had diminished more than he had ever thought possible.

As he'd told Reverend Kline, "I used to think about drinking all the time. Now I only think about it half the time."

"It's a struggle all right," the pastor had said. "But remember, even one drink can put you right back where you were before you passed out in front of our house."

Lucas didn't want to be on that road again. It should be easier to go straight since he wouldn't be working in a saloon, but sometimes, the urge to drink did seem stronger than he was. Would he be able to resist the urge, now that he'd returned to his room and the Klines lived several blocks away?

Standing near his bed, Lucas gazed around. He'd never seen the room looking so clean and neat. Mrs. Kline had washed and ironed all his clothes. Some were hung on the hooks that lined the wall, and the rest were neatly folded in the chest of drawers. He vowed to keep his room exactly as it was now.

Two letters had been placed on the little table by his bed—probably by his landlord. Lucas opened the first envelope.

Dear Mr. Scythe,
I was glad to get your letter. Everything here on your farm is fine as far as I can tell. The calves are growing bigger every day. If you come home soon, they should be ready to go to market.

My new wife and I took a little honeymoon trip to Hearten. Bobby looked after things here at the farm while I was gone. And you will never guess who I ran into in Hearten. Your niece, Miss Honor McCall. She is living at a boardinghouse there owned by a Mrs. Peters, and Mrs. Peters is the mother of a preacher, Jethro Peters.

I thought you would want to know. And I hope this means that I will get that reward of $30.00.
Sincerely yours,
John Alton Crammer

* * *

Lucas glared at the letter, digesting the news. Honor wasn't in Pine Falls. She'd probably been in Hearten all along. Why, that little... His old anger began to resurface, growing into rage. He felt as if his body might explode at any moment.

Lucas headed for the door, his mouth watered. He needed a drink. But reaching for the knob, he stopped. Yes, he wanted a drink, but could he survive without one? He paced back and forth in front on the door, trying to decide what to do.

Reverend Kline had insisted that Lucas could stop drinking if he really wanted to. God would help him.

He could pack his clothes and leave immediately, and that was just what he wanted to do. But where would he get the money to buy a ticket for the stage? Reverend and Mrs. Kline had given him food, but no money, and his job as the church caretaker had barely started. He hadn't been paid yet.

The letter had mentioned Jethro Peters, and Lucas suddenly remembered that was the name of the young preacher who'd come to Harriet's burial. Words he'd learned by heart from the Bible came to his mind: "For if ye forgive men their trespasses, your Heavenly Father will also forgive you."

A week ago, Lucas would have started out for Hearten at once, even if he had to walk. However, finding Honor wasn't as important anymore.

Maybe I should leave Honor alone—let her have whatever money she might have found. It probably isn't much anyway, he thought.

Lucas stopped, startled by his own thoughts. Had he really said in his mind that finding Honor and the money didn't matter anymore? Lucas shook his head. Who birthed those notions? Where was the anger? Was God changing him? Softening his heart? He didn't have any answers, but he meant to keep looking for them. He opened the second envelope. The letter was from Ruby.

Dear Lucas,
It was quite a surprise when I received your letter today. Frankly, I never expected to hear from you again. Will you be living in Pine Falls permanently? Or do you intend to move back to your farm in Falling Rock?

You said you had lost your job at the saloon and were looking for something else. Well, I had been searching for a job, too, and finally found one. I'm the new organist and choir director at the church where I attend. In your letter, you didn't even mention the argument we had just before you left. Maybe it was not important to you, but it was important to me.

I had just asked you to marry me. But that was then. Things are different now. I don't know if I will ever marry anyone, Lucas, but you will always be important to me. I still love you. But now that I know more about God and the Bible, I know I can never marry a man who doesn't share my faith and isn't a true believer in Jesus Christ.
Yours,
Ruby Ann Jones

Won't marry a man who don't share her faith, huh? Lucas clenched his fists. His jaw hardened. Who does Ruby think she is?

Then he remembered Ruby's beautiful face. Sure she was pretty, but Lucas had known a lot of handsome women in his life.

I still love you, she'd said.

What did Ruby know about love? Once, Lucas had thought he loved Ruby. Maybe he still did. He wasn't sure what love was. But he knew if he ever took another wife it would be— Who?

He'd thought he wanted to marry Honor. But now the name Ruby rippled through his brain.

Honor was hardly more than a pretty child. Ruby was a woman, perhaps more of a woman than someone like Lucas deserved.

At that moment, a grinding, gnawing sound interrupted his musings, and Lucas recoiled. He looked around. The noise came from the wall behind the chest of drawers.

Instantly, he thought of the horrible hallucination he'd had about the big rat at the foot of his bed. Rats had frightened him as a child. If he were honest, rats still disturbed him, but the gnawing sounds they made didn't bother him as much now.

Once he would have secretly feared that the rat would chew all the way through the wall and bite him in the dark of night. Now he felt safe somehow.

If there was a rodent behind the dresser, he needed to kill it. It also occurred to him that if he angled the heavy oak chest of drawers in front of the door, nobody could see his bed from the doorway, giving him a measure of privacy.

Lucas got on one side of the heavy piece of furniture and pushed with all his strength. It hardly moved an inch. When he shoved again, he heard something that sounded like a small object falling to the floor.

On his hands and knees, Lucas looked under the chest and saw something—something long and white. He reached in and pulled out Harriet's pearl necklace. He could not believe it. The strand must have been stuck in a crack of the chest all this time.

Lucas counted the pearls. There were forty-eight in all, just as he remembered. Reverend Kline had said he had prayed that Lucas would find the necklace. Now Lucas had. Could this be God's doing? Lucas was beginning to think it was.

On Friday night, Lucas wrote a letter to Ruby, apologizing for hurting her. He also requested Ruby's forgiveness for all the things he'd done in the past. He considered asking her to wait for him, but he didn't. He couldn't. He would never be the kind of man Ruby needed.

As it was, Lucas had said more in his letter to Ruby than he had intended. First, he wrote "I love you, too, Ruby." Then he marked a line through it and wrote "I wish you the best in your new job."

On Saturday morning, after he dropped the letter in the mail slot, he realized that one line through a sentence didn't completely block it. He would have known that if his thinking had been clearer, but it was too late now.

It snowed all day, and by the time Lucas got off work in the late afternoon, a thick coat of icy whiteness covered the ground. After hours of honest work, the cool air invigorated him. He decided to take a walk in the woods just for the fun of it.

He turned down a street he'd never visited before and saw a woman in a dark green cape, climbing the steps to the house on the corner. As he looked on, she went inside. His heart raced. Lucas couldn't be sure, but he thought the woman was Regina. His sister had worn a similar cape both of the times that he had seen her.

He'd been hoping to find Regina again. Although, at the same time, he hadn't known how he would be able to face her after all these years. After all that he'd said and done, why would she want anything to do with him? Regina was a lady, and Lucas was...a drunk.

A woman like Regina would expect her only brother to become successful in life. Yet Reverend Kline had defined prosperity differently from the way Lucas always had. To the minister, successful people needed only to repent for all their sins, invite the Lord into their hearts and lives, and then know that their names were written down in God's book.

Like the preacher, Regina was a Christian.

Lately, Lucas was thinking a lot about what it might be like for him to become a believer. But that would mean giving up drinking and gambling forever, and he didn't think he could ever do that. Besides, he had never been able to control his anger. He might be able to change for a while, but when things got bad, he knew he would always return to his old ways.

There were plenty of good folks in the world. Why would God choose a no-good loser like Lucas Scythe?

On the day he'd seen Regina at the café, he'd thought that her eyes had seemed kind. Her voice had sounded gentle, too, as gentle as Mrs. Kline's. And Regina had been dressed like a respectable lady, not like the women Lucas met at saloons.

He'd met Ruby in a saloon, but somehow she'd always seemed different from the other saloon girls. Maybe that was because she'd always claimed to love him.

Suddenly, a face peered out from behind the Christmas tree at the front window of the white house on the corner. Lucas squinted, hoping to glimpse Regina again. But it was a child who was looking out at the falling snowflakes, a handsome little boy with golden hair. He was smiling and appeared to be about seven or eight. Was Lucas related to that child? He desperately wanted to know.

Lucas waited a moment longer, knowing he wouldn't find answers tonight. Then, slowly, he turned and walked away.

From time to time, the general store in Hearten carried books. Honor had purchased one on the history of Colorado. On another occasion she found a book on kite-making and bought it for Timmy's birthday. Honor wrote a note and tucked it inside the box with the book.

Dear Timmy,
Happy birthday.
Besides this gift, Reverend Peters has a present for your birthday, too. He said he is gathering everything the two of you will need to build a new kite. Come spring, you and the pastor will start making a kite that will really fly.
Best wishes,
Miss Honor McCall

Then she wrapped the package in white paper and tied the red ribbon in a big bow.

After Miss Jordan's reading lesson on Monday, Honor walked to the little brick cottage at the end of the street where Timmy and his family lived. She cradled the package in her arms.

Honor knocked at the door. A pretty young woman with dark hair answered. She looked like Timmy.

"Hello. May I help you?" the woman asked.

Honor nodded. "Hello. I'm Miss Honor McCall, and I work over at the boardinghouse. I'm looking for Timmy Rivers. Am I in the right place?"

"Yes, indeed. Timmy mentioned you." The woman smiled. "I'm Mrs. Rivers, Timmy's mother. Won't you come in?"

"Thank you."

Honor followed her into the parlor. The woman turned to Honor and smiled.

"Timmy isn't home right now. He's playing with the little boy down the street. But please, sit down."

"I can't stay. But I bought this gift for Timmy's birthday." Honor handed the package to the child's mother. "Please see that he gets it."

The woman nodded, but Honor thought she looked confused. Perhaps she wondered why a perfect stranger was giving her son a gift.

"I was on that stagecoach," Honor explained, "the one that was robbed. One of the outlaws hit me over the head with his gun, and the doctor kept me in bed for a while after that. While I was recovering, Reverend Peters told me amusing stories about Timmy and his adventures with his kite. Later, Timmy came to the boardinghouse where I work and said his kite was broken. So I bought him a book on kite-building. I hope it's all right."

"Of course it's all right. You are very kind to think of buying it, Miss McCall."

There was an embarrassing pause. Honor didn't know what else to say. Mrs. Rivers wasn't speaking, either.

Honor drifted to the door. "As I said, I have to go now. But please wish Timmy a happy birthday for me."

"I will."

Honor reached for the doorknob. Then she glanced back and smiled. "He's a wonderful child."

"Thank you, Miss McCall. He thinks you're pretty wonderful, too."

* * *

After work on Monday, Lucas stood at a distance, hidden behind a clump of trees, watching the house that his sister, Regina, had entered. He longed to go to the front door and knock, but he couldn't find the courage.

All at once, the front door opened. Two young children in dark-colored coats and red neck scarves raced out of the house. The little boy who Lucas had seen at the window was pulling a sled, much like the sleds Lucas had owned as a child. The little girl had long, dark curls and carried a rag doll. Lucas heard their laughter and he could almost feel their merriment.

The door opened again, and Regina joined the children in the front yard. Lucas watched them talking and laughing, although their voices sounded joyful, he couldn't decipher their words, no matter how hard he tried.

Regina picked up a handful of snow and molded it into a ball. The children laughed, dashing around the yard, moving closer to where Lucas stood.

"You can't catch me, Aunt Regina!" the boy shouted.

"Me, neither!" the girl added.

"We'll see about that." Regina pulled back her hand and threw the snowball at the little boy. It hit his shoulder and splattered. The boy giggled. Regina scooped up another handful of snow and repeated the process. Only this time, she aimed for the girl. The snowball missed and landed near the girl's feet.

"See?" The little girl jumped up and down, giggling. "I knew you couldn't get me!"

"The day isn't over yet, Martha Marie Starling."

Martha Marie. His throat tightened, and a rush of warmth filled his heart. Martha Marie had been his mother's name.

"Can we go sledding now?" the boy asked. "You promised."

"We can if you two are very, very good and promise to do exactly as I say."

"We will," the children said together.

"Then, I guess it's time to go," Regina said. "Would you like for me to pull the sled?"

"I will," the boy said. "I like to."

"Very well, then, Sammy," Regina said. "Follow me."

Lucas followed, too, but some distance behind them, out of sight. Twigs cracked under his feet. The scent of pinecones and the slushy sound of boots on melting snow reminded him of other visits to the woods when he and his sisters were children. He might never get the chance to see his eldest sister, Clara, but it wasn't too late to connect with Regina—though he couldn't imagine that he would.

Now that he knew Honor didn't live in Pine Falls, he would be leaving town as soon as he'd saved enough for a stagecoach ticket. He had a farm to manage, calves to sell—and a woman to marry, if Ruby still wanted him. But before he left town, Lucas hoped to see a lot more of Regina, the children and the pregnant young woman—from a distance, of course.

Lucas continued to watch as Regina and the children climbed to the top of a hill that looked a little too steep for sledding.

"I get to go down first." The boy said, positioning the sled at the top of the hill and climbing on.

The little girl turned to him, one hand on her hip and the other clutching her doll. "You went down first last time, Sammy Starling. It's my time to do it first."

"Wait!" Regina exclaimed. "That side of the hill looks dangerous!"

But it was too late. Sammy started the downward slide at a rapid speed, and a tree loomed just ahead.

"Look out!" Regina shouted. "Sammy!"

Lucas stared in horror as the sled hit the thick trunk head-on. "No!" he charged out of his hiding place and raced toward the injured child.

Regina was already there, wiping blood from Sammy's forehead. As a former cowboy with a long history of cattle drives, Lucas knew some doctoring skills. When he reached them, he knelt, removed his jacket, and applied direct pressure to the child's head wound. It wasn't enough, but it was all he could think to do.

Chapter Eighteen

※

Lucas and Regina carried the unconscious child into the house. For days, Lucas had watched the Starling home from a distance, never expecting to go inside. Now, all he could think about was little Sammy.

"What happened to my baby?" a woman shouted, rushing forward.

"There was an accident, Margaret," Regina said, continuing down the entry hall.

"Mama!" Martha Marie called out. The little girl reached out to her mother. "Sammy's hurt, Mama. Bad."

The woman picked up her daughter and held her, but her eyes were on the injured boy. "Dan! Get in here! Quick!" she called.

Lucas and Regina entered a small parlor. A young man appeared before them. "Oh, no!" he cried, turning pale. "What happened?"

"Hit his head on a tree while he was sledding," Lucas said.

Lucas felt sorry for everyone. He assumed the man was the little boy's father. He'd already identified Margaret as the young woman he had seen that day at the Starling Café, as well as the child's mother. If only there was more he could do.

Lucas noticed only heavy green drapes and dark paneling as he and Regina made their way to one of the bedrooms. When they laid little Sammy on the bed, the entire household gathered around the injured child.

"I'll need sheets for bandages," Lucas said calmly. Nobody seemed to notice that he was a total stranger.

"Sheets?" Margaret glanced around as if she were confused. "I can't even think where they are."

Regina grabbed a sheet from a shelf nearby. "Here." She handed it to Lucas.

"Tear it in strips. And hurry!" he instructed.

"Dan," Margaret said in a shaky voice, "g-go get the doctor!"

"I'm on my way, dear," Dan said, heading for the door.

"Is Sammy gonna die, Mama?" Martha Marie asked.

"No, he's going to be fine." Margaret pressed the little girl's dark head against her chest.

Suddenly another woman, an elderly lady with gray hair, appeared near the door. She moved forward. "Come to Grandma, sweetheart." She reached for the child.

The little girl shook her head and held tight to her mother.

"Go with Grandma Starling, Martha Marie."

The woman took the child from her mother's arms. Then she carried Martha Marie from the room.

By the time Dan Starling led the doctor into the sickroom, Lucas had managed to stop the bleeding from Sammy's head wound. The doctor took one look as his patient and shooed everyone out, except the boy's father.

They all went into the parlor to wait, although Lucas longed to stay with the doctor and listen to what he had to say about the child's condition. The cut on the boy's head looked deep. The bump could be serious.

For several long minutes, no one spoke, then Dan joined the family in the parlor. Lucas thought he still looked very upset and discouraged. He sat soberly in a chair by the child's door. Then he stared at Lucas for a moment. At last, he turned to Regina.

"Aunt Regina, who is this man?"

"I'll explain later. But first, tell us what the doctor said about Sammy. Will he...will Sammy be all right?"

"Dr. Young didn't tell me anything," Dan Starling slumped in his chair. "He said he would talk to us later. We'll just have to wait."

Lucas sat in a maple rocker. He'd never liked chairs that moved, yet he found himself rocking back and forth. He also trembled, and, for the first time in years, he wasn't shaking because he wanted alcohol. He was truly concerned about Sammy.

"I think it's time we all prayed." Regina glanced at Lucas. "But first, I never got the chance to introduce our guest." She gestured toward her brother and then to the elderly woman Lucas saw earlier. "Mrs. Starling, I would like you to know my only brother, Lawrence Smith."

Lucas nodded. "Ma'am."

"Mrs. Starling is Sammy's grandmother." Regina's gaze shifted to the child's parents. "Dan and Margaret Starling and Martha Marie, I would like to present Lawrence Smith. As I just said, he's my brother. Clara's and mine. That makes him your uncle, Margaret—your uncle Lawrence."

"Glad to know you, sir," Sammy's father said. "And I appreciate what you did for our son."

Lucas nodded.

Margaret appeared to be trying to smile through her tears. "Hello, Uncle."

Uncle. Honor had called him Uncle until Lucas had told her not to anymore.

He gazed at Margaret. "Hello."

She was the one who reminded him so much of Clara. Margaret had been in the family way that day at the café. Now she held a baby in her arms.

"What's the baby's name?" Lucas asked.

"Regina Ann." Margaret turned to Regina. "She's named for Aunt Regina." Margaret paused, looking back at Lucas. "Haven't I seen you before?"

"Yes," Regina put in, "you have. But we won't go into that now. As I said, we need to pray. And since Lawrence is the oldest male member of this family—" She gazed at Lucas. "Will you lead us in prayer?"

He shook his head. "I'm sorry, but I ain't—I reckon I'd rather you did it."

"Very well, then." Regina bowed her head, closed her eyes and folded her hands just as the Klines had done. When she finished praying, she said, "Amen."

The others echoed it.

Lucas wanted to say "Amen," too, but didn't. He hoped the prayer would be answered. No point in messing up Sammy's chances with something he might tack on at the end.

He glanced at his niece, Margaret. Tears still streamed from her eyes. Regina wept, too. Little Martha Marie sat on the floor at her mother's feet, playing with her rag doll. But when she glanced up and saw the women crying, she began to sob, too.

Didn't they believe little Sammy would recover? Didn't they have hope? What happened to that Christian faith of theirs? Reverend Kline had said that God answered the prayers of those who truly turned to him.

The doctor opened the door, everyone turned, staring at him. Lucas looked for some indication that the news would be hopeful, but the doctor's expression didn't tell him anything.

Dan jumped out of his chair. Margaret got up, too, handing her baby to Regina. Then they just stood looking at the doctor, waiting.

"Mr. and Mrs. Starling." The doctor smiled. "I think your prayers have been answered."

Margaret moved toward him. "Do you mean...?"

"Yes. Sammy's awake and doing extremely well."

"Praise the Lord," Margaret whispered.

"When I first examined your son, I felt sure Sammy wouldn't make it. But a few minutes ago everything changed." Tears filled the doctor's eyes. He removed his spectacles and wiped them with a white handkerchief. "We'll need to keep watching him. But he's improved tremendously. I was amazed. Keep those prayers coming."

"The Lord healed our son," Dan stated firmly.

"Yes," the doctor said, "I know."

Later that evening, Lucas and Regina sat facing each other before the redbrick fireplace. They held cups of hot chocolate, and except for their whispered voices in the semidarkness and the sounds of the fire in the hearth, the house was silent. Lucas needed time to be with his sister, to discuss what happened that day and to think about all that had happened in his life since he'd last seen her.

Margaret was with Sammy in the downstairs bedroom.

Dan Starling, his mother, Martha Marie and the baby were all upstairs, sleeping.

Regina leaned forward, moving closer to him. "Tell me about your life, Lawrence. You're my very own brother. Yet I know absolutely nothing about you."

"I don't know nothing about you, either," he said. "Why, I don't even know if you're married."

"I was, but my husband died some years ago. His name was James Peters."

"Peters. I've heard that name somewhere or other."

"I doubt that you knew him. I met James a year or so after you moved away. We have a son."

"I'm mighty glad for you, Regina. Reckon I always wanted a son. Now tell me about Clara? Is she...?"

"Yes. Clara and her husband died of a fever five years ago. Now they are with the Lord."

"Is Margaret Clara's daughter?"

"Yes."

"Wish I'd known about Clara. That she died and all." He swallowed. "And Mama and Pappy?"

"They're dead, too, Lawrence. I'm sorry to deliver such bad news all in one evening."

"Don't fret none. Just give me a minute to get it all straight in my mind. My memory ain't what it once was."

"Neither is mine." She hesitated. "Are you married?"

"My wife died in October."

"I'm sorry. Did you have children?"

"She couldn't have any, but we raised her niece like she was our own. Then the girl ran away 'fore my Harriet was cold in the grave. Don't know why. I came to Pine Falls to fetch her home. Now I learned that she ain't even here. She's staying at a rooming house over in Hearten."

"Hearten?" Regina's eyes widened, and her voice sounded louder. "What's the girl's name?"

"Honor McCall. Why?"

"No!"

Regina's face paled. Lucas thought she might be about to faint.

"What's wrong, Regina? What did I say?"

A look of pure horror shone in her face. "Honor McCall is living at my rooming house in Hearten. And I think my son, your nephew, is sweet on her."

His heart seemed to be doing flip-flops. In that moment, all his hope for a relationship with his sister and the rest of his relatives vanished. He took a breath and exhaled, trying to hide the sense of loss he felt.

"Honor said she had an uncle. And my son told me that Honor called him Lucas. I think she was afraid of Lucas. Are you that man, Lawrence? Are you Lucas?"

His muscles tensed even more, the way they always did when hate and anger boiled deep inside him. His hands became fists. Lucas stood, his jaw like stone. He had to get out of the house before he hurt somebody.

"Are you Lucas Scythe?" she exclaimed. "Tell me!"

He glanced toward the door. "Yes," he shouted. "I am."

Without another word, Lucas ran out of the house and down the darkened street. His hands shook. He felt trapped, discovered. He stopped and glanced back. The house looked dark except for one dim light in the parlor by the fireplace.

He needed a drink. Now!

Lucas kicked the trunk of a nearby tree. Then he stood a moment longer, shivering in the snow and cold. He'd left his jacket back at the house, but there was no chance he would go back for it now. Besides, his jacket was soaked with blood.

A lamp glowed in the distance, a few blocks down the street. He started running. With the street lamp to guide him, he should be able to find the nearest saloon.

He should never have allowed that preacher to talk him into giving up alcohol. It was never going to work, not for a drunk like Lucas Scythe.

In the bright light of morning, Honor was polishing the pump organ in the parlor, but her thoughts were on Lucas. She couldn't get him out of her mind.

Mrs. Peters's six-shooter was still under her bed, and nobody was likely to find it there. But if the time ever came, would she be able to use it, to pull the trigger? She hoped it never came to that.

She inhaled the perfume of beeswax and continued her chore. Dipping the cloth into the can of wax again, she thought she heard something. She stopped and listened hard.

She heard the scrape of the entry door opening, and Honor turned, trembling.

Timmy Rivers bounced inside, followed by Jeth. The mere sight of them washed away all thoughts of Lucas.

"Timmy!" Honor smiled. "What are you doing here?"

"I came to see you, Miss McCall."

"Me?"

"Yes, you," Jeth said.

Honor looked behind the child, and her gaze met Jeth's. Time stopped—at least for her. She glanced away so her feelings for him wouldn't become apparent.

When she looked back, she noticed that snowflakes fell from Jeth's and Timmy's coats and caps onto the polished floor. Honor hardly cared.

Jeth frowned, looking down at his wet boots. "Why, we're tracking snow inside, Timmy." He looked at Honor

and smiled as though he hoped to make amends. "Sorry."
He reached out and pulled Timmy back into the entry hall.

"We forgot to wipe our shoes on the rug, Timmy. Guess
we better do it, don't you think?"

"Yes, sir."

Honor watched while they wiped their shoes and boots.
"Why don't we go into the kitchen?" she suggested. Honor
took their coats and hats and hung them on hooks in the hall.
Then she continued toward the kitchen.

"Hope your mother isn't sick again," Honor said to
the child.

"No, Mama's not sick. I came to thank you for my birthday gift." He grinned. "Thank you, ma'am. I like my book
very much."

"I'm glad. Have you read it yet?"

"No, but the reverend and I plan to, don't we, Reverend
Peters?"

Jeth nodded and grinned.

"We're going to read the book together," Timmy said.

Jeth held up the book on kite-making for Timmy and
Honor to see. Until that instant, she hadn't known Jeth had
it with him.

"Sit there at the table, then, you two," Honor said, "while
I get us some hot chocolate. Then you can tell me all about
those plans of yours, Timmy."

"The book has drawings in it." Timmy sat down at the
table beside Jeth. "And it tells exactly how to make a kite
that will really and truly fly. Reverend Peters and I are going
to study the drawings in the book today and learn how to
do it right, aren't we."

"We certainly are." Jeth pulled a roll of string from his
pocket and set it on the table. "And remember, Timmy, getting the right kind of string, the right kind of paper and the

right kind of wood is very important if we want your kite to fly. And we might need to take some wood off the sticks we use before making the frame. Heavy wood won't do with kites. You have to make the wood lighter. Ever done any whittling, boy?"

Timmy shook his head. "Mama won't let me play with knives."

"You have a wise mama. You can help cut the paper and wind the string." Jeth opened the book and pointed to one of the drawings. "Now, there's a kite!"

A few moments later, Honor set three cups of hot chocolate on the table. Then she came around behind them and leaned over their shoulders. The drawing they studied looked identical to all the other drawings in the book. She wondered what they found so unique about that one, but decided not to ask.

Jeth glanced at her over his shoulder and smiled. "We're going to start building the kite today, but Timmy probably won't be able to fly it until springtime. Now, isn't this the best set of plans you've ever seen for a kite?"

"Oh, yes," Honor said. "That drawing is special. Anyone can see that. I'm glad you boys chose that one instead of one of the others in the book."

Smiling, Honor sat down at the table and drank her chocolate. She didn't intend to say much. She didn't need to. Honor enjoyed just being there, watching the two of them have fun together on a snowy December day.

Jeth was going to make a wonderful father. She tried not to wonder who the mother of his children might be.

Lucas lay on the floor of his rented room. Some sound had wakened him. He yawned. What time was it? He glanced toward the east window. The window and wooden shutters were partly open. Snowflakes plugged the spaces between the slats, and more snow poured in from outside. He would get up and close the window when he found the desire to do it, not before.

A loud rap sounded at the door. Why couldn't people just leave him alone?

Lucas got up slowly, wobbled to the door and opened it. Regina stood on the landing outside, holding his jacket. Obviously, she'd washed it.

"Well." His sister sent him a smile he had not expected. "Aren't you going to invite me in? It's cold out here."

"Shore, come on in."

Lucas wasn't surprised to find snow on the ground, but he hadn't expected to see so much. Of course, he had no memory of anything that had taken place after he left the Starlings'.

Regina stood just inside his rented room, looking slightly bewildered.

"Let me warn you, Regina," he said, nodding toward his untidy room, "I ran out of wood for the stove."

"I'll keep my cape on."

Regina put his jacket on a hook. He closed the door, then shoved his dirty clothes from the chair and motioned for his sister to take a seat. When she did, he settled at the foot of his unmade bed.

She eyed the empty whiskey bottles. "Are you drunk, Lawrence?"

"Let's say I'm hung on the clothesline to dry."

"Then dry up. I have a lot I want to say."

"If you're trying to get me to stop drinking, save yourself the trouble. I ain't never gonna quit. I like drinking."

The pain that he saw in her eyes made him feel guilty. He glanced away.

"You know, Lawrence, there are some things we just shouldn't do, even if we enjoy doing them." She cleared her throat. "For example, remember how I always broke out in a rash when I ate strawberries?"

Lucas nodded.

"You might not know this, but I dearly love strawberries, especially when I dip them in honey. Nothing tastes better. But I can't eat strawberries because they make me sick. I break out. And your drinking makes you sick. That's why you shouldn't drink, no matter how good liquor might taste to you."

"Strawberries and alcohol ain't the same."

"No, but they affect some people in the same way."

Since he had no interest in hearing more on the subject, Lucas studied his bare feet. His toes felt like ice. He reached for a pair of dirty socks beside him on the bed and put them on.

It was time to look his sister square in the eye and try to change the subject. Either that or throw her out in the snow.

"How's Sammy doing?" he asked.

"Very well, thank you. God is good."

"Then why am I a drunk? I tried to stop, really tried. Even went to church once here in Pine Falls. I wanted to be a good person like the rest of my family. But it ain't working. Nothing ever does."

"You can't change yourself. Nobody can. You must become a Christian first. Let the Lord take care of your drinking habit."

"Well, with you and all them other good folks around, God don't need my name written down in that book of His."

Even as he said the words he regretted them. These past weeks, especially, he'd felt a nagging desire to belong in such a book. But he couldn't tell his sister that. She might think he was just making excuses for what he'd done to Honor and Harriet. Regina couldn't know that he'd hurt Ruby, too.

"You must mean the Lamb's Book of Life." She hesitated. "God loves you, Lawrence. He really does, and He wants your name written in His book. People whose names are written in God's book will go to heaven when they die."

"Then what must I do to get my name in that book you mentioned?"

"Repent! That's the first step."

"Repent? You mean, admit I done wrong?"

"Yes."

Was Regina out of her mind? Nobody would willingly admit to all the things Lucas had done.

She got down on her knees in front of her chair and motioned for Lucas to join her. But he wouldn't, couldn't. He didn't know how to be the kind of man everybody had always wanted him to be. Besides, it was too late—for him.

She closed her eyes, and her lips began to move. He knew she was praying. For the first time in years, he wanted to pray, too. If he knelt beside her, would she know he was there? And if it didn't work out, would she also know that?

Careful not to make a sound, he got down on his knees beside his sister and shut his eyes. But nothing happened. Now what? His mind went blank. Being on his knees didn't seem right. He wasn't worthy. He might as well face the fact that he could never be good enough. He started to rise.

"Get back down, Lawrence," she said.

He'd been so quiet. And she hadn't opened her eyes once. How had she known?

"We can pray together," she added.

"I—I can't, Regina. I don't know how to pray."

"Just repeat what I say."

Slowly, he got back down on his knees. He folded his hands and shut his eyes.

"Heavenly Father," she prayed aloud. *"I have not followed Your commandments or walked in Your ways, and I am truly sorry—"*

"Wait!" Lucas looked over at Regina and touched her wrist. "I'll never be able to remember all that."

"Say it in your own words, then. The Lord will like that better anyway."

Lucas nodded—more to himself than to Regina.

"Heavenly Father, I ain't never followed Your commandments or done much of anything right. Anyways, I shore am sorry. I'd be much obliged if You would forgive my sins and come into my heart and life right about now. Regina and Reverend Kline said You would come if I asked Ya to. Well, I reckon I'm asking. And I'm asking in the name of that son of Yours, Jesus. Like I used to hear Mama do. Amen."

Lucas remained on his knees for a long time. He wasn't exactly praying because he didn't know what else to say, but he wanted God to know he was available for service now. Alternately, he felt shy and ashamed, and then full of joy.

All at once, Lucas felt as though a heavy weight had been lifted from his shoulders. He was sure he must be ten pounds lighter. When tears moistened his eyes, he knew with certainty that he was in the presence of God. It was the first time in his life that he felt truly clean.

Reverend Kline had said that God saved a person as soon as that person requested salvation, but Lucas had spent a lot of years wrecking his life and the lives of others. Lucas would stay on his knees until he sensed that God had entered his name in the Lamb's Book of Life.

At last, he rose. A new sense of purpose and a well-spring of love that he planned to share with others filled his heart.

"I need to tell the Klines what I done," he finally said to Regina. "Let them know I repented and all. I also have to tell 'em I'm leaving Pine Falls."

"Leaving?"

He nodded. "I've got debts to pay and a ranch to run, and there's a woman I gotta see by the name of Ruby. I plan to marry her—if she'll have me." He gazed at his sister, searching for the right words. "And Regina, there's something I want you to do for me."

"What's that?"

Lucas went to the chest and opened the top drawer. He pulled out the pearl necklace and handed it to his sister. "I'd be obliged if ya would give these here pearls to Honor. They belonged to her aunt and to her grandmother before that. I think she should have them."

"Oh, Lawrence, I think so, too. I really do. And I know she'll be so grateful when I give them to her."

Lucas didn't know what else to say, but a new emotion swept over him. He smiled, wondering: Is this what folks call happiness?

Ten days before Christmas, rain and a cold wind swooped down from the north. Before getting out of bed that morning, Honor heard the patter of rain hitting the tin roof, then the sounds disappeared as the downpour turned into softly falling snow.

She snuggled under her covers, protected from the frosty air in her bedroom. The fire in the woodstove had died during the night. With her head on the feather pillow, Honor watched her breath puff out like smoke, curling, then slowly fading away. Needing to start her day, she gathered her courage, threw back the covers and got up.

Shivering, she stoked the black cast-iron stove and put in fresh firewood. In the dim light, she dressed quickly. Then she stood at her window, looking out at the golden sunrise, and at a white, fairy-tale world of incredible beauty.

A thick layer of snow covered the ground and the drive-way in front of the boardinghouse. Trees glistened like silver. Soon, children in brightly colored caps and neck scarves would be coasting down the hill beyond the road on wooden sleds with metal rims. When the water hardened, no doubt they would be skating on the frozen pond.

Honor was reluctant to leave her spot by the window, and by the time she went downstairs to the kitchen, Belinda was already there, rolling out biscuit dough.

"Are we ever going to have a Christmas tree?" Belinda teased. "The guests keep asking, especially Mrs. Clark and Mrs. Davis."

"Did Mrs. Peters put up a tree every year?" Honor asked.

"Always."

"Then I guess we should put up one, too." Honor grabbed the skillet from a hook hanging from the ceiling and reached for the bacon. "Belinda, would you like to go out later and look for a Christmas tree? Just the two of us? Might be fun."

"Why not get our pastor to help you find a tree?" Belinda suggested. "With all this cold weather, he probably won't venture out on church duties today. He should have time to help in your search."

"Belinda Grant, are you matchmaking again?"

"Me?" Belinda feigned innocence, pressed her hand to her chest and fluttered her eyelashes. "How could you accuse me of such a thing? So, are you going to ask our minister or not?"

Honor shrugged, pretending she had no idea what Belinda was talking about. "Ask him what?"

"To take you out to find a Christmas tree, of course."

"Oh, that." Honor hesitated, wondering how to reply. "Well, what if I should ask him and he says no. The reverend's a busy man, you know."

Belinda shook her head. "The reverend won't say no, Miss McCall. Not to you, anyway."

Chapter Nineteen

⚜

After breakfast, Honor noticed when Jeth left the formal dining room. Before he reached the door, he looked back at Honor and grinned. "That breakfast you fixed was mighty good. I gotta have another cup of your coffee."

Honor followed him into the kitchen. "Go sit at the table. I'll bring your coffee to you."

"I'm not about to turn down an offer like that, especially from a pretty lady in a blue dress."

Honor turned her back on him and grimaced, recalling Selma's green dress and the fiasco that had resulted when she'd worn it. The thought of Jeth's late wife made Honor wonder again who his future wife might be. Her thoughts settled on only one young woman: Lucy Jordan. Honor bit her lower lip. An instant before, she'd been in a good mood. Now all her good humor had turned sour. How quickly thoughts and emotions could change. Jeth had said that only the Lord could turn things around again. But for some reason, she didn't feel like praying.

"Speaking of pretty ladies," Honor said with a trace of sarcasm, "I won't be able to teach Miss Jordan's reading lesson this week, with all the work I have to do here and all."

"I told Lucy that we would delay the lessons until after Mama gets back," Jeth said easily, surprising Honor. "You have enough to do without tutoring besides."

"But I—"

"Need to make more money. I know. You mentioned that. But you'll still have the extra money you get doing alterations, won't you? And you've already paid me back for that coat. Why, you must have a bundle saved by now. What do you plan to do with all that money?"

"Pay my debts." She glanced toward the door leading to the hallway. "Now if you will excuse me, I need to check on the mess room."

But before she could make her escape, Belinda burst into the kitchen from the dining room. "Have you asked the reverend yet?" she queried.

"Asked me what?"

"I wondered if Miss Honor had invited you to escort her to the woods today. We need a suitable Christmas tree for the boardinghouse. Our boarders want one, and so do I."

"Then of course Miss McCall and I will go out in search of a tree this very morning." Jeth turned to Honor. "When can you be ready?"

"She can be ready as soon as we finish the breakfast dishes," Belinda replied. "And she need not be back in time to help with the noon meal. We're just having leftovers."

"Then, Miss McCall, I'll meet you on the back porch, as soon as you've finished your chores."

Honor closed her lips firmly. Comments were unnecessary. She'd been outranked as well as overruled.

When the last dish was dried and put away, Honor saw Jeth through the kitchen window. He was standing on the back porch, with a grin on his face that reminded her of the friendly circus clown who had paraded by the general store in Falling Rock once when she was a child. The clown, with blue hair and a red ball for a nose, had been dressed in a red, white and blue striped suit. He'd given Honor a special wave and smiled, just like Jeth was doing now.

Honor felt silly waving at Jeth for no good reason. She'd just talked to him and served him his breakfast. But when he kept waving and smiling at her, she laughed and waved back.

"Run along now," Belinda insisted. "If you don't, the reverend is liable to come in here to get you and track up my clean kitchen floor in the process. And don't forget your coat, your hat and your hand-warmer. It's cold outside."

Honor smiled, pulling her garments from the hook by the back door. She'd learned to love Belinda like an older sister. Still, sometimes she wondered if the feisty widow recalled that it was Honor who was in charge of the boardinghouse until Mrs. Peters returned, not Belinda Grant.

The flooring on the back porch usually creaked when Honor stepped out the kitchen door. That morning, the wooden planks were silent.

"Better be careful." Jeth offered her his arm. "The porch is wet and icy."

Ignoring his arm, Honor took another step and slid several inches. "Oh, no!"

Jeth grabbed her. "Easy there."

She stopped moving, but she still felt unsteady on her feet. Paralyzed with embarrassment and the fear of falling, she glanced up at Jeth. He grinned, looking amused. Seeing the humor in his blue eyes, Honor giggled. Then they were both laughing.

"Let's go over there and sit down," Jeth suggested.

"All right."

He helped her off the porch and down the steps.

Mrs. Peters had built a rock bench for her guests, so they could relax and enjoy the outdoors. The bare branches of plants and trees surrounded it. The shrubs, which had been cut practically to the ground, were covered with a sprinkling of snow and ice. Mrs. Peters had assured Honor that in the spring all those dead plants and trees would come back to life. Mrs. Peters called it a kind of rebirth, a gentle reminder that Jesus died and rose again.

"Sit here and rest a little." Jeth gestured toward the bench. "Just looking at you, I figure your heart is probably racing faster than a rabbit with a bobcat on its tail."

Honor went right over, sat down, and then immediately jumped up. She should have looked first. The bench was encased in frost. It was like sitting on a block of ice.

"Sorry, ma'am, I should have known the rock bench would be cold. Are you all right?"

"Of course."

Even with her coat, Honor was cold almost constantly now. However, she was determined not to complain and decided to change the subject.

"I noticed that you got another letter from your mother. Was she able to locate your uncle?"

"Not yet, but she's still trying." He grinned. "I expect her to find Uncle Lawrence any day now."

Honor wanted to question Jeth about John Crammer, to find out what else he knew. Perhaps she should simply blurt out what was on her mind and take her chances.

"Did you ever hear from John Crammer again?" she finally asked. "The man from Falling Rock who wrote to you?"

His smile faded. "I know who John Crammer is. But I never heard from him after the first letter I got."

Good, she thought.

Honor looked down at her snow-covered shoes, then back at Jeth. "I've been wondering if your cousin had her baby yet."

"Yes, Margaret had a little girl. Named her for my mother. And Regina Ann Starling weighed six pounds."

"How's the baby's mother doing?"

"Margaret's doing fine, but she's exhausted. Three children is a lot to worry about, I guess. She's trying to talk Mama into staying until after the new year. But Mama said no. Guess she's had enough of babies and children for a while."

Honor forced a laugh, but slowly, her laugh became a real one. Jeth had said that laughter was like a medicine. She was beginning to believe it.

"Maybe she misses Dr. Harris," Honor said.

"That's possible."

"When is your mother coming home?"

"She'll be home by Christmas. But I don't know exactly when she will get here."

Honor nodded. At least she's still coming, she thought.

"Shall we go on and find the tree now?" she asked.

"Absolutely."

As they strolled down the snowy path, Jeth pulled a sled by a rope. He put his free arm around Honor and gave her a quick squeeze.

A pleasant tingle shot through her. Honor glanced at his hand on her shoulder. He shouldn't be holding her, and she shouldn't enjoy it. But she did, even knowing that the sweet embraces would only make her leaving that much harder.

"I'm holding on to you so you won't slip," he insisted. "You wouldn't want to take the chance you might fall and hurt yourself, would you?"

"Of course not."

An icy wind whistled around the corner of the big house, blowing Honor's long hair in front of her eyes. She pushed back a stray curl and held it in place with one hand.

"What are you thinking, Honor Rose McCall?" he asked.

Surprised that he remembered her middle name, Honor gazed up at Jeth and grinned. "Why did you call me Rose just now?"

"I like your name. Honor Rose sounds good, to me, anyway. And by the way, you're shivering again."

"I am not." Looking down, she realized she was hugging her shoulders. "All right, maybe I am." She hesitated. "You said once that the Rose of Sharon was mentioned in the Bible. But I was never able to find anything about it. Would you mind explaining that to me now?"

"With pleasure." He smiled. "Sharon is a place, a beautiful location in the Holy Land where roses were said to grow. In the second chapter of the Song of Solomon, the Scriptures say, 'I am the rose of Sharon, and the lily of the valleys.' Jesus has many names in the Bible. Some believe that one of them is the Rose of Sharon. However, others think the passage refers to Israel and the church."

"That's interesting," she said.

"Yes, it is."

A wooded area just ahead captured Honor's attention. Jeth followed her gaze.

"What kind of a tree should we be looking for this Christmas?" he asked.

"Frankly, I like pines."

"Then that's just what we'll get." He looked away for an instant. "My late wife liked pine trees, too. In fact, in many ways you and Selma are much alike."

"Me? No." Honor shook her head.

Mrs. Peters had said that her daughter-in-law had been a wonderful Christian. Though Honor thought of herself as a Christian now, she could never meet Selma's standards. Jeth was merely being kind.

"I remember," he went on, "one Christmas season especially. Selma and I spent all day looking for a tree and never did find one she liked. At last I said, 'Wife, I'm tired of looking. I'm going to cut down the next tree I see.' And there it was. The prettiest pine I'd ever laid eyes on, and when it was decorated... Well, it looked beautiful." He hesitated. "You know, Miss McCall, you've never told me anything about your life before you came here. Did you and your family go looking for the perfect tree at Christmastime, too?"

Honor stopped. "If you don't mind, I'd rather not talk about my home life. Our house wasn't a happy place to be."

"But surely you can tell me something. Did you live in town or out in the country?"

"We lived on a farm. And that's all I'm going to say."

"Then I'll tell you a little more about my life. I grew up right here on this property. The house and grounds belonged to my grandparents. My father also grew up here."

"You never knew your father, did you?"

He shook his head and kicked a loose rock with the toe of his boot. "My mother said he loved to go fishing. He died in a boating accident soon after I was born."

Honor considered her options. He'd shared part of his past with her, and she had heard emotion in his voice, stronger than any she'd heard previously. She had the sudden urge to tell Jeth more about her past. She trusted him. But revealing all her secrets might inadvertently unlock a door that would be better left closed.

Jeth reached down, scooped up two handfuls of snow and molded them into a ball. Turning toward the horse pens, he drew back his arm and threw the snowball. It sailed threw the air and hit the wooden fence. *Plop*.

He turned back to Honor and looked her in the eye. "For a long time, I've had the feeling that your uncle was unkind to you. Was he, Honor? Did Lucas Scythe treat you badly?"

"I told you. We quarreled."

Honor wanted to be honest with Jeth, to tell him the truth about Lucas, but she would be leaving in a few days. There was no reason to bring up unhappy topics now. She needed to focus on something else. A beautifully shaped pine tree stood just off to their right. It looked about six feet high, and she imagined how it would look when it was decorated with popcorn, candy and paper flowers.

"That's the one," she exclaimed.

"What are you talking about?"

"That pine over there." She pointed to the tree. "It's perfect and just the Christmas tree I want for the boardinghouse this year."

"Okay, if that's the tree you want, that's the one we'll get— But sooner or later, you're going to tell me what really happened between you and your uncle."

On Saturday morning, Jeth sat beside Timmy Rivers in the covered wagon. He'd left the boardinghouse right after breakfast and had arrived at the Riverses' home early.

Timmy was Jeth's inspiration. Were it not for the boy, Jeth might never have come up with an idea for getting several young men and boys involved in church activities. Now he would find out whether his plan would work.

After a short visit with Timmy's parents, Jeth had invited the little boy to drive out to the Sharp Ranch with him. They were on the way there now.

Jeth smiled, looking down at Timmy. "You remembered to bring your book on kite-making, didn't you?"

"Yes, sir." Timmy lifted up the book that he'd gotten for his birthday.

"Good boy. And by the way, you're going to like Willie Sharp. He's a little older than you are, but he's a good boy, too."

Willie Sharp and his mother had attended services at the church on several occasions, but Jeth hadn't been able to talk to them. Each time, they'd arrived late and left before the service had ended.

Sheriff Green had asked Jeth to keep an eye on that family for him, to report anything unusual. Since Jeth wanted to visit the family again anyway, stopping by the ranch with Timmy seemed like the perfect solution.

Jeth had a lot to think about, and driving his team of horses always helped him to get things straight in his mind.

He'd wrapped Honor's engagement ring in white paper and tied it with a pink bow, but he hadn't put it under the Christmas tree yet. The gift was tucked in the bottom drawer of the desk in his bedroom. Honor wouldn't find it there.

Honor wasn't the Christian woman Selma had been, but she appeared to be growing in her knowledge of God and the Bible.

Jeth and Selma had grown up together. They'd been childhood sweethearts. He'd known everything there was to know about Selma before they married. But Honor's life before he'd met her was still a mystery.

The few things he did know about Honor were not encouraging. Some might say she could never be a proper minister's wife. And yet...

Timmy shifted restlessly. Jeth glanced down at the child, who had leaned his head on Jeth's arm and appeared to be falling asleep. Jeth grinned and looked back at the road.

The child's enthusiasm for kites would serve as Jeth's secret weapon. He hoped Timmy would convince Willie Sharp and the others that kite-making was fun and so was learning about the Lord. And if kites didn't appeal to Willie, there was always the hard candy that Jeth had put in his pocket as a treat.

Jeth stopped the wagon in front of the Sharp home. As he tied up the reins, he looked around. Three horses were penned nearby. None of them was red.

The carpenters were gone now. Apparently, the house repairs had been completed. Would he finally meet Mr. Sharp and his older sons? If not, he hoped Willie and his mother would be home.

He gave Timmy a gentle nudge. "Wake up, boy. It's time to go inside."

Timmy yawned. "Now, where did you say we were going?"

"To the Sharp Ranch. We're here now. The Sharps have a son, Willie. Remember, I told you about him."

"Is Willie the one who wants to build a kite?"

"Willie might not know anything about kites. You've got to be his teacher and invite him to church and to boys' fun night."

"Oh, yes. That's where boys my age get together at the

church and make things. When did you say fun night was going to start?"

"After the first of the year."

"And can we ring the church bell sometimes on fun nights? I sure think that would be fun."

Grinning, Jeth jumped from the wagon. "We'll have to see about that." He swung Timmy down. "Come on now. Let's go inside and talk about kites."

Mrs. Sharp's outlook on life seemed to have changed since Jeth's first visit. Her house looked clean and neat and so did her clothes. Her hair had a shine to it, and he saw a sparkle in her eyes. Jeth had thought Mrs. Sharp was an old woman the first time he came. She looked much younger now. Best of all, she and Willie were in church every Sunday.

"Where's Willie?" Jeth asked when they had settled in chairs in the parlor. "Timmy here wants to meet him."

"He's playing. I'll go get him." Mrs. Sharp got to her feet. "Now, you sit there. I'll be right back."

A minute later Willie raced into the parlor, smiling from ear to ear. "Did ya brung me any can—? Did ya brung me anything, Preacher?"

"Willie!" his mother scolded. "That ain't nice. Now sit down and behave."

"That's all right, ma'am," Jeth said. "I brought candy for the boys to eat later."

Willie's eyes glowed. "You did?"

Jeth nodded. Now all Jeth had to do was get Willie interested in church and the Bible.

"Have you ever made a kite, Willie?" Jeth asked.

"No, sir, I ain't never. Least, not one what will fly."

"Well, Timmy Rivers here knows all about kite-making, and he's got a book that tells just how to do it. Would you like for Timmy to show you his book?"

"Yes, sir, I'd be obliged."

"Then why don't you take Timmy to your room or someplace and talk, while your mother and I sit here and visit?"

"Yes, sir."

Jeth didn't find out much about the Sharp gang during the time he spent with Mrs. Sharp. But she promised to stay after church on Sunday long enough to meet some of the folks in the congregation. She also promised to drive Willie to the church on fun night so that he could learn how to build kites.

Jeth smiled as he lifted Timmy into the wagon. It looked like his plans for bringing the young people in his congregation to the Lord just might work.

On the morning of December twenty-third, Honor stood in the middle of the kitchen floor, sweeping. Her belongings were packed in a potato sack and ready to go, and she'd returned the six-shooter to Mrs. Peters's room. Her gifts for Jeth, his mother and Belinda were in the parlor under the Christmas tree.

Honor had saved enough to pay back what she had stolen from the church in Falling Rock, with enough left over to live on for a while. Her purse, with the money inside, and her other possessions waited by the front door. Mrs. Peters was expected home today or tomorrow. All Honor needed to do now was to find the words to tell Jeth that she was leaving Hearten, Colorado—forever.

It wouldn't be easy to leave Jeth. She knew now that she loved him. However, stealing money from a church was still on her conscience, and she was convinced that she wasn't a proper companion for a preacher of the Gospel.

Lucas hadn't come to get her after receiving John Crammer's letter as she'd expected. But she knew he would arrive in a week or two to see Elmer's filly, and she intended to be far away before then.

Jeth drifted inside and took a stance behind one of the kitchen chairs. Honor felt weak. She must tell him she was leaving now, and she still had no idea what words to use.

Honor glanced down at her broom. "You got another letter from your mother."

"Did I?"

"Yes." She couldn't meet his eyes. "It's on the desk in your office."

"Honor," he said with authority, "stop what you're doing and come over here. There's something I want to ask you."

Her heart gave a lurch. She remembered the ring Jeth had bought. The thought of it made her insides turn to jelly. But even if he were to ask her to marry him, it was too late. She was leaving.

She forced herself to remain calm and continued sweeping. "I thought you would be out back with everybody else," she said calmly, "looking at Elmer's new baby. I heard it's a black filly and that Elmer is really proud of her."

"There'll be plenty of time to see the filly. Right now, I need to talk to you. Will you please come over here and sit down, my dear?"

Dear. Had he said "my dear?" At last, she looked at him. Tender lights flickered in his blue eyes. Honor put away her broom and started toward him, as if she were drawn by an invisible string. He pulled out her chair. When she sat down, he reached for his chair and sat down, too.

"We need to talk about some things," he began. "But first, I'm going to answer some of your questions. And then I hope you'll answer some of mine." He reached across the table and took her hand in his. "Is that agreeable with you, hon?"

Hon? A thrill shot through her.

She liked the gentle way he spoke those endearing words. But what did all this mean? She couldn't allow herself to think that "hon" and "dear" meant anything.

"I know you were curious about what I said to Sheriff Green the day we saw the little boy on that red horse. We discussed some of this once before, but not everything." He pushed back a curl from her eyes with his forefinger. "You see, I hated to accuse someone of wrongdoing until I knew for sure he was guilty." Jeth leaned closer. "But under the circumstances, it's all right to tell you now."

He gazed at her tenderly and brushed her wrist with his fingertips. Honor felt warm all over but tried not to show it.

"The little boy, Willie Sharp, is the youngest member of a local family," he said as if nothing unusual was happening. "It's possible that some of his brothers are outlaws. Not only does the Sharp Gang own the red horse young Willie was riding that day, I think they were responsible for the stagecoach robbery near Hearten, as well as the one in Pine Falls. So far, the sheriff hasn't been able to prove anything, but I'm sure he will.... Do you have any questions?"

Is it me you love? she wondered. *Or Lucy Jordan?*

"Come on," he urged. "Can't you think of one little question? You've been wanting me to answer questions for weeks."

"Most of my Bible questions have already been answered by reading the Good Book and listening to your sermons."

"Wonderful."

What was the matter with her? She needed to tell him she was leaving. Why couldn't she bring herself to do it?

"Then please answer a couple of my questions," he said. "Let's start with your uncle. Was he cruel to you?"

Yes, she thought, averting her gaze.

She'd promised herself that she would disclose everything about her past today, and he'd provided a perfect opening, but she couldn't seem to speak.

"Honor, was your uncle cruel? Or not?"

She struggled to get out a reply. "Sometimes."

"Did he beat you and your aunt?"

She ran her forefinger around the edge of the sugar bowl in the center of the table, reluctant to meet Jeth's eyes. "When he'd been drinking, he..." She couldn't say more.

"He what?" Sympathy appeared to flow from him. "Lucas must have hurt you terribly. But as a Christian, you have to forgive your uncle, no matter what he's done."

Forgive Lucas? That was easy for Jeth to say. How could she forgive Lucas when she'd been unable to forgive herself for stealing church money?

At that moment, Belinda raced in the back door, out of breath. "Oh, Pastor!" she said, gasping. "Some riders came up while we were looking at Elmer's filly. A-and another stage was robbed! People were injured!"

"Injured? No!" Jeth shot out of his chair and grabbed his hat. "Where are the riders now?"

"They rode off to get the doctor."

"You and Mrs. Grant stay here," Jeth said to Honor. "I have to see if I can help. My mother could be on that stage."

Honor stood. "I'm coming, too."

Jeth set his wide-brimmed hat on his head. "It's too dangerous. You need to stay here, where you'll be safe."

"Not on your life. I'm going with you, like it or not."

Chapter Twenty

Sitting on the bench of the covered wagon next to Jeth, Honor wrapped a wool blanket over her head and around her shoulders. A cold, blustering wind was howling all around them. Four inches of frozen snow covered the road, trees and fields.

The horses labored to pull the load, stretching their tired muscles to the limit against the wind. Slowly, they plodded on toward the site of the robbery.

Jeth turned and said something to Honor, but the loud gusts of wind drowned out his voice.

Honor's mind was aswirl with thoughts and memories of her life since arriving in Hearten. She and Jeth hadn't talked since leaving the boardinghouse, but worry lines wrinkled his forehead. She guessed that he was terribly concerned about his mother.

Poor Mrs. Peters could be on that stage. She might be

dead, and there was nothing that Honor could say that might make Jeth feel better.

Finally, when the wind died down, Honor heard noises and turned in her seat. Two other wagons filled with folks from Hearten were coming up behind them. She swung back around and faced the front again.

At last, she could make out the outline of the stagecoach in the distance. As the caravan grew closer, she saw that the carriage was turned on its side. People stood around it, Sheriff Green among them, but Honor didn't see Jeth's mother.

Before the wagon had even drawn to a full stop, Annie and Simon Carr plodded toward them in the snow.

"Look," Honor exclaimed, pointing toward the elderly couple. "It's the Carrs!"

"Yes." Jeth sent her a half smile. "At least they're all right. We can be thankful for that."

Honor threw off her blanket and jumped down from the wagon, embracing Annie and Simon as if she'd known them all her life.

"We have more blankets in the wagon," Honor called out, "if anyone needs them."

"Thank you," Simon Carr said. "'Spect we can sure use them quilts. It's plenty cold out here."

Jeth had climbed down from the wagon. Honor was aware of him coming up behind her.

"Was there another woman on the stage with you?" Honor asked Mrs. Carr.

"Yes." Annie nodded. "A Mrs. Peters. She's all right."

"Thank You, Lord, for protecting my mother," Jeth prayed out loud. Looking relieved, he hugged the elderly couple. Then he handed them two feather quilts. "Where is she?"

Annie gestured toward the stagecoach. "Mrs. Peters is on the other side of the wagon, nursing her brother."

"Uncle Lawrence?" Jeth hurried toward the wagon.

Honor followed after him.

Dr. Harris was bending over a wounded man, examining him. Jeth hurried to his mother and hugged her.

"It's good to see you again, Mama. I'm so glad you're safe. We were worried."

"No need to worry about me," Mrs. Peters said. "I'm fine. It's my brother who needs our prayers."

Honor stood a short distance away, wondering if she should step forward and help, or if she would be in the way. She could see blood trickling from a cut on the man's head, but she couldn't see his face.

"Miss McCall." The doctor glanced a Honor. "Why don't you wait over there with Mr. and Mrs. Carr. You might not like what you see here."

"No." She shook her head. "I might be able to help, Doctor. I'm staying."

"What happened to Uncle Lawrence?" Jeth asked. "How was he hurt?"

Dr. Harris, continuing to treat his patient, spoke without looking up. "The stagecoach driver said that when he tried to outrun the outlaws, he made a sharp turn. The door flew open. Your uncle fell out and hit his head on something, possibly a rock."

Honor looked on while the doctor struggled to wind a white cloth around the man's head. Jeth and his mother crouched on the ground. Mrs. Peters handed the physician something from his black bag. The doctor turned the man's head toward Honor as he tied the white cloth in a knot at the back of his head.

Suddenly, Honor saw his face and felt faint. Lucas!

Stunned, she staggered away from the stagecoach, feeling weak and dizzy. Reaching out, she took hold of the closest thing she could find to keep from falling. Her fingers curled around the icy branch of a tree, and she paid no attention to the cold.

The name *Lucas* repeated over and over inside her head. No wonder she'd always thought that Jeth looked like her uncle.

The two men were related.

Fifteen minutes later, Honor stalked toward Jeth, who was standing under a tree on the other side of the stagecoach. Her emotional shock had turned to anger and most of it was aimed at him. How many times had she told Jeth that she and her uncle had never gotten along? Just because Jeth didn't know everything that happened back in Falling Rock was no excuse. Did he really expect her to help nurse Lucas back to health? At the moment, her fury was so great that she couldn't even look at him.

"Reverend," she snapped, "by now your mother must have told you that your uncle is Lucas Scythe." She put her hands on her hips. "You know how I feel about the man, and if you think I'm going to take care of him, your head must have dropped off and rolled down one of those hills out there."

"Somebody has to," Jeth replied calmly. "Mama and Mrs. Grant will have their hands full with the Carrs."

"What's wrong with Annie and Simon?"

"They did all right immediately after the robbery," Jeth said, "but now, witnessing a second stage robbery in two months has them both upset, especially Annie. Dr. Harris suggested bed rest for her. And besides taking care of them, Mama and Mrs. Grant have the regular guests at the boardinghouse to see to."

"But Dr. Harris will be with Lucas," Honor reminded him. "Why should I—?"

"The man's unconscious, Honor," Jeth interrupted. "Your uncle couldn't swat a fly, even if he wanted to." He gestured toward a red horse on the ground nearby. "That horse was killed in the shootout today, and it's the one that belongs to the Sharp Gang, I'm sure of it. I have to go back with the sheriff and sign a statement. Otherwise, the outlaws won't be arrested. It's not as if you have to take care of your uncle alone. The doctor and Mama will be there. Mrs. Grant will be there, too. And I'll be back to help as soon as I can."

Honor shook her head. She was quivering all over. "I...I can't do this."

"Yes, you can." Jeth put his hand on her shoulder. "You'll be able to do this, Honor. You're a Christian now."

She'd never told Jeth the real reason that she'd left the cabin in Falling Rock. Therefore he couldn't know how being alone in a room with her uncle would unnerve her. What if Lucas came to himself and started leering at her again? Grabbed her? She closed her eyes briefly to shut out the frightening thoughts forming in her mind. Memories of her uncle's improper gazes still made her feel dirty, as if it was her fault instead of his.

Honor knew she should have told Jeth everything the day she arrived at the boardinghouse. He would have listened then, but shame had held her back. Would he listen now? She shook her head, answering her own question.

Lucas was Lawrence Smith, Jeth's long-lost uncle, and his mother's only brother. *As Aunt Harriet had always said, blood is thicker than water.*

In a daze, Honor barely noticed when Jeth helped the doctor check the other victims for injuries. When it appeared no else was seriously hurt, Jeth and two other men loaded Lucas onto the back of the doctor's wagon.

"I'll be going into town with the sheriff," Jeth told Honor as he climbed up onto the bench of his wagon. "We need to discuss a few things about the robbery."

"What about me?" Honor asked.

"Would you mind riding in the doctor's wagon with my mother and going back to the boardinghouse with them? Dr. Harris could probably use your help."

Honor couldn't believe what she'd just heard. "You want me to ride in the wagon with my uncle?"

"Yes, if you don't mind."

Honor studied Jeth seated on his high perch. He seemed so cold, so preoccupied. What had become of the man who had called her "dear" and "hon?"

The muscles in Honor's stomach tightened as she climbed in the back of the doctor's wagon. All her old fears had returned, playing in her mind like the noise of a child banging on an out-of-tune piano.

Honor jumped down as soon as the wagon reached the boardinghouse. Lucas had remained unconscious, but who could say when he might wake up? What would she do if he did? She should have kept the six-shooter under her bed.

Belinda Grant stood on the front porch. "Glad you're home, Mrs. Peters," she said warmly. "You, too, Miss Honor. What can I do to help?"

Mrs. Peters smiled. "Thank you, Belinda. I'll take the Carrs to the bedroom upstairs. Mrs. Carr isn't feeling too well. I think you should put the injured man downstairs in the room next to Elmer's, near the kitchen. The stage driver and the man who rides shotgun will be eating here, but they'll be staying with Dr. Harris until the stagecoach can be repaired."

Mrs. Peters turned to Mr. and Mrs. Carr. "If you wouldn't mind going upstairs without me, I'll be there as soon as I can."

"We don't mind," Simon said. "Do we, Annie."

"No," Mrs. Carr said, looking too upset to say more.

"You'll be in the big corner room," Regina Peters said. "You can't miss it. There's a number five over the door. Make yourself at home. And just leave your bags at the foot of the stairs. I'll get them up to the second floor in a few minutes."

Simon took their carpetbags, one in each hand. "No need to worry about them bags. I'll have 'em up the stairs 'fore you can say, 'Colorado blizzard.'"

When the elderly couple left, Regina turned to Honor. "As soon as you get my brother settled in his room, please meet me in the kitchen. I have something to tell you."

Honor nodded. "Yes, ma'am."

By the time Honor got to her uncle's room, the men had already laid Lucas on the bed. At the mere sight of him, bile burned the back of her throat.

Both Dr. Harris and Belinda were looking after him, so Honor excused herself and went into the kitchen to wait for Jeth's mother. She didn't know for sure what Mrs. Peters wanted, but she assumed it had something to do with Lucas.

When Mrs. Peters arrived a few minutes later, Honor was sitting at the table, but she jumped out of her chair. "Can I get you something, ma'am? You must be exhausted after your ordeal."

"Please, sit down. I don't want anything now. Maybe later." She opened her drawstring purse and pulled out a small wooden box.

Honor's heart leaped in her chest. She could hardly believe her eyes. "Why, that's—"

"Yes, it is." Mrs. Peters smiled and handed the box to Honor.

After all this time, Honor was holding her grandmother's pearl box. She lifted the lid, and forty-eight perfectly matched pearls winked back at her. "Oh, thank you, Mrs. Peters. But how...?" She took a deep breath and tried to smile. "You can't know how much it means to me to get this back."

The older woman got up from her chair and stepped behind Honor. "Would you like me to help you put on the necklace?"

"Oh, yes, please do."

As Regina struggled with the clasp, Honor kept wondering how Jeth's mother happened to have the pearls. She couldn't bring herself to ask, she was so astonished to see the pearls that she had thought were lost forever.

When the necklace was fastened, Regina stepped in front of Honor again. "Let me take a look at you." She grinned. "Smile."

Honor beamed.

"Lovely. The pearls are as white and sparkling as your teeth." The older woman's pleasant expression faded. "Guess you're wondering how I got the necklace in the first place."

"Yes, ma'am."

She took in a deep breath and released it. "My brother, the man you call Lucas, wanted you to have them."

"Lucas? Why would he want *me* to have them? He should have given them to me himself years ago."

"He hadn't planned to stop in Hearten. He was on his way back to his farm in Falling Rock. But the stage robbers changed all our plans." Mrs. Peters hesitated. "And if it's any comfort to you, I know he's sorry for hurting you, Miss McCall, whatever it was he did. My brother said he planned to write you a letter. Do you think you can ever forgive him?"

Forgive him? At first, Honor didn't know how to reply. "I don't know right now, ma'am. We'll just have to wait and see."

* * *

Honor kept herself busy for the rest of the day, fixing meals, washing dishes, running here and there. She wanted to gather her belongings and just walk away, but it wouldn't be right until things settled down.

The boardinghouse provided rooms, nursing care, clean clothes and clean linens to all the victims of the robbery. Honor made a point of staying as far from Lucas's room as possible. Let Belinda tend to my uncle's needs, she thought.

Later, Honor put on her coat and knit scarf over her blue wool dress, and she and Belinda Grant went onto the back porch to do the weekly wash. The laundry consisted of soiled clothes belonging to the stagecoach passengers as well as the regular boarders.

From the porch, Honor gazed at the frozen ground and the hills beyond the pasture. A blanket of fresh snow partly masked the usual barnyard smells, but traces of unpleasant odors were still noticeable.

Elmer's mare and filly were penned near the barn. On wobbly legs, the baby animal followed her mother into the barn. Belinda had said the filly had a white dot on her forehead, and she had suggested that Elmer name her Star.

Honor looked down at the tub of hot, soapy water. The thought of touching the shirt and trousers that Lucas had worn made her feel sick. She handed them to Belinda. "Will you wash these, please?" Honor started down the rock steps. "Nature calls."

She went to the privy and shut the door, planning to stay there as long as possible. A few minutes later, with no excuse to tarry longer, she rejoined Belinda at the washtub.

Pinching her nose, Honor held up a pair of dirty blue socks filled with holes. "These must belong to the reverend."

Belinda giggled. "I think you're right."

Honor smiled. Belinda's giggle always lifted her spirits.

"A good thing you're giving him a pair of socks for Christmas, Miss Honor." Belinda went on. "Have you finished knitting them yet?"

"I've not only finished them, I've already wrapped them and put them under the Christmas tree." Honor reached down and picked up Simon's shirt. "I guess you've finished washing the injured man's clothes by now, haven't you?"

"Yes, but look what I found in his pocket." Belinda handed Honor a black Bible. "Guess he must be a religious man."

Honor put down Simon's shirt and took the Bible in both her hands. Opening to the first page, she read the dedication.

To Harriet Mary McCall
With Love,
Mother and Father

A mournful cry escaped from deep in Honor's throat.

Belinda grabbed Honor and held her close. "What's wrong, honey? You're shaking like a leaf."

"This...this Bible reminds me of one my late aunt had." She handed the Bible back to Belinda. "It was just a shock to see it, that's all."

"You've been working too hard." Belinda patted Honor's back gently. "Why don't you go up to your room and rest a while? I can finish the wash. I've done it dozens of times."

"No, I'm fine now." She held out her hands for Belinda to see. "Not even shaking." Honor forced a weak grin. "Besides, I'm your boss until Mrs. Peters tells us differently. And I say I'm going to finish this wash."

Belinda giggled and shook her head. "Well, if you're sure you're all right."

"Positive." Honor glanced at the hitching post in the backyard where Jeth sometimes tied his horse. Where was Jeth? She'd expected him back hours ago. Had something happened?

Slowly an image of Lucas replaced Jeth's handsome face in her mind's eye. She tensed. Uncle and nephew. Even their eyes were the same shade of blue.

Jeth was sure to become fond of his only uncle. If Lucas ever changed, that is. Lucas could become the father Jeth never had. Or was Dr. Harris expected to play that role?

The kitchen door opened a crack.

"Miss McCall," Dr. Harris said.

Surprised, Honor turned.

"Would you mind coming in here a minute, please?"

"Of course." She sent Belinda a smile spiced with amusement. "Here I go again. But I'll be back to help you finish the wash before you know I'm gone."

Honor followed the doctor to the front of the house. As she walked past the parlor, she glanced inside at the Christmas tree, which was charming, decorated with popcorn, paper flowers and colored ribbons.

Honor looked back at Dr. Harris, who now stood in front of the room Lucas occupied.

"What is it, Doctor?" she asked in as calm a tone as she could produce.

"I have to leave now to deliver a baby. Joe Miller stopped by to say that his wife's time has come. I'll be back as soon as I can. And Reverend Peters should be back shortly." He looked down at his pocket watch. "Frankly, I don't know what's keeping him, and I don't know where Regina is, either. Upstairs maybe. Until she gets back, you and Mrs. Grant are in charge of the wounded man."

"But—"

"But what?" Dr. Harris pulled off his spectacles and wiped the lenses with a white handkerchief.

"I'm not a doctor." Honor's knees felt like jam. "And I don't know anything about nursing sick people."

"Hogwash! The three of you ladies will do fine. But I'll admit this isn't the best way to spend the day before Christmas Eve, is it? Hope you've finished your holiday buying." He shrugged and put his spectacles back on his nose. "The gentleman inside isn't going to do much for the next few hours, except sleep. The best thing you can do for him is pray he wakes up."

"Is there a chance he might not?"

"Are you a praying woman, Miss McCall?"

She nodded.

"I thought so."

Honor noticed her hands shaking and hoped he hadn't noticed.

"I've seen you in church lately," he said. "In fact, you're a new member, aren't you?"

"I joined a few weeks ago."

"Joining the church is a good first step. But true Christians invite the Lord into their hearts and give their bodies as a living sacrifice to the Lord."

Worry lines formed on her brow. With thoughts of Lucas and what he might do to her flooding her mind, she was having a hard time concentrating on what the doctor was saying.

"Are you saved, young lady?" the doctor asked pointedly.

His question startled her—maybe because Jeth had asked her that same question several times. "I think I'm saved."

But was she?

"Don't wait too long to find out for sure," he said as if he'd read her mind. "And before I go, are you all right, Miss

McCall?" He studied her carefully. "You seem a little preoccupied."

"I'm all right," she said. "Anything else?"

"Just keep him nice and warm. I noticed the woodstove in his room could use a log or two."

"I'll see to it right away." She felt the blood drain from her face at the thought of being alone with Lucas.

"Then I guess I'll see you after the blessed event over at the Millers'."

Honor watched the elderly gentleman remove his coat and hat from the hall tree, put them on, and wrap a blue wool scarf around his neck. When he'd gone, she went out the back door.

Belinda still stood at the washtub. Honor could ask Belinda to bring in the logs and check on Lucas, but she might wonder why Honor chose not do it, and that would require an explanation. Honor would do the jobs quickly and that would be the end of it. Later, she would just walk away as she'd done on the day she left Falling Rock. Goodbyes were too difficult, too painful.

"I need to gather wood," Honor said to Belinda. "I'll be back shortly."

"Don't hurry. As I said, I can finish here."

At the woodshed, Honor gathered all the small logs her arms could hold. Then she swept back through the house. At the door to her uncle's room, she hesitated before going inside.

Lucas still slept, one arm across his chest, the other at his side. Honor had kept on her coat and bonnet since she planned to go right back outside to gather more wood for the upstairs bedrooms.

Bending over, she opened the little iron door of the stove with a wooden stick, then dropped a log on the hot coals. A small fire ignited, and the second log caused a quick blaze.

She closed the door. Warming her hands for a moment, Honor glanced back at Lucas.

His eyelashes fluttered a few times. Then his eyes opened.

Honor's heart raced.

Lucas blinked and rubbed his eyes. "Is that you, Harriet?" He hesitated, peering up at her. "Why, it's you, Honor, ain't it? How long have I been sleeping?"

Honor's hands at her sides became fists. "A while."

Her jaw tightened, looking down at him, she saw that his blue eyes looked clear instead of bloodshot. Could all the alcohol have worked its way out of his body? Was Lucas actually sober? If so, it was the first time in years.

Honor started for the door, eager to leave.

"Please," he pleaded. "Don't go!"

She heard distress in his tone and she glanced back. He smiled weakly, looking frail and helpless. Pity welled inside her, seeing her uncle so vulnerable. It almost made being in the same room with him tolerable.

He opened his mouth as if he wanted to say something else, but failed to utter a sound. Rubbing his throat, he motioned for her to come closer. Against her better judgment, Honor crossed to his bed.

"Is there something you need, Uncle?"

"W-water."

Honor poured water from the pitcher into a glass. Then she lifted his head so he could drink. He sent her a helpless smile instead of his usual mocking one. She put the glass back on the table by his bed with shaky hands.

She had thought merely touching the back of his head would send her running for cover. But compassion was the only emotion she experienced.

"Go get— Go get—"

"Go get what, Uncle?"

"Harriet's Bible."

Honor was flabbergasted. Lucas wanted a Bible? Could it be that he really had changed?

"Did you say 'Bible,' Uncle?"

"Yes, hurry."

"I'll be right back."

Honor raced through the kitchen to the porch. Belinda still stood at the washtub.

"Back already?" Belinda said. "I'm almost finished here."

"Would you mind handing me that Bible, please? The wounded man wants it."

"I knew he was a Christian. Here." Belinda handed Honor the Bible. "By the way, while you were gone, Mrs. Peters came down. She took the buggy into town. The couple up-stairs wanted a few things. She said to tell you that she would be right back to help."

Honor hurried back to her uncle's room and gave him the Bible. His hands shook when he opened it. A letter was folded inside. He gave it to Honor. "This is for you."

Honor put the letter in her pocket, planning to throw it away later. There was nothing Lucas could say or give her that was worth hearing or reading.

Lucas cleared his throat. "I'm...I'm a changed man, missy. And I forgive you for stealing the money what Harriet hid from me."

"Money? Aunt Harriet never had any hidden money. There was no money. Is there something else you need, Uncle?"

He grabbed her hand and held it like he was a drowning man, about to go underwater for the last time.

Honor froze. All her old memories of Lucas returned in an outpouring of angry thoughts and feelings.

His touch hadn't bothered her earlier. Now it disgusted her. She shook, more from rage than fear. Shaking her hand free, she raced from the room, down the entry hall, and out the front door of the boardinghouse.

"Where are you going?" Belinda called from behind her.

Honor didn't reply or look back. She just kept running, with no destination in mind. Being any place was better than being in the same house with Uncle Lucas.

Chapter Twenty-One

❧

At dusk, Jeth crouched behind a big rock, his six-shooter cocked and ready. The sheriff had deputized him, and a silver badge was pinned to the front of his jacket. The deputies had arrived in the wilderness area ten miles west of Hearten in late afternoon and had secured their horses and extra mounts in the brush behind the cabin. Now Jeth waited for further instructions.

It had all happened so fast. One minute he was the pastor of a church, the next he was also a special deputy. A gust of anger shook him. Nothing could keep Jeth from doing his part in bringing to justice the crooks who had knocked Honor unconscious and tried to harm his mother.

But that didn't make the job any easier. He wasn't even a very good shot.

Earlier, the snow had melted into a white slush. Now the weather grew colder by the minute. Despite the frosty air,

Jeth wiped moisture from his forehead with the back of his free hand.

The mountains had disappeared behind a bank of low-lying clouds, and a feeling of foreboding had come over him. Images of Honor unconscious on the road with a gash on her head still haunted him. When those same outlaws had robbed the stage coming from Pine Falls, with his mother on board, he had known he had to act.

Now, gritting his teeth, Jeth tightened his grip on his gun.

He should have tried harder to defend Honor during the stage robbery. He'd just stood there with his hands up. Jeth would never make another mistake like that one.

The sheriff had needed an extra deputy and he'd only been able to find a few men. So Jeth had answered the call, too. But was he doing God's will?

He thought of the story of King David in the Bible. David had been a man of the sword. When he was a boy, he killed a giant with nothing but a rock and his slingshot. Jeth had never thought of himself as a warrior like King David, but somebody had to bring the outlaws to justice. As long as they were out there, Honor, his mother and others could be harmed, not to mention Uncle Lawrence—the man Honor called Lucas Scythe.

Jeth squinted at the log house at the bottom of the hill. The Sharp Gang were holed up there. Sheriff Green stood behind a tree to Jeth's right. Several other men huddled in the bushes behind them.

The sheriff raised his right arm. Bob Grayson, one of the other deputies, moved into the open. Jeth tensed, ready to provide cover for him.

A crash like glass shattering came from the cabin. Had an outlaw hit a window with the butt of his gun for a better shot?

A rifle blasted.

Jeth fired back, and a *ping* sounded when his bullet hit an old piece of rusty farm equipment in front of the cabin.

Grayson crept behind the cabin and out of sight. The sheriff held up two fingers, giving the second signal. Two more deputies came out from behind Jeth and veered toward the other side of the cabin.

For several minutes, a volley of gunfire exploded. A man cried out, but it was impossible for Jeth to tell who had been hit.

Grayson threw a torch onto the shingled roof. A fire started, and the other two deputies lit their oil-soaked sticks and tossed them on the roof. Another blaze ignited. The cabin was quickly covered in flames.

Under the cover of the smoke, Jeth and the sheriff crept closer to the cabin. Jeth coughed and pulling up the red bandana from around his neck to cover his mouth.

"Come out with your hands up!" the sheriff demanded.

The outlaws tumbled onto the frozen ground, coughing, sputtering and holding their bellies. The sheriff's men surrounded them.

"I said drop your guns!" the sheriff shouted.

Nearby, in the thick cloud of smoke, Jeth saw the outline of a man pointing a gun at the sheriff. Jeth kicked high, and the gun sailed from the outlaw's hand. Jeth socked the man in the jaw, knocking him to the ground. Then he grabbed the unconscious man's hands and tied them. "Got one!" he called.

"Me, too," Grayson exclaimed.

"Well, boys, I guess we got 'em all," the sheriff shouted back. "Let's take these outlaws in and put them behind bars."

It was after midnight by the time Jeth got back to Hearten—cold, bone-tired and hungry. He didn't argue when Sheriff Green invited him to spend the night in his spare bedroom.

When Jeth finally hit the bed, all that had happened that day played in his mind, calling up uneasy feelings of guilt and remorse. The frontier was a dangerous place, and Christian men were expected to defend women and children, but did that include Jeth? He was a man of the cloth, not a man with a gun.

He'd planned to ask Honor to be his wife. But that morning seemed like a long time ago, so much had happened since then.

Jeth couldn't stop thinking about the man he'd knocked in the jaw. He also recalled the helpless look he'd seen in the eyes of one of the other wounded outlaws, a young man who Jeth had helped carry up the stairs to Dr. Harris's office. The fellow reminded Jeth of Willie Sharp—he must be one of the boy's older brothers.

Nobody knew who had shot the outlaw. It could have been Jeth. Thankfully, the man would recover, but if Jeth had been the shooter, was he worthy to continue as a pastor? Still, he knew that if Honor was in danger, he would defend her, always.

His thoughts drifted. Tomorrow was Christmas Eve. His mother was home from Pine Falls. Yet with all that had happened, he hadn't found time to visit with her and learn what had happened while she was away.

As a result of the gun fight, Jeth must decide whether to keep on the course he'd believed the Lord had given him or take a new direction in life. He prayed long and hard into the night.

By dawn, he had his answer.

The stagecoach from Pine Falls had parked across the street from the hotel in front of the general store. Honor watched from the shadows, clutching her ticket. She'd spent the night hidden in the cellar under the general store. During the night, her body shook—as much from a fear of rats as from the cold. Weeping always caused her to tremble, too, and she'd cried off and on until morning.

It wouldn't be easy, leaving Jeth, but it had to be.

A woman who Honor recognized from the church entered the general store, holding her little girl's hand. Honor moved behind a wall of the hotel to keep from being seen.

I'll never see Hearten or the people who live here again, she thought, swallowing hard. Goodbye, Jeth. I love you— and I always will.

When she thought nobody was looking, Honor got on the stage, her ticket in her hand. A few minutes later, the horses started off. The wheels rolled, slowly at first, and her heart churned with every turn, with every bump on the rocky road.

By now, Jeth and his mother would know she wasn't coming back. Would Jeth be sorry? Would he come and look for her? She was going far away, where he would never be able to find her. She wanted to look back, one more time, but Honor forced herself to gaze down at her hands folded in her lap.

The elderly gentleman seated beside her turned to speak. "Are you from Hearten, ma'am?"

Honor hesitated. "No, I'm just passing through."

"The ticket agent said there would be an hour stop in Falling Rock," the man went on. "And if the weather allows it, we'll be traveling on toward Cold Springs."

"And if the weather *is* bad?"

"We'll be spending the night in Falling Rock. In fact, the stage might not leave again until the day after Christmas. Ma'am, do you have family in Falling Rock?"

She hesitated. "I used to. Not anymore."

"Well, I hear there's a nice hotel in town. I planned to stay in the hotel myself, if we don't go on."

"Thank you for the information, sir. I'll keep that in mind."

Honor glanced down at her clothes. She wore her brown coat over her faded blue wool dress. It was the same outfit she'd worn to gather wood on the previous day, and she needed a bath. Honor didn't care, nor did she care where the stagecoach took her. All she wanted was to be as far from Lucas and all of her memories as possible.

When Jeth arrived at the boardinghouse, Belinda Grant waited in the kitchen. She looked distraught and began to cry as soon as she saw him.

"What's wrong?" Jeth asked. "Has Uncle Lawrence taken a turn for the worst?"

"He's doing much better. It's...it's Miss Honor."

"Honor!" Jeth's voice had cracked with emotion, making his feelings for the young woman all too clear. "What's wrong with her?" He felt his eyes widen. "Is she sick?"

"She's—" Belinda wept into her white handkerchief. "She's gone."

Jeth frowned. "What do you mean, 'gone'?"

"She just ran out the door yesterday afternoon."

"Yesterday afternoon," he exclaimed. "Are you saying she left here and hasn't come back?"

Belinda nodded. "We—" She wiped her eyes with the linen handkerchief. "Oh, Reverend, we haven't heard a thing from her since. Your mother and I have been worried sick about her."

Jeth yanked his hat from the kitchen table where he'd tossed it. "Where *is* Mama?"

"Upstairs. Mrs. Carr has a bad case of the blues today. Your mother sent Elmer out looking for Honor right after she ran away, but nobody's been able to find her."

He headed for the front of the house. "I'll find her!" Jeth set his hat on his head and kept moving. "She probably picked up her ticket and took the stage. I'll look there first."

"Wait!" Belinda called after him. "The noon stage had already pulled out by the time Miss Honor left here."

"I meant the noon stage today," he shouted back.

I'll bet that's just what she did, he thought as he reached the front door of the boardinghouse. Then he glanced over his shoulder. "Tell Mama I went after Honor."

As he turned the doorknob, Jeth saw a brown drawstring purse out of the corner of his eye. He paused. The purse was on the desk by the front door, and it was Honor's.

She'll need this now, he thought, and grabbed the purse.

Jeth raced outside to the place where he'd hitched his horse. His jaw firmed.

I'll bring her back, if I have to drag her.

Honor stood with the other passengers in front of a combination livery and blacksmith shop in Falling Rock, waiting to hear what Mr. Kraken would say.

"It's too cold to send the stage out again today." Mr. Kraken had made his decision. "And with the holidays coming and all, the stage won't be leaving again until the day after Christmas."

Honor walked from the depot toward the church. Christmas trees, burning candles and other cheery, holiday decorations appeared in the doors and windows along the way. On the rock porch in front of the church, Honor paused for a moment, remembering the last time she'd been here. Then, shivering, she opened the heavy, double doors and slipped inside.

A lit cast-iron stove stood to the left of the altar. Honor chose a pew next to it and warmed her hands.

Her gaze traveled to a Christmas tree to her far right. It looked about ten feet high. A shiny star at the top reflected the light coming from the stove and from the windows on both sides of the chapel. Gaily wrapped presents surrounded the tree.

She'd run away without the money that she'd saved, and now she had nothing to give Jesus to celebrate his birthday. Nor could she pay back the money she'd stolen, which caused a deep sorrow to spread deep in her heart.

Honor wiped away tears that had gathered at the edges of her eyes. Two Scripture verses came to mind: "Present your bodies a living sacrifice," and "Forgive others their trespasses and God will also forgive your sins."

Why had these Bible verses come to her at this particular time?

Jeth had assured her that God spoke to His people in many ways. Could this be one of them? And if so, what did it mean?

Honor bowed her head.

"I cannot know all that the scriptures mean, O Lord," she prayed. *"But I guess You want me to give my body as a living sacrifice. If that's what You want, I'm willing. But I'm not so sure about forgiveness. How can I forgive Lucas?"*

She'd hoped her prayer would destroy the dismal feelings deep inside her—that a rush of happiness would flow from her heart, but it didn't happen. Blinking back tears, she wondered: Did the Lord expect her to forgive Lucas no matter what he had done? Honor shook her head.

"I can't forgive yet, Lord. But I'll give You my body as a living sacrifice."

Honor found a pen and sheets of paper in the foyer. Seated at a writing desk nearby, she wrote the Lord a letter, promising to do what she could and thanking Him for loving her. Although she knew how to pray now, a letter still seemed right. When she finished, she dropped her letter in an empty collection plate exactly like the one from which she had taken the money.

Alone in the cold and drafty church, Honor prayed for a long time. She didn't know where she should go now, and sought God's help.

After Lucas had come into her life, Honor had withdrawn deeper and deeper into a shell, a private place where she'd been safe, but imprisoned. However, God's love had freed her from it and opened the doors of her heart. Honor knew that now, whatever happened, she would be all right. She no longer had to live in lonely isolation.

At sunset, she glanced out a church window just as a man rode up on horseback. As he dismounted, her heart jumped for joy. It was Jeth.

Why had he come? And what could she possibly say to him? Would he scold her for running away again? Or demand that she tell him about her uncle? She had no choice but to reveal the truth now. It wouldn't be right for Honor, a Christian, to lie to him, especially in a church on Christmas Eve.

His boots tapped the brick floor when he entered the sanctuary. Honor stood and faced him.

He strode down the middle aisle, eyes on Honor. "I knew I'd find you here."

She looked down at her high-buttoned shoes. How could she say what had to be said without crying?

He handed her the purse with the money in it. "Thought you might be needing this."

"Yes." Eyes lowered, Honor took the purse from him. "Thank you."

"I didn't come just to bring the purse."

She noted his serious, unyielding gaze. Did he know that she'd stolen money from this church? Had he always known?

"Guess you're wondering what I'm doing here," he said.

"That question crossed my mind."

"Why don't we sit down?" He gestured toward one of the pews. "This could take time."

"I have something I need to do first."

Honor went to the collection plate, opened her purse and placed all the money on top of her letter. *Merry Christmas, Lord.* A good feeling swept over her. Honor turned. As she started back up the center aisle, Jeth seated himself.

"I prayed you would give the money to the Lord," he said. "I'm so proud of you."

Honor stood in the aisle next to Jeth's pew, resting her hand on the carved arm of the wooden bench. For a long time, she'd thought Jeth had seen her take the money. Now she had to know for sure.

"You were the man standing in the foyer the morning of the first stage robbery, weren't you, Jeth?"

"Yes."

"And you've known I stole from this church all along, haven't you?"

He nodded.

"Then why didn't you tell me sooner? Why did you leave me dangling all this time? I kept wondering what you would do when you found out."

"I was waiting for you to tell me about it, and now you have."

"So, what will you do now?" she asked.

"You may recall that I have a question to ask you." He smiled. "The question I was about to ask you before Mrs. Grant rushed in the kitchen and told us about the stage robbery."

"What question is left to ask?"

He moved over, making room for her beside him. "First, will you please sit down?"

Honor did as he requested.

"Now," he went on. "I want to explain why I was late getting back to the boardinghouse after the stage robbery. Remember? I'd promised to go back and help you care for your uncle."

"Why didn't you?"

He told her about becoming a deputy, catching the robbers, worrying that he might have been the one who shot the wounded outlaw. Everything else that had happened after he left the boardinghouse tumbled out as well.

"I questioned whether or not I should continue as a pastor. But I've prayed a lot since then." He gazed down at his hands, folded loosely between his knees. "I think the Lord has given me some answers."

"What answers?"

Turning toward her, he put his arm on the back of the pew. "I'm to continue as a pastor."

"That's no surprise."

His arm curled around her. In his embrace, she felt safe and loved for the first time in ages. But it couldn't last. Why didn't Jeth know that?

"I've also done some thinking," he added. "And I want you to tell me about your uncle." He gently pressed his hand on her upper arm. "Will you please do that now?"

Honor's lips turned down. Tears gathered. She cleared her throat. "If I hadn't left when I did, he would have forced me to marry him. Or worse."

"Oh, my sweet darling." He kissed her eyes, her cheeks, her forehead.

He still held her close, and she thought she could hear his beating heart. She knew she felt hers.

"I love you, Honor. And I want you to be my wife."

A rush of joy filled her heart. But it was soon drowned beneath a flood of guilt and despair.

She could never be Jeth's wife. He was a minister of the Lord, an upright man, and she was a common thief. Why, she was no better than the gang of outlaws whom Jeth had brought to justice.

Honor had loved Jeth almost from the moment they met, and she had secretly hoped he felt the same way. Yet, even after she had revealed everything, she felt unworthy of his love.

"I have to get out of here." She broke free of his embrace and raced outside, into the cold night.

"Honor, wait!"

Everything that had happened since the day of her aunt's burial flashed before her. Even as she ran blindly through the darkness, she knew Jeth was right behind her.

His arms circled her. She felt his breath on the back of her neck.

"I'm not worthy to be a pastor's wife!"

"I'm not worthy to be a pastor. Nobody is. I'm not worthy to preach the Gospel of Jesus Christ, but the Lord called me to do it."

"It's not the same."

"Yes, it is." His soft breath tickled her ear. "A person's sins can be forgiven, Honor, every single one of them. But only if that person truly repents and believes in the Lord.

"Jesus paid for your sins on the cross, and He paid for mine. Believe it. In fact, Jesus paid for the sins of everybody who truly turns to Him." Jeth turned her body around, forcing her to face him. "Honor, I'm asking you to be my wife."

"I...I can't."

"Yes, you can."

His mouth found hers. Her pulse quickened, and her heart hammered inside her chest. A wonderful joy and sense of fulfillment swept over her.

She responded willingly, openly, lovingly. Even if he decided to walk away, she would have this moment to remember and cherish forever.

At last, he pulled his mouth from hers. "You said you wouldn't marry me," he said tenderly. "But your lips say that you will. Who am I to believe?"

Honor couldn't come up with an answer because she couldn't speak. Instead, she reached up on tiptoes and kissed him again.

He grinned. "I like the way you answer questions. And I take it that your answer is yes. Am I right?"

"Yes," she said breathlessly. "Yes, yes. yes."

Down the street, the church bells rang out seven times.

"If that's not a confirmation of our decision, I don't know what is," Jeth said.

Riding double, Jeth and Honor went back to Hearten, arriving before daylight on Christmas morning. In the darkened parlor of the boardinghouse, Jeth lit candles and started a fire in the hearth. Honor saw gifts under the tree.

He picked up a small wrapped package and handed it to her. "This is for you."

"Me?" Honor touched the soft material of a bow with a pink, silk rose in the center. "How beautiful."

"It's the Rose of Sharon."

"What a lovely thought." She studied the flower for a moment longer, then she turned back to Jeth. "I have a present for you, too." She handed him a package. "Please, open mine first. It's not much, but a lot of love went into making it."

Jeth sat down on the rag rug, pulled back the green bow, and ripped open his gift. Honor knelt beside him. In the glow of candlelight, Jeth's eyes shimmered with happiness. Lifting the blue socks from the box, he studied them closely.

"Thank you, Honor. You couldn't have given me anything I wanted or needed more."

Honor sat back on her heels and smiled. She knew she should open her gift slowly, carefully and soberly, the way her aunt had taught her. She took the pink rose and tucked the stem in the buttonhole of her brown coat. Then she tore into the tiny package with the same gusto that Jeth had shown, leaving white paper and pink ribbons in a pile on the floor.

An even smaller box waited inside the first one. She opened the lid, and a pearl ring stared back at her. The gold setting had been fashioned with gold filigree. The one pearl was large and white, gleaming against the red velvet lining of the box.

"Oh, how beautiful!"

"It's an engagement ring. And I bought it weeks ago."

"Weeks ago? Why didn't you tell me what you were feeling? I thought you liked Lucy Jordan."

"I do like Lucy Jordan, but I'm in love with you."

He leaned over and kissed her again. Gladness, as sparkling and glowing as a hundred flickering candles, filled her heart.

Her pearl necklace was hidden inside her clothes for safekeeping. She reached inside her collar and pulled out the pearls for Jeth to see. Lifting her pearl engagement ring to her throat, she placed the ring next to the necklace.

"See? They are a perfect match."

"Just like we are," he said.

"Yes, just like we are." Honor offered him her hand. "Put my ring on my finger for me, please."

"With pleasure."

In spite of the joy she felt, she still hadn't forgiven Lucas. As a Christian, she needed to. It wouldn't be easy, but if Jeth could take her into his home and heart, knowing what she'd done, could she do any less for Lucas?

Now she had another gift to give Jesus. "I've decided to forgive Lucas. It's time. As soon as it's light, I'll go and tell him, face-to-face."

Honor rose from the floor, walked to the east window and looked out. Beyond the hills, the sun was emerging over the horizon, bathing the entire valley in a golden glow. Jeth came up beside her and put his arm around her. Filled with contentment, Honor watched a glorious sunrise, safe in Jeth's warm embrace.

Later he gave her a tender squeeze. "I guess we should go on in and see our uncle now."

She nodded. "Yes."

Hand and hand, Honor and Jeth walked through the arched doorway and into the entry hall.

Forgive Lucas, Lord, she prayed silently. *He knew not what he did.*

Tears stung the edges of her eyes. For the first time since she'd arrived in Hearten, Honor thought she knew the Lord and His blessings in a personal way.

In one of his Sunday night sermons Jeth had said that a long time ago, Christians greeted each other by saying "Jesus is Lord." And others replied by saying, "He is Lord, indeed." Jeth had also said that only true believers called Jesus "Lord." She'd never understood the sermon's meaning—until now. Jeth had also preached that it was wrong to keep one's faith hidden from the world, that Christians should wear their faith proudly for everyone to see.

Now Honor turned to Jeth and smiled. "Jesus is Lord."

He nodded. "He is Lord, indeed."

Their gazes met, and she saw tears in his eyes. In that glorious moment, she finally knew what it meant to be loved.

Jeth's mother stood just outside Lucas's room, arm-in-arm with Dr. Harris.

"Merry Christmas," Mrs. Peters and the doctor whispered together.

"Merry Christmas to you."

"Did Mrs. Miller have her baby?" Honor asked the doctor.

"Yes, she had a boy. A big one, too, almost eight pounds. And mother and child are both doing well."

"What a blessing." Honor gazed at Regina Peters and motioned toward her uncle's bed. "How is he?"

Jeth's mother glanced up at the doctor and smiled as if she expected him to answer.

"He's doing amazingly well," Dr. Harris said. "I didn't give Regina's brother much of a chance when I first examined him, but he is already on the road to recovery."

"May I see him?" Honor asked. "There's something I must tell him."

Regina frowned. "He's sleeping right now."

"I won't wake him. I promise. But I must see him at once. It's important."

"Very well, then." She nodded. "Go on in. But don't stay too long."

Honor tiptoed to the foot of his bed. Looking down at the man who had hurt her for so long, she confronted the painful memories, every mean and hurtful thing he'd ever said to her, every beating, every insulting look. A deep sadness swept over her. Quivering, she had an urgent desire to turn and run, but she stayed and told herself: I will not give in to fear. Not now. Not ever again.

Wrenching all negative thoughts from her mind in the name of Jesus, she straightened her back. Once she'd thought Lucas was a monster, but he said he'd changed. In peaceful sleep, he didn't look like a monster.

All at once, she remembered something else that Jeth had said. Forgiveness didn't depend on what others did. Whether our enemies changed or whether they didn't wasn't important: "The Lord expects us to forgive others regardless."

"Lucas," Honor whispered.

He snored and turned his face away.

Honor stepped around the bed to look directly into his face. "Lucas, I forgive you for everything you've ever done to me. And when you wake up, I promise to say this again and loud enough for you to hear me."

Hate and resentment poured out of her. She *knew* she felt free, at last.

She watched Lucas for a moment longer. Then she glanced toward the ceiling as if heaven was only a few feet above her.

With forgiveness in her heart, Honor stepped joyfully from the room—and into Jeth's waiting arms, knowing that she loved Jeth and would walk with the Lord forever as a member of the family of God.

Epilogue

On her wedding day, Honor had gotten up early. She had helped Regina and Belinda prepare breakfast for the guests at the boardinghouse and then she had made final arrangements for the reception after the triple ceremonies. She didn't know what had become of Jeth, Dr. Harris and Lucas. Apparently, they had left the boardinghouse on the previous night and hadn't returned.

A washtub filled with cold water waited for Honor in her bedroom. At last, she carried a teakettle of hot water up the stairs to warm her bath. Then she would dress.

Her white, lace wedding gown, of the latest fashion, hung on a special hanger. Her lace veil had been draped across the back of the chair, and her white, satin shoes, her white stockings and her undergarments were spread out on her bed. She'd sprinkled rosewater on everything she would be wearing that day and also planned to dab a little more behind her ears before leaving for the church.

Honor poured hot water into the tub and put another log in the woodstove. It wouldn't make the water as warm as she would have liked, but she didn't have time to go downstairs and heat up the kettle again.

She removed her blue, wool work dress and everything underneath it, and stepped into the water. Shivering, she sat down. This would be a short bath.

As she rubbed lye soap on the white cloth, she thought about all that would happen that morning. Blushing, she also wondered what might happen in the bedroom that night with Jeth. Regina and Belinda had told her a few things, but not much.

Three weddings in one day. It seemed impossible. Yet that was exactly what was going to take place.

A knock sounded at her door.

"Are you ready yet?" Regina asked from the hallway.

"No, not yet."

"You better hurry. We wouldn't want to be late for our own weddings."

Jeth and his uncle had spent the night in the spare bedrooms at the two-story house owned by Dr. Harris. It wouldn't do for the grooms to see their brides before the ceremonies.

Besides, practically everybody in the town of Hearten, the Klines, the Carrs, Margaret and Dan Starling, and their families had arrived to attend the weddings. Even John Crammer and his wife had ridden over from Falling Rock to be at the big event.

Later, Mrs. Baker from the general store and her friend, Miss Bennett, would serve the big, three-layer, white wedding cake. Lucy Jordan would serve the coffee and punch, and Mrs. Clark and her sister, Mrs. Davis, would sit with Lucy's mother and keep her company during the wedding reception after the ceremonies. Elmer and Belinda Grant planned to deliver Honor, Jeth's mother and Ruby Jones to the church in the buggy.

In a navy-blue wool suit and royal-blue tie, Jeth rode his horse down the icy road. The country air felt cool and nippy on his skin, and a thin layer of snow covered the ground. The mountains that edged Hearten wore their whitest and tallest hats that morning, perhaps to celebrate this special day.

Jeth had expected to be the first to arrive at the church, but Timmy Rivers, Willie Sharp and the two Baker boys waited for him on the front steps.

"My," Jeth said with a grin, "the 'fun night boys' are up early. Are you ready to help ring the church bell this morning?"

"Yes, sir," the boys said in unison.

"You wouldn't happen to have none of that candy, would you?" Willie glanced at George Baker. "The kind what they sell over at his papa's store."

Jeth laughed. "I left candy I bought at Baker's in a sack in the bell closet. You boys can have it when you've finished your bell-ringing job."

"Thank ya kindly, sir." Willie smiled broadly. "We're much obliged to ya."

"We sure are, sir," Timmy said. "Can we ring the bell now?"

"Not yet. I'll let you know when it's time." Jeth started to walk inside the church building.

"Where do you want us to wait, Reverend?" Timmy asked.

Jeth stopped and looked back. "You might be in the way if you wait in the foyer. Why don't you all wait outside the door of the bell closet? But keep watching so you'll hear when I tell you to ring the bell."

"Yes, sir." Timmy gave a military salute.

The other boys mimicked him.

Jeth returned their salutes. "All right, then. I'll see you soldiers later."

The boys marched down the hall to the bell closet.

Jeth went into the sanctuary of the church. He'd only taken a few steps when he remembered that he'd left the Bible he planned to use during the service back at his office. Turning, he backtracked. He was about to go inside when four young boys stepped forward.

"Is it time?" Timmy asked excitedly.

"Not yet, but soon. I'll let you know."

Jeth had almost reached the pastor's chair to the right of the pulpit when he remembered that he'd also left his notes for the ceremonies on his desk. Where was his mind today? He was more of a forgetful groom-to-be than some of the young men in his congregation had been on the days of their weddings!

He retraced his steps and hadn't even reached the door to his office when the boys bumped into each other and surrounded him.

"Now, Preacher?" Timmy asked.

"No, but it won't be much longer."

They looked disappointed.

Jeth got his notes and stood in the center of his office for a moment, thinking. He didn't want to come back a third time.

Honor, in her white wedding dress, held a bouquet of pink silk roses and paraded down the aisle in front of

Regina and Ruby. She would first serve as a bridesmaid in the double wedding that Jeth was about to perform, joining Regina and the doctor, and Ruby and Lucas in marriage.

At first, she'd thought she would resent Ruby for stealing Harriet's husband. Certainly, Lucas and Ruby had been wrong to betray Harriet and the Lord by sinning in that way. Nevertheless, to Honor's surprise, she liked Ruby instantly, and she knew they were going to become good friends.

A groom wasn't supposed to see his bride before the wedding. Yet, as soon as she reached the front of the church, Honor felt Jeth's eyes on her above the white book he held. At last, he looked down at the book and began reading.

Jeth smiled at the two couples standing before him. "We are gathered here today to..."

Honor thought Jeth looked dashing in his new, navy-blue suit and hardly heard the rest of what he had to say. Ruby wore a light pink gown, and Regina wore a lovely silk dress in a darker shade of pink. Both brides carried bouquets of white silk flowers. Dr. Harris and Lucas also wore dark blue suits and looked almost as handsome as Jeth.

The double wedding ceremony ended, and the two couples moved to one side. Regina took Honor's pink bouquet of roses from her and handed her a bouquet of white silk roses that smelled like rosewater. Jeth stepped down from the podium, and his former father-in-law, Reverend Fields from Falling Rock, replaced Jeth at the pulpit.

"We are gathered here today to join this man and this woman in holy matrimony," Reverend Fields finally said. "If anyone has just cause why these two should not be joined together, let him speak now or forever hold his piece."

When no one spoke, Honor smiled. How could anyone object when God had so obviously placed them together?

The town of Hearten knew who Honor was now—and who she'd been. Yet they had accepted her with open arms and showered her with kindness. She would work to be the best pastor's wife it was possible to be and the perfect mate for her husband.

Jeth took Honor's hand and squeezed. Then the minister began speaking once more. Again, Honor was too excited and filled with joy to hear much.

At last, she said, "I do."

And when the pastor asked Jeth if he would take Honor Rose McCall to be his lawful wedded wife, he also said, "I do."

Thank you, Lord, she prayed, *for giving me Jeth as a husband—for as long as we both shall live.*

Suddenly, they were man and wife and running together down the center aisle of the church, followed by Ruby and Lucas, and Regina and the doctor. When Honor stepped onto the wooden floor of the foyer, she heard shuffling feet and children laughing. She glanced toward the sounds.

"Now, Preacher?" Timmy asked, peeking around the corner leading to the hall.

"Yes." Jeth laughed. "Now!"

The bell in the tower above their heads pealed loudly. For an instant, Honor remembered the day that she'd hidden in the church in Falling Rock and heard a bell ringing above her. Then those thoughts vanished, and joy filled her heart.

Timmy and the others were continuing to pull the rope. The bell clanged thunderously, again and again. Honor held her ears and counted the bongs. She glanced through the open doorway of the church and saw a cold mixture of rain and snow floating from the sky.

Jeth grabbed her hand. "Hurry! This sprinkle could become a downpour."

They raced to the black buggy. All around them, the others were rushing to their carriages, too.

Jeth frowned as he helped Honor up onto the wooden bench. "I told those boys to stop after seven pulls. But they're still ringing."

Gazing down at Jeth, Honor smiled. "I don't mind. Really. I love the sound of bells now, because from this day forward, church bells will always remind me of you, Jeth—the man I love."

His smile held a world of love and joy as he climbed in beside her. "I love you, too, Honor Rose Peters."

His tender kiss only proved what Honor already knew: The Rose of Sharon had finally come home.

* * * * *

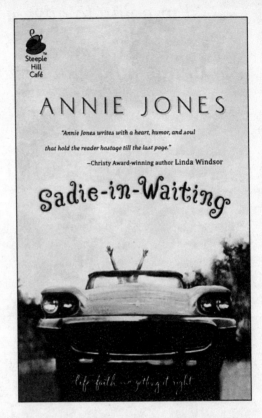

"I'm going to have a baby.
Me. Ann.
My dad is not gonna understand."

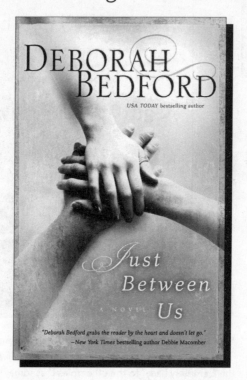

Fourteen-year-old Ann was right. Richard Small didn't understand.
Nor did he know how he and his daughter could have grown so far
apart. Missing his late wife more than ever, he arranged for a Big Sister
to offer Ann the support he felt incapable of giving himself.

What he didn't count on was falling in love with
the wonderful woman he brought into Ann's life
or that the very person who brought them together
could ultimately keep them apart....

Steeple
Hill®

On sale December 2004.
Visit your local bookseller.

www.SteepleHill.com

SDB530TR

FOR LOVE'S SAKE

BY

CYNTHIA RUTLEDGE

Jay Nordstrom thought his life had ended with his devastating car accident and he reluctantly returned to his hometown to heal. Nothing could pull him from despair…until teacher Rachel Tanner entered his world. His gentle caretaker showed him how much he'd missed by abandoning God, how faith could empower him…and how to open his heart to love.

Don't miss FOR LOVE'S SAKE.

On sale December 2004.

Available at your favorite retail outlet.